The Vote

The Vote

T. D. Patterson

Five Star • Waterville, Maine

First Edition
First Printing: September 2004

Published in 2004 in conjunction with Tekno Books and Ed Gorman.

Set in 11 pt. Plantin by Ramona Watson.

Printed in the United States on permanent paper.

Library of Congress Cataloging-in-Publication Data

Patterson, T. D.
    The vote : a novel / by T.D. Patterson.—1st ed.
      p. cm.
    ISBN 1-59414-239-4 (hc : alk. paper)
    1. Presidents—Election—Fiction.   2. Political corruption—Fiction.   3. Political campaigns—Fiction. 4. Washington (D.C.)—Fiction.   5. Legislators— Fiction.   6. Maryland—Fiction.   I. Title.
PS3616.A88V68 2004
    813'.6—dc22   2004053223

To Pamela, for never giving up on me—and never letting me give up on myself.

Acknowledgements

Sincere thanks go to the editors at Tekno Books, and especially John Helfers, for showing extraordinary faith and support in the publication of this book. Without John's persistence and expertise, the manuscript would still be only a dream.

Also, thanks to Gale and Five Star Publishing for seeing the possibilities, and allowing me to see them, as well.

Finally, I thank my family for creating an atmosphere of love, caring and compassion that helped me understand that one person can make a difference. Indeed, one person is all it takes.

Prologue

George Monroe pressed on the brake and brought the car to a sliding stop on the dirt road, then he did exactly as instructed: He turned off the headlights and engine, leaned across the seat and opened the passenger side door. He was careful to stare straight ahead at all times.

Hands trembling, he tried to calm himself by listening to the trickle of running water outside. A creek or riverbed was nearby. The rushing stream helped to soothe his nerves.

But then he heard footsteps coming up behind. When a twig cracked, George jumped and almost looked. Almost.

Finally, the car door opened wider, and he waited for the satchel to drop.

Five seconds. Ten. Fifteen. Nothing.

He stared straight ahead, feeling a set of eyes outside watching him. He felt the soft pressure of a body slipping inside the car and onto the bench seat. Out of the corner of his eye, he saw black tennis shoes on the floorboard where the satchel was supposed to be.

Still he stared straight ahead, his hands slipping on the wheel with the gathering perspiration. He wanted to speak, but he knew that might cancel the deal, too.

Another ten seconds. Twenty. Thirty. Nothing!

How long were they going to wait?

Suddenly, the stranger reached out and laid a gloved hand on George's thigh, rubbing him for a moment, as might a lover. When the man's hand lifted up and came down with a slap, George felt the tiniest of pinpricks. He looked down and saw a miniature syringe embedded in his thigh, sticking out from his pants leg like a tailor's mistake.

A chill swept over him like an ice-cold wind. It froze him on the spot. Literally. He could not move. Could not talk. Could not even blink. He sat there gape-mouthed, staring down at his own leg, which would not respond. He tried to scream, but nothing came. He tried to lift his hands from the wheel, but they were stuck there like mannequin hands, disembodied. Only his eyes worked. They flitted from side to side, up and down. To the man's face. Then to his own leg. Back to the man's face, where he saw his smile turn to a sneer.

Slowly, the man got out of the car and walked around to the driver's side. He popped open George's door, reached inside and pried his hands loose from the wheel, lifting him out as easily as picking up a plastic doll.

He moved quickly toward the side of the road where the creek rushed noisily now, sounding much more like a river than before. Holding George out in front, he forced his way through the tangle of bushes and tree branches to where the stream was lit by a full moon. He sat George there in the mud along the bank and began to straighten out his frozen limbs. Then he placed a hand in the middle of George's chest and pressed forward until he was flattened out on his back, staring up helplessly at the starry sky.

George knew what awaited him now. He wanted to beg for mercy, to swear he would never reveal what had happened on this night or on any other night, if the man would just let him go.

But George couldn't utter a sound.

Oddly, his breathing began to calm. The shaking in his hands stopped. He looked up at the night sky and began to feel strangely at peace, accepting of what was to come.

The giant man reached down and turned George's head so he could see across the water to a stand of trees where three men stood. Two of them were in business suits. One was dressed quite richly: An expensive three-piece suit with a red-white-and-blue designer tie. A small diamond stud—much like the one in the ear of the man hovering above him—was pinned in the middle of the man's tie, shining across the stream like a laser light.

George had never seen this man before. Nor had he seen the second man—dressed in all black. An ugly purple scar across the bridge of his nose gave him an especially sinister look.

But the third man George knew.

It was the congressman. He was the reason George was here tonight. He was the same man who had drunkenly run down and killed a girl on a bicycle two weeks ago. The congressman didn't realize he had been seen. But George had witnessed it all. If the girl hadn't been killed, George would have gone to the authorities. But nothing could bring her back now. So he decided to punish the congressman himself—and benefit a little financially in the process. Just enough to get by his last few years.

George watched the congressman and saw tears streaming down the man's face. He was being held in place by the scar-faced man and didn't want to be here, didn't want this to be happening. But it was. And neither George nor the congressman could do anything about it.

The fancily-dressed man whispered something into the congressman's ear, then turned and shouted out: "Do it, Steele."

The giant scooped under George's prone body and deposited him in the rushing creek on top of rocks and other debris, his face barely out of the water. George couldn't really feel anything. His body was numb inside and out. He could only sense the flow of water around his head and over his ears.

The huge man placed a foot in the middle of George's chest. The water rose up and washed over his eyes, the only part of his body that could respond. He tried to keep his eyelids open, not wanting to give up just yet, but the rush of water was too much, and his eyes pinched shut on their own.

George wanted to pray, but he was not a religious man. He wanted to say goodbye, but he had no one to say goodbye to. He was alone in this world, and he knew he would not be missed.

Chapter One

The giant blue-and-white helicopter, unmistakable Presidential seals affixed on either side, swept down out of a sapphire sky. Skimming the treetops for a hundred yards or so, the pilot dipped into a clearing and set the chopper down majestically, like a hawk into its nest.

Inside the twelve-person passenger section, Congressman Trey Stone, his wife, Jasmine, and their six-year-old daughter, Katie, gathered their carry-on luggage.

Trey pulled on a wool-lined mackinaw, and Jazz and Katie bundled up in ankle-length coats. This was a spur of the Blue Ridge Mountains, and the weather would be brisk, if not downright cold.

A steward opened the side door and lowered the exit ramp. Trey ducked through the door, and Jazz followed with Katie in hand. They stood at the landing on the top step and took in the glorious surroundings.

Camp David was even more incredible than they had expected. The site looked like a rustic Shangri-La, with twenty or so cabin-like buildings dotting the landscape around a lodge-like structure in the middle of a curved drive. The grounds were immaculately kept. Not a rock out of place. Not a blade of grass uncut. The compound rested on a plateau that looked out over the Catoctin Mountain Range. Its wave of unending evergreens gave the hillside the look of a calm, deep sea. The air was as fresh as could be, too, with a snap of cold that made their eyes rim with water.

Trey and Jazz took in as much as they could, then looked

at each other with a mix of excitement and a little fear.

For the first time, Trey looked down the stairs. At the bottom, looking up—as he knew she would be—Laura Weddington stood with her arms folded across her ample bosom, waiting for their descent.

"Welcome to heaven on earth," she called out. "It doesn't get any better than this."

Jazz led the way down the stairs and embraced her old school chum. They stood back and admired one another.

"I'm sorry to hear about Jack," Jazz said. "I'm sure everything'll be all right. The worst is over now."

Laura smiled grimly. "Honey, the worst is never over with that husband of mine." She knelt down and planted a kiss on Katie's forehead. "Baby, you look more like your mother every day. You definitely got the best of both parents."

"Thank you, Mrs. Weddington," Katie said, as she had been taught to do. "Where're the horses?"

"What makes you think we've got horses, darling?"

"Daddy said."

"He did?" She stood up. "That true, Daddy?" She turned to Trey as he reached the bottom of the stairs.

"That's what I hear. But you know about rumors in Washington—only half of them are true."

"The question is: Which half?"

They spoke this last line together and smiled fleetingly.

Trey leaned over and pecked her on the cheek. "How're you doing?"

"About as well as can be expected."

"That wayward husband of yours get home yet?"

"Briefly."

The response begged for more, but now wasn't the time. Trey handed two small bags and his briefcase to a porter.

"Let's go see your rooms," Laura said.

They strolled across the quad that led to a collection of cabin suites scattered around the central lodge, known as Aspen. Laura pointed out landmarks and sites as they moved along, including a two-story structure that served as a combination barn and storage facility.

"That," she said, "is where the horses are kept, Katie. Your Daddy's right."

"Yippee," she said. "Do we get to see them?"

"Later, honey. The President's got something planned."

"Is he here yet?" Jazz asked.

"Yes, he's in Hickory Lodge, meeting with a couple of Cabinet officers. He's anxious to get business out of the way and meet with his guests."

"What's the agenda look like?" Trey asked.

Laura glanced at her watch; it was a little after eleven. "They've planned a casual lunch for twelve-thirty in the small dining room. I'll show you the way later. It should be quaint and cozy—just you, the President and First Lady. Sort of an introductory get-together."

"That leaves us an hour and a half to get ready," Jazz said. "Plenty of time—even for me."

"After lunch, I'll give you a tour of the place. There's so much history here—the site where Anwar Sadat and Menachem Begin agreed to the Peace Accords. Dwight Eisenhower memorabilia. Roosevelt, Kennedy and Carter collectibles. It's an incredible place, just like a living museum."

She showed them into their cabin. From the outside, the place was a little more rugged than Trey had expected, but the interior was as tastefully appointed as a hotel suite. The Great Room rose up under a lofted ceiling, and a massive stone fireplace dominated one wall. Across from there, huge windows looked out onto the valley below.

Laura showed the way down a corridor to the first bedroom. The porter had already placed Katie's luggage at the foot of the bed. Further down, they passed through a double-door entry into the master suite, where floor-to-ceiling glass doors framed a breathtaking view of the mountains as the valley sloped away. It created a floating effect, as if the cabin were suspended in the clouds.

"I'm not leaving," Jazz said. "Tell the President it'll take an army to get me out of here."

"You haven't seen anything yet," Laura said. "Wait'll we get to the main lodge."

"I don't know if I can take it."

Laura checked her watch again. "We'll find out in an hour. That should give you enough time to freshen up."

"Just barely," Jazz said.

"In the meantime, I'm going to steal your husband. Hope you don't mind."

"Not for too long, I hope."

"A minute or two."

Trey followed her out the front door to a graveled path that meandered into the sheltered woods. The aroma of pine and sumac overwhelmed their senses.

They walked silently for a while, down a steep embankment made easier by small wooden steps. At the bottom of the slope, she took him by the arm and walked under a low umbrella of branches, holding him close to her. With each step, he could feel her softness move against him. She was braless beneath a pullover sweater, and he couldn't help but notice.

He tried to refocus on the issue at hand.

"You told us about lunch this afternoon," he said, "and that sounds innocent enough. But I assume the President's plans go beyond that?"

"Of course," she said. "He'll find *some* time to put the arm on you."

"At dinner tonight, I assume, or a meeting tomorrow?"

"Frankly, I'm not sure, Trey. All I've been told is a 'full court press' is planned. You had to expect that. Time's growing short. The President needs a commitment. He'll do whatever's necessary to secure your support."

"I came here because I believe he deserves to be heard, Laura. I didn't come to offer promises. It's too soon for that."

"I understand. But I want you to know extraordinary pressures will be applied. The President and his advisers can be awfully . . . persuasive."

"Then it's my job to keep their expectations in check."

She smiled—perfect white teeth against stark-red lips.

"That's what I love about politics," she said. "The conflicting interests. You never know the outcome until it's done. Even then, the outcome can be changed." She glanced at him out of the corner of her eye. "The perception is often different than the reality."

"And vice versa."

They came to a clearing beside a stream and watched a school of tiny fish feed in a rock pool. She held him tight, and he didn't try to pull away. The weight of her against him felt good in the fresh air as they stood in the sunlight and let it warm them for the walk back.

Before that, he needed to find out about another topic weighing heavily on his mind.

"You said Jack came home 'briefly'?" he asked. "What was that all about?"

"After the arraignment, he got home half in the bag. He was supposed to meet with his attorneys and PR people, but didn't. He and his dad got in this terrible argument, shouting and screaming." She glanced at him. "Your name came up more than once."

Trey took a deep breath. He hoped Jack's drunken comments didn't reveal more than they should have. Before he could ask, she went on.

"I did my best to keep the kids away. When I came downstairs, Jack was gone. I haven't talked to him since."

Trey turned and started back up the path. She moved with him, and quickly changed the topic. "I hope you don't mind me offering a little advice over the next couple of days . . ."

"I'm open to advice. I don't always take it, but I'm happy to listen." He winked as if he were kidding, but he wasn't.

"You have the chance this weekend to secure your political future, Trey. You've also got the chance to damage it, maybe even destroy it. I don't want to sound overly dramatic, but these are the stakes. Reelected or not, President Forsythe's an immensely powerful man. He and his circle of friends control Democratic politics today. That won't change, even if he's not returned to the White House."

"I'm painfully aware of that, Laura. It's exactly what I've been hearing from several different quarters."

She let go of his arm and stepped in front of him, placing both hands on his hips, inside his jacket.

"I realize you've got concerns about the effectiveness of his Presidency. They're legitimate concerns, and I don't mean to discount them."

Her hands slipped around his waist. She drew herself closer to him, her breasts resting against his mid-section. She looked up, unblinking, into his eyes. Her mouth was so close he could feel the warmth of her breath pass between them. He could see the brush marks in the deep-red lipstick that smoothed her lips, how it blended ever so carefully with the paleness of her complexion. She was an incredibly attractive woman. Her next to him like this, in this setting—with the mysteriousness of the forest all around—was intoxicating. It reminded him of the power of attraction, and how it could overcome all logic.

She moved harder against him, her hands going to the small of his back, her nails digging in through the fabric of his shirt.

"You have to leave the right impression," she said. "That's all you've got to do this weekend. Give them hope, Trey. Give *me* hope. It's my political future, too." She paused. "There's no telling how far we can go together. Maybe all the way to the top. Just hear them out and think about your future—about our future."

He didn't know what to say, or how to say it. He heard her words, but they didn't fully register. He stared silently into her dark eyes, watching as her face seemed to rise to meet his, her lips seemed to touch delicately against his.

Then he heard another voice call out in the woods.

"Daddy, Daddy!"

It was Katie coming down the path. He could hear the thump of her boots on the wooden steps.

He shouted out, "Over here, honey," and took a step back.

Laura stepped back, too, wrapping her arms around herself.

Katie appeared around a curve in the path and ran headlong into her father's arms. He swept her up and held her on his hip.

"What're you doing out here by yourself, young lady?" he asked.

"The guard said you came this way."

"You shouldn't be in the woods alone," he said. "You never know what you might come across out here."

"The guard said if I wasn't back in five minutes, he'd come after me."

Laura stroked Katie's hair. "It's impossible to get lost, Trey. The path only goes one way, and the guards keep close watch."

"Did your mom send you after me?"

"She said to hurry. We have to meet the President."

He put her down. "Come on, I'll race you back."

Katie ran off, and Trey hurried after her. Suddenly, he stopped and glanced back. Laura was still standing there, her arms crossed beneath her breasts, the sunlight reflecting off her face like a prism, shattering her silhouette.

For the first time, Trey wondered how much she knew, and when she knew it. Her talk of *his* future on the line; maybe she didn't realize how right she was. But his least concern right now was politics. He had far more . . . dangerous . . . thoughts on his mind.

To think, it had all begun so innocently with a Presidential election that was supposed to be a foregone conclusion—and had been anything but; and with a stupid favor for a friend who had asked once too often. Now, the intersection of these events was about to be his undoing. And maybe the country's, too. . . .

Chapter Two

Five Weeks Earlier

Trey Stone and a half-dozen congressional staffers stood inside the Cannon Building's third-floor conference room and watched the television monitor in stunned disbelief. Every one of them had believed the election was lost long ago. They and the rest of the country thought President Forsythe was destined to be a one-termer, and deservedly so. The Republicans were so confident of victory, they had already begun lining up positions in the new Administration. Even the Independent Party had predicted their man would fail to garner a single Electoral College vote.

They were all wrong.

"Despite recent polls showing a landslide victory for Carl Wardlow," the anchor said, "this Presidential contest is shaping up as one for the ages."

"Given the closeness of the count," his partner added, "we've got a long night ahead."

The two broadcasters laughed, knowing they were sitting on a political story as big or bigger than the historic Bush-Gore contest.

Trey sipped his lukewarm coffee and shook his head. He was supposed to be at a Democratic vote-watch in Annapolis tonight and knew he'd get nothing but grief for failing to show. He also knew his absence was one of the benefits of running unopposed. He would make a brief appearance at campaign headquarters to thank supporters, then head straight home for a quiet evening with his wife and daughter—for once.

He checked his watch. It was nearly seven. Already late for another family dinner . . .

He slugged down the last of his coffee and turned toward the door, nearly bumping into his senior staff secretary, Ellen Landers, who looked more concerned than usual.

"Mr. Stone, you have a visitor."

"Can't do it, Miss Landers. I'm late already. The missus is going to kill me this time."

She cleared her throat. "It's a White House official."

Trey did a double-take. Several people in the room glanced over with interest. It wasn't often the President sent an emissary to the congressional offices. He preferred the legislators come to him.

"What's it about?" he asked.

She shrugged. "All he said was it's urgent."

The remark got raised eyebrows around the room. Trey handed his empty cup to her and headed down the hall, glancing at his watch again. He knew his wife wouldn't understand, but a congressman couldn't dismiss a White House official, no matter how many dinners had to wait. He hurried into his office, finding his distinguished guest seated with his back to the door.

Trey walked around the chair, and reached out to shake hands. "I'm Congressman Stone."

He was left with his hand hanging in mid-air.

The White House man uncrossed his legs and brushed at his pants, then finally reciprocated.

"Archibald Longstreet," he said, his deep southern accent stretching the syllables out of shape. "You can call me Arch."

Trey smiled. "Arch it is."

He sat down behind his desk, noticing the family portrait had been moved; it was about to fall over. He straightened the frame and rested back.

"How can I help you, Arch? My secretary says your message is urgent."

"I hope I didn't alarm you."

"No, but I must admit I am intrigued. It's not every day a third-term congressman gets a personal visit from the White House."

"This isn't every day, is it?"

Trey pursed his lips. "I assume you're referring to the election."

"Of course."

"Sorry I can't help you there. The polls close"—he glanced at the wall clock—"in a couple of hours. Not much any of us can do at this point."

Longstreet nodded. "That's the conventional wisdom. I have a different view."

Trey smiled. "I'd love to hear it."

Longstreet stood. "Mind if I move around? I think better when I move."

"Feel free." Trey rocked back in his chair and wondered about this odd character. He had heard of him before, but had never met him. Trey knew he was the President's campaign strategist—had been for years. But Archibald Longstreet stayed well behind the scenes. Maybe it was because he didn't look the part. He was not an especially handsome man—a long, thin face; glasses that looked like goggles; dishwater blond hair combed ear to ear.

"Can I get you anything, Mr. Longstreet? Coffee, tea, soda?"

"Call me Arch. No, I've imposed too much already." He

paused. "I hope you don't mind my waiting in your office. Your secretary said it'd be okay."

"No problem."

Longstreet turned and sat against the windowsill overlooking Constitution Avenue, the Capitol Building looming behind him.

"I wouldn't want to cause a problem, Trey. I hope you don't mind if I call you that. I understand it's your preference."

"It's what my friends and family call me."

"I hope we become friends."

"I'd hate to make an enemy in the White House."

"I'd hate that, too. Of course, a lot of people don't think we'll be there much longer."

Trey picked up a bronzed Naval Academy keepsake from the corner of his desk and reset it in the middle, where it was always kept. "We should know the answer in another few hours."

"Some of us may know even earlier."

Trey nodded. "You have 'inside' information?"

"Always."

"Tell me, is it going to be the Republican challenger or the Democratic incumbent?"

"Neither."

Trey laughed. "Don't tell me the Independent candidate's going to pull this out."

"Funny you should put it that way. He'll have an effect on the outcome—a very dramatic effect."

Unlike most politicians, Trey didn't much care who won. If the Republican triumphed, Trey and his fellow Democrats would be faced with the opposite party in the Oval Office. If Forsythe won, the country would get another four years of a do-nothing Administration.

"Look, I don't mean to rush things here, but . . ."

"I apologize. I shouldn't take up your valuable time, but I wanted to impress upon you the importance of your role."

"My role?"

"I don't believe this election will be settled today, Mr. Stone. It's entirely possible a few congressmen will decide things in January." He paused. "I count you prominent among them."

Trey furrowed his brow. "You mean this election's going to the House? Good God, that hasn't happened in . . ."

"More than two hundred years."

"Why do you think it'll happen now? And if it did, why would my vote count more than anyone else's?"

"On the first question, let's just say, 'intuition.' On the second, your position in the Maryland delegation singles you out. You're the undisputed majority spokesperson. We believe that reputation's richly deserved."

Trey smiled wryly. "Thanks for the compliment, if that's what it is. I'm not sure the perception's all that accurate. We've got quite a few independent thinkers in the Chesapeake state."

"But very few with your background and credentials." He motioned around the room. "Exceptional family history. A father who was a war hero. A great uncle who was Chief Justice. You're an Annapolis graduate with high honors, and a successful congressman running unopposed." Longstreet smiled and shook his head. "You've built an enviable legislative record in only a few years, and you're known as a devoted family man with a lovely wife and daughter. In this town, those are as good as credentials get."

Longstreet stepped over to the desk and ran his finger along the top of the family photo. As he did, his suit coat fell open, displaying a small, silver-plated handgun belted inside.

Trey blanched at the sight. *My God,* he wondered, *why would a campaign strategist need to carry a pistol with the Secret Service at his disposal twenty-four hours a day?*

Longstreet buttoned his jacket and continued as if nothing had happened. "You have significant financial resources, you're a close confidant of the governor, and, I understand, you may have Senate aspirations—perhaps even national office down the road." He paused. "No, Trey, try to deny it if you will, but you're a powerful man in these parts. You should be proud of that." He lowered his voice conspiratorially. "In Washington, always use power to your advantage."

Trey was taken aback by Longstreet's remarks. They seemed so out of character for a White House spokesperson. Besides, why would the President's man know so much about him? Was Forsythe considering him for an Administrative position or a Cabinet post? If so, it didn't make much sense—not now. According to the latest polls, the President had little chance of winning the election. He trailed in the popular vote by landslide proportions and was even a distant third in Maryland. Why did Longstreet think a young congressman from Annapolis would have any role—let alone a critical one—to play in a Presidential election that was all but over?

"Mr. Longstreet—Arch—I must admit I'm a little confused by all this. Frankly, I'm also uncomfortable. I mean, the polls haven't even closed."

"I don't mean to compromise you or your office, Congressman. I simply want you to know the White House recognizes the contributions you can make. Should things go as we expect, we want to work with you. That's all."

Trey got up and moved around the desk to the door. He didn't like the direction of this conversation or the idea of being investigated without his knowledge. He didn't like Longstreet's vagueness, either, or his subtle intimidation.

"I'm honored the White House recognizes my political efforts," he said. "But I believe this discussion is inappropriate right now." Opening the door, he went back to his desk. "If and when a House vote occurs, we can talk. Until then, I don't have any more to say. I hope you understand."

Longstreet lifted up the family photo, staring at it for several long moments. Then he set it back slightly askew, just as it had been before. "You have an outstanding career in front of you, Trey. We just want to make sure nothing's . . . jeopardized."

"Jeopardized?"

Longstreet spun on his heel and walked toward the open door, speaking over his shoulder. "Congratulations on your re-election, Congressman, and give Jasmine and Katie all the best from me and the President."

Trey stood open-mouthed and watched him disappear. He sat down hard in his desk chair, realizing the palms of his hands were damp. He rubbed them over his pant legs, feeling like he needed a shower.

There was something utterly creepy about the man. Trey looked around the room and felt the oily presence of him everywhere—in his sickly-sweet after-shave and the odd smudges on the picture frames, and the wall portraits left slightly ajar. He had been touching things and leaving his mark.

Trey pulled out a handkerchief and wiped where Longstreet had been. He straightened the portraits, too. But the exercise did little to help. He couldn't erase the feel of the man. Nor could he forget the remark about "jeopardizing" his career. Trey had already come too close to that himself.

He looked at the picture of Jazz and Katie, and remembered he was supposed to be home more than an hour ago.

He grabbed his briefcase and hurried out, stopping only long enough to lock the door securely behind.

Chapter Three

The drive home went by in a blur. Trey kept turning Longstreet's words over in his mind. If he was right and Trey wound up in the middle of a House battle for the Presidency, it was the last place he could afford to be right now. And he had no one to blame but himself.

He cranked up the radio as the announcer turned to an election update: From all indications, the Presidential contest was tightening, just as Longstreet had predicted. Worse: Maryland and Maine were turning out to be the keys.

Only a few weeks ago, the two states had appeared locked up for the Republican. But in recent days, the Independent candidate—an industrialist with ties to both states—had flooded the airways with ads that attacked the two major party candidates with a vengeance of lies and half-truths. The strategy had worked. According to the exit polls, he had managed to grab a small lead in both states. With the rest of the Electoral College dividing up evenly, the national results were suddenly in question.

Trey wiped his mouth with the back of his hand, feeling a tremble he hadn't expected. Longstreet's visit was taking on even more ominous proportions.

He slowed the car to a crawl and pulled off the two-lane rural road onto a long stretch of drive leading up to his house on the hill. Listening to the gentle crunch of the tires over the gravel road, his nerves began to calm. A quarter-mile down the drive, a long line of towering oaks and maples gave way to a wide clearing around his spectacular Georgian manor home.

Trey parked in front, knowing he would need a quick getaway in the morning. He hurried inside, stopping in the kitchen doorway to watch Jazz stir something on the stove.

She looked up and flinched. "Damn you, Trey Stone. You scared the daylights out of me."

Across the room, Katie squealed and came running. "Daddy. Daddy. I made banana pie."

He tossed his suit jacket aside and caught her in midstride, planting a kiss on her nose.

"Hmmm, do I detect banana on your breath, young lady? Don't tell me, you've been eating dessert before the main meal!"

"It's not dessert . . . not yet, Daddy."

"You know banana pie's my favorite?"

"Mine too!"

"Good. We'll eat the whole thing tonight, and we won't save any for Mom. She's a cake eater, anyway."

"Oh, boy! Promise? Promise?!"

"You'll promise no such thing," Jazz scolded, shaking her spoon.

Trey grabbed his suit jacket. "In that case, I'm going upstairs to change and catch more of the election results."

Jazz turned off the fire. "I thought we agreed, no poll watching tonight."

"An update, hon, that's all. It's a close one. With this crazy third-party candidate in the mix, anything could happen."

"An update," she said. "That's it. Katie and I have other plans for this evening, don't we, honey?"

Katie nodded absently, once again consumed with her banana slices.

Trey turned and galloped up the stairs. In the bedroom, he went straight to the armoire to click on the television, immediately sensing the tension in the newscasters' voices.

"If the exit polls are accurate," the anchor said, "the Independent candidate could actually win a handful of Electoral College votes."

"If that happens," his partner chimed in, "he'd be the first third-party candidate since George Wallace of Alabama to win any Electoral College support." Then he added the punctuation: "For only the third time in history, a Presidential election could be thrown into the House of Representatives."

How could Longstreet be so right?

Trey turned to see Jazz walk in. She came to him and laid a hand on his shoulder.

"What'd he say about the House?"

"It's bizarre, Jazz. No one has an electoral majority. It means the House could wind up in the middle of electing our next President."

Her mouth fell open.

He shook his head. "Young's third-party candidacy is the key."

"I don't understand how anybody can support that man. He's so . . . disgusting."

"The far right's small but powerful. Add to that his favorite-son status around here, and he's got enough support to disrupt the national results."

"But Maryland never goes conservative."

"Half this state owes its livelihood to Young and his family. The same in Maine. People are voting their wallets on this one, not their heads."

"What would happen if he forces a House vote?"

"Each state delegation would get one vote. Majority wins."

She thought for a moment. "That takes the pressure off each representative at least."

"Theoretically. I'm not sure these things ever work the way they're supposed to."

She wrapped an arm around his waist and drew him close. "Does anything in Washington work the way it's supposed to?"

He pressed himself against her. "In politics, nothing is how it seems."

She held him tight and kneaded his back. When he bowed his head to kiss her, she slipped from his grasp and fell on the bed. He threw himself on top and wrapped around her, holding on as if it were their first time together.

"Where's Katie?" he asked.

"Downstairs with our faithful housekeeper. I gave Irma the night off, but she hasn't left yet."

"Thank God for that woman."

With the announcers droning in the background, Trey and Jazz waged a campaign all their own, making love as if it were their last private moment together. In the world of Washington politics, that was always a distinct possibility.

Chapter Four

Early the next morning, Trey woke with a start. He checked the clock: 5:30. He was already later than he wanted to be. He showered and dressed in minutes, then hurried downstairs for the paper, calling up the *Washington Post* on his laptop.

His mouth fell open when he saw the headline: *Presidential Election Goes to the House.*

So that's the way it's going to be.

He grabbed his cellular phone and dialed into the House voice mail system, knowing his mailbox would be overflowing with calls from reporters trying to reach him throughout the night. As he clicked through a series of messages, Katie appeared in the kitchen doorway, her eyes half closed. He motioned for her to come to him.

She crawled in his lap and dozed there while he rushed through message after message.

Jazz wasn't far behind. She headed straight for the coffee pot and poured two steaming cups, bringing him one on a saucer. She sat beside her small family and stroked Katie's hair, glancing at the computer screen.

"Congratulations, Congressman. Looks like you're about to either make a President, or break one."

He punched the "end" button on the phone, cutting his messages halfway through.

"Not me, Jazz. I'm just along for the ride on this one."

She sipped carefully from her cup. "Uh huh."

"Seriously, I'm just a lowly third-termer," he said. "It's not for me to choose."

"Right."

"You don't believe me?"

"I believe you." She smiled.

"Really, I'm planning to stay out of this one," he said. "Too much at stake."

"Of course."

She set her cup down and lifted Katie out of his lap. "You'll probably have to stay in D.C. for the next few days."

He rubbed at a spot on his forehead. "I suppose."

Katie began to stir.

"Want tomato juice, honey?" Jazz said.

Katie nodded. "And banana pie."

Trey and Jazz laughed. He reached over and ran a hand down her mass of auburn hair. "How about we have bananas on our cereal, instead?"

Jazz brought them two big bowls, and they ate hungrily. Afterward, Katie ran upstairs to prepare for school, as Trey and Jazz topped off their coffee cups and moved to the morning room. They sat close together on a white-cane couch and watched the day's sun break full over a calm bay.

"This vote's going to be a monster, isn't it?" she said.

He shook his head. "I don't know, hon. It's never been done—at least not in a couple of centuries."

"Have you thought about your position yet?"

"I'll have to find out how the voters feel first. Maybe I'll get lucky and my vote won't count for much."

Their eyes met quickly, then pulled away. They both knew nothing happened quickly or by luck in Washington.

He checked his watch, realizing he'd have to get on the road soon. "I've got a dozen calls stacked up from Democratic Party loyalists and the governor's office. There's another series of calls from reporters—the *Washington Post*, the AP, *New York Times*, all the networks. The other Maryland representatives are already asking for an informal caucus this week. It's going to be early mornings and late nights for the next few weeks."

"I thought Congress was out of session. Doesn't that include you?"

"I'm sorry, hon, but this is an extraordinary moment in history. Bigger than Watergate, bigger than the Clinton impeachment, bigger than Gore-Bush."

"But it's *always* something extraordinary," she said. "At some point the 'ordinary' has to count for something. Katie's starting to think you're a visitor around here. So am I."

Trey knew he didn't have an adequate response. As many hours as he put in, the work was still way ahead of him and never-ending.

"Who are you trying to impress anyway?" she asked. "If it's me, I can tell you it's not necessary. If it's the voters, that's a waste, too. The Republicans couldn't even find a candidate to run against you."

He smiled. "I've been fairly successful in my own district, I'll give you that. But the voters don't see what goes on behind the scenes, the constant negotiating and compromise. If I'm not there to speak for them, the issues become nothing more than a trade-off on their lives." He drank the last of his cold coffee and pinched his face at the bitterness. "Even if it keeps me away from you and Katie too much."

"Remember, this election includes another four hundred and thirty-four congressmen, Trey. You're not alone."

"I may not be alone, but sometimes I feel like it. This may be one of those times."

"What makes you say that?"

"The breakdown on yesterday's vote. Maryland went for the Independent, Marshall Young, but he's got no chance of winning. So it'd be a waste of our state's vote to support him. Logic would tell us to vote for Carl Wardlow instead, since he was a close second in the state."

"Uh huh."

"But he's a Republican, so the Democrats won't see it that way. The party'll do all it can to make sure we support Forsythe, even if he did finish a distant third in Maryland."

She shrugged. "Maybe it won't matter—one of the candidates could win without Maryland."

"If one man were going to win without us, he'd have already done it in the Electoral College. No, it's going to be a take-no-prisoners political war. We're talking about the most powerful office in the world. No one's going to give it up easily."

They both grew quiet and stared out at the morning sky. A marine-layer of fog drifted in over the water, darkening the horizon, creating a faint cherry hue. It reminded him of an old sailor's creed: *Red sky at morning, sailor's warning.*

Trey stood up. "One thing's for sure. This won't be decided until the final vote in January."

"That doesn't bode well for a merry December, does it?"

He kissed her lightly on the cheek. "Tell Katie I had to go."

"Are you staying in the city?"

"Only until Friday."

"You better call her later. She'll be upset."

"Me too."

He grabbed his suit jacket off the back of a chair and snatched his briefcase off the floor. Hurrying toward the front door, he didn't look back. For the next few days, he wanted to remember his wife as she was just a moment ago, sitting close beside him, wrapped in a white silk robe, her auburn hair tossed casually over her shoulders.

He closed the front door quietly, careful not to let Katie hear, knowing she would want a kiss and a hug, and he might never get away. He fired up his Lincoln Town Car and pulled out of the circular drive, watching in the rear-view mirror as the Chesapeake disappeared behind him.

His public awaited. So, too, did the pressures of a vote that, as Longstreet had intimated, would be one of the most contested in history. Trey knew the first order of the day would be to make sure Maryland's vote didn't become a bargaining chip between two opposing state factions, with him squarely in the middle—where he least wanted to be.

Off the coast, Sam Steele climbed a metal ladder to the trawler's wheel room and stepped inside. He picked up a pair of binoculars and focused on the back of the Stones' sprawling house more than a half-mile away.

"I hope these people don't get up in the middle of the night every day." He rubbed at his head, feeling the cold of the morning where his hair should be. "You get anything useful?"

Ridge Franks shook his head, his oversized earphones flopping from side to side. "Not much."

"What'd they talk about?"

"Mostly what a pain in the ass this election's going to be."

"We already knew that. Anything else?"

"It appears our congressman's got concerns about Forsythe. Stone says it'll be tough to support a man who finished third."

"We knew that, too." Steele turned to leave. "E-mail the

transcript to the boss. He'll want to know."

"Right away."

"Keep an eye on that wife of his, too. Both of 'em can't be as clean as they pretend to be. See if you can get a couple of shots through the windows." He laughed. "You know how the boss likes photos."

Steele yanked open the side door and caught a blast of early-morning chill off the bay. "This is gonna be a long few weeks."

"When it's over, we'll be treated to a nice Caribbean vacation for our troubles. You can be sure of that."

"That's if we win, Ridge. God only knows where we'll wind up if we lose this thing."

"We won't lose. The boss won't let that happen."

"He's counting on us, too, you know?"

"We won't let him down. Go on back to bed. I've got this under control."

Steele mumbled under his breath about always drawing the "short straw" on these assignments. He wrapped his jacket around himself and stepped into the icy cold, leaving his partner to his morning's work.

Chapter Five

The thirty-mile drive to D.C. took nearly an hour and a half, just as Trey expected. He wheeled his huge car off Constitution Avenue and maneuvered through a crowd on the sidewalk and into the underground parking garage of the Cannon Building, where nearly two hundred U.S. Representatives maintained their Capitol Hill offices.

When he saw a roving band of onlookers and reporters outside, he knew what awaited inside: Packs of journalists would be marauding the first-floor walkways, scouting out interviews and sound bites—anything to feed the voracious appetites of a worldwide audience.

He guided his car into its usual spot and parked quickly. Rushing through the basement entry, he jogged up the concrete stairs to the first-floor lobby, fighting his way through the expected crush of reporters. He tossed out "No comments" right and left, slowly making his way to the elevator reserved for representatives and their staffs. As the doors slid open, he stepped inside. Standing alone against the back wall, he looked out at the camera crews as they recorded his silence—which was, in itself, a comment to be exploited on the evening news.

When the doors reopened three floors up, he stepped into a hallway filled with staffers rushing everywhere. The tension was thick. Most congressmen were out of town, having flown home to celebrate their victories or mourn their defeats, but their staffs were still on the job, as always. Two of Trey's people fell into place beside him, talking over each other as he dodged his way inside their offices. Everyone stopped when Ellen Landers approached.

"Thank goodness you're here," she said. "The phones haven't quit."

"I returned a dozen calls on the drive in."

"You've got twenty more." She handed him a stack of call slips. "The other Maryland representatives want a meeting today to map out a position statement. The President's Re-election Committee called several times, and the reporters are phoning like crazy. They're insistent—they want an official statement within the hour. They're even threatening to make up something at this point."

He stopped in the middle of the room, his staff circled around him. "Here's our position," he said. "We *have* none, and we won't have one until we're damn good and ready. We won't decide on an issue this important just because the press has a deadline. Tell the reporters we'll conscientiously and lawfully represent the people of the state of Maryland. Period."

Miss Landers scribbled notes in longhand.

"Set up a luncheon in the Capitol dining room with the Maryland delegation," he said. "Nothing fancy, usual table. We'll need to decompress before the serious stuff starts."

A female staff assistant peeled off to a nearby telephone to make arrangements.

"You said the President's Re-election Committee called?"

"Repeatedly."

"Who?"

"Laura Weddington."

Trey fell silent. He glanced out the street-side window where the Lincoln Memorial loomed in the distance. It was barely nine o'clock on a chilly November morning and already the steps were covered with tourists. He watched them move about like visitors at an amusement park.

He turned back. "Put her off as long as you can."

"She says if you don't return her call in the next five minutes, she's coming down here in person." She handed him the call slip. "Lord knows we don't want that."

Trey stepped into his office and sank back in his desk chair, glaring at the phone, hoping his gaze might melt the instrument into a puddle on his desk. He hadn't seen Laura in months. He knew the last thing he needed was to talk with the governor's daughter-in-law, his best friend's wife. He also knew she might be his only route to Jack. If Trey had to go through Laura to get to him, so be it.

He reached for the phone. She answered on the first ring. "I knew my threats would get your attention," she purred.

"They did that and more. How've you been?"

"Good. How about you?"

"Fine. How're Jack and the kids?"

"The kids are good. As for Jack, God only knows. I haven't seen him lately. I've hardly had time to go home since before the election—and only then to shower and change."

He nodded. "It's good that these contests come around only once every four years. I assume you didn't get the results you were looking for yesterday."

"That's the understatement of the year. But we haven't lost this thing yet, Trey. I've been given the job of scheduling meetings with key congressmen to hear the President's case for re-election. I'd like to include you in that effort."

"I suspected as much. Our entire delegation wants to hear the President's position."

"I knew we could count on you."

"You've got to understand," he said, "we'll be meeting with the opposition, too."

"We just want an equal opportunity," she said.

"That's my middle name. When do you want to meet?"

"Right away. We want to do some fact-finding to determine your delegation's needs. Then we'll follow-up with the President and his top officers before making final recommmendations. We want to make sure everyone's questions are fully addressed."

"You've got a big job in front of you. Fifty state delegations. That's a lot of meetings, a lot of questions."

"We figure the decision will come down to a few strategic 'undecideds.' "

"It usually does."

"That raises another question, Trey."

"Yes?"

"I was hoping you might offer a little guidance," she said. "You're more knowledgeable on the issues than anyone. Would you consider meeting with me privately to go over a few of the . . . finer points?"

He paused, breathing heavily into the receiver. "You've got to understand, Laura, this could be the most sensitive vote I'll cast in my lifetime. I have to avoid all signs of favoritism."

"I'd never do anything to compromise your position, Trey, but I'm in way over my head. I don't know who else to turn to. I can't go to the governor. He hasn't got the right Washington connections. I need someone I can trust, someone who can offer a few pointers."

"I've just got to be extra careful on this one."

"I know, but—" She paused. "It's more than political advice I need."

"Oh?"

"I didn't want to tell you this—at least not this way. Jack's not well."

That was precisely the news Trey didn't want to hear. "The last time I saw him, he looked horrible. The booze is taking its toll."

"I can't go into it on the phone. I'd rather talk to you in person."

Personal meetings with Laura were always a dangerous proposition, but he had to know more. "When do you want to meet?"

"I'll come by your townhouse tonight at, say, nine. I'll bring Chinese. It'll be just like old times."

"Chinese it is."

"It'll be great to see you again. It's been too long."

"It's been a very long time."

"You're a doll. See you soon."

He pressed his phone into the cradle, holding it there as if it might leap up suddenly and bite. He wondered if he should call back right away and cancel the appointment. But the inside information on Jack was essential. It was always that way with the Weddingtons. Once you were trapped in their sphere, it was impossible to pull away, like sinking into a black hole.

The door to his office burst open, and Miss Landers stormed in, her sensible pumps clumping across the carpet. She had buzzed but he didn't notice.

"Mr. Stone, your calendar's overflowing. There're too many requests to accommodate. We need your guidance."

"Sit down, Miss Landers," he said calmly. "We'll go through them one at a time. Before we start, I want to add a request of my own."

"Yes?"

"Schedule an hour of private time for me between now

43

and noon to prepare a draft position document. I want to circulate it as early as possible to the other state Representatives—before they start making commitments we can't keep."

She held up a several-inch stack of call slips, memos and notes. "We don't have enough time."

"We'll make time." He gave her his best boyish grin.

She sighed. "I guess we will."

He took the stack of papers from her and dealt out piles of "to do's." For the moment, at least, he felt like a man calm in the midst of chaos. He wondered how much longer that would last; probably not much more than dinner tonight.

Chapter Six

Elegant as always in a jet-black suit—contrasting with the silvery white of his perfectly styled hair—President Benjamin Lamar Forsythe, Virginia Democrat, stepped behind his antique desk and folded his six-foot-four frame into a padded swivel chair. Crooking his elbows on the desktop, he held his head in his hands, and sat like that for what seemed an eternity. The only sound in the room was the voice of a newscaster tallying the results of a re-election campaign gone horribly wrong.

At least it had gone wrong in Forsythe's eyes.

Looking up, he slammed both fists on the desk, slopping his coffee from side to side, staining the blotter and a few randomly scattered papers. "Damn it to hell, Arch," he said. "We're going to lose this thing. I can feel it. Wardlow's got too big a lead in the popular vote."

Across the room, in a square of couches opposite the fireplace, his top adviser calmly set his teacup on a china saucer, then dabbed a napkin at the corners of his mouth. Only Arch Longstreet had the gall to make a flustered President wait.

"If I might be so bold, Mr. President," Longstreet said, "I wouldn't characterize what we're seeing today so negatively. The Electoral College will be our saving grace yet. Trust me."

Forsythe was at a loss for words, as he often was when Longstreet took the floor. The rest of the President's top advisers, known as the Southern Mafia, sat silently around the room, waiting for Longstreet to hold forth, yet again, on his controversial campaign strategy.

Vice President Fred McNally, standing closest to the television, stared at the news reports that showed his and Forsythe's intertwined political careers unraveling. McNally had been openly critical of Longstreet for weeks, as was Secretary of State Armand Gandolf, sitting nearest the fireplace. In fact, none of the officers present—not the chief of staff or top legal adviser—publicly supported Longstreet. But their opinions mattered little. The President rarely, if ever, listened to anyone's advice when it came to Archibald Longstreet. He had led Forsythe through countless successful political battles over the years, guiding his rise from congressman to senator to governor of Virginia. Four years ago, they teamed to seize the highest office in the land. They had never lost a major election or critical legislative battle together.

Longstreet didn't intend to start now.

"As I stated from the beginning of this campaign," he said, "our strength is and always will be the power of the Presidency. This is where we hold an advantage no one can overcome."

McNally, a balding, bloated man who seemed to have aged twenty years since taking office, turned from the television and walked to the bar cart to refill his spiked coffee. "It's too late," he said. "The power of the Presidency's lost. The votes have been cast—along with our political fates, I'm afraid."

Longstreet moved over beside Forsythe's desk, placing the President at his side for the rest of the room to view. "The votes have been cast," he said, "but the election's far from over."

McNally topped off his coffee with a shot of scotch and

sipped. "I don't want to hear your hare-brained theory again about winning this in the House. Remember, we've got a majority of Republican representatives against us. We've got a President who barely managed a win in his own home state." He looked to Forsythe. "Sorry, Ben, no offense." He looked back to Longstreet. "Do you really think we're going to carry a hostile House? Please."

The campaign adviser smiled and folded his arms across his chest, careful not to wrinkle his designer tie.

"Far be it for me to argue with the Vice President of the United States," he said. "But the best thing that happened to us in this election was the Independent candidate, Marshall Young. If not for him, the election would already be over. He saved our collective butts, Mr. Vice President. I, for one, intend to see his efforts do not go unrewarded."

Longstreet paced in front of the President's desk, hands clasped behind. "We've got to put aside all that's happened so far and look to the future," he said. "The electoral vote means nothing now. The popular vote means nothing. If the current results hold, the only vote that'll count is in the House of Representatives."

McNally snorted. "You can't make me believe the House is going to elect a President who lost the popular vote in a landslide. Governor Wardlow's taken most of the West and virtually all the South. He's got big majorities in Texas and his own home state of California." He stepped beside a U.S. map sitting on an easel near the fireplace. Picking up a sheaf of red "stick-on" dots, he thumped one onto Arizona and another onto Washington, filling out the Republican wins.

"Good God, Arch, we're behind in the popular vote by fifty-three to forty-five fucking percent," he said. "How're we going to command a majority in the House with national results like these? You really think a bunch of sniveling congressmen are going to risk their political careers to return to office a President who got creamed nationwide?"

Everyone in the room turned toward Longstreet, as if their heads were linked by an invisible wire.

Brushing at his suit pants—they didn't need it; he just liked dramatic pauses—Longstreet walked across the room and stood in front of the easel. His eyes, hidden behind fish-bowl lenses, moved over the map from one red mark to the next.

"You make a powerful case, Mr. Vice President, a powerful case, indeed. The job before us is a difficult one. But it's not impossible. Nothing's impossible when it comes to politics." He picked up two blue dots. "We've made things hard on ourselves, I agree. It's a habit we've had over the years, isn't it, Mr. President?"

Forsythe nodded, almost imperceptibly.

Longstreet looked back to the map. "I say again, this election's about the power of the Presidency. It's about where and how we apply that power." He turned to the room. "It takes two hundred and seventy electoral votes to win. Right now, Wardlow's four short. Since we're winning the same number of states he is, these four votes will be his undoing. Look, he's got twenty-four states, we've got twenty-four. Hell, we've even got twenty-five if you count D.C. Of course, they don't get a vote in the House, so our states will count the same as his in January. Don't you see?" He rubbed his hands together as if warming for the battle to come. "If the congressmen value their jobs—and they do—they'll reflect the wishes of the voters in their states. To do otherwise would be political suicide."

He looked around the room, watching the advisers accept his argument silently, grudgingly. He knew none of them liked him. That was all right. He didn't like them, either. More important, he didn't respect their political intelligence. But he knew they respected his. Everyone in the room admitted he was the sharpest, most conniving—most successful—campaign manager in the country. In all matters electoral, they had to give him his due.

"This means, gentlemen," he said, turning to the easel, "the election'll be decided by the two states now supporting our good friend Marshall Young." He stared at the northeast quadrant of the map. "Young knows he can't win, so he'll bargain away his votes. With the proper inducement, we'll convince him to throw his states our way." He placed a blue dot over New England's most northern state, Maine. "All we have to do is find out what he wants, and give it to him." He placed a second dot over Maryland, covering up Baltimore and part of the Chesapeake. Peeking out from one side was Annapolis, separated from the continental U.S. like an island broken off and floated out to sea. "Mark my words, gentlemen. Maine and Maryland. These are the states where the election'll be decided."

He looked around the room, waiting for comment, reaction. The advisers sat and stared, gape-mouthed. Finally, McNally reached over and refilled his cup.

"The power of the Presidency," Longstreet said. "No one can take that away. We've got the only candidate with the ability *right now* to deliver on his promises. Presidential power—Presidential promises—will win this election."

He turned on his heel, his tasseled loafers grinding into the royal-blue carpet. With no announcement or explanation, he stalked out of the room. Only Arch Longstreet would dare leave the President's office without permission. But he knew, even if no one else did, that the hard work was just beginning.

He also knew no one else on the President's team was capable of getting the job done—the only one with the guts to bring down anyone who stood in their way.

Chapter Seven

Trey hurried through the marbled halls of the Cannon Building toward the luxurious, glass-walled dining room. He entered and crossed quickly, listening to the room fall silent in waves behind him. Everywhere people stopped and gawked with forks halfway to their mouths.

Trey had decided to accept—or at least endure—his newfound celebrity. Fact was, he had little choice. In Washington social circles, his fame was spiraling out of all proportion. He was only a third-term congressman, but the political pundits were already talking of him as a potential Presidential candidate.

Certainly, he had the credentials for it: Good looks and money. His wealth was mostly inherited, but that made him no less a force. After all, the passing down of money and political power were as much a tradition in the U.S. as anywhere else.

As he neared the table, Trey saw Bobby Buckland and Miles Ogle had saved him a seat at the head. He unbuttoned his coat and sat down. For several seconds, no one spoke as they waited for conversation in the room to resume. When the clatter started, Trey signaled the waiter to bring his usual glass of iced tea. It arrived, and he toasted the table.

"Congratulations on successful re-elections all around," he said. "I only hope the voters forgive us for what we're about to do."

Everyone raised their glasses.

"And what are we about to do, Congressman?" Buckland said; he knew the answer, of course. They all did.

"Why, we're about to elect our country's next President," Trey said, mimicking Buckland's heavy southern accent. "We're about to make his-to-ry."

"Or chaos," Ogle said, sipping a glass of wine.

This obviously wasn't his first drink of the afternoon, or his last. Like too many public servants, Ogle had a fondness for liquid lunches. It was one of his few failings. He was a brilliant legal mind, a Constitutional expert, and upstanding in every other way, having grown up in one of Maryland's most respected families.

Buckland, on the other hand, was less formally educated but wiser in the ways of politicking. Nearing seventy now, he was close to the end of a distinguished career. Trey had learned many valuable lessons from both men over the years. Given the challenges before them, these lessons would be more important than ever.

"First things first," Buckland said. "We've got to make sure the election *gets* to the House—that the delegates to the Electoral College vote as they've been directed."

"The rules are clear, Bobby," Trey said. "The Senate and House can reject any state's electoral vote for cause. I suggest we write a resolution reaffirming this position. That'll get us out in front of any electors who think they've got a chance to manipulate things."

"I'll draft the document this afternoon," Ogle said. "We can make it available to the other representatives."

"Thanks, Miles," Trey said, realizing this was one job he could erase from his growing list.

"Have you thought about a position statement on our January vote?" Buckland asked. "Between the seven of us, we've got seven different ideas. We'd be happy to add yours to the pile."

"I could do that," Trey said, "but I'd rather propose something we can all agree on."

Buckland picked a handful of peanuts out of a communal bowl and popped them in his mouth. "Let's hear it."

"Our position is this," Trey said. "We will reflect the voters' wishes—no more, no less. We won't bargain away the office of the Presidency in any way, shape or form."

He sipped his tea and glanced around the table to read the faces of his colleagues. They appeared to agree.

Buckland popped another handful of peanuts. "We might have unanimous consent, for once."

Ogle cleared his throat. "We might," he said, "and we might not." Leaning back, he clutched his glass to his chest. "We can make a statement like that, Trey, and we might even believe it. The question is, will anyone else? The public's skeptical—the press even more so. Everyone knows this vote'll be subject to bargaining of the most difficult sort. To make them believe anything else, we've got a hard sell in front of us."

Heads nodded around the table.

"Let's think about that for a minute," Trey said. "What office does the public hold in highest regard? The Presidency. The public won't tolerate any backroom wrangling. Everyone found that out with Clinton's impeachment. Putting a President into office—or taking him out—is a sacred duty. We'd be drawn and quartered in the next election if we traded over the highest office in the land."

The nodding continued.

"The *only* position we can take is in support of the voters," Trey said.

Ogle finished his wine and signaled for another. "The fact is, political wrangling over the Presidency's a long and honored tradition in this country, Trey. The Gore-Bush election was only the most recent example. The House has elected Presidents twice, and both times it was a circus."

Ogle was warming to his topic. "First, Thomas Jefferson wound up competing against his own vice president, Aaron Burr. It took thirty-six ballots to settle that one. The next time was even worse. John Quincy Adams finished a poor second, then worked a deal with the fourth-place finisher, Henry Clay, to steal the election from Andrew Jackson."

Ogle smiled smugly. He had a remarkably facile mind and wasn't afraid to show it off. "Five times in history, candidates who lost the popular vote have been elected by Electoral College majorities," he said, setting his wine aside. "As of yesterday, the voters gave us no clear direction who they wanted. If they had, we'd have a President-elect today. We don't. The final results are in our hands, like it or not."

No one reacted for several seconds.

Then Trey spoke softly. "Times have changed a lot since Jefferson and Adams, Miles. The Presidency's the most powerful office in the world. We can't reduce the position to a crass negotiating tool. The nation deserves better."

Buckland brushed back a lock of caramel-brown hair. Amazingly for a man his age, he hardly showed any gray.

"Yesterday, forty-eight states told their representatives exactly who they support," he said. "They're the lucky ones—they've got clear mandates. But the results in Maine and Maryland threw everything into a cocked hat. No one wants us to waste our support on a sure loser, Marshall Young. If we support Governor Wardlow, we'll go against our own party. But if we back Forsythe, we'll stand behind a man who lost the popular vote in Maryland *and* nationwide." He shook his head slowly. "That's a helluva thing, no matter how you slice it."

Trey toyed with his tea glass and responded in a near whisper. "That's something we'll have to deal with when the time comes, Bobby. Meanwhile, our official position must be as I stated—no backroom deals. Whether we believe it or not, whether the public believes it, it's the only position we can take. Anything else, and we'll be crucified."

Waiters appeared with plates of pre-ordered food and served the table machine-like, then disappeared. Everyone dug in, except Trey. He nibbled a few fresh vegetables from a platter. But the meal reminded him of dinner tonight with Laura. The thought stole his appetite.

He drained the last of his tea and stood up. "I've got calls to make and paperwork stacked a foot high. My staff's about to mutiny. I hope everyone'll forgive me, but I must excuse myself."

He looked around for a show of objection. When there was none, he placed a reassuring hand on Backland's arm and moved away. All conversation in the room stopped again as he swept by the diners. Staring straight ahead, he tried to think only of the work ahead. He knew trying to maintain a sense of balance in the days to come would be tougher than ever. Miles Ogle was right. Bargaining over the office of the Presidency was the ultimate game in Washington. Maryland had little choice whether to play.

Like it or not.

Longstreet hurried past the West Wing offices like a man late for an appointment. It was the way he always moved, as if on a mission. Near a set of elevator doors outside the President's briefing room, he stopped beside two Secret Service agents. As if on cue, the metal doors popped open, and he stepped in, punching the button marked "B." In the basement of the White House was an underground

55

passageway to the Old Executive Office Building next door.

As the elevator descended, Longstreet checked his image in the polished doors, smoothing his thinning hair and adjusting his oversized glasses, making sure he was as meticulously put together as always, groomed to the point of ultraperfection. This was his style. Everything to the extreme. Looking at himself in the brushed steel, he was hardpressed to tell if his appearance tonight met his own high standards.

As the elevator settled to a stop, he stepped into the chilly basement of the two-hundred-year-old building, wondering once again why past Presidents hadn't spent more taxpayer money to rehabilitate the offices beneath a structure that housed the residence of the most powerful man on earth. Asbestos-wrapped pipes lined the cracked ceilings. Chipped tile floors were worn to the cement in spots. He shook his head and turned into a tunnel that led like a highway underpass toward the majestic structure next door—to the old Executive Office Building and his unofficial campaign central offices.

The EOB was a castle fit for royalty. Its high, granite walls and lofted ceilings fit the scale of a man of superior heights. Its steep, mansard roof and sculpted facade stood out from the rest of Washington like the central jewel in a king's crown. The place reminded him of one of the world's best universities or fine museums—an institute of higher learning and artistry, not like the tacky house next door, fit only for a public servant. The Presidency was above that. Longstreet was above that, too. After all, he was the power behind the Presidency. Forsythe knew this better than anyone. If the President's lackeys in the Oval Office didn't know, they would soon enough.

Longstreet rushed through the walkway, his leather heels

clicking on the tile floor, sounding like Morse Code in the empty space that wound its way beneath the nation's capital. He saw another figure approaching. The other person's shoes were soft-soled and silent, but his shaved head stood out like a beacon in the shadowed light.

They stopped in front of each other.

"How'd it go in Annapolis?" Longstreet asked.

"We've got a clear shot in. No problem, as long as the bay's not too rough. Gets pretty choppy out there."

"I'll have 'the fisherman' take care of that. He's got a whole fleet at our disposal. What about in Maine?"

"Haven't heard back yet. Shouldn't be a problem. The guy's out in the middle of the woods alone. Sounds like a piece of cake."

"Good. I want daily reports, Steele. These two men are the keys—just as I said they would be." He looked away. "I want your best men on them. They're the ones we've got to have."

"Will do."

Longstreet stepped around the intimidating figure of a man standing between him and a month's worth of work. "Everything's coming together exactly as I said." He could hardly contain the excitement in his voice. "It's all falling perfectly into place."

Steele called out behind him. "The President's with us?"

Longstreet stopped but didn't look back. "He's not convinced we can pull it off. But we'll make him a believer, won't we?"

Steele nodded, his bald head reflecting white light like an emergency flasher. "You got it."

Longstreet hurried off, thinking about the work ahead. His job was to pull off a political miracle between now and the House vote. He would do it, too. Whatever it took.

These were the times he lived for! Who would have believed the son of a failed postman from a backwater town in the heart of Dixie could have risen to such heights? Not his half-drunken father, who had done nothing but tarnish the family name. Not his embittered mother, who could never be satisfied with her son's achievements. She always said he would wind up like Longstreets of the past—men who had tasted victory, only to spit it out at the height of the moment. This was the family legacy, the mark of all Longstreet men.

He stepped into his top-floor suite where stained-glass windows allowed in a kaleidoscope of colors from the cloud-covered sky. He glided across the thick Persian rug to a broad picture window overlooking the White House next door. The Oval Office stood small beneath him, almost an anteroom to his own glorious office high above.

Turning back, he dialed a specially encrypted cell phone and was surprised to hear the call answered before it even rang on the other end.

"Good day, Mr. Longstreet," the clipped Asian voice said. "It appears your voting strategy is working after all. I must admit, we had our doubts. Your system of democracy is such a mystery."

"It's a mystery to our opponents, as well," Longstreet said. "But our victory is far from secure. We've been given the opportunity to fight again, that's all. The next battle will be even tougher."

"But it seems to me things have gotten simpler. Only two congressmen stand in our way, correct?"

"Yes, but there's no room for error. A single vote can make all the difference."

A long pause, then the Asian spoke again. "You'll see this one vote goes our way, won't you?"

Longstreet started to answer but the line went dead. He turned off the handset and tucked the phone back into his jacket pocket. Staring down at the White House complex, he saw President Forsythe click off a desk lamp and head out for the day, secure in the thought the Administration was still safely ensconced in the Oval Office.

As always, Longstreet would be the one to see they remained there.

Chapter Eight

Trey sat hunched over his desk, putting the final touches on a lengthy letter to his constituents, assuring them he would represent their interests above all else. He didn't know which candidate he'd support yet, but he would make a decision that reflected, as best he could, the voters' wishes, the state's interests and the country's needs. He would try to carry out his duties with integrity, hoping this would warrant their continued support.

His pencil hovered over the last few lines. Maybe it was too much. Maybe not enough. It would be easier, he knew—smarter, too—to crumple up the letter and throw it away. The voters were so skeptical these days, they wouldn't believe what he had to say anyway. But that hadn't stopped him from taking positions before.

Trey pulled out a fountain pen and signed his formal name at the bottom with a flourish: Thomas Josiah Stone III.

He scribbled a note for Miss Landers: *Mail copies as early as possible in the morning.*

He looked up at the large-face clock on the wall above his door and realized it was already eight o'clock, straight up. He barely had time to jog to his townhouse and grab a quick shower before Laura arrived.

He hurried to the basement gym and slipped into his running gear, then headed for the back exit. He started a slow jog, moving past the guard's booth and onto the sidewalk alongside Independence Avenue. At the corner, he laid out the route home: New Jersey Avenue north, past the Botanical Garden, around the back of the Capitol Building. He'd pick up Maryland Avenue to Constitution, then double back to Third, where his townhouse sat on a tree-lined street near the rear of the Supreme Court.

The air was crisp and damp, but he quickly worked up a sweat, running swiftly on the nearly empty streets. This part of town always cleared out at night. The "chic" residential sections were in the northwest quadrant, around Georgetown or near Adams-Morgan and Dupont Circle. But Trey and Jazz had found a perfectly restored Victorian townhouse on Capitol Hill, close enough for him to jog to the office. Of course, he would have preferred to drive home every night, but late hours and slow traffic would have forced him to turn right around and come back.

At the intersection of Maryland and Second, he slowed and checked for cars that could come from four different, sharply angled directions. No one in sight.

He stepped into the street. Then, halfway across, a gray sedan seemed to come out of nowhere, heading north. He caught a glimpse of the car out of the corner of his eye and stopped. The vehicle whizzed by without so much as a honk or a swerve, missing him by inches. He stood in the middle of the street and watched the car race up to Constitution and hang a squealing right.

Trey shrugged, wondering where D.C.'s finest were when he needed them. But this wasn't his first or last close call on the overcrowded streets of the nation's capital.

Within seconds, he was back up to full speed, cruising to 12th and the last lap home. He was in a comfortable pace now—easy, graceful strides that seemed disconnected from his body. He had always loved running. It was one of the times he could be completely alone with himself and his thoughts, not subject to the constant debate and compromise of national politics.

At the intersection before the last block home, he caught another red light and jogged in place. When the light turned, he started across the four-lane road. Then, just as before, a car came out of nowhere. This time, the roaring sedan shot toward the intersection at full speed. Trey turned quickly back toward the sidewalk, but the car was coming too fast. Looking sideways, Trey realized he might not make it. He dove toward the curb, sprawling on his hands and knees. The sedan screamed by, within a hair's breadth of running him over. When Trey sat up, the car's taillights had already disappeared. He wasn't sure, but he could have sworn it was the same gray limo. Sure, there were a lot of government vehicles that cruised this town, but something about this one—freshly washed and waxed, bright silver-spoke rims. The driver looked the same, too: a big guy with a shiny, shaved head.

Trey stared into the darkness, listening to the sound of the car's engine. Then he glanced down at the spot where the car had peeled by and saw a gleaming object lying in the skid marks. It took him a moment to figure out what it was—a bronzed replica of the Herndon monument. Just like the one on his desk in the office. Only this one had an odd object stuck on top. It was a President Forsythe campaign button pierced through by the point.

Trey grabbed the object in his fist and hurried across the street. On the sidewalk, he started to run again, this time full out, his heart pounding, the perspiration pouring off. He wasn't sure why, but someone was trying their best to intimidate the hell out of him. They had done one damn good job of it, too.

He arrived at the steps of his townhouse with his lungs

exploding. He paced in a small outside circle until his heart-beat returned to normal. Then he slowly climbed the steps. He hoped he was just being paranoid. Maybe the driver didn't *try* to hit him. Maybe it was just some crazy political junkie. This town was full of them.

He pushed the door open through a pile of mail spilled through the slot. It looked like all bills and third-class junk. He glanced at the grandfather clock in the hallway and saw he still had thirty minutes before Laura arrived. Enough time for a quick shave and shower.

The hot water felt like a baptismal, washing away the cares of the day. Stepping out, he wrapped a terry-cloth towel around his waist and headed for the phone for a quick call to Jazz and Katie, as promised. But on the way, the doorbell rang. He knew it would be his neighbor, Mr. Muldoon, who always collected overnight packages left during the day.

Trey galloped downstairs and flung open the door. His mouth fell open when he saw it was Laura.

She was dressed to the nines in spiked heels and a camel-hair suit slit to mid-thigh.

She smiled and stepped inside, her arms full of Chinese take-out. "It seems I'm always catching you in bath attire," she said, glancing down.

She breezed past him toward the kitchen, and he followed instinctively.

She pushed aside his pile of letters and set the packages down, then turned and kissed him on the lips, resting her hands on his hips.

For a moment, he thought she might come away with the towel in hand. But she turned back to the table and began to unpack. "I ordered one of just about everything they had," she said. "Szechwan chicken, one of your favorites.

Vegetable egg foo yong, one of mine. Sweet and sour pork—the best in town. And a light plum wine to wash it all down."

She wrapped her long, red-nailed fingers around the metal container of heated wine. "Still warm."

He hadn't spoken a full word yet.

She looked him in the eye. "You could use something warm."

"You're early," he blurted.

She poured the wine. They touched glasses and drank.

"I'm going to put on something more comfortable," he said.

She laughed. "You can't get much more comfortable than that, Trey."

"You'd be surprised."

He returned a few minutes later in casual slacks and a pullover sweater, his hair combed back. She had displayed the food on the dining room table with crystal dinnerware and lit candles. A soft CD played in the background. She was standing by the living room fireplace with gas logs burning. The flickering shadows danced tantalizingly over her. She had taken off her jacket, allowing a filmy silk blouse to display her white-lace bra underneath.

He took a glass of wine from her and sipped, his hand shaking slightly.

"You *do* look more comfortable out of shower togs," she said.

"And *into* something else." He tried to make light of the awkwardness, but her comment struck too close, as did a lot of things Laura said and did. This particular reference was to Trey's undergraduate years at the Naval Academy, when he often spent weekends at the Weddington family home. Once, when Jack's parents left for an out-of-town trip, Laura came over and the three of them stayed up drinking and talking until the early morning hours . . . Jack passed out, as usual, and Trey decided to grab a shower before heading back to the Academy. He stood under the pounding water, trying to sober up, when he heard someone enter the room. He pulled back the curtain to find Laura standing there in nothing but a towel. She dropped it at her feet and stepped in with him. He resisted at first—but not much. She picked up a bar of soap and lathered his back. He did the same for her. When she turned around, he found his hands gliding over her breasts like silk on glass. He tried to stop. He knew it was wrong, but she felt so good pressed against him. Without warning, she knelt under the water and took him in her mouth. He didn't remember much after that. When he awoke a few hours later, the two of them were on the bed, entangled in each other's arms. He got her up. She left without a word. It was their last time alone together.

Until tonight.

"Showers and us just go together, I guess," she said.

He slugged down the rest of his wine. "I'm starved," he said. "Let's eat before it gets cold."

He sat at the head of the table, she at his elbow. They ate silently for a minute, listening idly to a jazz combo in the background.

Finally, Laura broke the spell. "I came over here for a reason," she said, "other than just to see you—which is reason enough."

"It's a shame everyone's so busy these days," he said.

"We'll be a lot busier over the next few weeks."

He nodded. "I'm not looking forward to the politicking around a vote of this significance."

"But that's the fun of it, isn't it, Trey? The tough negotiations, the give and take, the behind-the-scenes strategy."

"Some people get their kicks out of that. I'm more into results than side deals—especially when the voters' interests always get lost in the process."

"Oh, Trey, the voters don't know what their interests are. That's why they elect people like you—to make the tough decisions for them."

He shrugged. "I used to believe that. But now I think the *only* people who understand the voters' interests are the voters. They've made some very good decisions over the years."

"They've made some real doozys, too. Nixon comes immediately to mind."

"Despite his flaws, he did some good in office. When everything went bad, the public pressure got him out. The voters still prevailed."

She dabbed at the corners of her mouth with a napkin. "What about Forsythe? What do you think of his chances?"

"He lost the popular vote," Trey said. "Which could be a mortal wound. But he's also a sitting President, and that counts for a lot. He'll use the power of his office to every possible advantage. He always does."

"The betting is that if he doesn't win on the first ballot, he won't make it. Wardlow's got too much popular support to lose in the long run."

"I wouldn't disagree with that assessment." He clinked his glass against hers. "For someone who's supposed to be a novice at these things, you appear to have done your homework."

"I'm learning." She poured more wine. "I also know the support of a few key congressmen is critical to our success. I'm *not* excluding present company, of course."

He nodded noncommittally.

She leaned forward. "Trey, this is a great opportunity for you. If you carry Maryland for the President, you know what that'd do for you with the Administration? You could write your own ticket. Your own *national* ticket."

He tossed his napkin on the table. "Let's go into the living room," he said. "It's cold in here, and the fire would be nice."

She picked up their wine glasses and followed. He stood by the mantle. She handed him his glass and curled up on the loveseat in front. He swirled his wine for a while, then set it aside and spoke solemnly.

"We're treading on dangerous ground here."

"How so?"

"I can't afford any hint of prejudice on this vote. I've sent a letter to that effect to my district. I promised the voters—and myself—I'd remain as impartial as possible. It's the least I can do on an issue of this importance."

"I'd expect no less. I'm sure your constituents feel the same. All I'm saying is, if you decide to support Forsythe, you can use that to your advantage."

"I appreciate your advice," he said. "It's funny—you came here to get my counsel, and I seem to be getting yours."

"It's just that you've got the opportunity to go places in this town. Sometimes I don't think you realize how much power you have."

"Sometimes I'd rather not know."

She swung her feet to the floor. "Statements like that'll get you in trouble around here. People will take advantage of you—of your good nature. You've got to reach out and take what you want, Trey. Nobody's going to give it to you. This is a 'take' town, not a 'give' one."

"I'm aware of that. All too aware." He sat in a lounge chair next to her, sinking back into it comfortably.

"Speaking of give and take," he said, "you mentioned Jack isn't doing so well. What's that all about?"

"It's an all-night story in itself."

"The night's young."

"But we're not, right?" she laughed. Her expression turned serious. "He's drinking heavier than ever. I hardly see him anymore, what with me working in the campaign and him on the boat all the time. He hardly goes into the office and only comes home to see the kids. I think he's in trouble at the bank."

Trouble at the bank.

The words hit Trey like a closed fist. He sat up. "What kind of trouble? Did he give any specifics?"

"Not really." She sighed deeply. "Something's wrong, but he won't tell me what. I thought maybe you could talk with him. He trusts you."

Trey wrung his hands. "He needs professional help, Laura, and I'm not qualified. In fact, I might be the worst possible person to counsel him. I remind him too much of the past. He needs to look to the future—and forget about what came before."

She started to respond, but the phone rang in the other room. Trey jumped up and went to the first-floor office to answer it, knowing exactly who it would be. He'd forgotten to call home.

Jazz wasn't completely understanding, either.

"Your daughter's an unhappy little girl," she said. "I told her Daddy'd call."

"I'm sorry, hon. Things are crazy here. Is she up?"

"She fell asleep in front of the TV, and I carried her up to bed."

"I'm going to be in trouble on this for a week. I'll get her something special."

"She wants you, Trey, not something bought," she said. "Me too."

"I'll be here one more night, hon, then home on Friday." He paused. "Tell me, what'd you do today?"

He rested back in his leather chair and listened to her talk, responding to her just often enough to keep her going. When they hung up, he went back to the living room and found Laura asleep on the couch. He grabbed a comforter and tucked it around her, then headed upstairs.

In the bedroom, he turned and bolted the door. He wasn't sure if he was locking himself in, or the world out. It didn't really matter. He just wanted a good night's sleep.

At the front of the townhouse a floor below, Sam Steele inserted a master key and turned with the slightest of pops. He opened the door silently and stepped in, then stood perfectly still for nearly a minute, letting his eyes adjust.

Slowly, he walked across the wood-plank flooring, finding all the solid spots. He knew every creak, every groan, and could avoid them with his eyes closed.

He slipped up next to Laura as she slept soundly on the couch, her heavy breathing a sure sign this was an alcohol-induced sleep. He reached down and pulled back the comforter to view her soft, radiant skin still glowing in the nearly lightless room.

He hoped he wouldn't have to damage these lovely goods. It would be such a waste.

He turned and walked toward the kitchen. By the breakfast nook, he found exactly what he was looking for: the small, bronzed Herndon monument. He picked up the keepsake and inspected it closely, wondering why people found such joy in faded memories of the past. In the morning, Congressman Stone would learn a lesson about what the present held. The Boss knew exactly the right pressure to apply: subtle at first, then increasingly obvious as time wore on, until the target broke.

Steele removed the campaign button and stuck it in his pocket. He set the replica back where it had been, knowing Stone would notice. A seed of doubt would have been planted—a seed that was destined to grow.

He turned and retraced his steps, pausing ever so briefly beside Laura once again, then crossed to the door and exited, leaving the lock undone: another small calling card, compliments of The Boss.

Chapter Nine

The gently curved façade of Maine's oldest inland resort, the Timbers, sat on the western shore of Nicatous Lake like a half-moon, lighting the way to the splendors beyond—Greenfield, Burlington, Passadumkeag and the Penobscot countryside. On a high floor of the hotel, overlooking the fog-shrouded water, Neil Van Deventer, senior Democratic congressman, shoved himself back from a long table laden with room-service food.

He stood up unsteadily and peered around the suite, listening to the loud chatter and bursts of laughter. Finally, raising his arms, he quieted the crowd. Resting one hand on the shoulder of Charlie Harris, his fellow representative, Van Deventer began softly.

"Ladies and gentlemen," he said, "and I use both terms loosely." Laughter erupted around the room. "Two months from now, the great state of Maine will play one of the most significant roles ever in electing a President." He paused. "Of course, this is exactly as it should be."

He was rewarded with applause and a few whistles, even a whoop or two. "On January sixth, in closed House chambers," his voice began to rise slowly, "we will once again put truth behind the phrase, 'As Maine goes, so goes the nation.'"

The men and women around the table began to applaud rhythmically. Several reached for their glasses to toast the moment. Van Deventer continued on, even more loudly now, the emotion swelling.

"For only the third time in this country's illustrious history, the congressional delegations from individual states will control a Presidential election. Ladies and gentlemen, I intend for the most important of these states to be Maine. And I intend for us to be richly rewarded for the power we hold."

An exuberant cheer went up from the crowd. Several people stood and clapped loudly.

Watching all this with delight, Van Deventer sipped his straight scotch whiskey and smiled knowingly. He had waited a lifetime for this moment—to be center stage in a dramatic national debate, to be the deciding vote in an issue of monumental importance.

Glancing down, he pulled at the bottom of his vest, trying to straighten the creases across his increasingly ample belly, the middle buttons threatening to burst. Van Deventer hadn't put on weight; it was simply the swell of the medication. He thought about putting on his jacket to hide the bulge, but that would be inappropriate for this crowd. The people around him had come from families of fishermen, longshoremen, and loggers. The Van Deventer name itself conjured up images of individualism and ruggedness across their home state. It was an image he had carefully crafted during his more than forty years in politics.

From town council to school board to county freeholder to state legislator and congressman, Van Deventer had always played the consummate New England politician. He had paid his party dues many times over, working fourteen-hour days, sometimes seven days a week, attending brunches and lunches and Rotary Club dinners up and down the coast and in inland areas you couldn't find without a compass. He had weathered brutal winter storms to knock on neighborhood doors and get out the vote. He had sacrificed everything to public life. And he wasn't the least bit sorry for it. He had achieved his objective. Over the next several weeks, he would hold the country's future in his hands.

Van Deventer knew he would never get another chance like this to appear on the national stage—or to use his position of strength to atone for the past. . . .

Holding up his arms, he drew silence from the crowd.

"Friends, for the first time in history, we have the power to make or break the leader of the strongest country on earth. Two states are uncommitted. Forsythe needs them both on the first ballot to win. He *must* have Maine."

Stepping back from the table, Van Deventer purposely placed himself in front of a replica of the state's flag. "To hell with those who say this decision should not be politicized. Our decision will be one that's best for Maine." Turning, he glimpsed the state's colors behind him and smiled. "And we can play the game better than anyone around."

The group rewarded him with exuberant cheers. Chugging their drinks, they poured fresh liquor all around. With the celebration reaching a crescendo, Van Deventer stepped over by a picture window looking out at the shining lake below. It was eerily quiet now. In a few hours the half-frozen waters below would be teeming with fishermen and commercial craft slashing through the icy flow. But for now, it was nice to see the countryside sleep. Maine needed all the rest it could get for the days ahead.

Van Deventer needed his rest, too. He checked the time—nearly nine o'clock. He had missed his last dosage of the day. Feeling the tightness in his chest, he gulped the last of his drink and began to work his way through the crowd toward the door.

"Retiring already?" Harris said. "Don't tell me you're leaving Maine's only other congressman alone with this crowd?"

"You can handle 'em, Charlie."

Harris leaned in and whispered. "The question is, Can I *stand* them much longer?"

Van Deventer looked at the raucous group and wondered the same. "I'm afraid you're going to have to—for two more years, at least."

They laughed and shook hands.

Van Deventer waved to the crowd and stepped out into the wide hallway. Walking slowly toward his room at the far end of the long hotel, he coughed and clutched his chest, trying his best to take a deep breath. He knew he would have to step up his dosage. He had to be at his strongest for the weeks to come. After all, this was *his* time. This was what he'd waited so long for, worked so hard for.

He wouldn't miss it for the world.

Van Deventer pushed open the door to his hotel suite, and the light from the hallway splashed across the carpet, triggering a remotely controlled camera in the ceiling fan. He shuffled across the floor, the scraping sound of his shoes starting up a digital recording device located in a black van parked in the lot below.

A man inside the van watched Van Deventer work his way through the darkened room to a desktop lamp. When the light clicked on, the congressman's hunched-over figure took on a three-dimensional view. Through a wide-angle lens, the man saw Van Deventer holding one hand over his mouth, bracing himself against the desk with the other. Van Deventer then turned and moved into the bathroom. Kneeling in front of the toilet, he began to retch, coughing up blood and sputum. He collapsed in a heap, his back against the bowl.

The cameraman got on a short-wave radio.

A static-filled voice came back: "Ridge here. What's up?"

"The old guy doesn't look good—kinda like you without the scar," the cameraman said, laughing. He peered closely at the image on his monitor. "He's coughing up all kinds of crap and popping pills like candy."

"We've gotta make sure he hangs on until the boss works a deal."

"He better work something fast. This guy won't be around much longer."

Ridge laughed into the mike. "The boss'll make sure it's fast *and* easy," he said. "It's his way."

The cameraman listened as Van Deventer coughed and wheezed several more minutes. Finally, the old man dropped off into a deep sleep on the bathroom floor.

Chapter Ten

The next morning, Trey brought his feet to the floor and rubbed his forehead. He felt a pounding in the middle of his brain. Too much plum wine. Standing, he stretched and tried to get the circulation going. He wanted to step under a steaming hot shower and wash out the hangover, but he didn't want to make noise and wake Laura. Besides, he had a three-mile jog back to the Cannon Building. He'd shower there and get a fresh change of clothes.

In the dark, he pulled on his running gear and tiptoed downstairs, hoping Laura would still be asleep. He found her curled up in the same position he had left her a few hours before.

He slipped into the kitchen and wrote her a note: *Drop the key through the mail slot. Thanks for dinner. Good luck in the election.*

He propped the note against a glass vase.

Then he saw the monument.

It was sitting where he'd left it the night before, but now it was partly obscured by a silk plant. He moved the leaves aside, and his mouth dropped open.

The campaign button was gone.

He looked around the table, on the floor and even around the counter behind the plant.

But the button was simply gone.

Laura must have gotten up during the night and taken it, he thought. But why would she want a meaningless campaign trinket? Unless she couldn't stand seeing it defaced. But that was silly. It was just a damn button.

He went to the front room and leaned over the couch, looking down. She didn't appear to have moved. He wanted to peek inside her purse, but couldn't make himself do it. He shook his head, realizing it didn't really matter. If she wanted the button, she could have it.

Unless, of course, she didn't take it.

Then who did?

He glanced toward the front door, and his breath caught. The door was unlocked.

He could have sworn he had bolted it when she came in. But he was so startled by her early arrival, he might have forgotten.

He went over and locked the door, thinking: *To hell with it. I've got ten better things to worry about.*

He turned and headed out the back door. In the pitch darkness, he saw the daily commute had already begun. But traffic was comparatively light, since most representatives and senators were still out of town.

With few distractions—and no close calls—he made decent time back to the office.

Inside the gym, he got a fresh towel from Billy.

"I'll wear my power suit today, Bill. The dark pinstripe with the solid red tie."

"Big doin's, Congressman?"

"You never know. Since I'm one of the few representatives around, I better look the part."

"Yes, suh. Power suit it is."

Thirty minutes later, Trey breezed into his office, hair still damp. He put on a pot of coffee, then flipped open the morning paper. There on the front page was a picture of himself staring back. The shot, next to one of Representative Van Deventer, accompanied a headline that read: "Two

States Key to Forsythe's Re-election."

The article restated the obvious—the President's return to office depended on his securing all the states supporting him in the Electoral College, as well as the two uncommitted delegations. Trey sat down with a hot cup of coffee and read an accompanying profile of himself and the man from Maine.

Van Deventer was a hard-line Democrat who hailed from a financially poor region that depended heavily on large cost-of-living increases for entitlement programs. Trey felt the payouts were too high and the age limits too low. His fiscally conservative position hadn't hurt him at home, but had damaged him with New Deal Democrats like Van Deventer who staked their re-elections on maintaining the status quo. Funny, Trey thought, two Democratic opposites now held the fate of a liberal president between them like a taut rope.

The rest of the article rehashed a lot of old stuff on Trey. It seemed old to him, anyway: *Kennedy-esque Party Hopeful. Annapolis Grad. Son of a Naval hero. Descendant of a long line of patriots. Boyish good looks. Multi-millionaire family man. "Chosen One."*

Most of the basic facts were true, but he knew nothing about this Kennedy-esque stuff, and certainly nothing about being "chosen." He just wanted to be a good husband, a good father and a good congressman.

He heard the outer-office door open and knew Miss Landers had arrived early. He smelled hot bagels and hoped there would be fresh fruit, too.

He walked out of his office, and she held out a fresh mug of coffee and a bagel on a napkin. Then she handed over a basket full of mail, and a sheaf of phone messages.

"Calls have been coming in all night," she said. "On the

train ride in, I copied the most important ones. They're stacked there in order of importance."

"Thanks," he said through a mouthful.

"The Speaker of the House and Minority Leader want separate strategy meetings with you this week."

"Uh huh."

"And the governor's office called twice. He's intent on getting you to a dinner party this evening at the Annapolis mansion."

Trey nodded and shuffled the notes.

"Most of the other messages were from reporters," she said.

Trey worked his way back toward his office.

"Oh," she said, "a message just came in from Laura Weddington."

He stopped.

"She thanked you for last night and said she left a twenty-dollar bill by the phone. Something about paying for long distance calls this morning."

Miss Landers spun on her heel and walked toward her office, wadding up Laura's note. "I'll make an appointment for you today in the barbershop."

He nodded sheepishly and went into his office, shutting the door with his foot. He wasn't sure why, but he felt a bit like a child who'd just been scolded.

He dropped the load of mail and messages on the desk and pawed through them absently. Three jumped out: The Speaker called and wanted a meeting this week. So did the Majority Leader. More important: Jack Weddington had finally called in. He needed to talk. Tonight.

Trey punched the intercom.

"Miss Landers, I want Miles Ogle to attend that meeting with the Speaker this week, and line up Bobby Buckland for the session with the Majority Leader."

"Right away."

"Then call Jack Weddington and tell him I'll see him at eight at the City Dock. Call my wife, too, and tell her I've decided to come home around midnight—earlier if I can get away."

"You have a conference scheduled at six this evening with the banking lobbyists."

"We'll have to reschedule."

"For next week?"

"After the first of the year. There's no rush."

He turned off the intercom and went back to the call slips. Two more caught his eye—one from Katie and one from his mother, congratulating him on his re-election. Miss Landers had written an aside on that one: *She sent flowers to the house.* He knew they would be black-eyed Susans, Maryland's state flower. He read his mother's message: *Running unopposed just means you scared away all the competition.* He laughed and checked his watch. Too early to call. Dad usually slept until ten a.m. or later. He would be awake long enough for a sponge bath and a bite to eat— maybe a brief call. He wouldn't talk, of course, but he could always listen. Sometimes, that was all Trey needed. He stuffed the note in his pocket as a reminder, then gathered the other messages from the press and punched the intercom again.

"Miss Landers, when the staff gets in this morning, have them return all these media calls." He flipped the pink slips into his out-basket. "I've got one response for everyone. The Maryland delegation has already stated its position. We'll have nothing more to say at this time on the Presidential vote."

He paused, checking the byline on the *Post* sidebar:

Mark Sarver. "And call my favorite reporter at the *Post*. See if we can meet for an off-the-record session."

Trey was curious about the media's take on the first House Presidential election in modern history. If anyone knew the public pulse, it would be Sarver.

He reached over and picked up the note from Katie. It asked him to check his e-mail this morning, saying a "special message" awaited.

He clicked on the computer and waited for it to warm, then read the last slip on his desk. It was from Jack Weddington. He had called in sometime before six. The transcribed message: *Give me a call, buddy, on the boat. Sorry, but it's important.* He flipped the note aside and stared at it warily, remembering Laura's words from last night. He decided to put the call off as long as he could.

When Trey turned back to the computer, he saw forty e-mail messages had already downloaded, mostly from the media, several constituents and a fellow congressman or two. Scanning the list, he found Katie's note and opened it. A three-piece graphic design popped up. The first part of the drawing was that of a big human eye, made by repeating the capital letter "I" over and over. Under it was a heart made out of electronic smiley faces. At the bottom was a big capital "U."

Eye—Love—U.

She had signed the artwork, *Your favorite daughter.*

He laughed out loud. She must have spent an hour designing the message. He clicked on the "reply" button and typed in a message of his own: *Your favorite Dad will see you in the morning,* and signed it, *Pops.*

Then he hit the "send" button and sat back to admire his daughter's handiwork, thinking how fun it was to be a father. At Katie's age, children were so trusting. They took and gave unconditionally. At some point, of course, they would turn into adults, and all the taking and giving would become nothing *but* conditional.

When his e-mail message said "sent," a new message from Katie came back in.

Odd, he thought. *She wouldn't be up this early.*

He opened the return mail and read: *Roses are red, violets are blue. Loyalty's sacred . . . How 'bout you?*

Trey re-read the lines again, his eyes fixed on the words, trying to make sense of them. Then he saw a second verse that read: *Peas porridge hot, peas porridge cold. The Presidency's at stake . . . No time to fold.*

The hair stood up on the back of his neck. He shook his head and re-read again, not believing his eyes. Katie couldn't have written these rhymes, even as amateurish as they were. He checked the "author" line. Sure enough, it was Katie's I.D. He scrolled down further, finding a third verse at the bottom: *Little Miss Muffet sat on her tuffet, eating her curds and whey; along came a wrong vote . . . by her Daddy's connote . . . and little Miss Muffet was never the same.*

Trey's hands trembled over the keyboard. *What in the hell?* He reached out for the intercom, but his mouth was so dry he could barely get the words out.

"Miss Landers." He cleared his throat. "Miss Landers."

"Yes?"

"Get House security up here right now."

"Is there a problem?"

"Someone's hacked into my e-mail system."

"I'll send for an information officer."

He clicked off the intercom and went back to the message, reviewing it time and again, trying to figure out how the intruder got access to Katie's I.D. The *why* was more obvious. Whoever sent the message—it was signed, *Ameri-*

cans for Forsythe—wanted to frighten Trey by showing the vulnerability of his family.

They had succeeded.

Underneath the salutation, a postscript read: *Do the right thing, Congressman, and we will all benefit from your support in January.*

A little smiley face served as the ending punctuation.

In his campaign headquarters, Longstreet sat alone, feet up on a circular table in the middle of the oval room, scanning a list projected on the wall that showed "Expected State Votes." When he got to the bottom, he shook his head and went back to the start, running through every possible scenario, recalling every congressman who owed the President, every representative the Administration had something on, every marker they could call. But every time the results were the same: Forsythe had his states, Wardlow had his. Neither appeared capable of taking the other's.

He drank from a cup of spiked coffee, then closed his eyes and felt the warmth of the brandy cut its way down. He laid his head back and swallowed a small white pill, and waited for the drug to course through his system, bringing his mind and body back to life.

He had been up all night, reviewing every file, exploring every option, knowing he could leave nothing to chance. This was the core of his success. Take no chances. Keep the pressure on. The other side would always break.

He pulled off his oversized glasses and ran his hands over his face, feeling a stubble of beard. He realized he'd have to shower and shave soon, before the staff arrived. Everyone else had left hours ago to catch some sleep. He had thought about making them stay through the night. They could ill afford lost time. But he decided to let them go, knowing he preferred to work alone. His mind operated differently than theirs. They slowed him down, distracted his energies, disrupted his flow.

He placed a new transparency on the projector and re-read a report on Congressman Stone. "No one can be that clean," he murmured. "There's got to be something."

Then he heard someone enter the room behind him. The sound of high heels clicking on the tile floor, the smell of delicate perfume in the air and the rustle of silk against silk as the visitor sat and crossed her legs.

Longstreet didn't turn around. "Don't keep me in suspense, dear," he said. "How'd it go?"

"Not all that well."

Her soft voice mixed perfectly with the darkness and shadows of the half-lit room.

Longstreet took a deep drag on his miniature cigar and let the smoke escape in a stream from his nostrils. "It's still honor before duty for our midshipman?"

"Too soon to tell, Arch," Laura said. "Publicly, he's neutral. Privately, he won't say."

Longstreet began to pace more rapidly, still not looking back.

"On the plus side, he hasn't decided yet," she said. "But on the negative side, he's not looking for a deal. He wants to make the 'right' decision. Whatever that is."

"Maybe that's not so bad. All we have to do is find out what makes Forsythe *right*."

"Easier said than done. Trey and the President might belong to the same party, but this congressman is no fan of Forsythe's."

"Then we'll have to make him one, won't we?" Spinning around, he smiled. He lit his cigarillo with a flourish and clenched it tightly between his teeth.

"Our bigger problem is the vote count," she said. "Forsythe finished last in Maryland. That's tough to overcome."

He sat beside her, blowing smoke over her head. "There's always a way, my dear, for *true* politicians."

"*We* may be politicians, but he's not. He's driven by ideals—high ones at that. What's important to him is honor and loyalty. And he can't be bought. He's got too much money for that."

Longstreet snorted. "Honor's a dangerous trait in politics."

"I told you, he's no ordinary politician. He sees himself as a public servant. I know it sounds old fashioned, but that's what we're up against. No one's more aware of how Maryland voted than he is."

Longstreet slammed his hand on the arm of the chair and came out of his seat. "Oh yes, someone is more aware—the fucking President of the United States, that's who. His job's on the line, Mrs. Weddington. His job and ours, too. We can't lose this election because a goddamned Boy Scout congressman from a backwater state decides he knows what's best for this country. *We* know what's best. That's why we're in the fucking White House. I don't know about you, but I intend to stay there."

"All I'm saying is he'll be extremely tough to sway. He's got principles."

"Sway? I'm not talking about 'sway' here. I don't know where you got that notion. I'm talking about doing whatever's necessary to *guarantee* his support. He controls Maryland. That means we *must* control him. No ifs, ands or *sway* about it." He stubbed out the cigarillo and swigged the last of his coffee.

She looked at the transparency projected on the far wall.

"Where'd you get this report?"

"I'm glad you asked, dear. It's time you learned." He knew he had to bring her in further. It was his protection. She had to have as much at stake as everyone else.

"That's a confidential FBI profile, Arch."

"You think I'd depend on anything less?"

She got up and walked closer to the screen. The report was dated yesterday and had Top Secret stamped across the top and bottom.

"Christ, this is like playing with a loaded gun," she said. "If anyone found out about this, it'd be a disaster."

"We need these reports to *prevent* disaster." He snatched the transparency off the projector and put a new one on. "This is what I've been telling you. We've got to get information any way we can—from anyone we can. That's the way we win, by having more ammunition than our enemies."

She turned to him. "Having these reports is illegal."

"Listen to me." He could feel his shirt collar tighten at the base of his throat. "Never—I repeat—*never* question my authority. Your role is to assure Congressman Stone votes exactly as we intend. Whatever it takes. I've given you one job in this election—Thomas Josiah Stone. If you can't handle him, I'll get someone who can."

"I said he was a friend of mine. I didn't say I controlled him, or he owed me or anything like that."

"If he doesn't owe you by now, he better owe you by to-morrow. If you don't control him now, you better control him by January sixth. I don't care how you do it, I just want it done. You're married to the man's best friend, for Christ's sake. If that drunk husband of yours can't help, God only knows who can. Use him or those feminine wiles of yours. My God, woman, the future of the Presidency depends on it."

He turned and marched out of the room, leaving Laura in the same position he was in earlier—staring at the light on the wall. He glanced back over his shoulder and saw the glare of the projector reflect off her powdered face. She looked drained, weakened. She didn't yet understand there was no right or wrong in this game. You were right when you won. Longstreet was one of the few who understood this rule. With a little work, she might learn.

He headed for his private, gold-gilded bathroom where a nice warm bath and another diet pill would make him as good as new.

Inside, he stared at himself in the mirror for a long time, seeing his father in the deep lines around his mouth, the thinning hairline, and long, thin nose that cut like a blade out of the center of his face. He was a replica of his father in all ways but one—he had his mother's eyes. They were small and steely, even behind thick lenses. She was the strong one in the family. The one with the intellect and drive. He had inherited these traits from her. Not the weakness of the Longstreets.

Bending down, he splashed cool water over his face, knowing he didn't have much time to clean up, to ready himself for the day and the skirmishes to come.

He repeated a family motto to himself, as he often did: "Never go into battle with one boot off." Always out-prepare the enemy. Get as much information as possible. Know more than the competition. Use fear and intimidation.

Plant doubt and seed anxiety.

Laura would learn. In politics, as in war, you never left room for choice or chance.

Luck was for losers.

Chapter Eleven

Aboard his long, black-and-white schooner moored alongside City Dock, Jack Weddington tossed back a straight whiskey and wiped his mouth with the back of his hand.

Standing at the rear of the boat, he looked out beyond Spa Creek to the clear waters of the Severn River where it merged in an unholy alliance with the southward flow of the Chesapeake. The sun had sunk fully beneath the horizon on the starboard side and a cool breeze rocked the schooner ever so slightly in its protected harbor. Which meant the bay would be churning right now—a sporting challenge for even the most experienced sailor. *Maybe Trey would be up for a nighttime sail,* Jack thought. The two of them could always lick the Chesapeake, even on a windy day. Bring on a squall!

Jack laughed and reached down to refill his glass, but the bottle was empty. He turned and made his way across the deck to the stairs below, where he had a fully equipped galley, sleeping quarters for eight, a ship-to-shore phone—even a small-screen television and a library of the best seagoing literature ever written.

Jack scrimped on nothing when it came to his boat. It was a breathtaking vessel of exceptional proportions—eighty-five feet from bow to stern. The narrow, sleek hull was made of the blackest teak, trimmed in white; seven ketch-like sails floated high above like billowy clouds. The flybridge, sundeck and pilothouse were all stained dark mahogany, and every square inch was polished to a mirror-like shine. At the mid-deck, two aluminum masts rose up like high-rises from a cityscape. Wherever Jack moored, the boat drew oohs and ahhs from even the most grizzled seamen.

Jack had commissioned the schooner to exact proportions for handcrafting by Scottish artisans on Nantucket Island, up the coast. The craft was five years old but still looked brand new. He spent every hour he could onboard spit-polishing every piece and part. The boat was known in every tiny harbor tucked alongside the mid-Atlantic coast. Jack always steered clear of the larger, touristy spots in favor of little-traveled ones where he could dock for free, hang out with the locals, drink and tell salty-dog stories throughout the night. Occasionally, he took his sons with him, but he had found he preferred sailing alone. The boys quickly tired of the work it took to keep a craft in tip-top condition. Besides, Laura complained the bay was too dangerous for a half-drunk sailor alone with two young kids. She never understood that sailing and booze go together like wind and sea. They're inseparable.

Rummaging around the bar, Jack found a fresh bottle of his best vodka. It was Trey's favorite drink, or at least it used to be, until he gave up hard liquor in favor of white wine and the occasional beer. But tonight, Trey would have at least one vodka straight up with a twist; Jack knew he could count on that for old times' sake.

He poured the clear alcohol over ice to let it chill, then grabbed a couple of glasses and headed back up. As he stepped on deck, he spotted his best friend sauntering across Bridge Street . . .

Trey pulled off his suit jacket and rolled up his shirt sleeves. Despite the breeze, the temperature was unseasonably warm—a major change from the cold front that had come through less than eight hours ago. But that was life on the Chesapeake. The bay was mild as a house pet one minute, snarling like a mad dog the next.

Trey knew he shouldn't be here tonight. Long ago he had learned Jack was always trouble. But with the pressures of the Presidential vote increasing by the minute, Trey had to get their stories straight. From everything he had heard since they last they met in July, Jack had been anything but straight from the start. Trey stepped onto the lowered gangplank and casually saluted. "Permission to come aboard, sir."

Jack grinned and saluted back. "Get your butt on deck, sailor," he growled. "Don't you know it's against regulations to leave the crew drinking alone?"

"It won't happen again, captain."

"I hope that's a promise."

"Sure, I'll promise anything. I'm a politician, remember?"

"Not when you're on my boat, mister."

Trey looked down and found his deck shoes to one side, where he knew they'd be. He kicked off his loafers and pulled on the rubber-soled sneakers, then took a full glass from Jack's outstretched hand.

"*Salud.*"

Trey sipped his drink while Jack gulped half of his. They sat back in deck chairs that faced the stern, looking out toward the pitch-black horizon, realizing it would be perfectly clear this evening. No clouds, no fog. Just the stars to guide by and a large-faced moon.

Trey glanced around the deck. "The boat's still in perfect shape. I don't know how you do it."

"A labor of love, my friend. I labor, and it loves me for it."

He laughed. "I'm sure the love goes both ways."

Jack smiled. "That it does." He drank again, nearly finishing his glass. "So," he sighed, "how go the Washington wars?"

"It's a losing cause, Jack, but at least it's a cause. Everybody's got to have one, right?"

"My cause is to eliminate all causes."

Trey raised his glass. "I'll drink to that."

Jack slugged down the rest of his drink and reached to pour another. "Speaking of which," he said, "I understand you're under a fair bit of pressure these days. It seems our state's congressional delegation holds the fate of the Free World in its hands."

"Just another day on the job."

Jack shook his head. "I've got one rule on this boat, mister. Work stops at the end of that gangplank. Aboard the *Herndon*, you're safe. No reality allowed."

They toasted again, and Jack filled Trey's half-empty glass. Sitting back, they stared up at the sky and listened to the sounds of laughter and music filtering across from the Main Street bars and bistros less than a block away.

It was another Friday night in Annapolis. There would be tourists and locals wandering up and down the tiny bricked streets until the wee hours of the morning, stepping into English-style pubs for a brew or two, then onto the next spot, the next round of laughter and seafood.

Trey and Jack had spent more than their share of nights in Annapolis celebrating with the locals and tourists. That was back when they both appeared destined to excel. At least one of them had done his best over the years to dispel that notion.

At one time, Jack was among the top in their class at the Academy, excelling in both academic studies *and* athletics.

But he was also an incurable romantic who never took himself seriously. He had a penchant for drinking too much and playing too hard. Halfway through his senior year, it all caught up with him. It caught up with all of them.

It was when he got Laura pregnant.

Trey found out the hard way. He returned one morning from guard duty to find Jack gone. He had up and quit the Academy to marry Laura. No explanations, no goodbyes. All his uniforms were packed and stowed; his street clothes and personal effects were gone. It was as if he'd never been on campus. Afterward, Jack never talked to Trey about it, and Trey figured he never would, so he never even asked.

Glancing over now, Trey said, "I saw Laura in the city a couple of nights ago. She's worried about you."

Jack shrugged. "She tells everyone that."

"I don't want to pry, Jack. It's probably none of my business, anyway. But remember, if you need anything, I'm here."

He scoffed. "I don't need anything." He jumped up and moved to the stern, facing away. "Everybody thinks I need something. But I don't need a damn thing. If I had my way, that's exactly what I'd get."

"What's that supposed to mean?"

Jack sat on the railing. "I'm tired, that's all. Tired of failing to live up to other people's expectations. You know, deep down I'm not a very good person. Everyone thinks I am, but I'm not."

His comment recalled Laura's earlier, ominous warning about trouble at the bank. Trey wanted to ask him to explain, but he knew Jack would only open up when he was good and ready. Which usually meant when he was half in the bag.

Trey sipped the last of his second martini. "This vodka's

going to my head," he said. "I haven't eaten since break-fast."

"You want to hit Chuck's?"

"I thought you'd never ask."

They stowed the alcohol and headed across the street to one of Annapolis' largest, most popular seafood hangouts.

Chuck's was a two-story bar and restaurant with the freshest shellfish around. Upstairs in an open room, diners sat at rickety wooden tables with paper tablecloths and pounded on crab and lobster with claw hammers. The place was always fun. You could let your hair down, toss back a brew or two and talk over the noise of a blasting rock band. They did just that, too, for more than an hour.

Halfway into their second pitcher, Trey had to get some fresh air. "I'm out of shape for this," he groaned.

"Come on, sailor," Jack said. "Time to give you a break before round two begins."

They trotted downstairs and stepped out to the cool, cobbled walks of the village. The temperature had dropped again. Trey tucked his jacket up around himself. As if on automatic pilot, they turned left out of the restaurant and onto Randall Street. It was a straight shot from there to the Main Gate leading to the middle of The Yard, the campus of the U.S. Naval Academy.

They had made this same walk so many times, they could do it in their sleep—and nearly had on more than one occasion. They stepped quickly, hands in their pockets. As they approached the gate, Trey flashed his I.D. badge, and the guard waved them through.

Jack made a quick left and led the way over to the tennis courts beneath Dahlgren Hall. Stopping there, he hung on the chain link fence and stared in like a kid who couldn't af-ford tickets to the big game.

"How many times did I whip your butt on these courts?" he said. "I've lost count over the years."

"You can't count to *one?*" Trey said. "If I remember right, I *threw* that match because I felt sorry for you."

"You never felt sorry for me—not on the tennis court, anyway."

"I admit, you're pretty tough to work up sympathy for."

Jack turned to him. "We need to get you on these courts for one last match—the championship of the entire known universe."

"Didn't I win that the last time we played?"

"That was for the *unknown* universe. Nobody cares about that."

"Go ahead, change the rules when you can't win. I've gotten used to it."

Jack looked at him sideways and grinned like he hadn't in years. "Get used to this." He grabbed Trey by the head and mussed his hair. Trey laughed like a little kid. Breaking loose, he tried to smooth down the swirled strands, but in the gusting wind it was a losing battle.

"I'd mess up your hair," he said, "except nobody'd notice."

"That's the beauty of not giving a damn about what other people think."

With that, Jack turned and walked off toward the center of campus. Trey caught up with him outside Buchanan House, the official residence of the Academy's superintendent. Inside, all the lights were on. It appeared a reception was underway. Trey glanced at Jack out of the corner of his eye.

"Don't even think about it," he said. "I can tell from that look in your eye, you're thinking bad thoughts."

"Me? I'm a good sailor."

"You're a lousy civilian, though, and I've got a reputation to maintain. I can see the headlines now—Congressman caught in hi-jinks on Navy campus. I'd prefer not to have to explain that one."

They watched the house for several seconds. Jack then opened his clenched fists, and a handful of pebbles fell to the ground. "Damn, you get it right too often to suit me, Lieutenant," he said.

He turned and broke into a sprint across Blake Road, running up to the gazebo near the entrance to the campus chapel. Trey came after him in a jog, joining him on a stone bench inside. They sat and stared out at Herndon Monument across the lawn.

"Despite everything," Jack said, glancing toward Bancroft Hall where they had roomed so many years ago, "I'm glad I left here when I did."

Trey didn't respond.

"I wasn't cut out for the Academy," he went on. "If I hadn't walked away when I did, something would've forced me out later. You know, some people couldn't stand the regimentation or the physical strain. I didn't mind all that. What I hated was just being here."

Trey got up and moved outside the gazebo onto the grass. "I didn't mind my years here. I guess I'm just a glutton for punishment."

"You just saw past all the military crap and bureaucracy. You had bigger things in mind, following in the footsteps of all those patriotic ancestors of yours." Jack stepped out and moved away. "I never liked the idea of ordering people around, or assuming responsibility for them. I don't even like assuming responsibility for myself." He laughed and took a few more steps. "Truth is, I don't like people much. I don't like dealing with them, don't like talking to them, don't like sailing with them—except for you, of course."

He laughed again, but Trey noticed it wasn't really a laugh, more an audible smirk.

Jack continued. "Yeah, it's nice to have a drink or two with somebody once in a while, trade a few stories. But in the end, I like being alone. Always have."

"Why'd you come to the Academy, then?"

"You know why."

"Do I?"

Jack glanced at him with a fierce look in his eye. "Yes, you do. I came here because Daddy the governor wanted me to. I was a fucking Weddington, by God, and I was gonna run this state whether I liked it or not." He leaned down and picked up a small rock and tossed it at Herndon Monument, missing badly. "The governor figured I needed a distinguished military record to make it big in politics. He knew my personality wouldn't carry me far."

Trey picked up a stone himself and skimmed it along the grass, leaving a trail in the dampness.

"Thing is, I never wanted his dream," Jack said. "You've got to want something bad to succeed at it. I never wanted to succeed at anything except failure. I've done one bang-up job at that."

Trey didn't speak for a moment. He wasn't sure how to respond. He had heard this same self-defeating sermon out of Jack too many times. It was like listening to a spoiled rich kid complain he had too much. The only thing Jack had too much of was sympathy for himself and not enough for those he hurt. Try as he might, Trey couldn't contain his anger anymore. When he spoke, the disgust was obvious in his voice.

"You wanted to succeed at a lot of things, Jack; the problem was you never had the guts to go after them. You wanted to write poetry, but you never gave it your best effort. You wanted to teach literature, but you never completed your education. You wanted a loving wife and family, but you never spent enough time with them to make it worth their while." Trey spit on the ground, something he rarely did, but this time it just felt right; he had to get the bitter taste out of his mouth—the bitterness of watching his best friend ruin his life and the lives of those around him.

He looked him square in the eye. "You never stood up for yourself, Jack. You always turned and ran. Damnit, stop blaming everyone else."

Jack looked at him gape-mouthed. He took a step back and sat down hard on the wet grass. "Christ, don't beat around the bush, Stone. Tell me what you really think."

Trey leaned against the gazebo, his breath coming in short bursts, as if he had just run a wind sprint. It was the first time he had ever lashed out at Jack. It felt good and bad at the same time, like letting out a deep, dark secret.

"I'm just worried, Jack. You can't keep going on like this. It's going to catch up with you sooner or later."

"You're not only a psychologist, but a fortune-teller."

"Call it what you will, I'm dead serious."

"So am I." Jack leaned back on his elbows, oblivious to the wetness and cold. "I'm afraid the 'sooner' part is here already, my friend." He paused. "I'm not running anymore. I'm taking my medicine like a big boy."

"What're you talking about?" Trey moved over to the front of the gazebo and sat on the step, his stomach tightening. It wasn't from the food and drink; it was more like watching a storm gather on the horizon.

"Maybe this'll clear it up for you." Jack got up and brushed off the back of his pants. "Remember the little bank problem we talked about, when I asked you to call off the federal inspectors?"

Shit, Trey thought. *Here it comes. I knew I shouldn't have gotten involved.*

"Yes . . ."

"The problem was worse than I thought."

"Christ, Jack. You assured me—"

"I assure a lot of people, Stone. You'd think they would learn." He smiled, but Trey wasn't smiling back.

Jack went on. "I couldn't take care of things like I thought. Everything's going to hit the fan next week."

Trey shook his head, unable to speak for a moment. He wanted to know more, but he didn't. He figured the less he knew at this point, the better. One thing was for sure— he had done all he could for Jack. No more favors. No more bailouts.

"Don't offer to help me, either," Jack said. "I'm going to take the hit. There's no other way."

"What do you mean?"

"I'm turning myself in. There'll be some jail time. Maybe a lot of it."

"Why didn't you come to me sooner? Do you need money? What can I do?" Trey heard himself rushing to the rescue again; he didn't know where the words came from. He didn't want to help, but he couldn't desert a drowning man—not even one who had weighed himself down.

"I've got no one to blame but myself," Jack said. "Isn't that what you said before—quit blaming everyone else? That's what I'm trying to do. Give me a break here."

Trey got up and began to pace opposite Jack; they looked like two warriors circling a common enemy.

"You've got a good job," Trey said. "Your family's well-off. How'd you get into trouble like this?"

"The Weddingtons aren't independently wealthy, despite the public's misperceptions. The governor's done all right, but not well enough to support me, a wife and two kids in the manner we've become accustomed to." Jack reached down and pulled out a few blades of grass. "Laura's playing in major league political circles these days. We've got an image to maintain. Designer clothes, imported cars, a showcase home. There's the damn boat, too. It costs a fortune."

"Look, we can manage this thing, Jack. We've just got to work together."

Jack shook his head and moved off. "It's not the money, Trey. That's the least of my concern. It's . . . other things. It's paperwork and authorization and signatures. Look, I borrowed funds without approval, okay? That's where they're going to hang me."

Trey took a deep, uneven breath. "Making restitution helps. At least we can do that."

"No, goddamn it! Don't you get it? I fucked up royally this time. You've got to stay out of it. You're in too deep already."

Trey's breath then caught in his throat. He sensed it would all come to this.

"What do you mean, 'in too deep'?"

Jack laughed that strange laugh again. "For an Annapolis grad, you're sure naïve sometimes. When I asked you to hold off the bank investigators, it was because I was already behind on payments. I thought I had a sure-fire way to make it up, only my plan misfired." He wadded up several blades of grass and flicked them away. "If I turn myself in, I can stop a deeper investigation—one that might implicate others, understand? You've got to stay away from me—as far you can."

"Good God, Jack, I . . . I don't know what to say." Trey grabbed a hold of a gazebo post as if strangling it. Everything began to overwhelm him. His head was swimming from the booze, the food, Jack's confession—and Trey's own role in possible bank fraud. He had really done it this time.

"Remember, you didn't have anything to do with this," Jack said. "We know the truth—you're innocent. But the investigators and press could make it look bad, real bad."

Trey sat inside the gazebo, staring down, unable to find words of support, or any words.

"I'm no damn good, Trey. I never have been. Let me do this one thing right."

With that, Jack turned and stalked off toward the main gate. Suddenly he stopped and looked back. "We can't see each other again," he shouted. "I'm poison. I've made too many people sick already. Let me do something right for a change."

He executed a perfect about-face and ran off, leaving Trey sitting alone in the quad, staring off toward Herndon Monument, feeling deserted by his best friend once again.

On Hanover Street outside Gate Three, Ridge Franks sat inside his late-model limo fidgeting with a knob on a receiver. He got nothing but static and an occasional squelch. The directional mike mounted on the roof wasn't high enough to clear the twelve-foot wall around the campus. He shut down the system and got on the encryption phone.

"Steele here," his partner replied. "What's up?"

"They're on the Naval Academy grounds," Franks said. "The wall's too high. I can't hear a thing."

"How long've they been there?"

"Half-hour, maybe."

"Did they give you anything useful?"

"Not a damn thing."

"Anything about women, drugs, money—something?"

"All they talked about on the boat was the old days at the Academy, sailing and sports—family stuff. A big zero."

Steele sighed. "We'll have to come at it from a different angle."

"Maybe we can lay a little money on him?"

"Nah, he's got too much for that."

"What then?"

"I don't know. It's Longstreet's call now."

"I could put a couple of dents in that pretty face of his." Franks whistled into the mouthpiece. "I wouldn't mind getting some of that stuff."

"The White House likes these things done delicately, at least until there's no other option."

"That'll only get us so far, Steele."

"Agreed."

With nothing more to say, they ended the call.

Franks slammed the car in gear and drove off slowly. As he watched in the rearview mirror, he thought to himself: *Another night wasted.* He knew they couldn't afford many more.

Chapter Twelve

The drive home felt like hours, though less than twenty minutes passed. Trey kept running the events over in his mind. When Jack had come to his office back in July asking for help with the banking regulators, Trey knew damn well to turn him down flat. But Trey was asked for favors all the time. Ninety-nine times out of a hundred, they were just that—favors. Who could have guessed criminal activity would be involved? Of course, with Jack's drinking and increasingly erratic behavior, Trey should have suspected the worst.

He turned left off the two-lane country road and cruised down the half-mile drive toward home. Within moments, the umbrella of trees gave way to plush willows and tall grasses lit by a full moon. Home. This was what he needed more than ever. Comfort and safety. Jazz and Katie.

Trey swung the car around the circular, bricked drive in front and stopped under the portico. He jumped out and hurried through the double-front doors into the paneled comfort of the great room. He found Jazz curled up on the couch, an open book by her side. Leaning down, he kissed her on the cheek. Her eyes opened sleepily, and she brought her arms around his neck, holding him for a moment.

He pulled back to watch the last of the fire dance in her pale, green eyes.

"I'm surprised," she said, sitting up. "You almost made it home on time."

He grinned. "It's barely twelve. I'd count this as being early."

"It's early all right," she said, checking her watch. "And getting earlier by the minute."

He kicked off his shoes and sat on the couch beside her, putting his feet next to hers on the coffee table. He ran a hand gently through her long tangle of auburn curls.

"How was it at the governor's?" she asked.

"I didn't make it."

"What happened?"

"I got a call from Jack and decided to meet him for dinner."

"Really? I haven't heard from him in ages."

"Count yourself lucky."

"You don't mean that."

He didn't answer.

"Is he still hitting the sauce pretty heavy?"

" 'Fraid so."

"What was the dinner about?"

"Nothing much. He just needed a little . . . advice."

"Where'd you eat?"

"Chuck's. It's got the cheapest booze in town."

"Have you talked to him about his drinking? The least he could do is sober up for those beautiful boys of his."

"It does no good to talk about his effect on the family. He's got to do it for himself."

He felt the anger—and fear—well up again. He got up and walked over by a table in the corner. Leaning down, he pawed through several days' worth of mail and faxes stacked on top. Most of the correspondence was from reporters looking to get exclusive interviews. But he came across one odd envelope with block letters written in heavy black ink. It was addressed simply to "The Stone Family." There was no return address or postmark. He ripped it open and pulled out a typewritten note. As he read, his hand started to shake.

Wife, daughter, loyal family pets. We treasure these things. Don't place them at risk. Do the right thing, and we'll all benefit from your support. It was signed, *Supporters of Forsythe.*

When he looked up, Jazz was watching him over her shoulder. He crumpled the letter and stuffed it in his back pocket. He walked over and sat beside her again. When he spoke, he tried his best to appear nonchalant. "How was our little girl today?"

"She got an A-plus on her American history assignment. You should've seen the map she put together. It was the cutest thing. She had little stick people for settlers, and Monopoly pieces for houses and barns. I'll have her bring it home."

He grinned. "I was supposed to help her glue everything down."

"She was just as happy having done it alone. She proved a little something to herself."

"She's getting awfully self-reliant."

"Before you know it," Jazz said, "she'll be asking to borrow the car."

He laughed. "By the way, I had the strangest thing happen at the office. I got an e-mail from her, and it appeared to have been altered, like someone hacked into her system."

"What did it say?"

"Nothing significant. It just didn't look like it came from her."

"Why do you say that?"

"The, uh, writing. It was an odd font style. I'm sure it's nothing she would've sent. The thing is, I was wondering— has anyone been around the house? Have you seen anything out of the ordinary?"

She looked at him askance. He knew he was raising more suspicion than he intended, but he had to know.

She shook her head. "I wasn't here most of the day. I visited the hospital, then came home to oversee repair work on the dock. By the way, the wood's looking pretty bad. We might have to replace the pilings."

"It sounds like you were busy. We need to get you some help. Trying to be a mother, a foundation member and manage a property this size is way too much."

"I also had to run media interference for you."

"What?"

"When I came home, I found a team of reporters camped out at our front gate."

"You're kidding."

"There must've been twenty of them. Mostly from Washington papers. There were broadcast reporters too, with cameramen and sound people."

"I don't believe it!" He sat up.

"They had three or four of those vans with dishes on top and everything."

"How'd you get rid of them?"

"I asked them to leave, but they responded by trying to interview me. They soon discovered I knew nothing about the Presidential vote and wasn't about to comment even if I did. I pulled into the property and called the police. A few minutes later, everyone was gone."

"I told the press I'm not going to comment further, not until we've heard from the candidates and voters. The damn journalists are like sharks. They keep circling 'til they see blood."

"A few of them left notes," she said, "including a smarmy-looking guy from something called the *National Tribune*. He called himself 'Ridge,' I think. His card's on the table with the others."

"What'd he want?"

"God, I don't know what any of them wanted. He called you 'Trey,' though, which I found odd—as if he knew you."

Trey frowned at this. Journalists were a cynical lot, but they always respected his position and title. "Did he have any credentials?"

"I didn't ask. The guy gave me the creeps." She paused. "He left a note, too. I put it on the table with the rest."

"The one with block lettering?"

"It might've been."

He wrapped an arm around her shoulder and pulled her close. "I'll check it out later, hon."

He watched the last of the fire die down. He realized he would need extra security to keep watch at the house, but without Jazz noticing too much. She despised the idea of being under scrutiny.

She brushed hair out of her eyes. "When do you have to go back to D.C.?"

"Tomorrow morning." He glanced at his watch. "Maybe I should say *this* morning. I've got paperwork stacked up a mile high—stuff I couldn't get to because of the election."

She pulled herself loose. "I've got to go to bed. I've got an early day tomorrow myself."

"I'll be up in a minute. I'm just going to glance at that pile of mail."

She shuffled toward the doorway. He watched her slippered feet barely lift off the floor.

"Hey," he called out, "let's go crabbing on Saturday. It's supposed to be nice, and it might be our last chance this year."

"Katie'll love that."

"Me too."

She walked off. He called out again. "I'll be gone by the time you get up."

Jazz came back and kissed him lightly on the lips. Without another word, she moved away. He watched her disappear around the corner. He thought about following her up, but knew he was too wound up to sleep—and she was too tired for anything else. It would be nice just to lie beside her, but he knew he would keep her awake by tossing and turning, which he always did when his mind was racing. It was certainly racing now.

He pulled out the wadded-up letter and smoothed it out, re-reading it twice. He wasn't sure if he was up against a harmless nut case or a serious threat. One thing was sure: He would give the letter to House security in the morning, and call for twenty-four-hour surveillance of his home.

Trey took a deep breath and laid his head back on the softly padded sofa, wondering why this Presidential vote was turning so ugly so fast. The occasion should be something to look forward to—for the history of it if nothing else. But politics these days seemed to be all about intimidation, threats, name-calling. Verbal combat.

He got up and scattered the last of the fire's ashes, then turned and headed toward the kitchen for a cup of hot chocolate, which always helped him get to sleep when he couldn't turn off the day.

Standing in the kitchen, he stared through the uncurtained windows toward the moonlit waters of the Chesapeake. He could see just enough of the bay to know it was still there, an endless black pool engulfing the eastern side of the earth. The distant, blinking lights told him that life on the water went on in spite of everything else. He felt secure in that, if nothing else.

On a small cotton tree just below Trey's line of vision, a miniature camera secured to the trunk recorded his every movement. Similar cameras were hidden in strategic locations around the property's perimeter with clear shots of the house, patio and private beach. They were invisible to the naked eye—unless you knew exactly where they were. And only a handful of people would ever know that.

In a darkened home office in the suburbs of Alexandria, the video signal from the cameras was clearer than expected, especially given the low level of light.

"What about inside the house?" a visitor asked. "What coverage have you got there?"

"We're shuffling your company's trawlers in and out of the cove. They're rigged with the best surveillance equipment—high-resolution telescopic cameras, directional mikes that can pick up conversations on his boat, in the kitchen and in the master bedroom."

"In the bedroom, huh? That must be fun."

Longstreet pulled off his coke-bottle-bottom glasses and pinched at the red spots on either side of his nose. "You're no better than those thugs I've got on this case."

"A young, virile congressman with a gorgeous redhead wife?" the visitor laughed. "We ought to at least find out if she's a natural."

Longstreet clicked off the monitor. "Mr. Young, I shouldn't have to remind you we're in this project for one reason only. We won't resort to unseemliness, unless of course it's absolutely necessary."

"Loosen up, Arch. I'm just having a little fun."

"Have fun at the right time—after we've acquired all the support necessary to win this election."

"I campaigned my ass off in Maine and Maryland, just like you asked. I spent a damn fortune, too. I've got as much at risk here as anyone."

"You mean to equate a few million dollars—half of

which we *gave* you—to holding the White House? There's no comparison. None! The Presidency's priceless."

"It's not priceless to me." Young slugged from a large tumbler of whiskey and ice. "In fact, it's got a very clear price, and it's not millions. It's *billions*—with a 'b.' "

Longstreet shuffled a couple of files on his notoriously uncluttered desk. "Don't worry, we'll keep our end of the bargain. Forsythe knows what's at stake here, better than any of us."

"He'd better." Young stood and pulled on his overcoat. "Just tell me what you want me to say, and when."

"When the time's right," Longstreet said, "you'll be called in and told precisely what to say and who to say it to." Standing by his desk, Longstreet crossed his arms defiantly. "Until then, you're to remain publicly uncommitted. We don't want anyone thinking deals have already been struck."

Young paused for a moment, staring down, his pencil-thin mustache looking like a dirty spot on his upper lip.

Longstreet thought to himself his real miracle in this election was Young's two-state victory. How they got a plurality of voters to throw away their ballots on slime like this was beyond even his own imagination. "It's amazing," he murmured, "what money can do."

"What'd you say?"

"Nothing."

Young shook his head and opened the door leading to a private courtyard. "This better pay off like you claim, that's all I can say. I don't know how I got myself into this."

"You said it yourself," Longstreet replied, sitting behind his desk. "It's billions, Mr. Young. With a 'b.' "

When Longstreet heard Young's limo pull away, he sighed deeply and held his head in his hands. He had kept up the strong front so far, but he knew the risks were getting more critical by the moment. Young was locked up. Even the Representative from Maine was all but a done deal. But from everything he had found so far, Stone was clean as could be. He had no weaknesses, no vulnerabilities . . . short of raw intimidation or physical threat. And these options were especially difficult against a sitting congressman.

He took a deep breath and shook away the momentary doubts. He would find a way. Tomorrow. Yes, tomorrow.

He always found a way.

He got up purposefully and headed for the basement of his ranch-style home. On the way downstairs, he unknotted his silk tie and pulled off his tailored suit jacket.

On entering the room, he laid the items delicately over a wooden butler's rack. He unbuttoned his fitted shirt meticulously, placing the pearl studs and cufflinks in a jewelry tray. He carefully pulled off the shirt and folded it beside his neatly-hung suit pants. Then he stood and stared at himself in the wall of mirrors directly in front. His powder-blue underpants looked almost like a pastel diaper against his pasty-white complexion.

He knew he shouldn't be doing this. Not with everything on the line. After all, how would it look if the President's man were caught? But he couldn't help himself. He loved getting pain as much as giving it.

He lifted up his arms and let the young boy behind him secure his wrists in sturdy leather straps, cinching them so tight he felt a tingling sensation in the tips of his fingers. The boy did the same to Longstreet's bare ankles. He forced Longstreet's legs apart, spread-eagling him like an animal for the slaughtering.

Not a word was spoken between them. It never was.

The boy stepped up close behind, pressing his bare chest against Longstreet's naked back. He brought a ball-gag up to Longstreet's face, forcing the protuberance into his mouth, buckling it tight behind his head.

This was taking a big chance, Longstreet knew. With the gag in, he couldn't utter the *safe* word to signal when he had had enough. And Longstreet didn't know this boy all that well. He never knew any of them, really. He couldn't afford to. It meant they would know him, too.

The boy moved slowly around the room, viewing his subject like an exhibit at a macabre museum. His face betrayed the disgust he felt for this loose-fleshed man with the ridiculously thick glasses and wispy, blond hair combed over a creamy white scalp. This was the reaction Longstreet had come to expect. It was what he deserved. He had gotten the very same look from his mother every time he failed in school or at sports or in "relationships."

Of course, now Longstreet controlled when and where the punishment was meted out. *He* made the decisions and issued the orders—and decided when to stop.

The young boy pulled off Longstreet's heavy glasses. Longstreet shook his head, trying to tell him "no." He wanted to see everything, not shadows and light. But when his tongue pressed against the gag, it almost made him retch.

The boy flipped the glasses aside and brought a hand up to Longstreet's crotch, squeezing until his knees gave way and the vomit rose halfway in his throat. Abruptly, the boy hocked up and spit in his face. Then, with both hands, he ripped Longstreet's underwear away and grabbed a metal paddle off the wall. He reared back and whipped him as hard as he could: once, twice, three times across the buttocks.

The boy was young and muscular and could hit harder than Longstreet had ever felt. The knifing pain shot through every part of his body. The boy whipped him again and again, until Longstreet felt the welts rise like blisters. The boy hit him in the legs, in the back, along the gut, and on the crotch. Longstreet tried to call out, but the gag only thrust deeper in his throat, and his breath went shallow. The dim lights in the room faded, swirling in his eyes, which were glassy with tears.

After what seemed like an hour, but couldn't have been more than a few minutes, the boy finally stopped. Half unconscious, Longstreet looked up and saw himself in the mirror, or what he could make out of the figure there. He was little more than a white apparition hanging limp and gasping, spittle running down his chin. He could barely see trickles of blood from his buttocks seep down the inside of his thighs.

Longstreet looked up and watched as his tormentor walked toward the stairs. He grunted, trying to call out for the boy not to leave him like this.

But it was too late. He was gone.

Longstreet turned back to the mirror, trying to focus on the disgusting reflection before him—the sick, twisted subhuman who, he knew, had gotten exactly what he deserved. Then he looked at the ceiling and smiled to himself, knowing the boy would be back.

After all, he hadn't been paid yet.

Chapter Thirteen

The next morning, Longstreet worked his way up the narrow, carpeted stairs leading from the White House basement to a hallway outside the Oval Office. With each step, he could feel the tightness across his buttocks and at the small of his back. He could sense the burn marks over his shoulders and along the backs of his thighs. The pain had softened now, but it still helped him to focus his mind, giving him the clarity he needed to think through his presentation and reassure himself the President would agree.

After all, Forsythe had no alternative—not if he wanted to win. And he wanted to win more than anyone. He *had* to win. They both did.

Longstreet reached the top step and turned into the hallway, stopping there for an instant to catch his breath. Switching his heavy satchel from one hand to the other, he stepped into the anteroom outside the President's office.

As was his custom, he paused in front of the gold-gilded mirror behind the secretary's desk, where he straightened his tie and smoothed his hair. He yanked at the sleeves of his jacket to hide the red marks around each wrist, then took a deep breath and marched through the open side door.

Inside, Longstreet found the President seated, as always, behind his huge oak desk with his feet up, hands folded across his increasingly ample belly. The windows behind him opened onto a garden scene, one that made Longstreet flash back to a similar moment nearly five years ago when he first came to Forsythe with another election plan.

They were in the Richmond State House then, in the governor's office, which was not too different from this one, overlooking an expanse of Virginia countryside. Longstreet had left an earlier meeting—as he did today—with financial "backers" who were willing to support Forsythe's run for the Presidency. After finishing a distant fourth in the New Hampshire primary, Forsythe's campaign donations had instantly dried up. His only chance to win was to get a huge infusion of dollars quickly. Longstreet had reached out to "overseas sources," Asian business connections who were willing to spend millions to establish a friend in the White House. The question was: Would Forsythe be willing to take the risk?

Longstreet wasn't surprised to discover he was. Forsythe's ambition, like Longstreet's own, was too powerful to be denied.

Ever since then, both men had come to realize the Asians got the better of the bargain. Forsythe was forced to pay back his supporters' largess with side deals and support legislation that left him exposed to charges of corruption. As long as he held the Oval Office, though—and remained in control of the Justice Department—he was able to keep the investigators at bay.

If Forsythe lost the Presidency now, the cover-up would come undone, since the President had not completed his payback; the Asians would have no further reason to protect him. This was why Longstreet was so sure the President would make the right decision today, just as he had before.

Longstreet set the satchel down and peered around the room. The rest of the Southern Mafia had taken up their standard places: Vice President Fred McNally by the bar cart; Secretary of State Gandolf and party chairman Lawton on opposite couches in front of the fireplace; Chief of Staff Wilmington on a Queen Anne chair farther back; Gaines, the President's "legal adviser," next to him.

"Good afternoon, gentlemen . . . and Fred," Longstreet said, smiling. He had used the line before. It never got so much as a chuckle.

McNally looked ready to say something, but he drank instead.

Longstreet walked over to the easel by the fireplace and planted his color-coded chart in the middle. Everyone had seen the display before. It showed the projected House votes broken down by state. On the right side, in red, were the votes for Wardlow. On the left side, in blue, were those for Forsythe. In the middle, in black, were the undecided votes of Maine and Maryland.

"I have excellent news to report," Longstreet said. "We have just had highly productive discussions with the top representative from Maine."

The President brought his feet down and leaned forward, elbows planted on the desk. Others in the room stirred as well, anxious to hear more.

"We're in a position," Longstreet said, "to secure the state's full support."

"Yes!" the President said. He stood in front of the rectangular windows looking out onto the Rose Garden and the south lawn beyond. "Great news, Arch. This means we're halfway there."

McNally set his scotch aside. " 'In a position,' you say?" he snorted. "What the hell's 'in a position' mean? Have we got his support or don't we?"

Longstreet stared down, lost for a moment in the room's azure blue carpet with its Presidential seal dead center. He

had to give McNally credit. The vice president was an ob-
noxious son of a bitch, but he had a way of cutting to the
core. With McNally, it was say it fast, say it straight, then
wait for the reaction.

Longstreet looked up, smiling. "Gentlemen, I can tell
you Maine's support is incumbent upon a *significant* mea-
sure of compromise on our part."

Forsythe stepped back to his chair and sat down. Others
in the room leaned back, arms folded.

"Define that," Forsythe said.

"The senior congressman from Maine is a tough old
bastard," Longstreet went on. "He knows how the game's
played. He may have even invented it." Looking around the
room, he saw smirks and smiles. Everyone knew how tough
a negotiator Van Deventer could be. The elderly congressman had out-maneuvered the Administration more
than once on House legislation.

"He's given us a short list of issues and positions he
wants us to support next year," Longstreet continued.
"Most of them are pork-barrel projects for his district, constituent favors, legislative arm-twisting . . . that sort of
thing. Nothing we can't accommodate."

"We've all dealt with Neil," Forsythe said. "His bark's
always worse than his bite. What's the problem this time?"

Longstreet paced in front of the fireplace, avoiding eye
contact. Here was the hard part. He had to get it out, gauge
the reaction, and negotiate the points one by one.

"The major project he wants us to support is a high-tech
operation based in Massachusetts. It's a small software
company bidding on a government contract. They haven't
had the resources to qualify. Good technology, but a weak
financial position." He glanced around and saw blank
stares. "Van Deventer wants us to float the company a low-

interest loan of twenty million dollars. After that, he wants assurances a federal contract will be awarded to the firm early next year."

Pausing, he let the gravity of the proposal gain weight. Van Deventer had presented them with a flat-out bribe, just one more step along the now-unending path to clear criminality.

Forsythe took a deep breath and looked around the room with raised eyebrows. "Why in hell does he want money funneled to a Massachusetts business? What's he get? Is he invested in this company?"

"In a sense, yes," Longstreet said. "I've had a little research done. Van Deventer's got a son, the child of an extramarital affair thirty years ago. For political and personal reasons, the congressman's never publicly acknowledged the relationship. My sources tell me he wants the financial support as a way of making up for the past."

"His son's connected to the company?" Forsythe asked.

"He's the founder and president."

"Oh boy," Forsythe said, shaking his head. "Oh boy."

Longstreet clicked on a laser pointer and quickly drew everyone back to the easel.

"But even with Van Deventer's support, we're still one state shy. To secure the last vote—Maryland's—we'll need the help of Marshall Young, the Independent candidate. With his endorsement, we could swing Maryland our way. Without his support, we stand little chance."

Longstreet listened to grumbling around the room. A few feet away, McNally slugged down the rest of his afternoon pick-me-up and went to get another.

The President sat back down and cut straight to the point: "What's Young want?"

Longstreet walked over to the bar cart and filled a glass

with mineral water. He swigged half of it, then set the glass back on the tray.

Looking up, he said, "Young wants sole commercial fishing rights to federal waters in key areas of the northeast."

Everyone in the room exchanged anxious glances. Another out-and-out bribe? Where would it stop? How much more exposed could they get?

Longstreet cleared his throat. "The commercial rights are open to bid every year. He wants to make sure his company wins. Simple as that." He paused to gauge the reaction further, realizing everyone appeared more confused than shocked. "He wants *guaranteed* contracts for as long as we're in office."

The roomful of advisers glanced at each other silently, reluctant to say out loud what they were thinking: Young's request was doable. But like Van Deventer's, it was utterly illegal. To meet his requirements meant adding even more corruption to the ever-growing list.

After a long, deadly quiet, Forsythe spoke. "So these gentlemen don't want us to *win* the election—they want us to buy it. Why should we expect anything less?"

Longstreet picked up his water glass and drained the rest. Setting the glass aside, he wiped his mouth with the back of his hand. It was an uncharacteristic gesture; he was always so fastidious, but the adrenaline was pumping now. He had managed to get out the worst of the news—and the best of it. Yes, Van Deventer and Young were blackmailing them, but at least they were willing to deal. What the President and his advisers didn't know was Longstreet had already agreed to their demands. The only question was: Would Forsythe deliver?

Longstreet looked around the room at each man, trying

to anticipate their reactions, read their faces. He watched as the President stroked his chin and stared out the windows at the south lawn. Everyone else watched the President, too. They would take their cue from him. His answer would tell them how far he was willing to go—how far they could go—to assure his return to office.

Longstreet stood silent, knowing he, least of all, could speak. He had a thousand things to say, justifications why they should agree to the demands. Hell, this was the White House they were talking about! Any sacrifice was better than losing the top office, losing the one protection they had against an open-ended congressional investigation. But he couldn't talk. It wasn't his place. He and everyone else knew the first reaction had to come from the President.

Forsythe held the sheer white curtains back with one hand and stared out blankly. The only sound in the room was his heavy, slow breathing.

When he did speak, his voice was unusually soft, almost a whisper.

"Gentlemen, I remember when we held our first meeting in this office. It was inauguration night four years ago. The weather was bitterly cold that night. I remember how the floodlights in front were so intense, it looked like daytime."

Turning around, he said, "I called it 'sunrise at night.' Remember that, Fred? 'Sunrise at night.' "

McNally nodded.

Forsythe moved forward and sat on the edge of his desk.

"I saw those bright lights as a metaphor for my election. We had high hopes then. We were going to change the system. Deliver on the will of the people." He toyed with a replica of a Harry Truman desk plaque that read: "The Buck Stops Here."

"It all seems so silly now, doesn't it? I mean, politics

doesn't operate that way. It never has, never will. It's a sleazy business we've chosen for ourselves, my friends."

Looking around for a response, he got none.

Forsythe stood and walked across the room. He stopped next to the easel and placed a hand on his campaign adviser's arm.

Longstreet stepped aside.

The President moved in front of the display, staring at it for a long, agonizing moment, head bent, shoulders slumped. Slowly, he raised a hand to the board and peeled the Maine and Maryland stickers from the center panel. He moved them to the left and stuck them at the top, then smoothed them down to make sure they stayed put.

Turning on his heel, he walked back to his desk and rested against it.

His decision had been made. Just as Longstreet knew deep inside it would be.

Longstreet reached over and poured another glass of water, his hand shaking. Gulping it down, he stepped back to the chart and started up again as if the last few minutes hadn't happened.

"I think we can safely move Maine to our column. I'm also sure we can't win Maryland without Young's support." Swallowing hard, he went on. "But even with the backing of the Independent candidate, we've still got our work cut out in the Chesapeake state."

"Good Lord, Arch," Forsythe said, exasperated, "first you tell me we can't win without Young, now you tell me that we can't win with him? Does the man help us or not? We better damn well know before we agree to anything."

"We're trying to fully understand the needs of the key Maryland congressman," Longstreet said. "I'm confident we can reach an agreement. He's a bit of a wild card, though."

"Wild card," Forsythe snickered, reaching for a cigar; his hand was perfectly calm and steady again. "That's to our advantage, isn't it?"

"Perhaps. But the leading congressman is Trey Stone, and his district supported Young in the general election. That's why we need Young on our side."

"So what else can we offer Stone?" Forsythe said. "A position in the Cabinet? Another goddamned government contract? What's *he* want?"

"We've been trying to understand that, Mr. President, but we've been unsuccessful so far."

Forsythe sneered. "We just put everything on the line for this election—and I do mean everything. It's time to get our congressman on board. I don't care what it takes."

"Perhaps it's a matter of impressing upon him the importance of our party retaining the White House," Longstreet said.

"Is this guy an idiot, or what?" McNally said, returning to his cantankerous self. He poured his third drink of the afternoon. "If a lowly congressman from a nothing mid-Atlantic state doesn't understand the importance of the White House to our party's political future, we're in more trouble than I thought."

Everyone in the room laughed at the outburst, breaking the last of the lingering tension.

Even Longstreet smiled. "Perhaps the President could set aside time to wine and dine the congressman," he said. "We should show him special attention—maybe reinforce our commitment to his special projects. As I said, I've found it difficult to understand exactly what he wants. Maybe an evening with the President would do the trick."

Forsythe walked behind his desk and sat down, feet up. "We'll kill two birds with one 'Stone,' " he said, grinning. "We'll invite him to Camp David for the weekend. It's beautiful this time of year. We'll have his family along. Do it up big. We'll helicopter them up to the Catoctin Mountains. Eat and drink on the taxpayers. Sleigh rides—the whole bit. By the time I get through lubricating him with a little southern charm—and a little Southern Comfort," he chuckled, "he'll wonder how the U.S. could survive without Benjamin Lamar Forsythe to lead the way."

Everyone nodded enthusiastically. Everyone except Longstreet.

"It's clearly the right thing to do, Mr. President," he said. "But Stone's not a big supporter of our Administration. He's not going to agree with us easily, I'm afraid."

Forsythe snorted. "Don't forget I was a congressman myself. I'd have given my eyeteeth for a weekend with the President. Hell, I'd have given my first-born son. I'll have that young man eating out of my benevolent Presidential hands by Sunday afternoon. You can count on that."

Gandolf and Lawton laughed and headed for the bar cart. It was their signal the business of the meeting was over. Time for a little fun on a Saturday afternoon, some "good ol' boy" drinking and story-telling.

Longstreet knew he was welcome to stay and join in, but he loathed these informal chat-fests at the end of the day. He had work to do. No one understood or appreciated the role he played. Without him, Forsythe wouldn't be where he was today. The President didn't fully understand this himself. Nor did he understand the critical nature of securing Stone's support. Without it, Forsythe and his Southern Mafia would be swapping war stories far from the White House come January.

Longstreet knew it was going to take a lot more than a little grinning and backslapping to get Stone's vote.

He gathered up his chart board and notes, then walked over and set the board beside the President's desk.

Lifting the Maryland sticker from the left side, he moved it back to the center, hoping this small, subtle gesture might serve as a symbolic reminder that a single state remained firmly in the undecided column. Until it came over, the Oval Office was still in ultimate jeopardy.

Chapter Fourteen

Jazz and Katie finished their breakfast leisurely while Trey sipped his fourth cup of coffee. He had surprised everyone—himself included—when he decided to work from home today. He knew Miss Landers would roast him good, but he had some private work to get done, and he knew his time was never his own in D.C.

He stretched his arms high over his head and stared out the windows that surrounded the breakfast nook. The sun was already halfway up a white sky, and the wind was moving up the coast at a good twenty-five knots. In another few weeks, snow flurries would start. He hoped a few nice days remained; he wanted to get the family out for one last sail before putting the boat in dry-dock.

He glanced at his wristwatch and saw it was a quarter after eight already. He first visitor of the day was due any minute. He had invited Mark Sarver, the *Washington Post*'s top political reporter. Later, he would meet with a House security man, disguised as a repairman.

When the intercom buzzed, he got up to meet Sarver out front as he pulled up in an early-model Ford with one hubcap missing. He jumped out and shook hands like a man in a hurry, which he always seemed to be.

"Good to see ya, Congressman," he said. "It's been too long."

"Thanks for coming, Mark," Trey said. "I would've done this by phone, but that seemed a little too impersonal."

"No problem."

They went inside and got coffee before retiring to Trey's study. After making themselves comfortable, they got right down to business.

"I can't stay long," Sarver said. "It's a story-a-minute in D.C. right now. And since this discussion's off the record . . ."

Trey nodded. "I wish I could be more open with you, and I will be at the right time. First, I need a little background."

"Shoot." Sarver gulped hot coffee, barely flinching from the sting of it.

Trey leaned back, legs crossed. "Ever hear of a paper called the *National Tribune*?"

Sarver shook his head. "Can't say I have."

"What about a D.C. reporter named Ridge Franks? A big guy with a nasty scar across his nose."

Trey flipped Franks' business card on the desk. Sarver picked it up and inspected both sides, then handed it back.

"That's bogus. No self-respecting news organization would hand out an I.D. without a phone number and street address."

Trey put the card in a drawer. "Another question: What can you tell me about Forsythe's background? The rumors of shady dealings are rampant. I'd like to know if there's more than just rumors."

Sarver whistled. He slugged down the rest of his coffee before replying.

"I've been trying to interview Forsythe and his top campaign man for years," he said. "Longstreet is supposed to be the brains behind the election campaigns. But for someone who makes his living in the public arena, he hates the bright lights. Never talks to the press."

"That hasn't stopped you from taking a hard look at him, has it?" Trey asked, grinning.

Sarver smiled back. "When somebody *doesn't* want to talk, that's when I listen the closest."

"I've noticed." Trey finished his coffee and asked Sarver if he wanted more. The reporter shook his shaggy hair out of his eyes, then sat back and warmed to his subject.

"At one time, I tracked him pretty close—right after Forsythe moved into Pennsylvania Avenue. But I must admit I didn't uncover much. I turned up a few items about his private life, stuff about him never being married . . . sexual proclivities, you know." He winked. "But Longstreet's not an elected official, so I was restricted. He's not an open target."

Trey nodded. "You ever follow the money with these guys—the reports of illegal campaign financing, illicit overseas ties?"

Sarver grinned widely, showing a gap between his front teeth. "All I can say is our investigation got about as far as the one in Congress did."

Trey laughed. The reporter had him there. Two House and Senate subcommittees had inquired into Forsythe's fundraising, but when the hearings threatened to spill into ongoing congressional races, most of the elected officials lost their enthusiasm. No one in Washington was totally clean.

"So Longstreet's on the straight and narrow, as far as you know?" Trey said.

Sarver hesitated. He got up and paced across the room. When he sat back down, he leaned in as if divulging a great confidence. "Congressman . . ."

"Please, call me Trey at home."

"Trey, from everything I found out, Longstreet, Forsythe and his whole Southern Mafia are dirty as the day is long. Don't quote me on this 'cause I can't prove it, but

Longstreet's the cover man. He protects Forsythe from exposure—gives him what they call 'plausible deniability.' "

It was a phrase from the Watergate era, meaning the less Forsythe knew, the more he could deny.

"Forsythe knows exactly what's going on," Sarver said, "but he's always one step away, with Longstreet as the man in-between." Shaking his head in grudging admiration, he said, "Longstreet's a slick son of a bitch. I'll give him that. Frankly, I think he's a dangerous one, too. We just haven't nailed him yet."

"But you haven't stopped trying?" Trey said.

"We won't, either—even if they lose the election." Sitting back, Sarver looked intrigued by the line of inquiry. "Mind if I ask; have you got something on him and the President?"

Trey looked away for a moment, wondering how much he should tell about the recent incidents—the gray limo, the "reporters" on the property, the e-mails and letters. But he knew everything added up to very little, especially when accusing White House officials of possible attempted coercion.

Fortunately, Trey was spared the decision when the phone rang. Seconds later, the housekeeper knocked.

Trey opened the door and asked, "Yes, Irma?"

"I don't mean to interrupt."

"Go ahead."

"The telephone's for you," she paused to gain composure. "It's the White House."

Trey and Sarver exchanged anxious glances. Trey had been called at home by many top government figures—from heads of bureaucracies to ambassadors to the Speaker of the House—but never the White House.

"I'll take it here," he said.

Turning, he shrugged at Sarver. The reporter waved a hand as if to say "no problem," and stepped out.

"I've got to run anyway," Sarver said, pausing in the hallway. "If you don't mind a word of caution: I'd be very careful around these guys. My sources indicate Longstreet's not afraid to use a little muscle on occasion."

Trey thanked him and watched as the reporter walked away, thinking to himself that Sarver might know more than he realized.

Shaking his head, Trey stepped back into his office and closed the door.

When he came out several minutes later, he found Jazz and Katie snuggled together on the family room couch, a comforter tossed casually over their legs. Irma stood off to one side. They watched him intently as he sat in his easy chair and picked up the newspaper.

Finally, Katie ran over and crashed into his lap.

"Was that the President on the phone, Daddy? Was it?"

"As a matter of fact," he said, "it was."

"Wow!" Katie's eyes got as big as saucers.

"Me and the Pres are old buddies, you know," he said.

"Are you?" Katie squealed. "You *know* the President?"

"Well, not personally. But I just got through talking to him. Isn't that worth something?"

"Will we get to go to the White House?" Katie jumped down, hardly able to contain herself.

Trey paused. "Not exactly."

"Oh, phooey," she said.

Jazz sounded excited, too. "You really talked to the President himself?" she asked.

"First his chief of staff was on the line, then he conferenced in the President. We talked for a minute or two. He was very pleasant."

"What'd he want?"

"Nothing much. Wished us a nice morning. Talked about the weather. Standard stuff."

"Right," she said. "The leader of the free world calls out of the blue to chat about the weather. Come on, you rat, you can tell us. We can keep a secret—can't we, Katie?"

"I can!"

"Me too," Irma said, sitting on the arm of the sofa, straightening the bun at the back of her hair.

Trey let them stew for a moment before answering.

"The President and First Lady have invited us to Camp David for a little holiday."

Katie jumped up and clapped. Irma patted her heart. Jazz's mouth fell open: "Wh—When?"

"Next weekend."

"Good Lord, I haven't got a thing to wear."

Katie clapped again, and asked wide-eyed: "What's Camp David?"

Trey and Jazz looked at each other and laughed.

"Come here for a minute, honey," he said, "and I'll tell you all about Camp David."

She crawled in his lap.

"It's what they call a 'Presidential retreat.' It's like a real big version of Camp High Hill, where you went last year with your class. It's got cabins, trails and stuff like that. The President uses Camp David for weekend getaways. He can relax there and meet with friends and foreign officials."

"Do we get to play games and go hiking?"

"I imagine so. I hear they've got horses, too."

She leapt out of his lap. "Wow, Mom! Horses!! Can you believe it?"

"Who else is going?" Jazz asked. "How long are we staying? We've got less than a week to prepare?"

"I'm afraid so. It's not kosher to turn down the President when he asks."

"But there's so much to do and find out about." She stood up and fidgeted.

"The chief of staff'll put us in touch with his people. They'll help us understand all the etiquette we'll need."

"I've got to get my hair done. My nails. I've got appointments to make . . . and to cancel. *Camp David!* I've always wanted to go, especially at this time of year. It's beautiful up there, you know."

"There's nothing more gorgeous than the Catoctin Mountains in the fall." He paused. "I forgot to mention something."

"What?"

"The President's sending his personal helicopter for us. He wants us there Saturday for lunch. We'll come back Sunday afternoon."

"A helicopter!" Katie yelled. She whirled around the room like a human top.

"That gives us only five days," Jazz said.

Trey smiled. "I'll call him back and cancel. . . ."

"You do and I'll . . ." She shook a pretend fist at him. "Irma, we've got to survey the closets to see what we've got and what we're missing. We'll have to make a list of necessities. I'll start calling around this afternoon to reschedule appointments."

She looked anxiously at Trey, who was staring into the flames of the fireplace.

"You don't seem very excited," she said. "We don't meet with the President every day."

"I'm excited," he said. "And a little concerned."

"About the reason for this sudden invitation?"

"That, and I'm more concerned about the appearance

our visit might create. I should have said 'no'. . . ."

"You can't refuse an invitation from a sitting President."

"You know that, and I know that, but the press and public might not agree." He slung one leg over the arm of the chair. "I only wish he'd invited the entire Maryland delegation. By going alone, it feeds the perception that I somehow control our state's vote."

"Maybe he invited the other congressmen."

Trey shook his head. "He would have said something."

"Do you think they'll react badly?"

"It shouldn't matter, since our delegation will be meeting with the President's campaign staff separately. We're also meeting with Wardlow's people. I mean, I'm not going to vote for Forsythe just because he invites me to Camp David for a weekend. The man deserves to be heard, though. He is the President."

Jazz sat on the footstool by his chair and put a hand gently on his knee. "You don't have to convince me. I know you'll do the right thing. Look, if you don't feel right about this, I'll understand."

Katie groaned.

Trey leaned forward and kissed her lightly on the cheek. "If I felt too uneasy about it, I'd have said 'no' when he asked. I expected something like this—maybe not Camp David for the weekend, but . . ." He sat back and put his feet up. "I hope you realize this is going to cut into our time for Christmas shopping."

"Oh no you don't," she said. "You're not getting out of the gift-buying season that easy."

"Not that easy," Katie chimed in.

"What do you think, Irma?" Trey asked. "Should I get out of Christmas shopping?"

She shook her head. "We ladies have to stick together."

"I guess you do," he said. "My voting record bears that out."

Jazz, Katie and Irma huddled together and headed off for the kitchen to make lists and prepare for the week to come.

Trey continued to sit in front of the fire. He picked up the *Post* again but couldn't focus on the news. He kept turning over in his mind the President's invitation, trying to figure out how the weekend might go. He knew it would be tough to accept the man's hospitality, eat his food, drink his beverages, enjoy the splendors of a magnificent mountain retreat, then walk away without offering a firm commitment.

Yet, he knew that was exactly the task at hand.

Chapter Fifteen

The sun was still well below the horizon when Trey drove through the iron gate of their estate the next morning. He saw an unmarked patrol car parked not more than thirty yards down the road. The House security people always used personalized licenses to identify their vehicles. He checked the lighted plate, smiled and waved to the driver, then pulled onto Route 31 for the long, dark drive.

He encountered only a few truckers and a commuter or two for nearly half the trip, but the closer he got to the Beltway, the more cars began to appear as if out of nowhere.

When he turned off Independence and into the Cannon garage, the building was still pitch black.

He stopped beside the guard booth and flashed his badge, then drove into his usual underground parking space. Before getting out, he took a long moment to survey the area. As far as he could tell, his car was the only one there.

No gray sedans lurking.

He let himself into the gym and quickly went to work on the weight machine, then moved to the treadmill. It was the first time in days he'd had the chance to run. It felt great to let out the built-up anxiety and tension.

Afterward, he stripped off his sweats and headed for the showers. All the cares and concerns of the last few days swirled down the drain in a few, brief minutes. When he grabbed a towel to dry off, he heard a noise in the dressing area—someone closing a locker door.

"Hey, Billy. 'Bout time you showed up," he called out. "What's a guy got to do for a heated towel around here?"

He waited for a response but heard nothing.

"Sorry I beat you in," he said. "It won't happen again."

Still no response.

"I said I'm sorry. What do you want from me?"

He wrapped the towel around his waist and walked into the locker room. As he stepped around the corner, his mouth dropped open. Somebody had been in the gym, all right.

But it wasn't Billy.

Scrawled across the wall next to his dressing area were words two feet high, spray-painted in red: *Forsythe. He's for you. He's for me. He's for America.*

Underneath the phrase was an additional line, painted in black: *Do it for your family.* Beside the word *"family,"* the artist had added two small circles—one with a smiley face and one with a frown. The effect was as intended. It made his skin crawl.

He heard the front door shut and sprinted through the exercise area to the entrance, but nobody was there. He yanked the door open and stepped into the hall. Still no one there. It was as if the intruder had vanished.

He started to check the exit leading to the garage, but realized he wasn't dressed for it. Turning, he rushed back inside and dialed three-one-one, the emergency line.

The phone rang four times before someone picked up.

"Security."

"It's about time. You guys always take this long?"

"Who is this?"

"Congressman Stone."

"You're in the gym?"

"Yes."

"I didn't realize anyone was here."

"I checked in at the gate."

"No one reported it."

"It doesn't matter. Someone just broke into the gym and sprayed graffiti on the locker room wall."

"Just now?"

"Yes."

"Did you see them?"

"I heard them. They ran out. . . ."

"Do you know which way they went?"

"I checked around and didn't see anyone. They must've gotten out through the garage."

The guard paused, taking notes. "All this just happened?"

"Two minutes ago."

"Some kids have hit the outside of the building before. But they've never gotten inside."

"This wasn't a kid."

"What makes you say that?"

"The graffiti was intended for me."

The guard paused. "What'd they write?"

"Look, I'm standing here in a towel, the guy who broke in is getting away. Do you think you could send someone after them?"

"Yes, sir. Right away."

Trey slammed down the receiver. He knew he shouldn't have been short with the guard, but you'd think a security officer would have a sense of urgency.

He walked back into the locker room and stared at the paint on the wall, trying to understand what the intruder was thinking. It was ludicrous to believe a scrawled note was going to influence his vote for President. Whoever was behind this was getting more brazen, though. Obviously, it was someone who had a lot to lose in this election. Which could be half the people in town.

Trey wasn't worried about the threats to himself as much as those aimed at his family. He decided to add private security at home and tighten the surveillance. He wanted guards on the property twenty-four hours a day.

He leaned into the locker for his cellular phone. Instead, he found a late-morning copy of the *Washington Post*. It hadn't been there before.

He unfolded it to the front page and read the lead headline: GOVERNOR'S SON ADMITS BANK FRAUD.

"Oh Christ, Jack. You did it. Damn you."

He scanned the first few paragraphs. Jack had turned himself in to federal marshals after midnight with no lawyer present. He had admitted to "mishandling" major corporate accounts at Chesapeake Savings and Loan. In a brief interview with the reporter, he owned up to "more than seven figures" in losses.

"What the hell were you thinking?"

The article indicated he was being held at a federal detention center in D.C. until a bail hearing later today.

Trey tossed the paper onto the damp, concrete floor and watched the front-page photo of Jack soak up pooled water, the black ink running together until his facial features were indistinguishable.

As he stared at the image, shaking his head, he wondered why the governor hadn't called to tell him. He reached back in for his cellular phone and flicked the switch.

The phone was dead.

That can't be, he thought. *I just replaced the battery.*

He popped open the back and saw that the battery was gone.

"Jesus H. Christ. What's going on?" he yelled out.

"Are you all right?" a voice said.

Startled, Trey swung around. The phone slipped out of his hand and slid across the cement floor, crashing against the wall. It took him a second to realize the other person was Billy.

Trey breathed a sigh. "Am I glad to see you."

"What's going on, Mr. Stone?"

"I wish I knew."

"Who put this paint on the wall?"

"We had an intruder."

"You okay?"

"I'm fine. Security's looking into it."

Billy walked over to the wall to inspect the handiwork. "You're in awfully early."

"It's the last time, too. I've had a helluva morning."

"Is there anything I can do?"

Trey sat quiet for a moment, trying to organize his thoughts, letting his heart rate return to normal.

"Warm up a towel for me, would you, Bill? I need another shower."

Dressed haphazardly, tie dangling around his neck, Trey was sweating again by the time he rushed into his office twenty minutes later. He clicked on lights everywhere before settling behind his desk. The red message lamp on his phone glared up. He knew there would be a backlog of messages about Jack. He speed-dialed the Maryland State House and asked to speak with the governor immediately.

"Tell him it's Trey Stone. He'll take the call."

A few seconds later, a female voice came on the line.

"Thank God it's you," Laura said. "We've been trying to reach you for hours. I guess you've heard."

"I just saw the front page of the *Post*."

"When Jack does something, he does it up big."

"How's the governor taking it?"

"He's pretty shaken. Jack called at four a.m. to say he was turning himself in. He gave a two-minute explanation, then hung up. I tried to reach you around four-thirty, but you were gone. I must have woken the entire household."

"That's okay."

"I tried your cell phone, too, but it wasn't working."

"The battery's out. Damn it, when Jack gets something in his mind, there's no stopping him. He didn't even have a lawyer present."

"The governor's been in contact with his attorney, who's supposed to meet with Jack before the bail hearing."

"When's that?"

"Two o'clock at the Federal Detention Center downtown. I don't know why they took him there instead of Baltimore."

"They wanted to avoid a conflict of interest by hearing the charges in Maryland. What's the attorney think bail will be?"

"He expects to get him out on his own recognizance. Since his dad *is* governor, that counts for something."

"It won't count for much if he insists on hanging himself. He's giving away every Constitutional right he's got. We've got to shut him up before he makes it worse. God, I wish he hadn't done this."

"He didn't have much choice. I think you know that."

Trey hesitated. He wasn't sure what she meant by that, and he didn't want to pursue it now.

"There's a little thing called the Fifth Amendment that gives him a choice—a lot more than he's using. Are you going to the bail hearing?"

"News crews will be all over the mansion in a few minutes.

I'll stay here to help out. I haven't told the kids yet, either."

"I'd do it soon. It'll be a lot worse for them to find out from the television."

"I'm working up the courage."

"I don't envy you. Tell the governor I'll come by after I've talked to Jack."

"Thanks for calling, Trey. It always helps to hear your voice—to know there's a thread of sanity in all this."

"Take care of yourself and those boys. I'll handle your wayward husband."

Trey hung up, but he still felt somehow connected, as if a strange magnetism trapped him in the orbit of the Weddingtons. No matter how he tried, he couldn't extricate himself. The family was like a black hole, drawing in all matter and light around them.

Looking up, he saw Miss Landers staring through the open office door. He jumped up and grabbed his suit jacket off the back of his chair.

"Cancel all my a.m. appointments and put the afternoon on hold. An emergency's come up."

She nodded. "Give him my best."

He hesitated at the hallway door, wondering how Miss Landers always knew what was going on. She had discovered the secret to success in Washington—always be first in the know. Trey was still learning.

"Call the firm I use for security at home, too," he said. "I want them to put armed guards on the grounds all day from now until the end of January."

"Yes, sir."

He took a deep breath and smiled. "I don't suppose you've got an extra bagel?"

She reached into a brown bag and pulled out a warm one with a napkin.

He took it and rushed out talking over his shoulder. "I don't know what I'd do without you, Miss Landers."

She called after him. "Neither do I, Mr. Stone. Neither do I."

Chapter Sixteen

Usually before an arraignment a suspect's lawyer and family members are the only ones allowed to meet with the accused privately. But when a U.S. congressman shows up unannounced at a federal detention center, even veteran marshals can be made to cooperate.

With little questioning, Trey was quickly escorted to a private office to meet with the facility's most famous, current resident.

Jack came in through a side door. Except for handcuffs and an orange jumpsuit, he looked pretty much like himself—better, even. He had a fresh shave, combed hair and a broad grin.

The guard undid his cuffs. Trey and Jack embraced awkwardly, then stood beside each other silently as the guard excused himself.

When he heard the door lock, Jack spun around.

The grin was gone.

"Damn you, Stone, I told you to stay away. We can't be seen together. It's not good for either of us."

"Damn *you*, Weddington. You gave a confession without a lawyer? What're you trying to do—commit legal suicide?"

"Think of it as a mercy killing." He sat down in one of two folding chairs facing each other in the middle of the room. He looked up sheepishly.

"I don't suppose you've got any smokes?"

Trey pulled out a new pack of cigarettes and fresh matches from inside his jacket; it was his little "care package" for the incarcerated.

"I thought you were going to quit these things."

"I said I was going to quit buying them."

Jack lit one and dragged deeply. The exhaled smoke emerged in a wispy cloud, rising to the ceiling like a fog lifting off the bay. "So, tell me, what brings you here?"

Trey sat down across from him and leaned in. "Frankly, I'm not sure why I came. You've already done all the damage you can do—talking to investigators, the press. God only knows who else. Everyone but a lawyer."

"Confession is good for the soul. I've been carrying this thing around too long. It was starting to bug me a little bit, you know?"

"Go straight to hell, Weddington," Trey said. He sat back, exasperated. "Go straight to fucking hell."

"Four-letter words from our distinguished congressman? My, my. What's the world coming to?"

"If you don't give a damn about yourself, at least think about your family. Do you realize what you're doing to them?" He looked down for a moment, staring at his own black wingtips opposite Jack's white, numbered tennis shoes. The contrast seemed to say it all. Looking up, he said, "You don't care about anyone but yourself, do you?"

Jack took another deep drag and blew the smoke straight out, forcing Trey to sit back. "That's where you're wrong. I care about everyone but myself. It's a hard lesson, but I've learned it well."

Trey struggled to find a way to talk sense to someone who saw logic as a disease. He knew the conversation was headed in the wrong direction. He hadn't come here to argue with a man intent on destroying himself.

"I don't care what you've said or who you've said it to, Jack. I just want you to do me a favor—I want you to shut up! Can you do that? You're not helping yourself, and you're sure as hell not helping me. You don't understand how this town works. The more you talk, the deeper everyone digs. The more you confess, the more everyone accuses. *Please,* shut up and get some legal advice. If you want to help me, that's the way to do it. *Capice?*"

"Oooh, I love it when you speak Italian."

"I've got a few foreign things I'd like to say."

Jack stubbed out his half-smoked cigarette. "I've never seen you so wound up. Take it easy. I've got this under control."

"No you don't. You're totally out of control. This whole damn situation is out of control. You've got to get legal advice—now. Before this goes any further."

"You're starting to sound like my old man's lawyer."

"You've already talked to him?"

"Yeah, but he's a public policy guy—not a 'criminal' man. They're sending over an expert from the firm. A shark who specializes in finance cases."

"When's he get here?"

"We'll talk before the arraignment. He says he'll get me out on 'O.R.' I should be back on the boat before the day's out."

"Did you ever think of going home to see your wife and kids?"

"I'm the last person they want to see. I've disgraced the family. They want me to dry up and blow away."

"That's where you're wrong, Jack. You can't tell me those boys of yours don't want their dad home."

"They did once—before 'Grandpa' got a hold of them. How is Pops? You talk with him?"

"Not yet. I understand he's pretty shaken. I mean, you call him in the middle of the night and drop a bombshell like this."

143

"It's the only thing he understands—explosions, fireworks."

"We *all* understand a seven-figure bomb. How'd you get in so deep?"

"It was pretty easy."

"Where'd all the money go, Jack? You don't live that extravagantly—except for the damn boat."

"I've been in over my head for a long time. Ever since Laura started running around in fashionable Washington circles, rubbing elbows with White House hotsy-tots. She's got an image to maintain, you know—the finest clothes, new cars, fancy restaurants, political contributions. You don't get on the 'A' list by being stingy in this town."

"That doesn't explain seven figures—not in my book. That's a hell of a lot of dresses and nights on the town."

Jack drew a deep breath, a smokeless one this time. For the first time, he looked serious. The smirk was gone.

"It started when I got behind on payments for the house. I was expecting a bonus at the bank. When it didn't come through, I shouldn't have been surprised. I didn't deserve it. But that hadn't stopped them before." He laughed. "I tried to make up for it in the financial market, trading interest-rate options. But I was always a day late and a few thousand dollars short."

He lit up another cigarette and inhaled half of it in one long pull. "That was when I showed up at your office. I was in deep, but I thought I could turn it around. I just needed a little more time." He sighed. "Then I was out on my boat when the Fed made a major interest-rate move. I couldn't react fast enough. My options got called, and I had to borrow more. Then I lost that. It was like watching money swirl down a drain. There was nothing I could do, except wait for the inevitable." He knocked an ash to the floor.

"Last night, the inevitable came."

Trey stood and went behind the desk to a small window that looked out on the enclosed office behind. The shade was drawn but he could make out the silhouettes of federal marshals on the other side, circling, closing in.

Turning, he leaned against the sill. "You've always been a fatalist," he said, "and it's not very becoming. Yes, you made a few mistakes—and they're doozies, but that doesn't mean you've got to make it worse. Seven figures is a lot of money, but there're ways to make restitution. You'd be surprised at the deals that can be cut. Just don't compound matters by working alone. Get professional help. Depend on your family, too. They don't hate you half as much as you want them to."

"I don't want them to hate me."

"You're doing your damnedest to make it look that way."

"It doesn't 'look' that way. That's the way it is."

Trey waved him off. "Listen, I'll do all I can to help—legally."

"I told you before, stay out of it. I don't want your goddamned help. I don't want anybody's help. Every time I get help, things get worse. Let me do this on my own."

Trey picked up his briefcase and went to the door. He knocked lightly. The guard opened it.

"Do it with a lawyer. At least give me that much."

"Yeah, a lawyer I'll take," he said. "I can't have 'em all out to get me."

Without looking back, Trey stepped away. Several officers turned to watch him walk off. He felt like a suspect himself—in the glare of naked lights behind one-way glass.

Hurrying across the room, he stepped through the front door and into the warming sunshine. He stopped on the concrete steps and stared across the chain-linked parking lot at the armed guards by a barricaded gate. There was something oddly reassuring about the place: ordered, precise, military. Standing there, breathing in the fresh air, he tried to clear his head of the anger inside. Then he realized he had left Jack for the first time without a handshake and salute. He thought about going back in, starting over, trying to reason with him. But he decided to wait until after the arraignment, when Jack was back on his boat. They could have a drink, talk this through like good friends. They would find a way to correct the mistakes. They just couldn't let the situation overwhelm them.

Trey slumped back in his car, fired up the engine and sped out of the lot, heading toward Annapolis.

Maybe the governor could stop the bleeding, before they all bled to death.

Chapter Seventeen

When Trey arrived at the governor's mansion, he drove straight to the back entrance to avoid the crush of media out front. He parked sideways, anticipating a quick get-away, then hurried through the kitchen door.

As he entered the long hallway leading to the front of the house, he spotted Laura at the far end. She saw him, too, and ran silently to him, falling into his arms.

He held her against his chest, entangling his hands in her long, thick hair. He expected to feel her sob against him. But she didn't make a sound.

For an interminably long moment, they stood like this, not speaking, holding onto one another, her arms draped around his neck.

Finally, he extracted himself and smiled at her self-consciously. She wiped under each eye, though tears were not evident on her cheeks.

He spoke first. "I saw Jack."

She nodded, little-girl-like. "How is he?"

"He's not taking this seriously enough. I don't think he understands what's at stake. He could wind up doing very serious time."

"I expect that."

"Don't you get fatalistic on me now. He hasn't even been arraigned, and everybody's got him convicted and sentenced."

"But he gave a full confession, Trey. It's not as if he's trying to fight this thing."

"He will—if I've got anything to say about it. He's got friends, a supportive family, a clean record. With a good lawyer and a repayment plan, miracles can happen."

"Miracles are not Jack's style. His family isn't as supportive as you think, either. The governor's fit to be tied."

"I assume he's recovered from his earlier shock."

"Yes, in a very big way. He's speaking to the press now, making a formal statement. Something about suspending judgment until the facts are in. He's using the standard 'out'—while the case is pending, he can't comment."

At the other end of the hall, the double doors to the press briefing room suddenly burst open, and Governor Weddington stormed out, leading two dozen reporters, cameramen and assorted hangers-on to the front entry.

The butler opened the doors, and the governor marched through. Standing on the landing, he showed everyone out. They tried to ask questions and thrust microphones, but the governor parried them all. He looked confident, but not overly so: the perfect mix of politician and father figure.

As the reporters emptied out, the governor turned and marched back inside, strobes popping behind. When the doors closed, he stopped and faced the long hall where Trey and Laura stood.

The three of them stared at one another for several agonizing moments, then the governor walked slowly toward them.

Trey met him halfway.

They shook hands and embraced, much the way Trey had done with Jack less than an hour ago.

The governor smiled grimly, and Trey thought he saw traces of tears rimming his eyes, but it could have been the rheumy look of a man of over-indulgence. Either way, there was little sadness in his voice.

"That bastard son of mine is out to ruin me," he said.

He took Trey by the arm and led him into the library. Laura followed at a safe distance. The governor headed to the bar and poured himself a brandy, then took a long sip.

"I'd like to say I'm surprised by Jack's admission," he said, "but I'm not. I always suspected him of financial mismanagement. The man has no head for numbers."

Trey sat on the edge of a couch by the fireplace. He wanted to defend his friend, but didn't know how. Jack's indiscretions had become indefensible.

"I got him a lawyer," the governor said, "and we're working up a PR plan. The media'll attempt to try this case in print and on television. That's where we'll wage our most fierce battle—where we'll win or lose it."

Trey nodded. "Jack didn't help his cause *legally* with a confession, but he may have helped himself in the court of public opinion."

"I doubt that's why he confessed."

"I'm sure it's not," Trey said. "Jack doesn't give a damn about public perceptions. He confessed out of some distorted sense of honor. I've never seen anyone with more of a martyr complex. He thinks everything can be made right by self-sacrifice."

Laura sat beside Trey and laid a hand gently on his knee. "We know that's impossible, don't we?"

For the second time today, he wasn't sure what she meant, and he didn't care to find out.

"Sacrifice is for victims," the governor said. He drank from the snifter again, then freshened his glass. "I don't intend to be a victim, even if Jack does. He might take himself down, but he's not taking me with him. That son of a bitch has been out to destroy my career for as long as I can remember. If I had my way, I'd let him hang. He knows I can't do that, so I'll save his scraggly ass—and my own—once more."

Moving closer to Trey, Weddington leaned against the fireplace mantle. Trey suddenly felt surrounded, as he often did in the presence of the Weddingtons. Only two other people were in the room, but they had him closed in. The governor on his right, his liquored breath barely a whisper away. Laura on his left, her hip against his, her hand lying lightly on his thigh. They both watched him intently, as if he could somehow make all their troubles disappear, as if he had some magic elixir they could drink to cure their ills.

Standing, he moved to the center of the room.

"This isn't going to go away fast or easy. It's going to be a long, protracted battle. The key is to conduct damage control up front. First, you've got to protect Jack from himself. In the process, you'll protect yourself. I wish I had the answers for you, but I don't. I'll tell you the same thing I told him—I'll do what I can to help, but the final results are up to you. You've got to work together. No accusations, no blaming, no finger pointing. The rest will take care of itself."

"It's not up to us, Trey," the governor said. "It's up to Jack. We're here if he wants us."

"I'm not sure he knows that, John," Trey said.

"He knows it all right." He tossed back another shot of brandy. "Jack'll claim we're out to get him, that we hate him—all the same old horse shit. The only person who hates Jack is Jack. I can't help that."

Trey shook his head. "I've been in the middle of this too long. If you want my help, I'll do what I can. The rest is up to you."

He moved toward the door. "I've got to get to D.C. I've got . . . work . . . to do." He started to say "real work," but couldn't bring himself to cut that deep.

"Wait!" The governor and Laura spoke together.

"Don't leave angry, son," the governor said. "We're all under a lot of pressure. We say things we don't mean."

"I'm not angry. I'm behind schedule, that's all. I've got conferences with House officers, voter polling to conduct. I've missed half a dozen meetings today. I'm sorry, I . . . I . . ."

Laura stood and embraced him again. "We shouldn't burden you with all this. Not with everything you're facing right now."

The governor took hold of his shoulder in one, large powerful hand. "You've always been like a rock, and we place too much weight on you because of it. But your advice is good, and we'll take it to heart."

Trey sighed. "All you've got is each other. When you give that up, you've lost everything."

"Agreed, son."

Laura rubbed her hand over his back, holding him tightly to her. For the second time today, he pried himself loose.

"I've got to go."

He kissed her on the forehead and reached out a hand to the governor, but Weddington would have none of it. He pulled Trey to his breast and held him like he would a young boy, rocking back and forth. Several moments later, Trey pulled away and walked to the door in a rush.

The governor called out. "Trey! You didn't tell us how the January vote's shaping up. Any inside word?"

He stared back before responding, wondering how the two of them could think about an election with Jack's freedom on the line. Could they be any more callous, any more calculating?

"We haven't completed phone polling of the voters," he said, "and we haven't met with the candidates' staffs. Too early to tell."

Turning, he headed down the hallway, but the click of Laura's high heels was right behind. She caught up and took him by the arm, leading him to the back door.

"Thanks for coming and for being so tolerant of us," she said. "This is a difficult time for everyone."

"Do me a favor, Laura—be tolerant of Jack, too. In his own way, he's trying to do what's right."

"I know he is. He thinks he is, anyway."

They reached the door, and Trey stepped onto the porch.

Leaning out, Laura kissed him on the cheek. "I'll see you this weekend."

He stammered. "But I'll—we'll—be away."

"I know," she said. "I'll be at Camp David, too."

She winked and closed the door.

Slowly, Trey turned and made his way to the car. Climbing behind the wheel, he let the engine idle for a while and wondered what the last few minutes were all about. Could the Weddingtons ever separate family and politics? Were the two inextricably linked—one fused to the other, indistinguishable from each another?

He spied a reporter coming around the corner of the mansion with a cameraman in tow. Jamming the car in gear, he skidded out of the back lot onto Church Circle.

At the corner of College Avenue, he stopped in the far right-hand lane. As traffic worked its way around, he looked longingly to the left, toward West Street. He felt drawn in that direction—toward home. Maybe, just maybe he should say to hell with everything else and head on back to the house. He could sit in front of the fire with Jazz and Katie and talk about the holidays to come. It wasn't even Thanksgiving yet, and he was already wishing for Christmas. For the end of the year. For the end of January.

He pulled out his cellular phone and dialed into the office, knowing he couldn't go home without checking with Miss Landers first.

She answered on the first ring.

"Am I glad you called," she said. "I've been trying to track you down."

"I'm in Annapolis at the governor's mansion. What's up?"

"We just got an urgent call from the Republican National Committee. Mr. Wardlow came into town unexpectedly."

"Yes?"

"He's requested the honor of meeting with the Maryland Congressional delegation tonight. He came on the line himself and apologized for the short notice."

Trey hesitated. "I suppose I can make it. I don't know about the others."

"We've been in contact with everyone. They're available."

"What sort of meeting does he want? And where?"

"He called it a 'get-acquainted' session. He reserved a room at Kinkead's Restaurant near the White House at eight o'clock."

"So he's already cozying up to Pennsylvania Avenue, huh? How clever."

"Should I confirm your attendance?"

He glanced out the side window and wondered why the route home seemed to be getting farther away all the time.

"It doesn't sound like I have much choice," he said.

"Are you coming back to the office now?"

"Things are piling up?"

"We can't see over all the call slips. Visitors are stacking up in the waiting room. The Speaker is frantic to hold a meeting with you and Mr. Ogle."

"I'll be there in thirty minutes."

He punched the 'end' button on the phone and slipped the transmission into drive.

Swinging a hard right, he floored the accelerator. The car rocketed down the four-lane road toward D.C.

The Beltway beckoned once more. As always, he responded like the proverbial lemming to the sea.

Half a dozen cars behind, Steel switched off his cellular monitoring system and got on the encryption phone. "The congressman appears to be tightening up," he said. "You get anything from our contact at the detention center?"

"They had a heated discussion," Ridge replied.

"Oh?"

"The congressman said, 'You think you're helping me but you're not.' And Weddington talked about them not being seen together. It's all very suspicious."

"Can we get a transcript?"

"It's on the way."

"Send a copy to Longstreet ASAP. Maybe he can make something out of it."

"Will do." He laughed. "This is getting to be fun."

Steele hesitated.

"It'll be fun when it's over."

He cut the call, pulled around traffic, gunning the engine after the town car in front.

Chapter Eighteen

Throughout the afternoon, Trey and his staff tried their best to hold off the flood of phone calls, faxes, e-mails, special deliveries and unexpected visitors. Congress was supposed to be out-of-session, but that did little to stop the unending stream.

Most of the day was taken up by meetings with everyone from the Speaker of the House—who was threatening to put a Republican vice president in the White House with Forsythe, if he won—and caucuses with the Democratic leadership, which was thrilled to learn of Trey's coming weekend retreat with the President. (The party faithful refused to believe the get-together was not a sign of Trey's impending support of the President.)

In the early evening, Trey ran everyone out of his office for a private, personal call.

Earlier in the day, he had asked a staff member to monitor Jack Weddington's arraignment. Now he wanted an update. The staffer reported, as expected, that Jack was released without bond. Trey's assistant volunteered to drive him home, but Jack declined, saying he would meet with his attorneys well into the night.

Trey thanked the assistant for the report, then went back to work, trying to put Jack's troubles as far from his mind as possible, hoping they would stay away. He knew this was wishful thinking at its worst.

He pored over paperwork until nearly seven o'clock. After showering in the House gym, he met his two closest congressional teammates, Bobby Buckland and Miles Ogle, for the ten-minute ride to Kinkead's.

For a few, fleeting moments together in the back of the limo, the three friends laughed and poked fun at one another. Buckland and Ogle remarked that, for the first time in their careers, the national press seemed to care what they thought. Buckland said he could get used to all the attention. "This privacy thing is overrated," he joked.

The conversation went on this way until the car rolled up in front of the restaurant, where the scene was madness. Trey had hoped the meeting would be an unannounced affair, but the sidewalk and streets were filled with reporters, gawkers and police.

The cops cut a pathway to the front door, and the limo driver worked his way through the crowd. When they stopped in front, Trey hesitated before opening the door, looking over at Buckland and Ogle.

"Privacy's overrated, huh?" he said. "We'll see how long that attitude lasts."

With the help of officers holding back the crowd, Trey led the way through the front door, squinting against the flashes and strobes. Then he discovered inside the restaurant wasn't much better than out. The place was packed with campaign workers and advisers.

Trey was greeted by an assistant to Governor Wardlow, a young woman who told him the governor and Maryland's other congressmen were waiting upstairs.

Trey and his two partners bounded up to a private room designated for the meeting. When they opened the door, it was like entering the eye of a storm.

The place was eerily quiet. At one end, a large table was set with china, silverware and goblets. Around it sat five congressmen, munching on condiments and sipping wine.

At the other end, Governor Wardlow stood by himself, staring out a one-way window at the mob scene below.

Buckland and Ogle joined their fellow representatives. Trey didn't want to leave the guest of honor alone. He walked up beside Wardlow and stared out the window with him.

"Looks like your little unexpected visit has caused quite a commotion, Governor," he said. "I imagine you've seen a lot of this over the last few months."

"Indeed I have," he said, smiling. "This is what Presidential elections are all about—stir up interest, generate excitement. Sometimes it becomes a monster you can't control."

"Everyone likes publicity in *theory*," Trey said. "But the press seems intent on covering only the negative, even when it doesn't exist."

"You sound like a man who speaks from experience."

"I'm learning."

"That you are."

Wardlow turned full to him and extended his right hand. "It's an honor to meet you, Congressman Stone."

"The honor's mine, sir."

They shook hands respectfully, like two warriors from opposite sides before the battle.

"Speaking of publicity," the governor said, "most of the media pundits feel you hold a key vote that could decide my political future. Any truth to the rumors?"

Trey shook his head. "I'm only one of four hundred and thirty-five, Governor. No more, no less. The media likes to find heroes and villains. When they can't, they make them up."

"You may underestimate yourself, Trey. I hope you don't mind if I call you that. I understand it's your preference."

"Yes it is. Feel free."

"Only if you'll use my first name. It's Carlos."

"I thought you always went by Carl."

"That's my campaign name," he laughed. "My 'handlers' felt the public would react badly to an ethnic name. Hiding minority status, I'm afraid, is the nature of national elections these days."

"Carlos it is," Trey said.

Despite his Spanish ancestry, the governor looked every bit the mainstream Presidential candidate. He was a tall man, two or three inches taller than Trey, with salt-and-pepper hair that receded slightly at the temples, forming a distinguished widow's peak. His skin was smooth as paper, with a golden tan undoubtedly aided by his genes. His eyes were the lightest blue, too, like two oases in dusky sand. More important, he had a calmness about him, an inner strength that emanated through those eyes and through the easy grin that turned up the corners of his mouth.

"I understand we have a military background in common, Trey. You're an Annapolis man?"

"That's right. I didn't serve out my full Naval commitment, though. Congressional duty called."

"I'm a West Point man, myself."

"I understand you made quite a name for yourself in Vietnam."

"Many good men gave a lot to that losing cause. I made some great friends there, and lost some great ones, too."

"It was a tough war, fought more in the political chambers than on the battlefields. But I envy the opportunity you had to put your military training to the test."

"The purpose of a military is to preserve the peace. When war's our only option, we've failed."

Trey nodded. "You sound like my father. He fought in

two wars and despised them both for all the senseless death and destruction."

"But he gave a good account of himself. Quite a hero, I understand. I hope he's feeling better."

"Not any worse."

Trey looked out the window at the growing crowd. The onlookers had attracted other onlookers. A feeding frenzy was on.

Turning back, he went on. "My father says his best days were at the end of his career, when he taught war history to Naval recruits at Annapolis. He wanted them to learn from the mistakes of the past."

"It's an honorable calling."

"Ever been to The Yard, Governor?"

"No. I'd love to go. The campus must be ripe with history."

"I'd be honored to give you a first-class tour."

"After this election's over, we'll set it up." He smiled broadly. "You can count on that, whether I win or lose."

They shook hands on the deal, then the governor's assistant beckoned them to the dinner table.

Most of the rest of the three-hour evening was spent in innocent chatter around the table. Wardlow gave a brief, informal presentation, followed by an even more informal question-and-answer session on the economy, crime, entitlements, foreign trade.

The Maryland representatives didn't ask anything that hadn't been asked before, but it was reassuring to hear from a candidate who spoke off-the-cuff. It gave everyone a feel for whether Wardlow truly believed in his publicly held positions.

Trey liked what he heard. Wardlow showed himself to be a fast-thinker, articulate and well informed. Most impressively, he didn't try to buy their support. He simply built a strong case for himself, pointing out he had won the popular vote in a landslide. Except for the oddity of a far-right candidate winning a handful of electoral votes, he would already be President-elect today.

"It would be a shame," he said, "even a tragedy, to take away from the voters what they've already given."

It was a good case, well stated by a man obviously qualified to fill the job.

Then Trey asked a question of increasing personal interest: "Reports are you're encouraging an investigation into Forsythe's campaign financing. Is that something you would pursue in office?"

Wardlow's brow furrowed. He stared hard at Trey as he responded. "Campaign financing at all levels needs a closer look. I've opened up my own records. I expect Forsythe to do the same—no matter who wins."

Trey nodded. He began to see why the President might view Wardlow as such a threat.

The governor's assistant appeared. She said their next appointment awaited. Apparently, Wardlow was flying out tonight for the West Coast.

The candidate stood and went around the table shaking hands with all the guests, graciously thanking them for attending the dinner on such short notice. He knew a little something personal about each one, and used his knowledge like a master craftsman, carefully assembling the whole.

Trey was last. The two men stepped away from the table toward the stairs.

"I can honestly say it's been a pleasure," Wardlow said, "and somewhat of a surprise meeting you this evening. You're very different than your public persona—much more down to earth than the press would have us believe."

"I was about to say the same about you."

Wardlow threw back his head and laughed heartily.

Then he went on. "I could say I came here tonight bearing gifts—political gifts. But that's not my style. With me, what you see is what you get. My word is my bond. Win or lose, that'll always be the same."

Trey looked him in the eye and gave him a subtle nod of the head. With that, the governor was off.

As he moved away, his advisers and staff gathered around him like migratory birds in flight; the assistants trailed back from his lead position in a perfect, inverted "V" formation. Reaching the stairs, Wardlow started down. Before disappearing below, he looked up and tossed out a quick, almost imperceptible salute.

Trey flicked one back. Then the governor was gone.

When Trey got back to the dinner table, the other congressmen were leisurely sipping wine and chatting. Everyone was impressed by Wardlow's performance. Even hardline Democrats expressed admiration.

"Our own candidate, Mr. Forsythe, is much less impressive than the gentleman we just broke bread with, as much as I hate to admit it," Ogle drawled. "That could have something to do with the fact that our President all but abandoned his pledge to support increased aid to education and defend Social Security against funding cuts."

Buckland nodded agreement. "Or that Forsythe oversaw tax relief for the wealthy and increased military spending at a time when real income for the middle-class is declining."

Trey piled on: "Of course, the rumors of illegal campaign financing are troubling, to say the least, as are the charges of suspect trade deals with corrupt foreign governments."

All the Democrats at the table glanced furtively at one another, knowing their own party helped block a congressional investigation into those most serious allegations—part of the payback to Republicans for their failure to pursue equally serious charges against previous GOP administrations. More importantly, though, all the Democrats knew Forsythe was all they had. Possible felonies aside, the party could not afford to lose the one branch of government they controlled by a thread.

Looking around the table, Trey did the quick arithmetic: Three of the four Democrats present would back Forsythe come January, no matter what. The lone Independent, who always voted with the left, would do the same. That made the fifth and deciding vote on the President's survival Trey himself—just as everyone had been saying all along. The only problem was, his *deciding* vote was the most undecided of all. And he was about to meet face-to-face with the one man who needed him more than anyone else. Indeed, Trey was mere hours from finding out the lengths Forsythe would go to secure his own safe return to office.

Chapter Nineteen

Camp David

The anticipation—and the helicopter flight—were invigorating. But after Trey and Laura's interlude in the woods (there was no other word to describe their meeting), Trey began to feel an increasing sense of dread. Something about the urgency in her voice. She almost appeared on the verge of panic.

After leaving her behind on the sheltered path, he returned to the cabin with Katie, cleaned up quickly and escorted his wife and daughter across the grounds to Aspen Lodge for lunch.

Walking arm-in-arm across the quad, he hoped his concerns were the work of an overactive imagination. And they appeared to be just that when President Forsythe opened the door. The President offered up a big smile and a hearty handshake.

"Welcome, Stone family!" he bellowed. "I'm honored to have you here." Dressed in khaki pants and a turtleneck sweater, he looked every bit the grandfatherly host.

Trey had heard the President was powerfully attached to Camp David. He always lit up—physically and emotionally—when on retreat here. His eyes even took a renewed sparkle, much like they had during his first campaign for President four years ago. That brightness had faded during his first term in office; it was good to see the effects were not necessarily permanent.

The President introduced his wife, the First Lady, as Mrs. Forsythe.

"Call me Madge," she insisted. "I won't have it any other way."

She looked kindly, almost spinsterly, with white hair, weathered skin and round shoulders. She was the same age as her husband, but looked a good ten years older.

She started off the afternoon with a brief tour of the giant lodge, which served as a combination residence and Presidential office.

She recited facts and figures obviously memorized over the years. "Every President since Roosevelt has slept in this same bed," she said, showing off the master suite. "And Bess Truman had this living room redesigned shortly after World War II." "This sitting room was added by Mamie Eisenhower." "Lady Bird Johnson had the library reconstructed."

On it went, like a history lesson in still-life. It could have continued, too, but Forsythe shortened the tour by announcing, "Soup's on."

A team of White House chefs was on premises to handle all meals. The settings included top-grade dinnerware arrayed across a checkered tablecloth. Steaming bowls of split-pea soup sat in front of each chair. Trey was surprised to see seven places set. He had expected only five.

The President pointed out seating arrangements as two other diners appeared. "I believe you know this young lady," Forsythe said. "Laura Weddington." Smiles all around. "You may not know this gentleman," he went on. "Congressman and Mrs. Stone, please meet Arch Longstreet."

Trey's mouth fell open; he was sure his complexion turned several shades of gray and white.

Longstreet smiled and reached out to shake hands. He held on a little too hard and a little too long. Trey unhooked himself by gesturing to his left.

"This is my wife . . ."

"Mrs. Stone," Longstreet said. "You look familiar. Are we acquainted?"

She shook her head. "I don't believe so. Call me Jazz—everyone does."

He held her hand too long, too, until an uncomfortable silence engulfed the room.

The President then cleared his throat and announced: "Let's eat."

When he pulled back his chair and sat down, the rest followed. The conversation quickly turned to typical lunchtime topics—the weather, food, their surroundings. Trey extolled the benefits of Maryland and its diverse geography, claiming the state never got its due for being one of the country's best-kept secrets. Everyone agreed.

After lunch, they retired to the family room for coffee and tea. With the raise of an eyebrow, the President signaled his wife to begin the next item on the agenda—a girls-only event. The First Lady invited Jazz, Laura and Katie for a walk around the grounds.

As they departed, Forsythe asked Trey and Longstreet to join him in Hickory Lodge for a little "boy talk."

They didn't don jackets for the quick walk across the compound to the second-largest lodge. Marching single-file, Trey behind the President, Longstreet at the rear, they moved up the wooden steps and into the main meeting room.

Trey wasn't surprised to find three members of the infamous Southern Mafia inside, sitting on leather couches near a roaring fireplace.

The President introduced him to Vice President McNally ("Good to meet you, Congressman"); Secretary of State Gandolf ("Call me Army, everyone does"); and Chief of Staff Wilmington ("Hope everything's as you expected").

Forsythe offered Trey a drink from the bar, but he asked for tea instead. As a waiter delivered a steaming cup, the President lit a long, thick Cuban cigar, and McNally followed suit.

Trey struggled to keep his sinuses under control. He took a seat in a chair as far from the smoke as possible. Sipping his tea, he watched the "chosen ones" as they watched him. He couldn't help but think this was a good-old-boys' club of the highest order. He envisioned the members sitting around with cognacs in hand, recounting glories of political wars past, trophies prominently displayed on the cabin walls—the head of a wayward senator here, the skin of a disagreeable governor there. Smiling, Trey thought of his own head mounted, horns and all, over the doorway of the lodge. *I might be the most important quarry of all.*

The President fired the first round.

"Gentlemen, we're honored today to talk with a man who appears to control our political futures," he said.

"Here, here," McNally said, raising his glass to Trey.

The vice president swigged a brandy. Others in the room drank from their respective glasses and cups.

Trey didn't salute back.

"Mr. President," he said, "you give far too much significance to my single vote. I'm only one of four hundred and thirty-five congressmen—all of whom will do a fair job of representing the country as a whole."

"Four hundred and thirty-five men and women," Forsythe said, "but only fifty states. That narrows the odds quite a bit, right there."

"But no one man controls the votes in a single state," Trey responded, "except in those cases where only one representative serves. That's certainly not the situation in Maryland."

"No, but let's look at those single-representative states." Despite his reputation as a slacker in office, Forsythe had a facile mind, capable of recalling facts and figures precisely and with little prompting.

"Alaska," he said. "The state went nearly seventy percent for Wardlow. I think it's safe to say the single representative from our largest state will support the conservative."

Trey nodded and sipped his tea.

The President rose from his chair and stood in front of the fireplace.

"Delaware," he said. "Our smallest state. More than seventy percent of the electorate went for Wardlow, again. I think the state's single representative is a safe bet for supporting my opposition."

Everyone around the room moved their heads up and down, staring at Trey as he listened.

"Montana," Forsythe said. "One of my favorites." He smiled and re-lit his dying cigar. "It's another Republican stronghold, though. Nearly sixty percent of the vote went Republican. I think it's safe to say Montana's another good bet for Wardlow."

He paced in front of the hearth, the cigar protruding from his mouth like a giant pacifier.

"North Dakota," he said. "We thought we had a shot in North Dakota this year." He glared at Longstreet. "But the state went for Wardlow fifty-five to forty-five. It's safely in the Republican column." Stooping in front of the fire, he warmed his hands. "South Dakota is another Republican state, as was Vermont this year. Tack up two more for the competition." Turning, he folded his arms across his chest and rocked back and forth. "Wyoming. Another gorgeous state that always goes Republican. Chalk up yet another for Wardlow."

Forsythe stared at Trey for what seemed an interminably long time, then he walked to his easy chair and sat down. The silence grew like a cloud, filling every corner and crevice of the room.

Trey wanted to speak, wanted to debate the President's points, but he couldn't. Forsythe had done his homework. He knew the seven single-vote states were in Wardlow's pocket. Nothing could change that between now and January.

The President harrumphed. "I could go down the list of two-congressmen states," he said, "but I won't bore you anymore. You know the vote better than I do."

"I doubt that, sir."

Forsythe winked. "The only undecided two-congressman state was Maine," he said. "It's also the one state, other than yours, where the Independent candidate won a plurality. A few days ago, Marshall Young asked his home state of Maine to cast its ballots for me in January." Forsythe swished his index finger in the air. "Rack up one for the home team." Unable to sit still, he stood again in front of the fire, displaying an almost manic energy that kept the room on edge.

Trey sipped the last of his tea and set the cup aside.

"Can we refresh that for you, Congressman?" the President asked.

"No thanks. I've exceeded my limit."

"Maybe we can offer you something stronger?"

"Later, perhaps."

"Are you a smoker, Trey? I've got a private reserve of the

world's best cigars. Cuban, of course." He winked. "Don't
let that out."

Trey shook his head and smiled. *Clever,* he thought. *Pull
me into your confidence. Trade a little secret for a secret. I won't
tell if you don't.*

The President went on.

"Marshall Young made another suggestion. He said the
one other state where he achieved plurality support should
back me, as well. He hasn't made *that* position known publicly. He wanted to do it one-on-one, first."

Forsythe looked over to an open doorway where a man
emerged and took several steps into the room, then stopped
and waited to be introduced.

"Mr. Stone," the President said, "I give you the Independent candidate, Marshall Young."

Trey nearly lost his tea right there. He had expected a
"full-court press," as Laura described, but this was beyond
reason. Obviously, the President had worked a deal with
Young.

To Trey's way of thinking, though, Young won Maine
and Maryland only because many in the states owed their
livelihoods to his family's corporation. This aberration
didn't entitle him to a say in the final vote. Yet, here he
stood at Forsythe's side, bearing a message of support for
the current Administration.

Over the next few minutes, Young laid out his position:
"I won more than thirty percent of the vote in Maryland,"
he said. "Add that to the President's total, and we exceed a
majority. This should be enough to warrant your support
for his re-election."

He offered other justifications, as well—briefly-stated ar-
guments and positions—but Trey didn't really hear them,
or care to. As far as he was concerned, Young had earned

no role in the selection of a President.

Even Forsythe himself appeared embarrassed by the moment. He listened to Young's memorized, five-minute appeal, and smiled sheepishly. At the end, he thanked him and raised a hand to show him the way out.

Forsythe then sat and stared into the fire for a moment. When he spoke again, a lot of the earlier energy had left his voice.

"Mr. Young's words may or may not influence you, Trey. But in my mind, they should have a powerful effect. He did win Electoral College support in two states. Despite his inexperience in national politics, he deserves a say in how the House votes."

Forsythe checked the end of his cigar and saw it had gone out again. Setting it aside, he leaned forward in his chair. "Tell me, do you believe Young's support will have an effect on the House vote?"

There it was—the question Trey had been expecting. He thought the President would ease his way into it. Take his time. Build their relationship. But Forsythe was no political connoisseur. He was a meat and potatoes guy. He wanted to know where he stood. If it wasn't where he needed to be, he wanted the rest of the weekend to change it.

Trey got up and moved over by the fire, standing with hands behind his back as if at attention before a firing squad. All he needed was a blindfold and a cigarette.

"I can't speak for the other states, Mr. President."

"Call me Ben. You're among friends."

"I can't speak for Maryland, either, Ben."

Forsythe slumped in his chair.

"We're polling the voters in our districts, meeting with the candidates and their staffs—your people included. Until that process is finished, I can't say where the state will come down. I could stand here and tell you I know who we'll support. But I won't tell you something just because you want to hear it—not on an issue as monumental as this. My vote in January is as close to a sacred duty as I'll ever face as an elected official. I can't play politics with my position or that of my state."

Folding his arms across his chest, Trey stood spread-legged in front of the fire, waiting to take the shots. He was satisfied with his statement. He had spoken from the heart, and it had worked out just fine.

Forsythe picked up his gnarled cigar and re-lit it once more. Apparently, smoking was only a ritual with him, a distraction. He seldom puffed.

"Playing politics," he said. "Funny you should choose that phrase, especially since so few people elect a President. Only about half the country is eligible to vote, and only half the eligible voters actually cast ballots. This means about twenty percent of the population actually votes for the man who wins. It's pretty scary, when you think about it. A fifth of the population elects the leader of the most powerful nation in the world." He took a deep drag on his cigar and coughed hard. "Of course, with everything getting thrown into the House this year, percentages mean nothing."

He cleared his throat and went on. "Maybe it's right that people who have dedicated their lives to politics should decide who leads this country. After all, they're the ones who have to work with the man." Pausing, he said, "I'd like to make a difference in office. I'm not satisfied with what I accomplished during my first term. I did some good things, but I made my share of mistakes. Four years is not enough time to fix all the wrongs. Only two-term Presidents ever accomplish anything of substance. That's what I'd like to do. It's probably self-serving, but what isn't these days?"

The President didn't really want an answer. Trey listened silently, trying to figure out where the conversation was going from here. He had made his point. He wasn't going to commit his vote. What more could he say?

"An airline pilot told me a funny thing one day," Forsythe rambled on. "He said, ninety-nine percent of piloting today is pure, mechanized boredom. Pilots are in the cockpit for rare moments when something goes wrong. It takes a steady hand and years of experience to deal with that—to know when to pull back on the throttle, or lower the flaps, or whatever the hell they do. I don't know, I'm not a pilot." He tossed the dead cigar aside and leaned forward in his chair. "I am President, though, and I know how to deal with crises and how to play politics. I also know how to win elections, and I damn well intend to win this one."

Standing, he brushed stray ashes off the sleeves of his sweater. "The office of the Presidency's immensely powerful. The office shouldn't be trusted to untested hands. A Chief Executive can make and break people. You may call it a game, but it's a game with the highest possible stakes. It's one I don't intend to lose."

For the first time, Trey realized what a tall and imposing figure Forsythe could be. On television and in publicity photos, the weight of the office had appeared to diminish him, rounding his shoulders, darkening his eyes. But now, caught in the firelight, his long shadow sweeping up the wall behind, he was once again his full six-foot-four. Hands on his hips. Chin up. Eyes piercing.

"Time's short, son," he said, "and my patience isn't much longer. I need you to make a commitment to your party, to your President and to your own political future."

He looked over to his circle of advisers. "Join me back in Aspen Lodge, gentlemen." He stuck out a hand to

Trey. "Excuse the abruptness, but I've got business to conduct."

They shook hands and Forsythe stalked off, his officers trailing behind.

Trey didn't move. He felt frozen in place. Camp David had suddenly taken on a cold presence. He felt isolated. One against many. One against all. He moved away from the fireplace and leaned against the chair where he had been before. The palms of his hands were slick against the leather. He sat on the arm and took a deep breath.

Longstreet, the only other person in the room, walked over and sat where the President had been. Sinking back into the folds of the leather, he stared at his fingernails, bitten to the quick.

"President Forsythe can be a forceful man," he said. "The very nature of his personality changes when he's challenged." Looking up, he added, "He's a vicious fighter, and an undeniable winner. No matter what it takes and at all costs."

When Trey replied, his voice was shaky. It was his first time in the presence of the President and his advisers—men who had dominated the front pages of major dailies worldwide, dueled with heads of states and commanded the earth's most powerful armed forces. Trey had seen a flash of anger he hadn't expected, wasn't prepared for. He felt like a college kid dressed down by the Commander of the Fleet.

"I wish he'd shown that same intensity during the campaign," Trey said. "It might've made a difference in the vote."

"You didn't see him in personal appearances, informal meetings, one-on-ones," Longstreet said. "Everything gets filtered through television these days. It's impossible to get to every voter, to shake every hand. If he had the opportunity to meet more people, it would've been a different story. But the President's buffered away from the people. It gets harder to connect, to be yourself."

"Wardlow suffered the same restrictions, I'm sure. He had to fight his way through large crowds and commanded a pretty good-sized entourage himself."

"That's nothing like being a sitting President. A visit by Forsythe can shut down an entire city. People resent him for coming into town. Besides, only a small portion of the population cares one way or the other."

Trey wasn't up to arguing campaign strategy with a man who made his living at it. Besides, he wasn't sure what was next on the obviously well-planned agenda. One thing was sure: He hadn't heard the last from the President. They had just been through round one. This little chat with Longstreet was just the toweling off for the rest of the bout.

Longstreet stood and warmed his hands in front of the fire, much as Forsythe had done earlier. "The President's restricted in other ways, as well," he said. "Being an official of the government, he's not in a position to offer, shall we say, *opportunities* in exchange for support."

Trey stared ahead, not acknowledging the point.

Longstreet continued. "As you might guess from what the President said between the lines, these opportunities are open-ended. Everyone's got to get something. We understand that."

Standing, Trey moved behind his chair, resting his elbows on top. His breathing began to return to normal. He listened a little more attentively.

"What are you driving at?"

"Perhaps that's a question I should ask you. Let me put it this way: What do you want? What'll it take?"

"Are you asking what it'll take for my vote?" Trey said. "Please be perfectly clear, Mr. Longstreet."

"What'll it take for your vote, Congressman? Can I be any clearer than that?"

Trey let the question hang in the air to gain gravity. Trey wasn't willing to *negotiate* his vote, so Longstreet was asking if they could buy it. This was politics at its dirtiest. This was what Trey hated about the system, what it had become.

He shook his head. "Absolutely nothing. That's what it'll take to get my vote."

Longstreet moved over to Forsythe's chair and re-seated himself, one leg slung over the side. "Let me make sure I understand. You're saying you already support the President, so there's no need for further . . . assistance . . . to secure your vote."

Trey stepped away, closer to the door. "Nothing you can offer me will alter my vote one way or the other. I'm not for sale, Mr. Longstreet. You can pass that along to the President. He's a powerful man, and he can give and withhold a lot, but I don't work that way. I'll vote my conscience. It may sound like a cliché to you, but that's my commitment to the voters."

With that, he turned on his heel and walked out, slamming the door behind.

On the front porch of the lodge, he caught a glimpse of Laura seated inside an anteroom off the main meeting hall.

He mouthed a question through the window, asking: "Where's Jazz?"

"In your cabin," she said, her voice muffled by the glass.

He turned and walked away as Laura called out behind—something like "How'd it go?"—but he ignored the question and kept walking, across the open grounds, through the fresh mountain air. Taking several deep breaths, he tried to clear his sinuses of the cigar smoke and his head of the emotional haze left behind. His instinct was to get back to the cabin, pack up and go—to get the hell out of this lovely forest setting besmirched by politics of the ugliest kind. But he was the President's guest and had to finish his stay, like it or not.

Longstreet walked to the door of the lodge and found Laura standing in the hallway, watching Trey rush away.

"I assume things didn't go well," she said.

"That's an understatement."

"What happened?"

"I offered him a deal, and he took offense. Honestly, I don't think much of your friend's political skills."

"He sees himself as a servant of the people, whatever that is."

"I seldom deal with his kind—so stubborn, so *righteous*. There's no place in politics for that today."

"He just doesn't understand how much he's hurting himself," she said. "No one'd blame him for cooperating. Good Lord, it's *expected*."

"We've got to get more leverage," Longstreet said. "I had hoped Young's support might do it, but Trey doesn't owe him. We've got to find out who he owes. Otherwise, more stringent measures may be required."

"What's that supposed to mean?"

"If we can't find his weak spot, we'll have to create one. My rule is—if you can't win, stop others from winning. It's what we did with Young in November. We may have to do it with Stone in January."

"What are you talking about?"

"You don't think Marshall Young won Maine and Maryland on his own, do you? Hell, I funded his campaign—

swung as many votes to him as possible."

Standing, he paced in a tight little circle, his eyes blinking wildly behind his thick lenses. "I fixed those two states' elections. I knew Forsythe could never win there. The only chance was to split the vote and keep Wardlow from a majority. It worked perfectly."

"Good God, Arch, if that ever got out we'd be crucified," she said, pacing beside him.

"It won't get out. Young owes us too much. He'll owe us even more after the election."

Stopping, he faced her and brought his magnified eyes down close to her face. "We have to do whatever's necessary to retain the Presidency. If that means breaking our little Maryland congressman and his precious family, that's what we'll do."

Laura turned and walked into the adjacent waiting room. She sat on a flowered couch and stared out the window at the forest beyond.

Outside, fall was taking its toll. With every small breeze, the few remaining leaves took flight, spinning into the air for a flash of color before slowly drifting to the ground to turn brown and rot. That's the way it was with politics, too, she knew. Win or you're yesterday's refuse. Trey didn't understand this. He didn't realize the damage he could do to himself and those closest to him by failing to play along. He needed help, even if he didn't know it. Sometimes, that help had to come in the most unexpected ways. This was more true in Washington than anywhere. People like Trey—good people, innocent people who could be permanently damaged by the war-like atmosphere between the parties—had to be protected against their own instincts. Laura could never stand by and watch him be hurt—even if he never understood how . . . or why.

She felt a chill in the room and curled up the collar of her sweater against her face. Glancing at Longstreet, she patted the seat cushion beside her and scooted over, giving him room to sit.

"Arch," she said in a whisper. "We need to talk."

He came and sat next to her, leaning in.

"I think I can give us more leverage with Trey," she said. "It has to do with him and my husband."

Longstreet nodded knowingly.

Chapter Twenty

For the second time today, Trey crooked his left elbow, and Jazz threaded her arm through. He took Katie by the hand and led them across the grounds of Camp David to Aspen Lodge.

On the way, he felt vaguely like a prisoner of war leading his troops to an interrogation. He was more unsure than ever of what to expect and had come to realize this was all part of the President's method: Keep the competition off balance. Expect the unexpected. Be pleasant and congenial at first, then challenging and confrontational. An unsure enemy is a weakened enemy.

Trey certainly felt like an enemy tonight.

When they climbed the steps to the plank-board porch, the President pulled open the front door and motioned them inside, smiling broadly. Apparently, he had decided on warmness and collegiality as the evening's M.O.

"Season's greetings," he announced, pumping Trey's hand enthusiastically. He kissed Jazz on both cheeks and patted Katie's head. The perfect, affable host.

The Stones were last to arrive for dinner.

No doubt, that was planned, too.

They quickly discovered the crowd had grown. More than a half-dozen people had been added to the camp's retinue. One face was missing, though: Marshall Young was nowhere around.

The President handled introductions, starting with his oldest daughter, Bonnie, and her husband, Beau. *Their* daughter, Barbie (the three "Bs"), was the same age as Katie. The two girls shook hands formally, then hurried off with the First Lady for a playroom in the back.

The lodge was decorated with autumn wreaths, ribbons and Christmas ornaments. Seasonal music played in the background. Everyone seemed in a joyous mood, sipping festive drinks.

Trey and Jazz each took a cup of eggnog and toasted the crowd. They were then introduced to two newcomers—Grace Stanton and her "companion," Rick. Grace was a well-known recording star in gospel and country-and-western; she had been added to the guest list, apparently, as part of the evening's entertainment.

Final introductions were to Maine's two congressmen, who arrived only an hour earlier. They were staying for dinner and flying back tonight.

Trey had worked with the state's senior representative occasionally. But he didn't know either of them well. With so many people in Congress, most representatives were less familiar with their colleagues than the public generally thought.

Trey exchanged handshakes with Neil Van Deventer, the elder congressman, then Charlie Harris, the junior representative who was just starting his second term—the equivalent of a rookie in the House pecking order.

The two Maine men looked oddly out-of-place. Both were dressed in business suits rumpled from the trip. Everyone else was dressed in casual attire—slacks, sweaters, loafers. Van Deventer looked pale, too, his complexion a ghostly white. Maybe that was to be expected from a man who hailed from the far north. But he obviously felt well enough to carry on an animated conversation. He had a good sense of humor, too, chiding himself for showing up in the woods dressed for the streets. He tossed back a straight whiskey and unabashedly called for another.

Trey and Jazz made their way through the crowd, chatting amiably, discussing everyone's plans for the holidays. The gathering was a boisterous one, led by the President, his deep, guttural laugh reverberating around the room. After thirty minutes or so, Forsythe pulled himself loose from a conversation and announced that dinner was on.

The meal was served in a large dining room off the kitchen, where four rectangular tables were fitted together in a perfect square. Name cards showed everyone to their spots. The President sat in the middle on one side, his wife at his left. Other diners spread out from there. Katie and Barbie were allowed to dine away from the adults, on card tables in the game room.

The conversation consisted of light-hearted one-on-ones. The size of the crowd made group discussion impossible over the laughter and piped-in music.

But Congressman Van Deventer, seated on Trey's left, managed to whisper a point or two about the upcoming vote.

"Forsythe make a big play for your support?" he asked.

" 'Big's' not exactly the word I'd choose," Trey said. "But I can't blame him for trying his hardest. I'd do the same in his position." He took a sip of spiked cider.

"I hear Marshall Young was used as part of their ammunition," Van Deventer said.

"Yes, part of it," Trey said. "Perhaps the biggest part, unfortunately."

Van Deventer squinched his face, showing his own distaste for Young's role. "I hate to admit it, but he did carry our states," he said. "We can't ignore that—try as we might."

"Young squeaked out plurality support," Trey said, "running on a platform that called for stripping federal waters of environmental protection in the name of increased profits. As far as I'm concerned, that doesn't give him a say in who holds the Oval Office."

Van Deventer rolled a whiskey tumbler in his hand. "I hope you don't mind a little advice from an old political geezer," he said. "Politics is about compromise. Neither of us are big Forsythe supporters, but we owe it to our states to get the best deals we can. We're in the driver's seat. We can take the President where we want him to go. He's just along for the ride."

Trey toyed with his food, not looking up. He knew there was a large element of truth in what Van Deventer said, but he also knew compromise didn't have to mean giving up your principles.

"What's best for each of our states," he said, "is what's best for the country."

Van Deventer shrugged. "This vote's about getting what you can while you can. We're in the perfect position to deal. I plan to take advantage of it."

Trey glanced around the table, hoping to find a way to change the subject; he had had enough debate on Presidential politics for one day.

"Would you mind passing those string beans?"

The meal continued for nearly two hours. Finally, everyone retired to the Great Room for after-dinner drinks, coffee, and tea. As the drinks were served, Grace Stanton seated herself at the grand piano and played a soft melody. Before long, with the President's urging, she was in full song. With her companion accompanying on guitar, they ran through a medley of holiday tunes and carols. Everyone had a great time. It wasn't every night this crowd got to sing along with a major recording star in the hospitality of a Presidential retreat.

After nearly forty minutes, she closed with a moving rendition of "White Christmas." There was hardly a dry eye in the house. When the last note was struck—as the guests rewarded her with enthusiastic applause—Forsythe stepped to the front by the fireplace. With fresh wood crackling beside him, he picked up an old meerschaum pipe from the mantle and tapped it against his brandy glass.

The lights dimmed ever so slightly.

"Ladies and gentlemen," he said, "I want to thank you for joining me and my family tonight in Shangri-La." He cast his eyes downward, pausing melodramatically. Then he waved to his wife to join him. He wrapped a huge arm around her shoulders and kissed the top of her head.

"Friends," he began again, "you're with us tonight on a very special evening—one that has nothing to do with politics." He held up his hand. "I know it's hard to believe, but other things are sometimes more important. You see, Madge and I have grown awfully fond of Camp David during our time in office. We've had wonderful times here. We've had a few difficult moments, too. This is where we found out about the loss of our grandchild." He didn't need to retell the story. Bonnie and Beau had lost their second child after a difficult birth. The news devastated Forsythe, who had never had a son of his own.

"That was two years ago tonight," he said. "So you can imagine this is a very special evening of remembrance for me and my family. I thank you for sharing it with us and for tolerating my melancholy memories."

Looking down at his wife, he used a thumb to gently wipe a tear from her cheek.

"This is also a special night because it may be our last at

Camp David. Which depends, of course, on the House vote in January."

A few boos rose up from supporters in the room. Several of the guests glanced at Trey, who fully understood the purpose of this little show. It was a barely disguised emotional plea to the young, Democratic congressman to return this caring, concerned family man of a President to his rightful place.

"No, no," Forsythe protested, "I only make mention of this as a reference for what's about to come. I ask you to indulge me in a little capper to our celebration. I've planned an outdoor event for our finale. I know the weather's cold, but we've got plenty of blankets. We've also got hot cider and other spirits to keep us toasty. I want everyone to join us for a sleigh ride around the compound."

Everyone oohed and ahhed.

"I know there's no snow on the ground, but that's never stopped us before. If you care to join me and the First Lady, I've taken the liberty of preparing horse-drawn sleighs."

The crowd clapped loudly and gathered their jackets. Katie and Barbie, fast friends already, galloped out the front door. Trey and Jazz came right behind. A short walk down from Aspen Lodge, several sleighs stood in a row, horses harnessed and ready. Each was attended by a Marine guard. The President's family took the first sleigh, others piled in randomly behind. The Stones got in a small one by themselves, the three of them snuggled under a heavy wool blanket.

The horses cantered slowly around the dirt roads of the complex, occasionally drifting onto dew-slicked lawns. Then the drivers followed one another down an embankment behind Aspen Lodge. In the summertime, the field served as a three-hole golf course. In the winter, the slope was used as a sledding area. Tonight, the damp grass glistened in the light of a new moon as the sleighs stopped near the bottom of the hill next to a wooden rail.

The President climbed out and led everyone to the edge. Without a word, he stared out over the valley below, where the trees appeared to merge into a pool of blackness. Miniature lights twinkled up through the low-lying fog, marking the homes and businesses below.

Recorded music began to play in the distance. Low at first, gaining in volume, the sound rose up out of the woods as "God Bless America" filled the air. Then a single flare shot up, piercing the sky. Another followed that, and another. Before long, fireworks were bursting everywhere. The effect was exhilarating. It drew gasps from the crowd. Several people even hummed the song under their breath.

Trey watched it all wide-eyed, holding Katie's tiny hand in his. When an eruption of fireworks drew her and Jazz running off for a better view, he started to follow, but someone stepped in-between.

"Quite a sight, isn't it?" Longstreet said.

"Incredible," Trey replied. "I only hope those sparks don't start a fire."

"They're specially prepared explosives. By the time they hit the ground, they're cool as can be."

Trey nodded and looked past Longstreet, hoping to join his daughter and wife.

"I'm afraid the same cannot be said of your best friend," Longstreet said.

"I beg your pardon?"

"Jack Weddington. He's not 'cool as can be' right now."

Trey was taken aback by the comment and felt compelled to respond.

"Jack'll be all right—if it's any concern of yours."

"Normally, it wouldn't be," Longstreet said, leaning against the rail. "But these aren't normal times, are they?"

"I'm not in the habit of discussing a friend's legal issues with strangers."

"I hope I'm not a stranger, Trey," he said. "Besides, this goes far beyond Jack Weddington, doesn't it?"

"I don't know what the hell you're talking about."

"I think you do."

"It's time we ended this conversation."

Trey started to move away.

"The House Banking Committee."

He stopped.

"It wasn't a coincidence earlier this year," Longstreet said, "when the committee delayed its investigation of Weddington's savings and loan, was it?"

Trey walked back to him and stood close, so close the cold vapor from his breath washed over the man's face.

"The banking committee delayed its investigation for procedural reasons," he said. "We had no idea about Weddington's legal troubles."

Longstreet smiled and looked out at the fireworks as another burst of light lit up the horizon. "That's not the way I hear it. I understand you recommended the delay after meeting with Weddington privately this summer. You knew he was in trouble at the bank and agreed to help."

Trey couldn't say anything. He was dumbstruck. How in the hell did Longstreet find out about their meeting? He cursed himself under his breath. He *knew* he should have refused Jack's request, sensing there was more to it at the time. But he *didn't* refuse him. He never refused the goddamn Weddingtons.

"If that information were to leak out," Longstreet said,

"it could prove career-ending—maybe even worse." Shaking his head slowly, he added: "It wouldn't look good to the authorities. Not good at all."

"You don't know what the hell you're talking about." Trey tried to sound confident, but he heard the tremor in his own voice. "You're not trying to threaten a sitting congressman, are you, Mr. Longstreet?"

Longstreet turned full to him, his smile suddenly gone. "I can't threaten you, but you can threaten yourself by being dumb about this. No one has to know about your little meeting with Weddington. It can stay between you and me. All you have to do is the right thing in January."

He turned and started to walk away, speaking as he moved off. "But it's all up to you."

Trey leaned against the wooden rail, supporting himself with both hands. *God, you've done it now, Stone,* he thought to himself, *you got yourself in a helluva fix.*

Trey knew Longstreet's charges could be made to look bad. Very bad. Bordering on criminal. He couldn't deny the basic facts, either. The meeting *did* take place. He *did* recommend a delay in the investigation. He didn't know illegal activity was involved, but that didn't matter now. In politics, appearances are everything—and the appearance here was a major conflict of interest, even collusion.

Katie suddenly ran up beside him and grabbed his pant-leg. "Daddy, isn't it fun?!" she cried. "Come on, Mom wants you."

"Okay, honey," he said. "Tell her I'm coming."

Katie ran back to her mother's side. The two of them stood next to each other looking out at the dark sky veiled in hues of red, white and blue. Another song began to play—"The Star Spangled Banner." Streaks of light and colored haze wafted across the horizon, and the crowd began to sing out in full voice, hands over their hearts.

Jazz turned to Trey and held out her hand.

He walked over to her, joining them in the final few bars, or at least he tried to. His voice wouldn't cooperate. He simply mouthed the words. Land of the free. Home of the brave. He couldn't focus, couldn't even applaud as everyone around him clapped wildly.

Along with the others, he shook the President's hand, and thanked him for the evening. But the words were perfunctory, hollow-sounding. He couldn't put together a good, clear sentence.

He listened blankly as the President spoke.

"Everyone's welcome to stay as long as they like," Forsythe said. "But I must retire now. I thank you for sharing this special evening with me and my family, and I look forward to seeing you here sometime in the future. God bless America."

The President and his family climbed into their sleigh and drove off into the darkness, two other sleighs of Secret Service following closely behind.

Trey stood at the rail, mute, watching wisps of smoke disappear into thin air. He could smell the phosphorous—it was the stench of rotten eggs. The music had stopped. The lights had died. He was left staring into the blackness.

"Was that an incredible show or what?" Jazz said.

"Incredible."

"What's wrong?"

"Nothing."

"You look like you've seen a ghost."

He wiped a hand over his brow. Despite the cold, he felt a trace of wetness.

"No ghosts," he said. "This was the real thing."

Chapter Twenty-One

The next morning, the Stones ate a late continental breakfast in Aspen Lodge with the President and a few of his guests. Everyone else had left. The President wasn't far behind. But at his insistence, the Stones decided to stay a little longer to let Katie enjoy the outdoors—and the horses.

When they finally departed, they completed the ride back to Annapolis in near silence, the President's helicopter delivering them back to the Naval Academy dock where they had departed less than thirty hours before.

During the drive home, Katie chattered on, but Trey barely responded, lost in his own thoughts, which had little to do with the splendors of Camp David or the emotional celebration the night before.

When he pulled up in front of the house, he took all the suitcases upstairs, then got out of Jazz's way while she unpacked.

A few minutes later, he heard her walk up behind him as he stared out the kitchen window toward the bay, watching its gray waters stir in an offshore wind.

She wrapped her arms around his waist and rested her chin on his shoulder, whispering into his ear: "You ready to talk yet?"

"Not really. But I don't have much choice."

"You've got *no* choice, bud. I have to know what happened last night. I've never seen you look like that. It scared me."

He nodded, his late-morning beard scratching against her cheek. "It scared me, too."

She stepped in front of him. "So what happened?"

"Let's go for a walk."

They got jackets from the hall closet and stepped out the back toward their private beach. When they got down by the tide line, Trey picked up a few shells and skimmed them into the water. Then he started in:

"Last night during the fireworks show, I had a conversation with the President's campaign adviser, Longstreet."

"He's one of the creepiest guys I've ever met. What'd you talk about?"

"It's a long, difficult story."

"I'm not going anywhere."

He took her hand and walked up shore, toward the dock that led into the semi-protected waters. The family yacht was moored at the end, rocking in the swells. As they made their way toward the boat, Trey told her the story of Jack's visit to his office and of his request for "temporary assistance." He also told her of his own stupidity for agreeing to help without first checking Jack's version.

"Christ, Trey, I've told you time and again," she said, "you're too damn loyal to that man. He's trouble. Always has been."

"More than I realized."

They stepped onto the boat and went below. Sitting across from each other at the galley table, they held hands over the top.

"Let me guess," Jazz said. "Your talk with Longstreet was about the meeting with Jack?"

"That's right."

"He knows about your offer to help?"

"Yes."

"And now he's trying to claim you were protecting a friend illegally."

"Yup."

"But you didn't know he was stealing. No one knew."

"I never should've agreed to a delay in the investigation until I'd looked into it further. It was stupid. But I believed Jack when he said it was a paperwork thing—that he'd take care of it. He made it sound like nothing—a little bureaucratic foul-up."

She let go of his hands and stood in the small walkway between the galley and sleeping quarters.

"So Longstreet's threatening to divulge everything," she said, "if you don't support Forsythe."

"That's right."

"How could you do it, Trey? You're smarter than that! If it had been anyone but Jack, you never would have left yourself open like that."

She fell back into the seat across from him and stared out a porthole window toward the coastline of the Chesapeake, lost in her own thoughts and agony. He looked out the same window with her, thinking it would be nice to weigh anchor right now and point the boat due north, just follow the wind as far as it would take them, away from all this sordid business.

That's exactly what Jack would do.

"For the life of me, I can't figure out how Longstreet knew about the meeting," he said. "Jack assured me no one knew. When he turned himself in, he promised to keep me out of it."

"You're sure Longstreet knows—that he's not just guessing?"

"He's aware of when and where the meeting took place. He knows about my recommendation to the committee. He knows everything."

"You're sure Jack told no one."

"He wouldn't do that."

"What about Laura? She works for Longstreet."

"First of all, she knows nothing about it. Second of all, she would never do that, not to me. You know that."

She raised her eyebrows disapprovingly. "Yes, I know that—all too well." She sighed. "Then it *had* to be Jack. It's the only way."

Trey slammed his hand on the tabletop. "It was not Jack!"

They both looked away, wondering what to say next, what to do next. They had been faced with tragedy before—when Trey's Dad became ill, and when Jazz's younger sister died of cancer. But this was different. Trey was not an innocent victim of circumstances; he had brought this on himself. He was in a position to stop the damage, too. All he had to do was support the President's re-election. He also knew if he didn't, the consequences could be worse than federal charges. The *Post* reporter had said Longstreet wasn't afraid to resort to violence.

Reaching over, he ran a hand down Jazz's hair, smoothing the windblown mass. "Promise me one thing: You'll keep the security officers close to you and Katie at all times. I don't know how far these guys will go. We've got to trust each other."

She looked up, tenseness etched in her eyes, and nodded silently. He helped her up and they went topside, trying to calm himself by fussing around with deck items—checking sails, making sure everything was battened down.

Finally, they walked back toward the beach, not talking, just listening to each other's thoughts. Two gulls glided lazily overhead, scanning the water below. One of the birds suddenly pointed its black beak straight down and fell out of the sky, plunging under the water. A split second later, it broke the surface, a prized fish grasped in its mouth. If only politics were so easy, so natural.

Jazz broke his reverie.

"What're you going to do?"

"Longstreet's got me trapped—or I've trapped myself. Either way, there's no easy way out."

"You still hold the key vote. He can't take that away. They've got as much at risk as you do."

"But I won't stoop to his level, Jazz. Whatever happens, I've got to vote for the best man. I won't bargain with Longstreet over that."

"Do you think the President condones his tactics?"

"He's been given a free hand to get my vote. From what I saw at Camp David, Forsythe's determined to win. He doesn't care what it takes."

They turned toward the house and climbed the rugged rock stairway, Jazz leading the way. Halfway to the top, she stopped and turned around.

"Don't forget," she said, "the White House can't bear to lose, and that makes them vulnerable—maybe more vulnerable than you are right now."

Looking up at his wife, the afternoon sun blazing over her shoulder, Trey watched the light gather around her hair like an aura, and he wondered where he would be without her and Katie.

He stepped up next to her and kissed her deeply. Then, brushing away a lock of hair, he stared into her emerald-green eyes. They appeared darker, deeper in the reflected light of the bay.

"I could make this very easy on us," he said, "and do what Longstreet wants. I know you wouldn't want that, though, and that means everything to me."

193

They turned and climbed the stairs arm in arm, silently supporting one another. Trey took comfort in the strength she gave him. It was what attracted him to her the most. Most people only saw the public woman, the soft-spoken political wife. But she could be so tough underneath. It was a trait he drew on constantly, knowing he too often depended on the approval of others, when all he needed was the approval of the one person closest to him.

He also knew that no matter what happened, he would always have Jazz and Katie. No one could take away his family. Not the President. Not his advisers. Not the court of public opinion. In the end, this was his ultimate strength. Certainly, it was something Longstreet hadn't counted on.

In a lavishly equipped radio room aboard an offshore trawler, Ridge Franks pulled off his headset and looked up at Steele, smiling.

"The vise is tightening on our little congressman."

Steele nodded. "He's on his heels, but he's resisting. Until he commits, we have to keep the pressure on."

"You mean the fun's not over?"

"This won't be over 'til January, my friend. The way Longstreet works, we never leave anything to chance."

"I'm starting to enjoy this little family. It's nice to see the rich can be weak, too."

"Don't have too much fun. We missed that whole bit about the banking investigation. The boss ain't happy about that."

Franks put his headphones back on. "That won't happen again. I've got Weddington's house and boat tapped. No more 'secret' conversations."

"Let's keep it that way. Meanwhile, I'll give Longstreet a

call and let him know we've still got work to do with our Mr. Stone."

Franks didn't respond. He just gripped the earphones tighter and went back to his listening duties.

Chapter Twenty-Two

The next morning, Trey arrived at the downtown City Dock of Annapolis at six-fifteen. The sun was just clearing the horizon, and a gentle, ten-knot breeze had already escorted the morning fog out to sea. The temperature was rising fast, too, expected to hit sixty by mid-day. A perfect sailing day.

He spied Jack at the bow of his boat, weighing anchor. Stepping onboard, Trey dispensed with the usual "request permission" stuff. He reached down, cast off the moor line and grabbed the helm.

"Fire up the engines, sailor," he said. "We've got serious sailing to do."

Jack nodded and went below to set the diesel engine for a slow cruise through the narrow inlet of Spa Creek. In less than ten minutes, they would be in the middle of the Severn River; in less than fifteen, in the bay itself.

As they entered open waters, Trey set sail for a southeasterly course, planning to dip down toward Cambridge, make a wide arc and skirt up the western shore. The trip would take an hour, most of it on the northward route.

They sailed silently for twenty minutes, Trey at the wheel with his chin up, eyes moist from the wind. He felt the keel cut through the water like a knife, and had to admit captaining Jack's boat was the epitome of sailing. The craft was as responsive as a cat. A small jibe here, a subtle turn there, and the boat responded as if anticipating his next move.

He steered the craft through a cove, then began the long, slow turn that would take them north again. Jack offered him a bloody Mary, but he asked for coffee instead. Standing behind the giant wooden wheel, they stared out the starboard side, toward the Atlantic, sipping their drinks and wondering why it couldn't always be like this.

Trey finally broke the silence between them.

"We've got trouble," he said. He went into the story of Camp David and how he was being pressured to support the President in exchange for saving his own reputation. He told Jack how their "private" conversation was on the verge of going public in a very big way.

"How'd this happen?" he asked. "You said you had a 'paperwork' problem, not a goddamned federal crime. You said no one knew about your visit to my office. You dragged me into a cover-up! I don't understand how or why."

Jack swigged the last of his drink and sat in a deck chair at the stern of the boat.

"This is exactly what I was trying to protect you from," he said. "No one knew about our meeting. Longstreet's got to be guessing. There's no way he knows."

"He told me exactly when and where we met. He knew the substance of our conversation."

Jack sat stunned, looking down. "Maybe they had your office bugged."

Trey made a minor adjustment in their course, then locked the wheel. "Security officers sweep the offices regularly, checking for taps. Besides, why would they have bugged it before the election? No one knew how the vote would turn out."

Standing, Jack moved across the deck, holding onto guy lines as the boat tacked more steeply. "You've got to believe me, buddy. The information didn't come from me."

"I'm not blaming you, Jack. I'm just trying to get to the bottom of it."

Jack sat back down, looking crestfallen. His worst fears had come true. He had tried to sacrifice himself to protect his best friend, and it had done no good.

He looked up, squinting into the sunlight and said, "Let's deny it. Hell, there's no evidence. I'll back you up. We'll just say the conversation never occurred."

Trey unlocked the wheel and eased the boat into the wind. "I won't lie. The conversation *did* occur. It was a conflict of interest. There's no denying that."

"But there *is* denying it, Trey. Who's to know? We'll say it never happened. Nobody's got to incriminate themselves."

"You're forgetting one thing: Somebody *does* know— Longstreet and whoever told him. They must have evidence—how else could he figure it out? What happens if a tape turns up? I'd have a perjury charge on top of a cover-up. No thanks."

Jack sat with his head in his hands, not speaking for several minutes. Trey didn't speak either. Slowly, he walked to the bow and struck the spinnaker. When he returned midship, Jack had gotten out a bottle of whiskey and was chugging from it straight, leaning back in his chair, face into the sun.

"The night we met in Washington," he said, "I took your advice for once. I got a cup of black coffee and went home to see my wife and kids. We had a nice night. Ate a late supper, talked around the table. Just like a real family." He grinned for a fleeting moment. "Later that night, in bed, I told Laura how you'd come to my rescue again. I didn't give her details of our conversation. I swear it, Trey. I just talked in generalities." He took a long pull from the bottle and wiped his mouth on the sleeve of his jacket. "But she's a pretty smart girl. She may have figured it out after the charges broke. That's the only thing I can think of. She works for Longstreet now—that's where her loyalties are. Not with me and not with you. Hard as that is to believe." He gulped more whiskey and looked out to the horizon.

Trey watched him and let the enormity of what he'd said sink in. Maybe he was right. Laura was the only one in a position to know. She could have told Longstreet at Camp David after it became obvious Trey was less than committed to supporting their candidate. After all, she had put everything on Forsythe's re-election—she freely admitted that.

He steered the *Herndon* cross wind, cutting her at a forty-five-degree angle. The mainsail caught full and the craft began to scream now, twenty-five knots through rising swells, the bow slashing violently into the tide. Freezing water exploded into the air in a soaking foam. He felt the moisture pour down onto him; the taste of it was bitter on his tongue, and the coldness stung his eyes.

He laid the boat to its side and picked up even more speed, holding himself against the helm, riding the pitch and yaw like a part of the boat itself. Then, glancing back, he saw Jack's feet braced on the bulkhead, holding himself upright in the flimsy deck chair, oblivious to the movement of the yacht, its crashing against the flow. Jack stared absently out to sea, one hand in his jacket pocket, his collar turned up against the howl.

Trey ran the boat as fast as he could for nearly twenty minutes, until they reached calmer winds near shore, where he brought the speed down for a slow sail up the coast, back from where they'd come.

Relaxing his grip on the wheel, he tried to calm the rage

he felt inside. Why would Laura turn on him like that? They had been so close. He thought they had something special between them. He didn't want to believe she could be so cold, so calculating, but there was no other logical explanation. Of course, logic had failed him in the past. No matter what the explanation, one fact was unassailable: Trey had to be more careful than ever about who he opened up to—and when. He could trust no one but his family from here on out. Too much was at stake. For the moment, even long-time friends were now the enemy.

Trey spent the rest of the time back to port asking Jack about his legal defense. How bad were the charges? Did his lawyers give him much of a chance in court? Did the attorneys think he would do time?

The answers were what he expected: Jack's only defense was mercy. Yes, he'd probably do time. How much remained to be seen. He had a clean record, good references and the governor's political connections on his side. After making restitution, he'd probably do a year in minimum security.

As they neared port, Trey struck the rest of the sails and fired up the engine for the cruise into City Dock. Jack still had not moved. He was locked in place at the back of the boat, feet up, a nearly empty bottle in hand.

Trey cut the engine and tied the moor line, then walked to the shore side of the boat, standing with his hands on his hips, staring at his long-time friend, who looked like a lifeless body in a deck chair.

When he turned to walk away, Jack spoke out.

"What're you going to do?"

Trey answered without looking back. "I'm going to admit my part. That's all I can do. After that, I'll resign from office."

Jack nodded. "You're sure there's no other way?"

He sighed. "But I won't resign until after the vote in January. I don't want to give the President's henchmen the satisfaction of winning this election by default."

Jack swallowed the last of his whiskey and tossed the bottle overboard. "I wish there was another way, pal."

"So do I, Jack."

"You're an honorable man, Lieutenant," he said. "Too damn honorable, if you ask me."

"If that were true," he said, jumping onto the dock, "I wouldn't be in the position I'm in now. But I'll get myself out the only way I know how."

Jack rocked gently back on the legs of the chair, chin to his chest. "All I can say is, I'm sorry. I've said that a lot, I know. But I won't have to say it again. I promise."

Trey turned and walked away. "Right, Jack. Never again."

Trey drove the small, familiar streets of Annapolis for nearly an hour before heading home. Whenever he was under pressure, he liked to reacquaint himself with the town he felt a part of, born to.

When he finally drove to the house, he parked in the garage and entered through the covered walkway leading to a large mudroom. He cleaned up there and went to look for Jazz and Katie, eventually finding them in the living room.

Both of them were still in their pajamas, trimming the Christmas tree. Normally, their holiday preparations would have been done a week ago, but Camp David had put them behind schedule.

Katie ran and jumped into his arms. Hugging her tight, he wished her a good morning. She smiled and went back to her tinseling job—placing long, silver strands on the tree one by one, carefully draping them like icicles off the branches.

Jazz unpacked bulbs and ornaments. "You look cold. Been out on the water?"

"I went to see Jack. The bay's the only place you can find him these days."

"You want hot cider? It'll warm you up."

"Sounds great."

"I'll get it!" Katie said. Jumping up, she ran to the kitchen.

"Want to give us a hand here?" Jazz asked, holding up a tangle of tree lights.

"Hand 'em over." He took the ball-sized bunch from her and sat in a barrel chair to begin the task of untying the lights. Every year he promised himself he would carefully pack the decorations after taking down the tree. Every year, he got in a hurry and forgot.

Katie returned with his cup of cider, walking slowly across the room, trying her best not to spill a drop. He took the cup and set it aside, forgetting to thank her. He was too engrossed in his untying task, staring into the knots.

"How's Jack doing?" Jazz asked.

"Same as always. Drinking and sailing—in that order."

"Kind of early for alcohol, isn't it?"

"It's never too early for Jack."

She hung a few bulbs on the upper branches of the tree, reaching as high as she could. "Did he help *clarify* anything?"

"Does he ever?" He pulled angrily at a knot that wouldn't break free. He suddenly realized he should tell Jazz about Laura's possible betrayal; she would find out sooner or later, anyway. But then Jazz would start in again about how he always let friendships and personal loyalties get in the way.

She hung a few more bulbs and stepped back to inspect her work. "I can't believe how far behind schedule we are. Tomorrow's Christmas Eve, and we still haven't got your parents' gifts. We're supposed to see them tomorrow night."

Trey yanked on the snarled wires, realizing he hadn't figured out how to tell his parents about the pending accusations. He couldn't let them find out from anyone else.

Jazz came over and sat in the chair beside him, resting one hand on his knee. "Have you figured out what you're going to do?"

"The way I see it, I'm going to have to suffer the consequences, Jazz. There's no other way."

"By 'consequences,' you mean resignation from office?"

"Yes, and the legal actions that will come afterward."

He sipped from the hot cider, his hand shaking ever so slightly as he brought the cup to his lips. The prospect of leaving office under these circumstances nearly took his breath away—not so much for the personal embarrassment, but the agony it would bring to those around him.

"There's another option, too," Jazz said. "It's one Longstreet hasn't thought of, I'll bet."

"What's that?"

"Hold a press conference. Announce your mistake. Apologize and ask for understanding. The voters are forgiving, Trey. They'd probably understand."

He stood and paced in front of the chair. Then he noticed Katie was listening intently. She could tell something was wrong, but didn't know exactly what. He managed to gulp the steaming cider down and asked her to refill his cup. When she left, he turned back to Jazz.

"It's not a bad idea, but I doubt it'll do any good, not with the White House working against me. Longstreet's got a multi-million-dollar publicity machine at his disposal. He'll use everything he's got to make my recommendation to the Banking Committee look like a criminal breach of trust. No matter how much I deny it, the regulators and media will savage me. Forsythe and his gang won't let up. They're vicious. No part of our lives'll be untouched. They'll probe every decision I've made over the last four years. They'll question every vote, every relationship, every family investment. We'll be in court for years. They'll try to break us emotionally, physically—maybe even financially." He shook his head, the Christmas lights dangling from one hand.

"What if you vote the way Longstreet wants," she said, "and the President loses anyway? He couldn't blame you, could he?"

"Longstreet knows Maryland holds the tiebreaker. If our state supports Forsythe, he wins. Simple as that."

"You've always said nothing in politics is how it appears."

He sat cross-legged beside the tree and pulled at the wires, un-knotting a long section. "I was wrong. Some things are as they appear—and this is one of them."

The rest of the lights unexpectedly came undone. He stood up and draped the wires over the tree branches, Jazz lending a hand. When they finished hanging the last of them, creating a perfect spiral from top to bottom, he plugged them in, and they stood back to view their work. The reds, greens and yellows of the holiday sparkled like colored stars.

It reminded him of the night sky over Camp David.

He wrapped an arm around her and drew her close. "How about no more political talk tonight? I'm up to here with Washington."

She kissed him on the cheek. "Me too."

Katie returned from the kitchen carrying a fresh cup of steaming cider. He took it from her and set it aside, then swept her up in his arms.

"What do you think of the lights, Katie?"

"They're beautiful."

"Just like you."

She grinned broadly, displaying a missing tooth in an otherwise perfect smile held in place by dimples on either side.

"Do we get to finish the tree now?" she asked.

"Me and you are on tinsel patrol. Mom's on bulbs."

"I can do more than you."

"You've got to put them on nice and straight. Mom's going to inspect."

He winked at Jazz, and the three of them went to work. A few moments later, Trey started a fire, and Jazz put on an album of Christmas music. Irma brought in snacks. With Red Dog napping nearby, all thoughts of politics and other distractions disappeared.

Trey knew it was an all-too-temporary pause.

Longstreet prowled his top-floor suite like a caged animal, his cell phone pressed so hard to the side of his head his knuckles were going white. He did his best to control the rising tension in his voice.

"I can't believe this goody two-shoes will risk everything he's got over one lousy vote," he snarled. "We've got him nailed—he just doesn't know it yet. We'll have to step up the pressure and show him there's more at stake here than just a congressional career."

"Hate to tell ya, boss, but that's what we've been telling you all along," Steele said. "This guy's a tough nut to crack. It's going to take 'extra' measures."

"Nothing too violent yet. Just enough to throw a good scare into him."

"We've already thrown a scare at him. He just increases security. He doesn't frighten easily."

"We can't afford to raise too much more suspicion. He's talking about bringing in the FBI. That's the last thing we need right now. Still, we've got to let him know what's at stake."

"Let me handle it, chief. I can do *subtle*."

"I don't want anybody dead—not yet. We haven't reached that point."

Steele sighed loudly. "The only thing he understands is physical intimidation. Anything else, and he'll blow us off."

"The key word is 'intimidation.' Remember that."

"I'll remember. And so will our congressman."

They hung up, and Longstreet stood in the dark calculating his options. He knew Steele was right. Extraordinary measures were required. But Longstreet knew he couldn't trust two thugs with this delicate job. It required someone they would never suspect. An insider.

Fortunately, this was exactly what Longstreet had prepared for all along. He had already made sure the right pieces were in place.

He dialed the Maryland number emblazoned in his memory. He wasn't surprised when the voice on the other end came back tentatively, uncertainly, as if wondering who might be calling at this hour.

"I want you here tomorrow night," Longstreet said.

"What happened?"

"Our congressman is still reluctant. We've got to make additional preparations."

"Preparations?"

"Don't play dumb with me. We've been through this. Should we need it, it'll be quick and easy."

"You can't put me in this position. He's a friend, for Christ's sake. Just give him a little more time."

"We've given him plenty of time. We're getting too close to the end. There may be no other choice."

A long pause, then the voice came back again, pleadingly: "I can't do it. *Please,* anyone but me."

"You're the only one close enough to get the job done, if we need it. I'll have no more discussion. We all know the consequences. Be here tomorrow at midnight." He paused. "We'll go over the procedures one last time."

Before hearing any more protests or whining, Longstreet pressed the "end" button on his phone, severing the connection. Then he looked out his office window at the White House below, and quietly repeated the family motto to himself: "Never go into battle with one boot off." In war and politics, it was all about life and death. The sooner everyone understood this, the better.

Chapter Twenty-Three

To keep reporters and onlookers away from the front of their estate, Trey asked the local police to work with his private security force in clearing the road. They obliged gladly, realizing the crowds made driving hazardous on the two-lane route. Trey also rented a nondescript sedan—and traded cars every few days—so the family's movements were difficult to follow.

The afternoon of Christmas Eve, he wheeled the boxy, four-door rental car through an open gate into the park-like grounds of the Bethesda Naval Hospital annex.

Signaling the security car behind him to wait by the gate, he pulled up in front of a collection of quaint, single-story cottages that made up a miniature retirement village a few minutes' walk from the main hospital.

Everyone piled out of the car, grabbing a load of Christmas presents. Katie was first inside, running through the door held open by her grandmother. She placed her packages under the small tree in the corner of the room, kissed Grandma hello, and hugged Grandpa.

Trey and Jazz straggled in behind, arms full of presents and plates of food. They stacked everything wherever they could find room, then settled in for an afternoon of Christmas celebration.

Trey had brought along a CD of seasonal music. He put the volume on low and poured everyone drinks, then took up a chair near his father's bed, watching him drift in and out of sleep as everyone talked.

Later on, Trey assumed the role of Santa Claus, handing out gifts and Christmas stockings. When Grandma opened Katie's gift, her eyes lit up like the holiday lights on the small tree across the room. It was a collection of Katie's best artwork, carefully catalogued in a photo album. The drawings were of family members gathered around each other in various settings. The last one showed Katie and her grandmother sitting where they were now, beside Grandpa on his hospital bed. A note attached read: *Whenever Grandpa sleeps, we are in his dreams.*

Grandma held Katie close, then had to excuse herself.

When she came back in a few minutes, everyone sang along to Christmas songs. Trey did his best to enjoy the festivities. But he was subdued. His mother stood behind him, hands on his shoulders.

"How're you doing, honey?" she asked.

He wondered if this might be the time to tell her about the charges against him—how he was about to face a White House-inspired publicity campaign that could destroy his reputation and the Stone family name; how he had done the one thing he swore he'd never do—brought dishonor on himself and those closest to him.

This wasn't the time, of course. The last thing he wanted was to ruin Christmas on top of everything else.

"The vote," he said, "it's turning downright ugly."

"That's what I hate about politics," she said. "There just aren't enough good people involved—like you, hon."

He smiled grimly, thinking she had just offered up the perfect opening.

"I forgot to tell you," his mother said. "I got a visit from the press. It made me almost feel like a celebrity."

He turned around to face her. "A reporter came here? When?"

"A couple of days ago. Two of them. I think they worked for a tabloid—something called the *National Tribune*. Are you familiar with it?"

He stood up and spoke deliberately. "I'm *extremely* familiar with it. What'd they want?"

"They asked a lot of personal questions—about the family business, how your father got sick, that sort of thing."

"How long were they here?"

"Long enough to make me a little uncomfortable. I told them I didn't think I should be answering their questions, then asked them to leave. For a moment, I thought about calling security."

"This is incredible." He paced in a tight circle; stupidly, he hadn't considered Longstreet might go after his mother and father. "Did they leave a business card?"

She picked a card off the nightstand and handed it to him. It looked like the one Jazz had gotten at the house: *National Tribune. Washington, D.C.* A few other flourishes and logos. No street address or phone number.

He stuck it in his pocket. "I'm sorry to put you through this, Mom. It shouldn't have happened—and it won't again. I'll make sure of that."

"Don't go to any trouble, Trey. They're just looking everywhere they can for information." She paused. "One thing did concern me, though."

"What's that?"

"They wanted to photograph your father."

"What?" Trey nearly shouted. "You didn't let them take any shots, did you?"

"That's when I asked them to leave. They finally did."

He filled his cup with cider and drank it down. "Did they give you their names?"

"One did. A gentleman named 'Ridge.' He was a very large man with a scar across his nose. I use the word 'gentleman,' but he didn't act that way."

Trey sat down on the side of the bed and collected his thoughts. This Ridge character was obviously working in tandem with the shaved-head thug—and both were working for Longstreet. Proving it, of course, was another matter. But they were getting too damn close. Trey decided, right then and there, to have his security guards stay with his parents tonight, until he could make permanent arrangements tomorrow.

He moved over by the window and looked out onto the hospital's campus-like grounds. It was a crystal clear day outside, perfect for an afternoon stroll. Turning back, he said, "It's beautiful out today, Mom. Kind of chilly, but clear as a bell. You shouldn't stay cooped up."

"I need a walk to work off some of these calories."

"All of us could use that." He patted his waistline.

"Let's do it, then," she said.

Katie ran to get her jacket, and Jazz stood and brushed crumbs from her lap.

"I'll join you in a couple of minutes," Trey said. "I want to talk to Dad for a second."

"We'll take the long way around—behind the hospital. You can catch up with us."

"I'm right behind you."

When the door closed, he scooted his chair up next to the head of his father's bed. Leaning forward, he brushed hair from his father's forehead. Dad's eyes opened partway, and Trey thought he saw a smile turn up the corners of his mouth. He rested a hand on his arm and felt the bones jut sharply through the sheet.

Trey remembered when this once-robust man with

weathered skin thick as canvas took his family for daylong cruises up and down the coast. That was back when he manned the yacht like a full crew. He'd prowl the deck, trim the sails, tie the ropes, steer the boat—all the while teaching his son the craft of sailing. That was Dad in his element. It was hard to believe this frail, wizened figure was the same person. The only evidence was the color of the ocean in his eyes; their cobalt blue had not faded a bit.

Trey talked to him in a whisper, knowing he could still hear and understand. "You look good today. I think you may have put on a pound or two."

He seemed to nod, ever so slightly.

"I'd love to be out on the water with you." He rested his arms on the side of the bed and clasped his hands together. "It's a perfect day for a sail. The boat could use a little of your attention, too. I've let it go. There just aren't enough hours in the day." He wiped a spot of perspiration from his father's forehead and asked, "Would you like something to drink? Some juice or water?"

Dad's eyes closed, then half opened. Trey took this to mean, "No thanks."

"The boat's not the only thing I've let go," he said. "There're some other things I haven't done such a good job at. I've made a few mistakes. We all do, I suppose, but mine was a real zinger."

His father's eyes opened wider. He stirred slightly and turned his head. It was the first time in weeks Trey had seen him respond.

"I don't want to burden you with the particulars," he said. "But I've got a tough decision to make. There doesn't seem to be a right way to go. I've put myself in a difficult spot." He struggled to find the right words. "I always thought right and wrong were obvious. On this one, I don't know. I'm, I'm . . ."

His Dad cleared his throat. It was the sound of a baby's cough, weak and testing. Trey filled a water cup and gave him a sip. Then Dad started to speak. It was barely intelligible at first—just a mouthing of the words. Trey leaned in close, their faces almost touching, until he could make out the sounds.

"Right or wrong," he said, "is always clear, son." Barely lifting a hand, he tapped his chest, then his head sank back into the impression left in the pillow.

Trey realized the effort to speak had taken everything out of him; Dad fell into a deep sleep. Trey wanted to rouse him, to ask him more. It was the first time in nearly a month he'd actually spoken. Trey wanted to tell him everything—the mistakes he'd made, the pressures of the vote. Here was a man he trusted implicitly, who could help him decide the right course in a moment.

Trey sat back, hands in his lap, and silently watched his father rest. The more he thought about what he had said, the more he knew he'd said enough.

He pulled the woolen blanket up around him and tucked it tight. He stood up and put on his jacket and gloves, continuing to watch his father sleep and wondering how he summoned the strength to go on—and why. Maybe it was for the rare moments like these when he could still offer something to a family that needed him so.

Clicking off the lights, Trey walked out into the fading afternoon and took a long, deep breath to clear away the medicinal smell.

The sun was low on the horizon, casting elongated shadows across the grounds. He zipped up his jacket and hurried off to catch up with his family.

★ ★ ★ ★ ★

Later that night, Trey pulled off West Street in downtown Annapolis onto the straight, tree-lined road that led out to their estate. The sky was jet black. A low layer of clouds blotted out the little natural light that may have helped show the way. This was always a dangerous drive—nearly three full miles down an unlit country road; one small lane either way, deep ruts off the shoulders.

As the headlights burrowed two solid beams into the darkness, Trey's eyes followed the white line, his thoughts drifting.

Dad's brief advice had been welcomed, but it was a long way from resolving his problem. Trey liked to keep things simple: *Yes, no. Right, wrong. Black, white.*

Of course, the real world wasn't like that.

Trey held the steering wheel tight and guided the car over a road made slick by moisture from a gathering layer of fog. He let up on the accelerator and checked the rearview mirror. In the distance, a pair of headlights was approaching fast—much too fast for these wet conditions. The driver had his high beams on, too.

Trey moved his car to the right, the passenger-side wheels skirting the shoulder.

The other car moved alongside.

It was crazy to be passing at night, he thought.

The other car surged ahead for a moment, then fell slightly behind. When it pulled alongside them once more, Trey waved the driver on, letting up on the accelerator to allow him to pass.

But the other car slowed, too.

Oh Christ, here we go again, he thought. He suddenly wished he had called for additional security before leaving the hospital.

"Go on by!" he yelled.

His voice woke Katie, sleeping in the back. It startled Jazz, too, who was dozing in front.

"What's going on?" she said, sleepily.

"The idiot beside us is playing games."

"Slow down and let him pass."

"I tried that."

"What's he want?"

"I don't know, and I'm not about to stop and find out. Get on the cellular phone and call the cops."

Jazz reached for the handset as the other car moved closer, squeezing them to the side.

Then the car began to lightly bump into the driver's side of the rental.

Trey heard Katie cry out in the back. The car's right wheels were off the pavement now, sliding through the loose gravel beside a drainage ditch. He tried to straighten it out, but the other vehicle came alongside again, crashing harder into the driver's-side door.

Trey had no choice. He stood on the brakes and tightened his grip on the steering wheel, but he couldn't hold the car straight. He felt the car slip into a spin, suddenly rotating twice before coming to a sliding stop in the middle of the road with the engine stalled.

He sat stunned, hands slick with sweat, watching the other vehicle race ahead, its taillights fading into the night.

"Is everyone all right?" He checked front and back.

They were shaken but unhurt.

He looked around the floorboard for the cell phone. Then he heard Jazz's voice.

"Trey . . ."

It wasn't a scream, or a yell—just a small, trembling sound. He looked up and saw a pair of high-beam headlights wailing down the road at them. The oncoming car had its engine full out, growling like a low-throated animal.

"Oh Jesus." He grabbed the ignition key and turned. The engine cranked but wouldn't start. He pumped the accelerator and tried again. More churning and grinding. The other headlights were coming fast. He unsnapped his seat belt and screamed at Jazz to jump out.

She struggled with her belt.

"Get Katie," she cried.

He crawled over the front seat, but it was too late. The other car was on them. He threw himself on top, closed his eyes and held on.

Everything seemed to happen in slow motion. He heard the crunch of metal against metal. The car rocked violently, glass blasting through the interior like sleet. He felt the car slide sideways, back-end first, into the ditch. The front end came down after it, falling into the muddy grass and weeds.

He held onto Katie as tight as he could and looked through the broken glass. The other car had stopped and backed up. It sat there beside them, idling. At the wheel was the man with the shaved head, his diamond-stud earring reflecting light like shattered glass.

Trey moved toward the front seat, reaching for the phone.

But the bald-headed man jammed his car in gear and squealed away.

Trey listened to the sound of the fading engine. When he looked back to Katie, her eyes showed a terror he'd never seen before, never wanted to see again.

He brushed particles of glass away from her face and helped her sit up. But the car was leaning at such an angle it was difficult to stay upright. The left side door was too mangled to open. He checked the window edges for shards of glass, then hoisted himself out and reached back in for his daughter.

Then he heard his name called out again.

"Trey."

It was that same small, trembling sound he'd heard before.

Jazz!

He raced around the car and found his wife lying in the field beside the road, face up, her legs twisted and bunched beneath her.

He jumped down beside her. "Oh my God, Hon, are you all right?"

"I don't know. I think—I don't know." She reached down and grabbed her left leg and pulled. "I can't move my legs, Trey. The car's on top of me."

"Don't pull. Give me a minute. Are you bleeding?"

"I can't tell. They're numb. I'm scared, Trey."

"Hang on, babe."

He scrambled up from the ditch and ran back to the driver's side for the cell phone. After calling for help, he looked around for something to dig with. Finding two long pieces of bumper several yards down the road, he used one piece to brace the car and dug furiously with the other, sliding dirt away from his wife's legs while Katie held her mother's scraped and bloodied hands.

By the time the ambulance arrived, Trey had freed her completely. But he refused to let her stand. He forced her to lie in the mud, using his jacket for a pillow.

"I'm think I'm okay," she kept saying.

But he knew she wasn't, and he couldn't stop blaming himself.

Chapter Twenty-Four

With Jazz in a neck brace and strapped tightly to a cot, the paramedics wheeled her in for X-rays. Trey went to find a quiet room where Katie could sleep. When she was soundly dozing, he tiptoed out of the room—and went looking for the police.

He found them huddled together outside the emergency room door. "Have you found the other driver?" he asked.

"Not yet, but we'll get him. He couldn't have gotten far."

"I want that bastard tonight. I don't care what it takes. If you've got to bring in extra people, I'll pay the cost. He tried to kill us."

"I understand, Congressman. We're doing all we can."

"Apparently it's not enough."

"We've got patrols all over the area—cruisers, choppers. We're checking every building between the accident site and Annapolis. We'll get him."

"Accident? This was no accident. The bastard ran us down on purpose."

"That's what I meant."

"That's not what you said."

"It was just a word. I didn't mean . . ."

"What *did* you mean?"

"That it was . . . I mean wasn't . . . an accident."

"You don't know what the hell you're talking about. Some son of a bitch tried to kill my family. He's driving around in a smashed-up auto on an empty country road, and you can't find him. Why am I not surprised?"

"We're doing the best we can. Hit-and-run is a horrible crime. But what makes you so certain the collision was done on purpose?"

Trey started to answer, then caught himself. Could he afford to accuse the White House of attempted murder? With virtually no hard evidence on his side, he'd look like a lunatic in the press and to the public at-large. No, he had to have more to go on before leveling charges that would explode across the political landscape and damage himself more than the opposition.

He took a deep breath. "The man stopped and smiled at what he'd done, officer. He obviously took enjoyment from his . . . work."

The officer raised an eyebrow. "I understand your reaction, Mr. Stone. If it were me and my family, I'd feel the same way. Look, we're doing all we can to track him down. We're doing our best. That's all we can do."

"Are you *really*, officer?"

"Yes, sir."

"Then your best isn't good enough. I want that man found. If you can't do it, I'll get somebody who can."

Turning, he stalked off, leaving the patrolman shaking his head in frustration. But Trey didn't care who he angered now. As far as he was concerned, everyone was his enemy. Until he knew different, no one could be trusted.

He found his way into a waiting room and sat in an old worn chair, trying to calm himself. But the same questions kept swirling through his mind: If these guys worked for Longstreet, would they really resort to *murder* for the President? If so, why? What could be so important about the Oval Office they'd kill to keep it? Maybe they were just trying to scare the hell out of him. Certainly, they had done that. But could Forsythe know about this and condone it? Or was Longstreet out of control?

Trey looked up when the swinging doors opened. A young doctor clad in a white coat and tennis shoes walked in, stopping in front of him.

"How is she?"

"Banged up and bruised," he said. "But no broken bones. None I can find, anyway."

"Thank God." Trey sank back into the chair. "No concussion or head injuries?"

"No."

"She complained of numbness in her legs."

"Probably from the circulation being cut off, or the cold. We couldn't find any nerve damage."

Trey sat back and let a lungful of air escape. For the first time in the last hour, he could let down—but not too far down.

"When can she go home?"

"We'd like to keep her twenty-four hours for observation."

"But this is Christmas Eve."

"I understand," he said. "How about we keep her another eight hours? I'll have her home in time for a late breakfast. If there's a problem, you're not far away."

"She'll appreciate that. So will my daughter."

Standing, Trey shook the young man's hand. The doctor then turned and hurried out to the next emergency.

Trey came out after him, going straight to Jazz's room. He found her asleep from the pain medication. Sitting at her side, he watched her for several minutes and listened to her breathe. He couldn't believe how close he'd come to losing her.

He kissed her on the cheek, then got up and went to get

his daughter. He knew Katie would want to be in her own bed come Christmas morning, even if she had to wait before opening her presents.

In the hall, he passed the small group of Maryland state officers. He glared at the patrolman he had chewed out earlier. The cop looked back sheepishly and shrugged. Trey kept on walking. He was starting to believe no arrests would be made—not tonight or any other night. Whoever had assaulted them was long gone by now. The only question was: Would he be back?

Longstreet sat back in his swivel chair behind his perfectly ordered desk and wondered, as he often did these days, if the President fully understood the risks they had taken—the extremes to which they had gone—to return him to office. Just so they could avoid what might prove to be the inevitable, anyway: a congressional investigation that would bring them all down. So much for service to country.

He didn't look up as the door opened and the sound of soft shoes squeaked across the parquet floor. When the visitor was seated comfortably in front, Longstreet spoke quietly.

"Nice job."

"Intimidation," Steele replied. "It's my specialty."

"But you gave him a clear look at your face," Longstreet said. "They've got your description plastered all over the place."

"I had to give him something to remember me by. I want him lying awake tonight thinking about me, about what I can do—what I *will* do."

"If they believe this was anything other than an accident, the FBI could be put on the case; then we'd have the press all over the story. You may have raised the stakes too high this time."

Steele laughed. "Stone's not going to level charges without proof, Boss. He's got nothing. He'd look like a crazy man." He laughed again. "In fact, I think he already does look crazy." Longstreet breathed heavily for several minutes. Steele was right. If Stone were going to go public, he'd have done it by now. Obviously, his public image was still ultimately important to him—further evidence they were on the right track with this guy.

"The next step is to put pressure on where it hurts the most," Longstreet said. "We have to close the deal."

"And where might that be?"

"Where do you think it is?"

"That pretty face of his?"

"Not hardly."

"Where then?"

Longstreet let the tension build, then spoke in a whisper: "Does the name Katie Christine mean anything to you?"

Before Steele could respond, Longstreet got up and walked out of the office, leaving his partner sitting alone in the dark, pondering their next move.

Chapter Twenty-Five

Trey stood at the front-room window, arms clinched across his chest, and watched a police cruiser emerge from the woods. It was followed by an ambulance, red lights flashing, no siren. Two other unmarked cars trailed behind, their headlights blazing, as if joined in a funeral dirge.

He met them out front. Two orderlies jumped out of the ambulance, wrapped Jazz in a blanket and carried her through the open front door in a wheelchair. Inside, she jumped up and caught Katie running into her arms. Both of them nearly tumbled to the floor.

Trey escorted the orderlies back to the ambulance, then came in the house and found his wife and daughter in the living room about to open presents.

He went straight to Jazz and held her tightly. No kisses. No words. Just a long embrace.

Afterward, they turned to the business of Christmas—exchanging presents and snacking on Irma's treats.

When Katie went outside to ride her new Christmas bike, Jazz turned to Trey with the question she had wanted to ask all morning:

"Did they get the guy?"

He shook his head. "He's long gone."

"What was it all about? I don't understand."

"They were sending me another message: Support Forsythe or else."

"We could've been killed, Trey. It's a miracle Katie wasn't hurt. This is insane."

"I've hired additional security guards here and at the hospital for Mom and Dad. The Washington and Maryland police are on alert, and I briefed the FBI, too."

She pulled her quilted robe up around herself and stared deeply, silently into the fire. Trey watched her for a moment, wondering what else he could do to calm her fears—and his own.

He finished his coffee and got up to freshen his cup. "You want more?"

"Yes, please. I'm drowsy from the pills they gave me."

"Mom will be over for dinner around four o'clock," he said. "I called her and told her about the 'accident.' As far as she knows, it was just an accident. I convinced her Dad would be all right for a couple of hours while she had dinner with us."

"I wish she'd spend the night."

"Maybe we can talk her into it."

He went to the kitchen, cups and saucers in hand.

Halfway down the hall, the phone rang, and Irma came running in after him.

"Mr. Stone. It's for you. The White House again!"

He hesitated, searching for an excuse to avoid the call. Then he thought: *Maybe this is exactly what I need.*

He went to his office and closed the door.

The conversation began perfunctorily. Forsythe wished him a Merry Christmas and reminisced about Camp David. They both hoped each other's families would have a great New Year.

"I know you're under tremendous pressure," the President said. "I've been in the same position myself on a few occasions."

"I can appreciate that."

"If any questions come up I can answer—anything I can

do to help you decide, I want you to call. My secretary's got instructions to put you through."

"Thank you."

"We can do great things together, Trey. You've got wonderful ideas and a powerful sense of what's right for this country. I can use that in my Administration. It would strengthen our party, too. It would strengthen our nation." Pausing, he went on slowly. "We can accomplish a lot with both of us in the White House."

The President's comment was another lightly veiled bribe, perhaps vaguer than Longstreet's but no less pointed: Work with us, and you can name your price.

But Trey's thoughts weren't on politics right now. He was focused on the car assault. Given his suspicions of Longstreet, he couldn't resist probing.

"Mr. President, please don't take this the wrong way. . . ."

"Yes."

"A man in your position is often the target of radical political supporters."

"More than you can imagine."

"It's all new to me, and I've been getting threatening calls and other activity that has me quite concerned."

"Yes. . . ."

"I have reason to believe supporters of yours are behind it."

The comment seemed to take Forsythe by surprise. He hesitated before responding.

"What makes you say that?"

"The threats are clear—I better vote for you or else."

He laughed uncomfortably. "Let's hope your support is not contingent on physical violence."

"Of course not. It's just that I've decided to call in federal officers to investigate. I hope they might get access to your, uh, campaign officials," he was struggling to find the right words, "to help determine who's behind this."

"You believe someone on my staff is involved?"

"Your people might know where to go, who to talk to—who's capable of extreme measures. It's someone who has a lot at stake."

"Everyone's got a lot at stake. You included."

The comment was like a slap in the face—exactly the opposite reaction Trey had hoped for. He didn't want to anger the President, but he had to get to the bottom of the violent threats. He had hoped Forsythe would be more understanding.

"I apologize if I've offended you, Mr. President."

"Threats are the nature of our profession. You'll learn there's one sure way to deal with these lunatics—give 'em what they want."

Trey didn't know exactly how to react, or what to say. The President could be joking, but Trey wasn't in a joking mood—not when the safety of his family was at stake.

Then the President abruptly changed topics, as if Trey's request wasn't even worth considering.

"We're having a dinner party at the White House on New Year's Eve," he said. "We'd love to have you and Jazz here. Nothing too formal. A few close friends and supporters. Maybe we'll have something special to toast."

Trey let the invitation hang in the air for several seconds.

"It's an honor to be invited, Mr. President. Unfortunately, Jazz is laid up right now. We had a little accident last night."

"Nothing too serious, I hope."

"She'll be fine. A little sore, that's all. But she won't be ready for a night out anytime soon, I'm afraid."

"That's a real shame. Give her our best."

"I'll do that."

"You're still welcome to attend."

"It's not often I turn down a President, but I'd hate to leave my wife alone on New Year's, especially given the circumstances." He knew Forsythe assumed those "circumstances" were Jazz's injuries. The fact was, Trey wasn't interested in meeting with the President now or anytime.

"I'll give your condolences to the First Lady."

"Give her our best for the coming year, too."

With that, they hung up.

Trey stood and stared at the phone, startled by the fact Forsythe was so unsympathetic to his concerns—he seemed almost *glad* for his supporters' tactics.

The more Trey thought about his reaction, the more he was sure Forsythe was not only aware of Longstreet's threats, he could even be directing him. He also sensed the President's civility was stretched to the breaking point. He could almost hear the strain in his voice, like the threads popping in the fabric of his Presidency.

He went back to the living room and found everyone else gone—Jazz off to bed, Irma in the kitchen, Katie outside. He poured a fresh cup of coffee and went to his office to get comfortable, then the phone rang again. When he answered this time, he wasn't surprised to hear Governor Wardlow's voice on the other end.

"Merry Christmas to you and yours," Wardlow said.

"Same to you. I hope you have a great New Year, too."

"I've got a feeling next year'll be a wonderful one. In fact, I've got an especially good feeling about January."

Trey decided to let the comment go.

"I'll be in Washington the middle part of next month,"

Wardlow said. "I'd like to take you up on that offer to tour Annapolis."

"Name the day and time, and I'll make myself available."

"As soon as my schedule firms up, I'll give you a call."

"I'm looking forward to it."

A brief moment of silence, then Wardlow spoke again. "I want you to know, no matter what the outcome of the vote, it's been a pleasure dealing with you. I sense you're a man of integrity. It's a trait all too rare in politics these days."

"I could say the same thing about you."

"Thank you, friend, and *salud*. See you next year."

"Vaya con dios."

Trey hung up the phone and rested back in his leather chair, feet propped up on the desk. There was something about Wardlow he basically liked, even though he knew the man wasn't totally altruistic. No one at the highest reaches of public office was. Wardlow did his fair share of avoiding the hard line on unpopular positions, but he was also clear on where he wanted to go and how he wanted to get there. One thing they agreed on implicitly: Politics was what you do, not who you are.

When the phone rang yet again, Trey let it go this time, unable to handle one more conversation.

A few minutes later, Jazz straggled into his office.

"What're you doing up?" he said. "I thought you'd snooze half the day away."

"Your mother'll be here in a few hours. I want to help Irma with dinner and setting up the dining room."

"I'll do all that." He took her by the arm and led her toward the living room. "I want you to rest."

"Oh, Governor Weddington just called," she said.

"Then I'm glad I didn't answer it."

"He wished us a Merry Christmas."

"A pretext for prying out more information on the vote."

"I told him you were out. Hope you don't mind."

"Mind? I owe you."

"But he said he'd call back later."

"I was afraid of that."

"Apparently, he's looking for Jack," she said. "No one's seen him since the day before yesterday."

"I thought he'd at least spend the holiday with his family. Have they tried his boat?"

"Yes. No one's seen him at City Dock or any of his usual hangouts. They alerted the Coast Guard, but no one's seen him on the bay at all."

"That's strange."

They sat where they had been before, Jazz warming her hands in front of the fire.

"I'm worried, Trey. Jack's boat is like a magnet. Everywhere he goes, he attracts a crowd. You'd think *somebody* would've seen him."

"They probably have, and they're not talking. He's been known to disappear before."

Trey stirred the embers, and the fire started to roar. Jazz curled up her legs. Soon, she was napping again.

Trey watched her for a while, then pulled himself away to help with dinner. On the way to the kitchen, he decided to forward the phone to their answering service. No more calls. No more intrusions. The outside world could stay there for a while.

In a small inlet of Weems Creek north of Annapolis, Jack maneuvered his craft toward open water. Over his shoulder, the sun was halfway down the horizon, simmering reddish pink through a layer of low-hanging clouds.

He expertly steered into open waters, then tacked starboard. The wind, like a welcoming friend, came up behind him, helping the *Herndon* get up to running speed.

He walked forward, along the slender path between the cabin and rail, and opened the spinnaker; the boat immediately gained another three or four knots. He went back to the helm and held the craft on a course for the dead center of the bay. The *Herndon* was full out now, moving smoothly with the current.

Jack sailed for an hour, due south, with no one else on the water. No one was crazy enough to be on the Chesapeake on a cold December day, not with the sun disappearing as if dropping away forever.

When he cleared the mouth of the Patuxent River, shore was barely visible in the last moments of light. Jack felt as if he were sailing in a dream—all alone and with all the time in the world.

He swigged from a plastic jug of tomato juice. Normally, he would have spiked the drink with hundred-proof vodka. But not this afternoon. For once, he wanted to be sober, to embrace the remnants of a day on the bay, to feel the wind at his back and the sea beneath his feet.

He locked the helm in place and stepped back by the rail and peered in the direction of Annapolis, due north. There was nothing but miles of blue sea between himself and home. In a sense, it had always been that way. There had always been a gulf between him and others. Sure, he had a few good friends and a loving family, but they had always been much better to him than he had been to them. Now, here he was delivering the final insult. Forever spoiling the one holiday of the year his family had always so much enjoyed together. He shook his head in self disgust, then finished the last of his ice-chilled juice and stuffed the jug inside the bulwark.

Stretching his arms wide, he watched the top edge of the sun sink behind the disappearing shoreline. In a last, explosive burst of light, the day was gone, slipped beneath the horizon, leaving behind purplish clouds bruised by their encounter with a force larger than life itself.

Jack snapped off a smart salute and took in a deep breath of fresh air. It was the best he'd felt in months, maybe years. He should have tried sobriety before.

Calmly, confidently, he stepped over the rear gunnel and glanced back over his shoulder for one last look.

Then he leaned down and silently slipped over the side.

Holding the back of the boat in a one-handed grip, he let his legs flow out evenly with the surface of the water, as if treading in its wake.

Then he let go and watched the *Herndon* sail off without him.

It was a shame to let a good craft go on its own like that. He hoped the boat would be found in good shape, and its next captain would take as much care and pride.

Floating on his back, Jack watched the night sky, its faint stars gathering like lightning bugs, one by one, until there were too many to count.

Slowly, he closed his eyes and felt the freezing cold of the water numb him inside and out.

Inevitably, sleep came—more easily than he had imagined. Reaching out, he pulled the surface of the Chesapeake up around him like a blanket and took in one last, watery breath.

That night around the dinner table, everyone's mood was buoyant. Trey regaled his mother and Irma with tales of Camp David; Katie described her helicopter ride. Jazz told everyone about her family members, most of whom she'd spoken with earlier in the day. She didn't tell anyone about the car accident, of course, not wanting to worry them on a holiday.

The only interruption was an occasional jangle from the phone before the answering service picked up.

At the end of the meal, with everyone relaxing around the table, Irma could take the ringing no more and went to get the messages.

When she returned, Trey was leading everyone out for tea and dessert.

"Mrs. Weddington called several times," Irma said. "Apparently, it's urgent."

Irma looked to Trey first, then to Jazz.

Finally, Jazz went to return the call.

Several minutes passed before she returned from the kitchen. Standing at the doorway, she waved for Trey to come. He got up and followed her down the hall. She spun around and took his hands in hers, tears welling in her eyes.

"What happened?" he said.

"They found Jack." Her voice broke. "He's dead."

Chapter Twenty-Six

In an exclusive, gated community in Alexandria, twenty minutes from D.C., a gray limo with blacked-out windows pulled into the driveway of a stately, bricked colonial home. The car drove to the garage at the back of the property and waited for an overhead door to swing open. The driver pulled inside, and the door fell shut behind in an echoing thud.

Inside the house, Arch Longstreet hurried to the back door to meet his visitor. The two men shook hands warmly, but Longstreet knew this meeting would be anything but cordial. It was only the second time President Forsythe had ever asked to speak with his campaign adviser in the privacy of his own residence.

"I've got ten minutes, Arch. No time for anything but cold, hard facts." The President led the way to the back of the house, into a den darkened by shuttered windows.

"Here it is," Longstreet began. "Weddington's death hurts Stone more than it helps him." He waited for the President to sit before he took a chair himself.

"Why's that?" Forsythe asked.

"His death eliminates the legal maneuvering that could've delayed an investigation about his relationship with Stone."

"But now there's no one to prosecute," Forsythe said. "The investigators won't go after a dead man."

"No, but they'll go after Stone if we point them there. He's as liable as ever—maybe even more so. His only witness is gone. He'll have a helluva time defending himself."

Standing, the President paced across the room and back again, then stopped in front of Longstreet. He towered over his campaign manager, who had slumped back in his chair. "Give it to me straight, Arch—did your people have anything to do with Weddington's death? Are we vulnerable there, too?"

"God no, Ben. The man was a drunk. We had no idea he'd kill himself. But the suicide doesn't hurt us. Nothing's changed. We've still got Stone up against the wall."

"His death doesn't *help* us, either, not in the court of public opinion. If we push for an investigation, it'll look like what it is—an attempt to intimidate Stone."

Forsythe went back and sat on the edge of the seat where he had been before. Staring down at the intricately patterned carpet, he thought for a long moment before going on: "I talked with him on Christmas Day. He wants me to authorize the FBI to talk with you and others on the campaign staff. He's on to us, Arch. He knows where the threats are coming from. We're in way too deep. The last thing we need is the Justice Department rummaging through our files, talking to witnesses, putting the pieces together."

Longstreet sat back, trying to look confident, though his own legendary over-confidence had been shaken by recent events; Stone was much tougher to break than he had ever imagined.

Longstreet spoke softly, in the steadiest voice he could summon: "We'll stall the FBI by claiming a witch hunt. We'll say Wardlow is behind the allegations of intimidation and tampering. We only need a few weeks. After the vote, nobody'll care what Stone thinks. He'll just be another second-rate congressman."

The President rubbed his chin and stared off into the distance, obviously pondering more than Stone's intransigence. Longstreet knew every member of the President's vaunted Southern Mafia was running scared. The inner circle had been cautioning Forsythe to cut his losses and sacrifice his own campaign manager to the opposition. After all, someone would have to be offered up. Why not Longstreet? He had the least to lose. He wasn't a government official. The Justice Department would go easier on him than on Cabinet officials—or even on the President himself.

When Forsythe looked up, Longstreet noticed his eyes—so bright and piercing at Camp David—had begun to sag again; the light was fading as fast as his Presidency.

"We still haven't answered the biggest question of all," Forsythe said. "How're we going to nail down Stone's support? Time's about run out."

"He's ready to break. I can feel it."

Forsythe shook his head; he had heard this once too often. Without a word, he got up and started for the door. Longstreet jumped up and followed him. Halfway down the hall, the President stopped and spun around.

"I don't have to tell you how much we've got riding on this," he said. "How much *all* of us have at stake."

"Of course not."

"We've got promises to keep, agreements to deliver on. We can't do it *out* of office, that's for sure. If I lose this election, our Asian support will vanish in a second. They'll have no reason to protect us, and we'll be exposed like we never have been before."

"I realize that, Ben."

"Our overseas friends didn't fund my campaign so I could lose."

Forsythe smiled fleetingly. Then he glanced around at the lavishly decorated home: the crystal chandeliers, the perfectly kept antiques, the designer drapes and hand-loomed Persian rugs.

"We all have expensive tastes," he said. "If we want to continue in the lifestyle to which we've all become accustomed, we better get things right with our reluctant Representative." He paused. "There aren't carpeting and drapes in Leavenworth."

Longstreet grinned, but he knew the President was right. Everything still hinged on Stone. "I haven't let you down yet, have I?"

The President turned and walked to the back door, grabbing the polished knob in one giant hand, holding it tight, staring down at the white tiled floor that showed not a speck of dirt or wear.

He spoke almost as if to himself. "No, you haven't let me down. And this is no time to start."

He opened the door and stepped out.

Longstreet called after him. "I've still got a trick or two left. You'll see—tomorrow at the funeral."

"I'm not going to that spectacle," Forsythe said. He crawled in the back of the limo. "I'm sending Fred."

Longstreet grimaced. "How ironic. One drunk acknowledging the demise of another."

Forsythe sighed. "It's just our way of showing support for the governor, that's all."

"I plan a 'show of support' for Stone, as well. Something that'll really get his attention."

"You do that, Arch," Forsythe said. "I just don't want to know about it." He slammed the limo door. The automatic garage door lifted open, and the driver pulled out expertly, gunning the engine down the driveway.

Longstreet stared after the car for a moment, then punched the button to re-close the door. He went back inside, knowing his options were more limited than ever. He had been around Washington long enough to understand how to read between the lines: He had to solve the Stone question once and for all, or Longstreet himself would be the one to suffer.

He wasn't about to let that happen. At any cost.

Chapter Twenty-Seven

That weekend, the Stones arrived on the grounds of the U.S. Naval Academy in a black stretch limo driven by a private security guard. A second guard rode shotgun. With all the military police and government security agents expected at Jack's funeral, Trey decided two guards were more than enough for the family's protection.

Trey and Jazz had debated long and hard about whether to bring Katie. Funerals were tough enough on adults, but she had held up well after her first good cry, and she did so want to say goodbye to her "Uncle Jack."

Eventually, Trey and Jazz relented, knowing the experience would help prepare her for other losses to come—like her grandfather's, which wasn't far away.

More than a thousand people were expected to attend the ceremonies. Included on the guest list were the Vice President, Fred McNally; Maryland's entire contingent of congressmen, state senators and assemblymen, plus administrative officials and staff, and several ambassadors from nations Maryland traded with. Most of them attended in honor of the governor, not his son. But that made the occasion no less of a spectacle for media outlets nationwide.

The crowds were expected to swell to two thousand or more, an overwhelming number for the hamlet of Annapolis. Arrangements for the funeral itself were a major project. Jack wasn't an Annapolis graduate, and chapel rites were usually reserved for military heroes. To make an exception, the two days after Jack's death were filled with negotiations between the governor's office and campus officials. As Trey understood it, the White House finally intervened, and the school's superintendent gave in.

The Stones' limo driver maneuvered through scores of spectators gathered around Gate Three, then swung the car onto Blake Road and parked in front of the chapel.

When everyone got out, the driver pulled away, leaving the family standing in the one-lane road, staring up at an imposing tiered dome that rose two hundred feet into a blindingly bright sky. Even with dark glasses on, Trey had to shield his eyes beneath the bill of his Navy cap. The sight was awe-inspiring. It took him several seconds to tear himself away; he found himself standing alone as everyone else moved toward the marble steps in front. Buttoning his dress-blues jacket, he quickly caught up, joining them on the stairway between two massive stone anchors.

Trey introduced the Navy chaplain to his family. They awkwardly shook hands all around. Then the chaplain asked Trey to step inside the chapel. The two men entered through the huge bronze doors and stopped in a small waiting area preceding the main sanctuary.

Chaplain Porter was a large man, but well proportioned. Draped around his neck, a purple and gold prayer cloth set off the silver of his hair.

He dispensed with pleasantries and went right to work. "I'll begin the service precisely at eleven," he said. They checked their watches; twenty minutes to go. "We'll start with music selected by the family. Then I'll offer a prayer from the scriptures before moving onto a prepared statement from the governor. Mr. Weddington isn't saying a lot." He bowed his head. "I don't think he's quite up to it yet."

"He's taking this hard," Trey said. "Lots of regrets there, I think."

Porter nodded. "The sons of the deceased will lay wreaths at the altar, beneath their father's ashes. At that point, it'll be time for your eulogy."

For the first time, Trey's hands began to moisten and his mouth became dry. He had spoken before large crowds many times, of course; he wasn't nervous about that. Rather, it was the thought of eulogizing a best friend who had died so much before his time—in a way that made no sense—that disturbed him. Trey wasn't sure he could ever forgive Jack for what he'd done, or himself. He knew he should have seen it coming. When Jazz first told him of the drowning, Trey realized it was no accident. *Jack had taken his own life to prevent a deeper investigation.* It was so typical of him; self-sacrifice was his mantra.

"We'll close with another musical selection by the family," Porter said, "then the Navy hymn."

Trey was only half listening.

"The Weddingtons will lead the procession to Santee Basin where a captain's skiff will be waiting. The scattering of ashes should take thirty minutes. By the time we re-dock, the other mourners will be gone. That's the plan, anyway. Traffic may slow things a bit."

"It always does." Trey tried his best to smile.

They shook hands, and Porter asked Trey to bring in his family, encouraging the others to follow.

Trey stepped outside and took Jazz and Katie by the hand, leading them into the sanctuary. They moved slowly down the length of the nave, absorbing the splendor of the place like visitors to a holy shrine. Which they were.

He ushered them to a front-row seat on the left side, opposite where the Weddingtons would be. They listened to the soft chords of the pipe organ as others shuffled in.

The service began precisely at eleven, as the chaplain

said it would. All the parts were played to perfection.

That was, until Trey stepped up to offer the eulogy.

Starting off in a strong, sure voice, he spent time remembering his friend, Laura's husband, the governor's son, the father of two wonderful sons. He held up fine until it came time to close with a poem by one of Jack's favorite writers, Henry Van Dyke.

Trey got through the first verse all right, but he nearly came apart during the second, speaking the words in a quavering voice, tears trickling down his cheeks.

Who will walk a mile with me
Along life's weary way?
A friend whose heart has eyes to see
the stars shine out o'er the darkening lea,
And the quiet rest at the end of the day
A friend who knows, and dares to say,
the brave, sweet words that cheer the way
Where he walks a mile with me.

He pulled himself together for the close:

With such a comrade, such a friend,
I fain would walk til journey's end.
Through summer sunshine, winter rain,
And then? Farewell, we shall meet again.

He looked up from the lectern to find a chapel full of mourners also overcome. Trey wiped away the tears, folded the poem and stuck it inside his jacket. When he stepped down off the altar and sat beside his wife, they both stared ahead stoically, Jazz weeping quietly into a handkerchief as the choir sang "Amazing Grace."

After a short benediction by Porter, the service was completed with the Navy hymn. Porter then led the mass procession a half-mile across the grounds to the school's river port, where a small Navy cruiser waited. As planned, the governor and Laura stepped onto the gangway; Trey and Jazz were right behind.

Chaplain Porter spoke out loud enough for everyone to hear: "Jack Weddington . . . son, husband, father . . . we pray for your soul."

A trumpeter blared out "Taps," the mournful notes piercing the air like steel arrows. Porter then crossed himself and looked up to the crowd. "Thank you, ladies and gentleman, for joining us today."

And everyone began to disperse.

Kneeling down, Trey kissed Katie on the forehead. "We'll be back in a few minutes, hon."

He followed the others onboard, calling back to Irma: "We'll meet you by the chapel steps."

The skiff pulled away, and a crush of sightseers aboard a fleet of small boats trailed them out of the basin and into the bay. Because of the heavy crowds, it took longer than expected to complete the burial at sea. Through the entire ceremony, Trey barely spoke with the Weddingtons. He exchanged a few brief words and an embrace with the governor. But they were both too overwhelmed to carry on much of a conversation. It felt better simply to stare out across the water and admire the only environment that gave Jack a sense of joy and belonging.

At one point, Trey exchanged furtive glances with Laura, but he couldn't bring himself to talk with her or even comfort her distress with a gentle hand. Jazz stepped in to offer up the family's sympathies, and that seemed to suffice, especially since Laura appeared determined to stay as close as possible to her children, struggling all the while to hold herself together.

But Trey could work up no concern for her well-being. If anyone were responsible for Jack's death, Laura had to take the ultimate blame. Jack was always an unstable character, and maybe he would have found another excuse somewhere down the line. But that his own wife would betray him—and Trey—was utterly unconscionable. For a man who valued loyalty and love above all else, Trey would never—could never—accept Laura's treachery.

Forty-five minutes after having pulled out of port, the skiff finally arrived back at the dock. As it slowly pulled in, Trey stood at the rail on the starboard side to see if all the onlookers were gone.

And they were.

All but one.

Standing at the dock where they had left less than an hour before, he saw the last face he expected: Irma was standing where they had left her.

And she was alone.

Chapter Twenty-Eight

The captain's skiff nestled up to the dock, and Trey vaulted over the side, landing on both feet with a thud. He barely paused to catch his balance. Then he rushed up beside Irma.

"Where's Katie?" he yelled.

She was crying so hard she could hardly speak.

He grabbed her and forced her to look him in the eye. "Where's Katie, Irma?"

She barely got the words out. "I . . . I don't know, Mr. Stone. God forgive me, I don't know. We went to the restroom. After that, she was gone. We couldn't have been apart more than thirty seconds."

Trey didn't need any more than that. He tossed his hat aside and took off in a sprint. The half-mile back to the chapel was a blur. He could think of nothing but Katie. If anyone had harmed his daughter, no law would deny him revenge. She was an innocent child. Nothing in the world was worth risking her safety—certainly not politics.

He covered the distance in two minutes flat, arriving beside the limo with his lungs heaving. One bodyguard was on the car phone; the other one was gone.

Trey leaned through the open door and grabbed the driver by the lapels, screaming into his face, "Where the hell's my daughter?"

"I, I don't know, sir," he said. "We're getting a search underway."

"You're damn right you are. I want every cop, every

guard, every military policeman we can find. I want the entire campus sealed off right now, goddamn it. Where the hell were you guys?"

"Right here, sir, all the time. She couldn't have gotten far. It was only a few minutes ago."

"A few minutes . . ." Trey was spitting with rage. "You weren't supposed to take your eyes off her!"

"She went to the bathroom with your housekeeper. . . ."

Trey turned away. "I'm calling the FBI."

He ran as fast as he could across Blake Road to the chaplain's quarters and took the steps three at a time. Bursting inside the office, he snatched a phone off the first desk he came to.

A clerk approached him warily but said nothing as he dialed an emergency number and waited for the phone to ring.

In the subdued light of a low-ceilinged chamber, Arch Longstreet took the little girl by one hand and led her to a central exhibit.

Roped off in the middle of the circular room, an enormous casket sat in spotlighted splendor, a testament to American naval heroes past, present and future.

The paunchy, middle-aged man and slightly-built child stood silently viewing the display before them.

Longstreet glanced down, a silly grin replacing the crooked sneer he usually wore. He knelt on both knees in front of her and inspected her lips. White cream smudged the edges of her mouth ever so tantalizingly. He reached up with a paper napkin and dabbed carefully. Then he licked the napkin clean and dabbed her face again, making sure to get every last drop.

Standing, he walked next to the macabre display in the

center of the room, pulling her along with him. She came quietly, innocently, unaware of who this man was; she knew only he professed to be "Daddy's friend," and that she should be unafraid.

Longstreet stopped in front of a twenty-ton sarcophagus, a giant box-like crypt fashioned out of black-and-white marble, supported by life-like bronze dolphins. Like a tour guide, he recited the history of the display: "This is the gravesite of our nation's most famous naval hero, Admiral John Paul Jones," he said.

He read from a brass-plated inscription set in the floor: "Admiral Jones gave the Navy its earliest traditions of heroism and victory." Looking down, he smiled at the little girl beside him. "You know your Daddy can be a hero, too, Katie?"

She nodded. Longstreet went on.

"He can decide, almost by himself, who our next President will be."

She nodded again, tentatively.

"This is a big honor," Longstreet said, trying to sound paternalistic, "and an even bigger responsibility."

Katie shrugged. Like a typical first-grader, she turned and wandered off toward other displays and memorabilia, obviously bored by the meaninglessness of it all to her.

Longstreet followed her next to a life-sized bust of Admiral Jones. Part of the funeral eulogy was etched in stone below the bust: "The fame of the brave always outlives him," Longstreet recited.

He turned to Katie, frowning. "Let's hope this is not true with your father."

The police seemed to take forever, but only a few minutes passed before squadrons of officers swarmed the small streets of Annapolis.

They went door-to-door inquiring whether anyone had seen a lost little girl. They broadcast an all-points bulletin for a six-year-old who looked like a hundred other first-graders in the area; except this one was wearing a dark, formal funeral dress.

The state police sealed off all routes into and out of the hamlet and began checking autos one-by-one, opening up the trunks and pulling out the back seats of especially suspicious vehicles.

Overhead, news choppers hovered in a deafening roar.

In the middle of all this, Trey managed logistics and manpower like a soldier in a losing battle. He tried his damnedest to remain civil, but the rising panic in his voice left an edge few had ever heard before.

After nearly thirty minutes of shouting instructions and making sure all available manpower was mobilized, he decided to take a moment to talk with Jazz. He knew he needed to reassure her everything would be fine, whether he believed it or not.

He found her beside the limo out front. She was standing there like an after-school mother waiting for her child to appear from class. She was in her bare feet, having abandoned her high heels at the boat dock before racing across campus. She held Katie's sweater in one hand, as if her daughter would arrive any moment to claim the wrap and jump in the back of the car for an uneventful ride home. The only sign anything was wrong appeared in the odd combination of deadness and terror in her eyes. Despite the strain, Trey knew she was doing her best to remain strong.

"We'll find her, hon, don't worry," he said. He wrapped his arms around her and felt her shiver. Pulling off his Navy jacket, he draped it over her bare shoulders. "They couldn't have gotten far."

In fact, he knew they could have gotten very far; every minute that went by could take them even farther away.

Looking down at his wife, Trey knew she was on the verge of a breakdown; he was in about the same shape. This was their worse nightmare come true. From the day Katie was born prematurely, they had done everything to make sure she had the best possible care. After Jazz's difficult pregnancy, they knew they could never have another child. Now, their one and only was gone, stolen right out from under them. For what? An election? A public office? A damn political contest?

Jazz looked up and asked, "Who would do this? Why would they want our baby?"

He held her tightly, unable to find a good answer. Even though, in his heart, he knew exactly who was behind the disappearance. Proving it was another matter. He had already asked the FBI to check Longstreet's home. The agents obliged with a visit, but they found no one home. Without a warrant, they couldn't enter the property.

Trey wondered whether he should go there himself. He didn't give a damn about warrants or legalisms at this point.

Then he heard someone call out his name; a police officer was asking for him to come back to the chaplain's quarters to handle more questions.

He kissed Jazz lightly on one cheek and hurried across the quad to the office, pushing his way impatiently through the crowd.

In the dim light of the crypt, Longstreet's eyes caught Katie Christine looking up innocently. He watched her as she spoke in that little-girl voice of hers, which sounded so much like her mother's: "Please, mister," she said, "I better go see my Daddy."

"Soon, Katie. Soon," he said, thinking to himself: *Just a little longer; they must twist a little more.*

He knew he had selected the perfect spot for their seclusion: right under the frantic searchers above. The buried crypt was closed to the public. No one would think to look for them mere steps from the family. The police would be combing the highways, closing off escape routes, halting traffic, searching everywhere but right under their feet. When questioned later, Longstreet would profess to know nothing of the search. He was simply watching over a lost child.

He knelt next to the little girl and placed a soft hand in the middle of her back, holding her gently. "We need to talk a little more about your Daddy, Katie Christine, and what he has to do. Okay?"

She nodded, accepting the adult's instruction, as she had been taught to do.

"Come with me," he said. "Let's sit in the corner and practice again."

Longstreet took her by the shoulder and walked toward the far wall of the room, next to a tiny spotlight beside a metal door. She stood facing away from him. He bent down behind her and brought his hands to the collar of her dress, grasping one button carefully with his fingertips.

She stood perfectly still as he manipulated the button, sliding it through the narrow slot to re-secure her dress.

"Your top came loose, dear," he said. "We mustn't have that."

She turned and thanked him—just as she had been taught to do.

"Remember what I told you earlier?" Longstreet said,

fluffing the sleeves of her dress.

She mumbled something that sounded like "yes."

"Put your jacket on, honey. It's cold outside." She did as instructed. He held her arms firmly. "Do *exactly* as I said, dear, and only talk to Daddy, okay?"

Her head moved up and down. Then she leaned forward and pecked him lightly on the cheek. Turning quickly, she hurried toward the doorway, held open by Longstreet's assistant. Scurrying out of the room, she ran toward the daylight that spilled into the darkened chamber like an unfriendly intruder.

On the chaplain's phone, Trey spoke with as much patience as he could muster, explaining to the FBI agent once again how Longstreet's home and office had to be *searched;* the agents had to understand the man was key to Katie's disappearance, whether Trey could prove it or not.

"There must be clues there," he said. "The longer we wait to get access, the farther away they get."

He listened to the federal officer drone on, explaining once more how no judge was going to issue a warrant without more to go on. While the agent spoke, Trey tried to ignore the commotion behind him. But the noise was too much. He whirled around to quiet the uproar.

He was stunned by what he saw.

Katie was standing there in the open doorway surrounded by cops and guards, her new Christmas doll clutched in one hand.

"Good God." He dropped the phone and rushed to her.

Was this a dream? Was she really safe? Had she simply been lost all this time?

It didn't matter. He could feel her in his arms and hear the sound of her breathing in his ear.

She *was* here. Safe again.

He pressed her to him, harder than he realized. "Where in the world were you?" His voice was louder than he intended, and she started to cry.

He brushed back her hair, trying to calm her, and himself. Then he asked again: "Where were you, baby? You scared us."

"I went to the bathroom," she said, sniffling.

He grabbed a tissue off the clerk's desk and had her blow her nose.

"A man took me for an ice cream. He said he was a friend of yours."

Trey wiped her face where it was streaked with tears. "A friend of mine?"

"Uh huh. He took me to the commissary."

Kneeling in front of her, he held onto her tightly, unable to let go. "Where is this man?"

"We went through the big door under the chapel."

Trey knew exactly where she meant. At the side of the chapel, a granite stairway led down to a massive steel door that protected the entryway to the John Paul Jones crypt; Trey had visited the site many times during his under-grad years.

"Let's see if we can find your mother," he said.

He swept his daughter up in his arms and walked outside, spotting Jazz not far from where she was before. She was talking with Irma, who was still distraught and blaming herself. Trey met them in the middle of the road and handed Katie to her mother.

"Go to the limousine," he instructed. "I'll meet you there."

"Where was she?" Jazz asked, tears flooding down her face.

"She'll tell you all about it."

"Where're you going?"

"To meet someone who says he's my friend."

Trey turned and marched off toward the chapel, his arms swinging wildly. He had no idea what he'd do when he saw this so-called friend, but if his growing rage were any indication, it wouldn't be good.

He swept around the corner of the chapel and down the steps to the double doors. Before entering the crypt, he paused to let his eyes adjust to the light. As he stepped inside, he saw the elaborate sarcophagus in the middle of the room slowly come into view.

He glanced around, catching glimpses of memorabilia displayed in wall niches here and there.

On the left side, he spotted an older man viewing a large bust of Admiral Jones. Opposite him was a second man, standing well over six feet—*shaved head and a diamond-stud earring.* Trey raced over and grabbed the first man's shoulder. Spinning him around, he slammed him up against the wall, knocking his thick glasses sideways.

"You ever touch my daughter again," he screamed, his voice breaking, "I'll rip your heart out." His hands moved to the man's neck, squeezing until his fingers dug into the loose flesh.

Longstreet made a choking sound, holding onto Trey's arms with both his hands, trying to speak.

"I . . . I helped your little girl," he managed to cough. "I thought you'd be glad."

"I'm no idiot. I know exactly what you're up to."

He looked over at the bald-headed thug and was seized with the urge to bash in his face, too, to push both their heads straight through the concrete wall.

But then he heard the sound of a weapon being cocked behind him. Looking back, he saw a Marine guard standing

252

with his rifle at ready-arms.

"I don't know what's going on here, gentlemen," the guard said, "but take it outside. This is hallowed ground."

Trey relaxed his grip.

"That's not necessary, corporal," he said. He looked back to Longstreet with disgust. "As far as I'm concerned, we're done here."

He walked to the exit. Before stepping into the sunlight, he stopped and spoke over his shoulder: "No government office in the world is worth my family. You want my vote that bad, you can have it. Just leave us the hell alone."

His hands trembling, Longstreet tried to smooth down his mussed hair. He didn't say a word; he only grinned that incessant, sickening smile of his.

Trey stalked out of the room into the harsh mid-day light. Outside, he paused for a moment to stop the shaking inside. Then he hurried back toward the limo.

As he approached the car, he saw Governor Weddington and Laura standing several vehicles away. Laura held up his Navy cap and called out: "Trey, your hat."

But he didn't acknowledge her; he jumped in the back seat and wrapped an arm tightly around Katie.

"Get us home now, driver," he demanded.

The car pulled away slowly.

"Hurry it up," Trey said. "Run over anybody who gets in our way."

The limo roared out of the drive, just as Longstreet came up the steps to watch them depart.

He turned to his companion with a look that could only be described as utter satisfaction. "I told you the daughter was our best weapon."

Steele shook his head and sauntered off, leaving Longstreet to revel in his total victory.

Chapter Twenty-Nine

Trey pulled up the collar of his old pea coat jacket and buttoned the top. A bitter, biting wind came out of the north, nipping at his face. He knelt at the shore end of the weathered dock that stretched like a fallen mast into the sea. Jazz was right. The redwood planks where the pilings were affixed were rotted underneath. He cursed himself for not paying more attention. Dad never would have let it get this way. He was vigilant about maintenance on the house, on the boat, on the dock. He was relentless about taking care of things. But Trey had waited too long. The entire decking would have to be replaced, before the rot spread and the pilings were split beyond repair.

He stood and walked to the far end of the dock and rested one foot on the bulwark of the family boat, feeling it rock rhythmically in the morning swells. He heard an osprey cry out overhead. The bird, a giant in the species, had nested on the Stone property for years. Its smaller, female mate was back at the nest feeding their brood of one high up in a towering oak along the gravel drive.

Mesmerized, Trey watched the dark-winged hawk glide effortlessly over the drafts of air, like a tail-less fighter kite.

"Osgood on the hunt again?"

He turned and saw Jazz walk up quietly. He reached out and took her by the hand. "He's not a happy camper. Slim pickings this time of year."

Osgood was Jazz's name for their largest feathered resident; she called the smaller, gray-toned spouse, Abigail.

254

She had yet to come up with a name for the baby. She had to see the youngster in flight first.

They stood, hand in hand, and watched Osgood scout the waters near a commercial trawler anchored far offshore.

"I'll bet he has more luck than that fishing boat," Trey said.

"I've seen a few of them moored around here," Jazz said. "But I haven't seen them bring in anything yet."

"This isn't the best season for commercial hauls," he replied.

They didn't speak for a minute or two, allowing the fresh, cold air to wash over them, sweeping away the residue of the last few days.

Jazz let go of his hand and moved over by the yacht. "Did you *really* tell Longstreet he could have your vote?" She knew the answer, of course. It was just her way of re-opening a topic Trey had hoped he had closed.

"I didn't have any choice. The man's capable of anything, and I can't take any more chances—not when it comes to you and Katie. This isn't a war, it's a damn election. I choose not to fight."

"Why don't you go to the President, Trey? Forsythe can't possibly condone what Longstreet's done, or threatened to do."

"What's he done? I've got no proof he was involved in the letters or the car crash. At the funeral, he bought a little girl an ice cream. Is that a crime? We've got no evidence, Jazz. If I went to Forsythe, I'd sound like a lunatic. The FBI already thinks I'm paranoid. I told them I've been followed, but they haven't seen anyone. They know I've gotten anonymous e-mails and calls, but name me a congressman who hasn't? Especially one who's at the center of a Presidential election."

He stepped aboard the boat and faced Jazz, who was looking away from him, refusing to acknowledge his argument.

"You didn't hear the President at Camp David or on the phone the other day," he said. "He's determined to win this election. He doesn't give a damn what it takes. He may not agree with Longstreet's behavior, but he won't stop it either. The only person who can stop Longstreet is me—by giving him what he wants."

She swung around and looked into his eyes. "Whatever you decide, I'll support you."

"Then it's Forsythe in January."

"If that's what you want, I'll back your decision. If you think it's right, that's all that matters to me."

"It's right."

"You're sure?"

"I've got my priorities straight."

"You're absolutely sure? There's no turning back, you know."

"Jesus, I feel like I'm being interrogated. I'm sure—I'm absolutely sure. Positively sure. What do you want from me?"

"I want to believe you, Trey, and I don't. When you believe it, I'll believe it."

He turned away and looked at Osgood again. The bird was still on the hunt, relentlessly swooping overhead, his eyes like scopes on the water below, scanning the surface, waiting for the precise moment to dive and strike. *Sometimes,* Trey thought, *Jazz was like that damn hawk. Her words could grab like talons.*

"I've got one possibility to explore," he said. "It's a long shot—a very long shot."

Jazz tucked her arms inside her jacket, hiding her claw-like nails.

"If I can arrange it," he said, "I'm going to talk with the senior congressman from Maine."

"Van Deventer?"

"Yes. If I can get a hold of him, I'll fly up there right away."

"What's this last-ditch idea of yours?"

He took a deep breath. "I've been thinking about what you said when we got back from Camp David."

"What was that?"

"You asked, what would happen if I voted for Forsythe and he still lost? He couldn't blame me, right?"

"I wouldn't think so."

"That's why I've got to talk with Van Deventer."

He looked at her sideways, then pointed a mock-menacing finger at her and said, "If this doesn't work, I'm sticking with plan 'A'—support for Forsythe. I don't want any second-guessing."

"Second-guessing from me? Please." She turned toward shore, and Trey followed. He watched her walk in front, gazing at the wispy red hairs that spilled out from underneath her beret, the strands playing at the nape of her neck. Normally, he would take her arm and walk with her through the sand, up the embankment to their house on the hill. But his mind was elsewhere. His thoughts were focused on the vote—for the millionth time.

Only one week to go before the election, and he was no more decided now than when all this began nearly two months ago. But his family's safety and his own political future were more at stake than ever, and he was about to hinge everything on a backwoods congressman from Maine, a man Trey barely knew—a man who had no good reason to help, and a lot of good reasons not to.

Chapter Thirty

Trey peeked out the porthole window of his chartered jet. The runway below looked shiny in spots. A thin coating of fresh snow obliterated the lines and signs. He was glad Jerry Rogers was at the controls. Rogers was an experienced wartime flyer who could land a plane on the deck of a rowboat if he had to.

As expected, Trey's handpicked pilot brought the Lear down softly, expertly, then threw the engines into reverse, powering down in a perfect, sweeping right-hand turn. When they stopped in front of a small, private hangar, Trey pried his fingers loose from the arms of his seat and gathered his briefcase and overcoat.

The steward opened the door. Trey thanked his two-man crew for getting him here safely, and briefly argued with his bodyguard one last time.

"This is something I've got to do alone, Rick," he said. "I appreciate your concern, but I'll be fine."

Everyone agreed to wait for him at the airport, knowing the visit with Van Deventer could take all night.

Trey ducked through the exit and onto the clanky metal stairs, feeling a blast of cold air like needles on his skin. He hurried down the steps and met Van Deventer walking out of the hangar.

The senior congressman looked older than Trey remembered. His complexion was a pale yellow, and he was hunched over against the gale-like winds that blew snow sideways across the runway. Van Deventer reached out a bare hand. Trey pulled off his glove to shake.

"Welcome to Winter Wonderland," Van Deventer said, trying to smile through a frozen face. "There's nothing like Maine in December."

"Except Maine in January, February and March," Trey said, smiling.

Van Deventer laughed and pulled his hand away to cover his mouth as he coughed.

"Let's get out of this weather before we both get pneumonia," Trey said.

Van Deventer led the way through a chain link fence to a parking lot. He motioned Trey to climb in the passenger side of a Range Rover by the gate.

They slammed the doors to seal off the brutal world outside. Van Deventer fired up the V8 and cranked on the heater; Trey pulled off his gloves to warm his hands by the vent.

"My cabin's thirty minutes from here," Van Deventer said. "It's not a bad ride. Roads are pretty clear."

He jammed the vehicle into gear and pulled away a little faster than Trey would have liked in these conditions.

A wet, sleety snow plastered the windshield as they pulled onto a four-lane road leading east toward the hills above Bangor. They drove for less than ten minutes before turning off the highway and heading due north on an unlit, two-lane road.

Through the headlights, Trey could make out giant fir trees and other evergreens rising like a picket fence on either side of the shoulder. Not much room for error out here. Not another car in sight, either. No homes or businesses. It was not the kind of place to break down during a storm. The only comfort was a mobile phone mounted on the console between them.

"My place is beside Nicatous Lake, about twenty minutes from here," Van Deventer said. "Ever been to this part of the country?"

"I've visited Maine on occasion," Trey said. "Mostly around Portland and Kennebunkport."

Van Deventer smirked. "Typical tourist spots."

"At a typical tourist time of the year, too," he replied. "Summer."

Van Deventer chuckled. He seemed in a jovial mood. Trey figured he didn't get much company this time of year. He knew Van Deventer's wife had died not long ago, and he had no children. He lived by himself in a cabin in the woods. It probably got pretty lonely around the holidays.

"I'm about to show you paradise," Van Deventer said. "There's nothing like celebrating winter with a new snowfall on a crystal lake in the Maine woods. You'll see that for yourself."

"I appreciate your meeting me like this, Neil. Especially on such short notice."

"I'm just thankful for the attention, and for the opportunity to show off the nation's most beautiful state. No offense intended to you Chesapeakeans, of course."

"Of course."

"I've lived in this area all my life," he said. "The same as my father and his father before him. The first Van Deventers founded much of this land. They developed the first businesses, too, always with an eye toward preserving the environment."

"From what I can tell, they did an outstanding job."

Van Deventer swung the truck through a sharp left-hand turn, the headlights following a split second behind.

"If you've got time, I'll show you around," he said, "It's important for all congressmen to experience the culture of other areas. Helps to understand where your colleagues are coming from, you know?"

"Most of us don't take the time, unfortunately. We're too concerned with our own voters to worry about others."

"When I first came to the Hill, there was a gentleman's understanding—you never openly criticized your fellow representatives. Things were much more pleasant then. We got just as much done, but in a more civil way."

"It's a lost art, I'm afraid."

Van Deventer slowed the vehicle to a crawl and pointed out the left side to a valley that opened below. A few lights sparkled up the hillside through the foliage.

"That's why Maine's called the Pine Tree State," he said. "It's dominated by evergreens, so it's beautiful year-round." He stopped the car like a tour guide at an historical monument. "Not many people know it, but Leif Ericson landed here five hundred years before Columbus. Maine had the first settlement in North America, too, though Jamestown got the credit. We also had the first naval battle of the American Revolution." He grinned broadly, as if he'd been there with them.

Trey was glad to see a fellow congressman so enthusiastic about the history and accomplishments of his state.

Van Deventer gunned the engine and wheeled around a tight curve, then steered off the paved road onto a dirt stretch that wound through deep woods to a clearing beside a giant lake.

He ground the vehicle to a stop next to a two-story log cabin. The two men sat and looked out over the shrouded water silently, reverently. The snow had stopped, and the moon came out from behind a cloud; Nicatous Lake emerged like a shimmering jewel from the fog.

Trey shook his head. "Wow." It was the best he could

manage. It was more than enough.

"That's the reaction this place always gets," Van Deventer said. He drew himself up closer to the view outside. "We have a motto here. *'Dirigo.'* It's Indian for 'I lead.' Around here, you have to lead. You learn that real quick walking these hills."

They gathered up their belongings and made their way toward the back door. The snow was nearly four feet high in spots; Trey followed as Van Deventer cut a path.

Inside the mudroom, they yanked off their coats and boots. Van Deventer pulled on a pair of old leather slippers and handed a new pair to Trey.

Van Deventer then led the way to the front of the house. As he clicked on lights, the interior seemed to come alive. They passed a large kitchen and a formal dining room to a step-down family room with a massive rock fireplace, where a small fire was still alive, nudged by a gas flame. The house had the look of a cabin but the feel of a home. A woman's touch was evident throughout—from the coordinated furnishings to the lacy curtains over the window frames.

"Can I fix you a drink, Congressman?" Van Deventer said, stirring one for himself.

"Whatever you're having's fine."

"I'm a hot toddy man. Warm cider with a shot of cold Turkey."

"Make that two shots and you're on."

Van Deventer grinned. "You're a man after my own heart."

Trey picked up a poker and stirred the logs. "I hope so, Congressman. Believe me, I hope so."

Van Deventer handed him the drink, and they toasted.

"Make yourself comfortable," Van Deventer said, gesturing toward an easy chair, one of two facing the fireplace.

"I've got beef stew on the stove and homemade bread in the oven." He checked his watch. "Ought to be done in a half-hour or so."

"You're very kind, Neil. I don't know how to thank you."

Van Deventer rested back in his chair. "It's my pleasure. Besides, you may not want to thank me at all by the time your business is done."

Trey sipped the hot cider. It warmed him all the way down, like the first nip of a perfect martini. The fire began to roar, creating a warm glow inside and out. "I take it the lovely lady in the photo there's your wife," he said.

"My dear, departed wife of nearly forty years, Emily. She died last year 'bout this same time. Went fast, though. Didn't suffer. I thank God for that."

"I know how tough that must've been, and still is."

"I have my moments."

"I've got a lovely wife of my own," Trey said. "I can't imagine going on without her. You're to be commended for holding up so well."

"Emily'd have it no other way." He slugged down the rest of his cider and coughed for several seconds. Resting his head back, he slowly regained composure. "Emily's the reason I got into politics. She got tired of hearing me belly-ache about the incompetence of the local town council. She said, 'Put up or shut up.' Next thing I knew, I was mayor, then county freeholder, then state assemblyman, finally, congressman. I had a hankering to move into the Senate," he said, "but never could get party backing. Too much of a maverick, I suppose."

"I sensed that about you, Neil," Trey said. "That's why I'm here tonight."

Van Deventer got up to freshen his drink. "Is this where we talk business?"

Trey nodded. "I've done nothing but think about this conversation for the last twenty-four hours. Now that it's here, I'm at a loss."

Van Deventer handed him a new mug of cider. "Maybe this'll loosen you up."

Trey set the drink aside. Moving forward in his chair, he faced Van Deventer square on. "From our brief conversation at Camp David, it was apparent to me you've worked out an attractive agreement with the Administration to support Forsythe's re-election."

Van Deventer shrugged. "It's not attractive for me personally, but for the state of Maine—for my constituents. I owe them that and a whole lot more."

"I don't question your right to serve the voters of your state, Neil," Trey said, "but I came here to ask you to reconsider." He waited for a reaction; Van Deventer stared ahead, unflinching, and Trey went on. "Forsythe doesn't deserve to win this election. He doesn't deserve to be President."

Van Deventer got up and stood by the fire, one foot on the riser. "I can't worry about who deserves what in this election, frankly. I promised Forsythe I'd deliver Maine, and I intend to do it."

Trey stood next to him. Here was the moment he was dreading. He would have to tell Van Deventer everything. It was the only way to prove the President and his people had had thrown away all integrity, all principle to win. It was the only way to convince him Forsythe was trying to extort his own re-election.

"Mind if I tell you a short version of a very long story?" Trey said. "It might help you understand why I feel as I do."

"Have at it."

Trey went on to tell of the threatening calls, the letters,

the intimidation, the car "accident," and how he was sure the President's people were behind it all. He told about the meeting at Camp David where Forsythe made it clear he'd do whatever was required to secure his own return to office. He also told about the Christmas Day conversation with the President, and the confrontation with Longstreet at the funeral.

Van Deventer occasionally interrupted with questions and clarifications; Trey's short story turned long. The two men moved into the kitchen and ate steaming bowls of stew and hot buttered bread.

At Van Deventer's suggestion, they pulled on heavy coats and moved onto the front porch for a cup of coffee and a breath of fresh air—and to watch the last of a fading moon disappear behind gathering clouds.

Trey leaned on the porch rail and took in the awesome silence that always accompanies new-fallen snow. The scene was like something out of Currier and Ives. Evergreen branches laden with white. A perfectly still lake shining up through the trees like a tinted mirror. The temperature had warmed up ten or fifteen degrees, as often happens after a storm. They stood in their slippers and gazed into the distance like two explorers on the edge of a beckoning frontier. In many ways, that's exactly what they were. But their frontier was seven hundred miles south—in the marbled halls of Congress, where history was about to be made. One way or the other.

Trey brushed snow off the railing and sat on it sideways. "I have to admit I haven't told you everything, Neil."

Van Deventer sat in a low-slung wooden chair. "I thought there might be more."

"Earlier this year, I made a big mistake—a very big mistake. I helped out a friend during the course of a banking investigation. At the time, I didn't realize federal laws had been broken, but they were—not by me—but by my friend. Still, it could be made to look like I was involved. I swear to you tonight I was not. I was stupid, yes—criminal, no." He took a deep breath. "But the White House has made it clear they'll level criminal charges if I don't support Forsythe."

Van Deventer whistled. "These boys are playing hardball. What happens if you do support Forsythe—they'll let the charges go?"

"Yes. Not only that, the President essentially said I could name my price. He offered me a position in the Administration."

Van Deventer tried to get comfortable on the hard, damp seat. "Let me see if I've got this. If you don't support Forsythe, you could go to jail. If you do support him, you'll go to the White House. Does that sum it up?"

"I can't make it any clearer than that."

"Can I be honest with you, Mr. Stone?"

"Please."

"Most people'd say, 'I don't see the problem here.' "

Trey nodded. He stepped over in front of Van Deventer, and the old, slump-shouldered congressman leaned back and stared up. "But you're not 'most people,' are you, Neil? I get the feeling you're as uneasy about this as I am. You don't like Forsythe and his slimy ways any more than I do."

"I'm no fan of the man," he said. "I've never made any bones about that. But this vote's not about my personal opinion of the President."

"Sure it is." Trey took a step back. "We're two men who, like it or not, hold enormous power right now. We can 'thumbs up' or 'thumbs down' a sitting President. That hasn't happened often in the history of this country—may never happen again. Now's the time to make a decision that's good for the nation, not for just ourselves."

Van Deventer ran a hand over his face and got up. Moving away a few steps, he suddenly turned back.

"Just for the sake of argument, let's say I agree with you. What difference would it make? If either of us withholds support from Forsythe, the man loses. What do you need me for? Why don't you just vote your own conscience and leave me out of this?"

"Call it selfishness. I don't want to give the President and his henchmen the pleasure of bringing me down with them," Trey said. "That's part of it, anyway."

"What's the other part?"

"The safety of my family. I don't know how far these guys will go to get my vote—and I don't want to find out."

Van Deventer rubbed his chin thoughtfully. He paced a little more, then stared out at the lake again, speaking in a low, resigned voice. "I never trusted Forsythe—few people do. But I've already promised him my support. I'm not in the habit of going back on my word."

This was where Trey knew he had to offer something more than a simple change of vote; he needed more leverage with a man who prided himself on loyalty and tradition.

"You promised the President you wouldn't support Wardlow, right?"

"That was my commitment."

"I'm not asking you to change that," Trey said.

Van Deventer turned to him, confusion etched in his eyes. "I don't get it."

Trey took a step closer, realizing he had captured the fascination of this old political warhorse who could still take pleasure from a well-conceived legislative strategy.

"Maine's voters were split in November, right?" Trey asked.

"As split as they could be."

"That's how I want you to vote in January—divided."

"What the hell's that? I'm not sure we can do that." Van Deventer began to pace the length of the porch.

"You can do it all right," Trey said. "During the election of 1824—John Quincy Adams versus Andrew Jackson—the House passed a rule. It says this: If a state delegation can't support one candidate, they can cast a 'divided' ballot. It amounts to a pass. The rule's still on the books."

"I wasn't aware . . ." He sat down. "But what's this 'divided' vote accomplish?"

"It guarantees a second ballot."

Van Deventer thought hard for a moment, a finger pressed to his lips. "You're saying, with a big Republican majority in the House, a second ballot assures Wardlow's election."

"That's my belief."

Van Deventer turned and walked over to a canvas-covered porch-swing. Sitting down, he stared at the floorboards beneath his feet.

"So if Maine votes divided," he said, "neither of us can be the deciding ballot."

"No matter what Maryland does, no one gets a majority."

Van Deventer didn't seem to know what to say next; Trey went on quickly. "Look, Neil, this is not about me or you, or Maine or Maryland. This is about whether our country can afford four more years of an ineffective, corrupt Administration. Can we afford a second term by a President who's so afraid of losing power he'll run over anyone who gets in his way? This is about a President who'll resort to bribery and extortion to get what he wants."

Trey paused to calm himself; he felt the anger building inside and didn't want to come across as vindictive.

"This is also about a candidate who deserves the Oval Office," he went on. "Wardlow won the election. He'd be taking the oath of office next month if not for an Independent candidate who's trading his votes like baseball cards. Ask yourself this: Do we have the right to go against the voters of this country? They elected a new President. Wardlow won the popular vote in a landslide, and he won the most Electoral College support. Whatever I think or you think—whatever sweetheart deals we've worked out—we owe the voters of this country their man. You said it before: This is about leading, not following. This is about creating firsts, not settling for second best. It's about each of us— you and me—doing the right thing."

Van Deventer rested back, watching the last of his coffee grains swirl in the bottom of his cup. He didn't respond for several long, agonizing minutes. Finally, he placed a hand on the arm of his seat and hoisted himself up.

"It's getting chilly out here, Congressman. Can I interest you in a warmer-upper?"

Trey followed him inside. Van Deventer poured two cognacs in large snifters and sat back in his easy chair. Trey stood by the hearth. After awhile, Van Deventer spoke in a near whisper.

"When I first went into politics, I didn't like it all that much. Too much arguing, not enough *doing*. Eventually, I learned the power of compromise—how to give up something to get something. The trick's not to give up too much."

Trey rolled the cognac around in his glass, watching the amber liquid paint the sides an orange-ish brown.

"In all my years in public service," Van Deventer said, "only a couple of times did I truly regret a compromise I struck. One of those times was a few weeks ago."

Trey looked up, intrigued. "Why's that?"

Van Deventer glanced away. In the firelight, he appeared even older than before. The flickering shadows seemed to wash the features from his face, leaving behind a flat, emotionless expression.

"You've been honest with me, Trey, and you deserve the same in return." He leaned forward. "I loved my wife—more than life itself—but I wasn't always faithful. That's something I've had to live with for a long time."

He sighed, and Trey could tell he was struggling to get this out; he leaned in closer to listen.

"Thirty years ago, I got another woman pregnant. It's a long story. The woman used to work for me. I tried to convince her to have an abortion. At the time, I couldn't afford the scandal. It would've ended my political career."

Trey shook his head. "Thirty years ago, adultery was still a sin for politicians," Trey said. "Times have changed."

Van Deventer went on. "The girl wouldn't do it. I never could figure out why. I was gonna pick up all the cost, get the best doctor—everything." He sat back. "She gave birth to a bouncing baby boy. I helped her out with financial assistance—whatever I could do, but I never acknowledged him as my son. I didn't want to hurt Emily, you know?"

Trey shifted in his chair, wondering what all this had to do with the election.

"Funny thing is," Van Deventer said, "Emily knew all along. I found out the night she died. She said I should 'get to know' the one person I had stayed away from for too long." Smiling to himself, he appeared to remember those last few hours together. "When I asked her to explain, she told me *she* was the one who convinced the other woman to keep the child. She never said a thing to me—to protect me, I guess, the same way I tried to protect her."

"Sounds like something out of O Henry."

"Yes, 'Gift of the Magi,' and all that."

A comfortable quiet slowly grew around them. Neither man felt the need to fill the silence. Still, Trey wondered what the story meant and why Van Deventer felt compelled to tell it now. He figured it was just an old man reminiscing after a little too much to drink.

But then he went on.

"I don't need to go into particulars tonight. Suffice it to say, part of my deal with the President concerned that son of mine. I wanted to do something special for him. I took this opportunity to do that."

Trey squinted at Van Deventer through the firelight, wondering just what kind of deal they had struck; this election was getting sleazier by the moment.

"They got the better of me," Van Deventer said. "I struck a devil's bargain. It wouldn't have made Emily proud, I can tell you that."

Trey saw Van Deventer wipe away a tear, and he thought to himself, this election had gone more wrong than anyone could have imagined. It was all about deals cut and threats made while real people were getting sacrificed in the process. Trey also realized both men had bared their souls tonight. They needed time to reflect and recharge; this wasn't the time to continue the conversation.

He set his drink aside. "I better make a phone call. I should let my wife know when I'm coming home."

"I've got phones all over the place. Grab any one you want. There's one in the guest bedroom."

"While I'm at it, I think I'll hit the sack, Neil."

"Sounds like a capital idea, Congressman. I'm right behind you."

Trey walked to the hallway at the rear of the room, and

slowly turned back. "Thanks for the hospitality and for taking the time to listen."

Van Deventer waved over the back of his chair. "Same to you. That's what we politicians ought to do more of—listening. We'd all be better served."

Trey headed down the hallway, listening to Van Deventer hum a mysterious, haunting melody. Trey told himself he'd have to ask about the song in the morning. But tonight, he could think of nothing but sleep. He was exhausted from the trip, the food, the drink and especially the conversation. Trey knew he had taken a big chance telling his story. He might wake up in the morning to find out the risk was for nothing. But right now, he didn't care. He just wanted to collapse into a deep, dreamless sleep where his mind could escape from itself.

And maybe Van Deventer's would do the same.

In a camouflaged radio truck parked deep in the woods a quarter mile away, Steele warmed his hands over a space heater and smiled to himself. Pulling off his oversized headset, he tossed it aside.

"That's enough for tonight," he said. "Tape Stone's phone call, then give me a copy of the whole conversation."

The second man in the truck slipped a CD in the recording drive and flipped a switch.

"Beautiful," Steele said, grabbing his belongings. "Just beautiful. This recording is going straight back to D.C. tonight. That beady-eyed Longstreet is gonna get out of bed to listen to this. I told him it's going to take a lot more than 'intimidation' to bring this guy around."

Steele pulled on a heavy overcoat and knee-high boots. "One of these days that 'suit' in the White House is going to learn I know what I'm talking about. You don't play 'cutesy' when everything's on the line. You go for the jugular."

He grabbed the CD from his partner, shoved it inside his briefcase, and stepped into the icy cold. "Stone has left us no other options. It's time to end this."

He slammed the door and headed out into the night.

Chapter Thirty-One

Trey pulled back the comforter and shielded his face from the morning light glinting off newly-driven snow. *Good Lord,* he thought, *it must be nine o'clock.* He checked his watch: eight twenty-five. He swung his feet to the floor and rubbed sleep from his eyes. He knew he'd have to call Jerry immediately and get him to warm up the plane; Trey had wanted to be on his way home by now.

He jumped up, dressed quickly and headed for the front of the cabin. But he came across his host in the kitchen.

"Morning," Van Deventer chirped. "Coffee's on the stove. If you want cream or sugar, it's on the table. I'm scrambling up some eggs and frying us a little Maine-cured bacon. You game?"

"I'm hungry as a bear," Trey said, pouring a cup of pitch-black coffee. "I'll have to eat fast, though. I've got to get back before my wife and daughter disown me."

"Won't take but fifteen minutes to cook this up. You'll need it for the trip home."

"Thanks, Neil. Mind if I clean up a bit?"

"The bathroom's all yours." Van Deventer pointed a spatula down the hall, and Trey hurried off.

With a quick shave and a comb through his hair, he figured he'd be presentable enough for the plane ride at least. After a splash of ice-cold water to rinse the sleep from his eyes, he hurried back to the kitchen.

Just as Van Deventer had predicted, breakfast had taken fifteen minutes from pan to plate. Trey found two heaping portions of eggs, bacon and buttered toast on the table.

The two men ate with gusto, the meal helping to clear their heads from a night of too much whiskey and cognac.

Neither of them mentioned the conversation from the evening before; Trey knew Van Deventer would need time to mull over his proposal.

"Too bad you can't stay longer," Van Deventer said. "It's the perfect time to explore these hills. I've got snow-shoes in the shed and ski poles. Sure you don't want to enjoy a fine winter day while you still can?"

"I've already enjoyed myself immensely, Neil. You've been the consummate host. I can't thank you enough for your graciousness and hospitality."

"But you've got to go, anyway, right?"

Trey smiled.

"A grizzled old mountain man hasn't got a prayer against a beautiful wife and lovely daughter. I don't blame you. If it were me, I'd do the same."

"Are the roads clear enough to get us to the airport in thirty minutes?"

"I can make it in twenty."

"No, no." Trey waved a hand. "Thirty's fine. It takes the pilot that long to warm up the plane."

A half-hour later, they climbed into the utility vehicle for the drive back. On the way, Van Deventer took a few moments to stop and point out a landmark or two, including a stone monument to Maine's Civil War brigade.

As the two men sat there viewing the statue cut out of rock, the old congressman began to hum that same, haunting melody from last night. Trey asked him about it.

"It's an old Dutch folk song," Van Deventer said. "It's a story about a little boy who loses a precious gem. He blames the error on his friend, then winds up losing the friend."

Trey nodded. "Those old folk tales always seem to capture life so perfectly," Trey said, "and so truthfully."

Van Deventer glanced at Trey out of the corner of his eye. He appeared ready to say something, but jammed the truck into gear and silently drove on down the road.

A few minutes later, he wheeled into the same parking spot they had left less than fourteen hours ago. It seemed as if a week had passed. In the last several hours, Trey had laid his career on the line and trusted a man he barely knew with information that could destroy him, or put an end to an Administration that did not deserve to go on.

They sat for a long time silently staring out the windshield at the warming jet. Then they both slowly crawled out of the jeep and walked side-by-side to the waiting plane, stopping at the bottom of the ramp. Trey reached out and took Van Deventer's hand in his.

"I can't thank you enough, Neil. No matter how this vote goes, I owe you a lot just for hearing me out. One word of caution: Be extra careful. These guys play for keeps."

"I'm always careful when it comes to politics." Van Deventer looked away for an instant. Then he spoke again in a low, hesitant voice.

"I know it wasn't easy for you to come here, but I appreciate your making the pilgrimage. I learned a few mighty important things last night. One of them was to remember a promise I made to myself."

"What was that?"

Van Deventer rested a hand on Trey's shoulder. "When I got elected to office the first time, I said I'd be willing to compromise on the issues, but not on my principles. It's a commitment I'd forgotten over the years."

Trey nodded solemnly, wishing he had kept a similar commitment the last few months.

"I remembered something last night, too," Trey said. "It was what my Dad told me a long time ago. He said doing the right thing isn't always easy, but it's always right." He laid a hand on Van Deventer's shoulder. "I just hope we both do the right thing in the coming days, Neil."

Without waiting for a response, Trey turned and jogged up the metal steps. When he got to the top, he wheeled around and waved.

Van Deventer spoke out from the bottom of the stairs, his voice sounding stronger than before. "You've got a long, bright career in front of you, Congressman. One day, I'll be able to look back and say I had a little something to do with your success."

Trey knew it was a subtle message, but a clear one. Van Deventer was telling him he had made his decision.

The aging politician then stepped back and shouted over the whine of the turbines. "Remember our state motto. *Dirigo.*" He waved once, then turned and walked away.

Trey called out: *"I lead."* But Van Deventer was too far away to hear. Trey grinned and ducked inside the jet, the door slamming behind him. He strapped himself in for the two-hour flight home, thinking the ride just got a whole lot shorter.

Chapter Thirty-Two

After an uneventful flight home, the Lear touched down at Washington National at the stroke of noon. Trey hurried out of the jet and jumped behind the wheel of his waiting town car. With his bodyguard riding shotgun, he pulled out in a hurry for the fifteen-minute drive to downtown D.C.

On the flight in, Trey had made a series of phone calls. The first one was to Jazz and Katie, telling them he would be home by three; both of them were just glad to hear he was back safe.

The other calls were to his fellow congressmen from Maryland. Four of the seven representatives agreed to meet him on short notice at the Cannon Building at one o'clock. The rest were to tie in by conference call.

Trey's plan was to put the second piece of his voting strategy in place by telling his congressional colleagues whom he planned to support in the election. When he announced Forsythe, everyone would automatically assume the President had locked up his re-election.

Only Trey and Van Deventer would know any different.

The ride to D.C. passed in a flash. Trey pulled into the underground garage and parked. Scrambling out of the car, he rushed through the building's basement entrance with his bodyguard trailing a half-step behind.

Inside the cavernous facility, the halls were like a mausoleum. But Trey was anything but somber. He could even hear an extra bounce in his own step. Yesterday at this time, he was at his lowest point, resigned to helping reelect

Forsythe for no other reason than to protect himself and his family. But now, with a little political luck and some help from an unexpected source, he was about to beat the White House at its own game.

Trey opened up his office and swept through the place, turning on lights. He put on a fresh pot of coffee, turned up the thermostat to ward off the winter chill and stationed his security guard outside.

Just as he began to check voice mail and e-mail, Bobby Buckland showed up—early, as usual. They greeted each other like the good friends they were and chatted idly about the holidays.

Miles Ogle wasn't far behind. He made himself comfortable, then two more representatives arrived—Steven Easterbrooke and Donald Moyers. Everyone got coffee and chatted about Christmas for a few minutes. Trey then set up a conference call with the state's other three representatives in the all-male contingent.

After a little general conversation, they got down to business.

"Gentlemen, I appreciate your taking time out of your holidays to join me for this informal conference," Trey said. "I promise not to take much of your time. With the vote closing in, I thought we'd better finalize our strategy."

As a lead-in, Trey reviewed the difficult position they all had found themselves. The entire contingent had been inundated with calls, letters, e-mails, articles, press conferences and unending public and private conversations about the election. It was as if the Presidential vote had become their only job.

"Despite the pressure, we have yet to take a formal nose count," Trey said. "Still, my intuition tells me I'm the tie-breaker. After all, the rumor mill isn't always wrong."

Everyone laughed nervously.

"The other Democrats and our lone Independent are supporting Forsythe, right?" They all nodded. "And our three Republicans are supporting Wardlow." He looked around; no disagreement. "If I side with my own party, we'll support Forsythe five to three. If I side with the other guys, we'll have a four-four split. Then we could try to reach a consensus, or we could vote divided."

Only Miles Ogle knew a divided vote was even possible. Trey quickly explained the legislative maneuver. He waited for questions.

Ogle was first to speak, going straight to the point. "Which is it, Trey? You've built enough suspense. Are you going Democrat or Republican?"

Trey looked around the room silently to let the tension build; he had to make this look as real as possible. While the others in the room fidgeted, he finally responded with the name few expected to hear.

"Forsythe."

Bobby Buckland sat back and breathed a sigh of relief. Miles Ogle nearly dropped his teacup. The other two Republicans slumped in their chairs; they had hoped Trey would go with Wardlow, since the two men had obviously hit it off. Also, Trey hadn't been shy about demeaning Forsythe's first-term record. Apparently, party loyalties had won out anyway.

After the announcement—and the animated conversation that followed—the meeting wound down with Trey trying to explain his public position for supporting Forsythe, saying he had "assurances" from the President of positive changes during his second term.

Looking around the room, Trey hoped his public posturing was convincing. He didn't believe his own words, but he had to make sure others did. From everyone's reaction, they appeared to accept his rationale, even though all the Republicans disagreed vehemently. Trey only hoped Forsythe and Longstreet would be convinced as easily.

One-by-one, everyone dropped out of the meeting. Trey knew they were anxious to spread the word. He was sure the "secret" announcement would sweep the streets of Washington like a howling winter storm. He shook hands with Easterbrooke and escorted him out, leaving only Buckland and Ogle alone with Trey.

The three men sat quietly for several moments before Ogle spoke.

"I hope you realize," he said, "your decision will lead to a divided White House. The Speaker is serious, Trey. If Wardlow loses this election, he'll see to it we get a Republican Vice President."

Trey nodded. "That's a bridge we'll have to jump off when we get to it, Miles."

Ogle cast his eyes to the floor, unable to find an adequate response. He stood up and collected his belongings.

"This election is shaping up to be a helluva thing for ourselves and our country," he said. "Let's hope for Democracy's sake it never happens again."

As Ogle walked out, Trey turned to face his most trusted adviser and confidant.

Before Trey could speak, Buckland jumped in.

"My, aren't you full of surprises today?" he said. "A few days ago, I was afraid you'd decided to go with Wardlow. Now you announce Forsythe out of the blue. Honestly, I'm stunned. You've never been one for partisanship—especially not when principle's at stake."

Trey sat down and leaned back in his chair, hands folded in his lap. "You think principle is at stake here, Bobby?"

The old congressman shook his shaggy head of hair and stared off into the distance, his coffee cup paused halfway to his mouth. He struggled to find the right words.

"You know better than anyone that principle is *always* at stake in our jobs."

Trey got up and moved over by the window looking out onto Independence Avenue. The Capitol Building appeared so close he could almost reach out and touch it. It was also farther away than ever, like an apparition barely out of reach. Trey knew Bobby was right. Principle was always at stake in political decisions, no matter how politicians tried to avoid the inevitable. The problem was, principles were never absolute. They changed according to the person and the times. No better example existed than this election.

Trey spoke over his shoulder. "As a fellow Democrat, I'm surprised you sound so unenthusiastic about my decision. I thought you'd be pleased."

Buckland shrugged. "Old age is gettin' to me, I guess." He sipped carefully from his cup. "I only wish there was another way, that's all. Forsythe's got all these charges hanging over him—suspect foreign deals, campaign irregularities."

He sipped again, watching Trey over the rim of his cup. Trey turned and leaned against the windowsill, intrigued by Buckland's newly found conscience.

"You sound like a man who'd prefer to support Wardlow himself."

Buckland shook his head vigorously. "I've been a Democrat for more than half a century. No one's going to find this old political warhorse putting the opposite party into office. I'll leave that up to others."

"Like me?"

He set his cup aside. "Let's say I'm glad you decided to support the President. It's the only reasonable decision.

You've got too much to lose to do anything else. We all do." He got up and moved toward the door. "We might as well face it, Forsythe's got another four years, and we'll just have to make the most of it."

Trey looked down, doing his damnedest to remain silent. He wanted to tell Bobby about his voting strategy, to explain the extraordinary pressures he was under, and how he had to resort to legislative manipulation to get the right result. But he could say nothing. An admission now might wind up undoing all his earlier preparations.

Instead, he remarked: "Maybe Forsythe'll win, and maybe he won't."

Buckland looked surprised. "What's that supposed to mean?"

"Just that no one should jump to conclusions. Forsythe hasn't won this thing yet."

"No, but he's won Maryland. That's essentially the same thing."

"He needs Maine, too."

"Maine announced its intentions weeks ago."

Trey gathered together a bunch of papers strewn across his desk, packing up his valise for the trip home.

"Political intentions have a way of changing under the right conditions, Bobby. You told me that more than once."

Looking suspicious, Buckland pulled on his overcoat. "You know something I don't?"

"Yes, that I'm late to see my wife and daughter."

Buckland held the door.

On the way out, Trey stopped and reached out a hand to his long-time mentor. "Happy New Year, Bobby," he said.

Buckland hesitated before reaching back. He finally took Trey's hand in both of his and held on tight.

"Let's hope it's a happy new year for everyone's sake," he said, solemnly.

Trey nodded and walked out.

He knew Buckland's legislative mind was churning as fast—if not faster—than his own. The long-awaited Presidential vote was finally reaching a crescendo. The only thing left to do now was figure out how to capitalize on the results. No one was better at that than Buckland. But the old legislator's prized pupil was learning fast.

Chapter Thirty-Three

Trey's drive home went by in a snap. At the house, he parked in the garage and walked through the enclosed breezeway to the back door. Entering the house quietly, he searched around the rambling first floor for his wife and daughter, finally finding them in the family room. Jazz was reading by the fire. Katie was at the card table cutting out party favors for New Year's Eve.

Trey got the warm reception he expected and gave the same in return. Jazz went to fix him a cup of hot cocoa, while he joined Katie at the worktable with scissors in hand. She was having two girlfriends over for a sleepover tomorrow, and Grandma was coming, too. That was the extent of the Stones' plans for celebrating the end of one year and the start of another.

When Jazz came back with a cup of chocolate and two Christmas cookies, she asked bluntly, "How did it go?"

He looked up from his confetti chores and winked. "A plan 'B' can be better than an 'A.' You were right after all," he said, smiling broadly.

She rubbed a hand over his back, watching him cut up colored paper with his daughter. "Maybe this won't be such a bad New Year's after all," she said.

"We'll know soon enough," he said. "One week to election day—and counting."

After dinner, Trey and Jazz decided to take CARE packages of cookies and chocolate out to the security force stationed around the property. They stayed a few minutes by the front gate to chat with a handful of reporters holding fort, hoping to be first with the political story that would not go away. Jokingly, Trey apologized for not being able to give them "hot news on a cold night."

One reporter asked the obligatory question: With the vote closing in, did the congressman have a statement to make on the election? The reporter hinted of rumors Trey was supporting Forsythe.

Trey gave the obligatory answer: No comment. He knew the rumors would be more powerful than a publicly-announced decision at this point.

He wished all the journalists a warm evening, then went back to the house arm-in-arm with his wife, walking the quarter-mile into a gentle breeze. When they arrived, shivering cold, they warmed themselves with a sherry by the fire and listened to one of Jazz's favorite recordings. Managing to avoid all reference to politics, they sat with their arms around each other, heads pressed together.

Finally, Jazz got up and went to bed.

But Trey was still too wound up. He decided to watch a college bowl game. With the score out of reach, his attention wandered; his eyes closed involuntarily. Still, he couldn't seem to drag himself away; the hum of the TV was like a safety line, holding him between sleep and wakefulness.

Then an announcer came on to promo the newscast to follow: "We'll wrap up the day's football scores," he said. "Afterward, we'll take you to the White House, where the President and First Lady hosted a formal dinner tonight for friends and supporters."

Trey grabbed the remote to click off the set; he had no interest in watching footage of Forsythe.

As he searched for the off button, the announcer went

on: "We'll also bring you a sad report. One of the country's longest-serving congressmen passed away today."

Trey stopped up short.

"Representative Neil Van Deventer was found dead earlier this afternoon at his Maine cabin home."

Chapter Thirty-Four

Trey dropped the remote on the coffee table, leaving a jagged crack in the tinted glass.

He fell back on the couch and stared slack-jawed as the broadcast returned to the game. He was unable to move a muscle or utter a sound; he simply watched the TV screen blankly, all color drained from his face.

When he finally recovered several minutes later, he rushed to his office phone, immediately calling Van Deventer's office in Bangor, then the Maine State Police, three Maine news outlets, the state governor's office—anyone and everyone who might provide more information.

But reports were sketchy.

All indications were Van Deventer died of natural causes. The authorities reported he had been undergoing treatment for a cancerous tumor during the last year. Apparently, it was inoperable, and he had been told it was only a matter of time. This was all Trey could uncover.

He sat back at his desk in a state of shock. Having seen Van Deventer earlier, Trey knew the man was not well, but not mere hours from death. It didn't seem possible he could go so quick. Trey held his head in his hands and wondered what would happen with the vote now.

When he glanced up, Jazz was standing in the doorway.

"What's going on?" she asked. "Haven't you been to bed?" she said.

He was too dumbfounded to find words of explanation. He sat silent, shaking his head, then finally uttered the only words he could. They sounded surreal in their stark simplicity:

"Van Deventer's dead."

She gasped and slumped in the visitor's chair by the door. "Oh, God, that can't be. You just saw him."

He attempted the best explanation he could summon. "He didn't answer his phone last night, and a friend got worried. When the police checked in, they found him curled up in bed—dead. No struggle or foul play, apparently."

"From what?"

"Natural causes. It turns out he had cancer."

"Did he look ill when you spoke with him?"

"Maybe a little under the weather. He had a nasty cough. I'm no doctor, but he didn't look that sick to me—certainly not hours from death."

"I'm so sorry, Trey. I know how you were counting on him." She got up and came around the desk and hugged him tightly, then asked the inevitable question: "What will this do to the election?"

He laughed, not meaning to embarrass her, but out of his own sense of disbelief. "That's the million-dollar question."

He stood up abruptly and grabbed his coffee cup. Staring into the emptiness at the bottom for a moment, he wondered if he should start another pot. Maybe an overdose of caffeine would help distract him from the implications of Van Deventer's demise and the simultaneous death of Trey's voting strategy. "I tried to call the junior congressman from Maine," he said. "Harris is in the best position to know how this'll affect the state's vote. But he hasn't called back yet."

"The whole thing is too amazing," she replied, "and too

coincidental—right after you set up everything."

He shook his head slowly, also doubting the too-true-to-be-believed circumstances. "I can't blame a guy for dying, but the timing of it. It's simply unbelievable."

Trey dangled his arms by his side, the coffee cup hanging from one crooked finger. With a deep sigh, he turned and headed for the kitchen. He had to find something to do with his hands, because his mind was racing out of control at the implication the White House could be involved in murder.

Jazz followed him to the kitchen.

"You don't think Longstreet had anything to do with this, do you?" she asked. "I know he's a bastard, but *murder*. My God, is that possible?"

"Frankly, I don't know how far that son of a bitch will go—or has gone."

He stepped over by the kitchen sink and fussed with the coffee grounds, but he didn't have much success, spilling a handful on the counter. Jazz took over the job, and he leaned back against the breakfast bar to watch, arms folded across his chest.

"The thing is, no one knew about my conversation with Van Deventer," he mused. "Even if they did, I can't believe they would resort to killing a sitting congressman—to murdering *anyone*, for that matter. . . ."

Jazz started the pot brewing and went over to sit by a window in the breakfast nook, staring out the tinted glass at the morning sun, now nearly half over the horizon. She sighed deeply and looked back to her husband.

"What are you going to do?"

"I've got to think it through. Everything was set up. Now it's come apart. It's like starting over again."

"But you don't know how Harris will vote," she said.

"Maybe things haven't changed. You need to find that out before making any final decisions."

He came over and sat across from her and took her by the hand. He looked deeply into her eyes, thinking how much he appreciated her unemotional logic during this time of insanity all around them.

"One thing's for sure," he said. "I can't let Forsythe win. Whether he was involved in Van Deventer's death or not, the President and his people have disgraced the Oval Office. They ought to be in jail, not the White House."

Still holding her hand, he went on, hesitantly.

"When I spoke with Van Deventer the other night, I realized this vote isn't about me or the mistakes I've made. I've got to live with those. As long as I know you and Katie are safe—and I'm reasonably sure you are—I've got to do what's right. Whatever the consequences."

"But Longstreet's unforgiving," Jazz said, playing devil's advocate. "He'll come after you with everything he's got. He'll see to it your reputation's destroyed."

"I realize that."

He turned his head and looked out the window at a distant point beyond the shore, beyond the horizon. The days to come played out in his mind like a bad movie. He knew he would be disgraced in the public's eyes. Worse, he might be fighting not only for his reputation, but his freedom in a court of law. He couldn't understand how the circumstances around him had spiraled so far out of control.

Staring at the scene outside, he spoke to Jazz in a near whisper. "What about you, hon? Can you handle the pressure? We're talking about a full-blown public spectacle here. Investigations, charges, hearings, prosecution . . ."

She dismissed his question with a wave of the hand. "Don't worry about me. I can handle it."

"What about Katie? If I lose in court, there could be jail time. Do we want to inflict that on her?" He turned and looked to her, holding her eyes with his.

"You won't lose," she proclaimed. "The truth will out. Remember that phrase from Watergate? The truth always comes out. It will this time, too."

Trey loved her confidence in the face of catastrophe. Smiling, he replied, "Even if I do win, they could make it awfully tough on us. The publicity, the scandal, the financial cost. One thing's for sure—I'd be out of office."

She paused for a moment before responding, then asked pointblank: "Are you wondering if I can handle this, Trey— or are you wondering about yourself? You *know* my answer. Nothing means more to me than you. Not the money, not the house, certainly not the political office. As long as we can trust each other, we have everything we need."

He closed his eyes and nodded to himself. Then, his voice shaking, he said, "I hope you remember this conversation a few days from now, when the headlines are blaring, and our friends and family members are looking at us in a whole new light."

"To hell with what everyone else thinks," she said. "I'll remember this conversation a lot longer than a few headlines and TV stories," she said.

Jazz patted his hand and motioned toward the kitchen counter. "Get me a cup of coffee before I decide to go back to bed on you."

He jumped up, but before he could get to the pot, the phone rang, startling them both. Trey hoped it was Congressman Harris on the line.

He snatched the receiver off the wall: "Trey Stone here."

"Thank God I got you."

His stomach knotted at the sound of Laura's voice on

the other end. They had hardly spoken since Camp David. Even at the funeral, he completely avoided her. He certainly wasn't in the mood to chat now.

"I'm surprised to hear from you so early, Laura," he said, raising his eyebrows at Jazz. "How're you doing?"

"I've been better."

He heard her turn from the mouthpiece and speak to someone else.

"Leave it there," she said. "Thank you."

"Where are you?"

"At the Watergate."

He was also surprised to hear she was back in Washington so soon after Jack's death. "I hope the boys are okay," he said.

"They're fine. Grandpa's with them today."

He could sense a strain in her voice, as if she were about to come apart. He was on the verge himself, in large part because of her words to Longstreet. Still, he couldn't completely hate her for the betrayal. He truly hoped there was a logical explanation. After all, so much remained between them. He refused to believe she had hurt him intentionally; there had to be something more behind it.

Suddenly, he found himself reaching out to her again, as he had done too many times before. "You and the boys are always welcome here. Anything we can do to help."

"Right now, we've got to talk privately, Trey—and I mean right now. This is important. *Extremely* important."

He wasn't sure their meeting was such a good idea. His emotions were still too raw. But his words seemed to come out on their own: "I'm listening."

"I can't do it by phone. I've got to see you."

"When are you coming back to Annapolis?"

"Not until tomorrow."

"We'll meet then," he said. "Come by the house."

"We've got to meet now. I hate to ask this, but you'll understand when you get here."

He glanced over at Jazz and shrugged, as if to say: Why me? But Jazz looked away. She could never understand his weakness for the Weddingtons. He couldn't understand it himself, and especially not now, not after what she'd done. But he also knew their relationship went well beyond payback for the governor's kindness years ago. It was more like a misplaced sense of loyalty, a constant need to feel needed. One thing he knew for sure and didn't want to admit: he had been attracted to Laura for as long as he could remember. Too often, he looked for reasons to be near her. There was something magnetic about her passion for life, her sense of risk-taking and danger. Like so many others, Trey felt electric when near her, and he found himself coming back to her time and again, like the proverbial moth to the flame. Even when he knew he would regret it later.

He sighed deeply, feeling a strange mix of anticipation and raging anger. He knew he should slam down the receiver now, while he still could. But also sensed she had important information he could little afford to ignore. Once again, he heard the words come out on their own. "Let's meet at the governor's mansion. You need to get out of Washington for a while, anyway. Maybe we all do."

"I can't. I'm attending a re-election committee meeting today. There's no way I can miss it. You'll understand when you get here. *Please*, Trey, it's critical. It's . . . even more than that." Her voice broke.

He cupped the phone to his mouth and tried to whisper the words to her: "What time?"

She sniffled and composed herself. "I'll be in session

until this afternoon. Can you come here around three or four?"

"Where?"

"Room eight-oh-five."

"I'll be there at five-thirty. First, I've got a lot of phone calls to make to the other Maryland representatives. I assume you heard—Congressman Van Deventer died last night."

"That's why we need to talk."

He paused, wanting to ask her more, but he'd been on the line too long already. He knew that from the cold stare in Jazz's eyes.

"I'll see you later."

"Thanks, Trey. You won't regret it."

Famous last words, he thought to himself. "Just take care of yourself. It's awfully soon after . . . you know."

"No, it's not *soon* after. It's late, very late," she said. "I only hope it's not too late."

She was talking in riddles now, and he didn't have time for guessing. He ended the call with a quick "goodbye" and hung up the receiver with a thud, looking up just in time to see Jazz walk out.

Chapter Thirty-Five

Trey drove as if in a race, weaving in and out of traffic, cutting off several other drivers and swerving through openings that barely existed. He had run out of all patience at this point, and he wasn't in the mood for anyone or anything to get in his way. Within thirty minutes, he swept his Lincoln off the highway onto Constitution Avenue and into the curved driveway of the Watergate Hotel, roaring up to the front. Two plainclothes security guards followed a split-second later in an unmarked car. The bodyguards wanted to ride with him, but Trey couldn't talk openly on the car phone with them along, and he demanded they trail behind.

He jumped out of his car, and all three men jogged through the entry, crossing the marbled lobby to a bank of elevators. They caught an empty car going up.

Trey punched the button marked *eight* and rested back against the mirrored wall, wondering what new emergency awaited him high above. He had given up trying to predict the next turn of events. All he knew was he would get in and out as quickly as possible.

The elevator heaved to a stop and Trey stepped out. He found Laura's room down the hall where a set of doors announced "Suite 805." *Typical Laura,* he thought. *Why get a single room when a suite would do?*

He stationed the guards at each end of the hall, then rang the doorbell.

A moment later, Laura swung the door open and motioned him inside.

"Thank God you're here," she said, slamming the door behind.

He was surprised to find her wrapped in a bathrobe, hair disheveled. She was smoking, too. Something he hadn't seen her do in years. She pointed her cigarette toward a couch in the living room.

"Can I get you a drink?" she asked.

He sat on the edge of an easy chair and looked down at an ashtray full of butts and a whiskey glass with the residue of liquor and ice. "No thanks. I'm driving."

"One drink won't hurt you. You're a big boy."

She picked up her own glass and went to a bar.

Behind an elegant marble counter, rows of glass shelves were stocked with every kind of alcohol a drinker could want. He glanced in the dining room. It looked like something out of *Architectural Digest*. Huge oak table, towering glass chandelier, an imposing grandfather clock. Further down the hall, he could see two elegant bedroom suites decked out in the finest designer bedding.

This was a place fit for a king—or a president.

She handed him a straight bourbon. "You're going to need this."

He took the tumbler and held it in both hands, rattling the ice against the sides but not drinking. He spoke with a little-disguised edge to his voice.

"It appears the President's re-election committee is doing all right. You must have leftover funds you're trying to get rid of."

She waved her hand around the room. "You mean this? It's for a 'foreign dignitary' arriving tomorrow." She put quote marks around the words with her fingers. "Longstreet said I could use it tonight."

Her words were slightly slurred. He watched her move a

little unsteadily to a loveseat opposite him.

She sat on the arm of the chair and took a long sip from her drink and an even longer drag, letting the smoke out slowly, languidly.

"Look, I'm here, Laura, but I'm not here for long," he said. "Do you want to tell me about this *'extreme'* emergency of yours, or not?"

She rested back. "I'm having little trouble getting started."

"I noticed."

She slid off the arm and onto the cushion. When she crossed her legs, he couldn't help but notice bare skin all the way up. She did little to hide the view.

"Where to start?" she said. "How about with mistakes? Lord knows I've made a bunch of them."

"I can identify with you there." He paused. "Did you have any *particular* mistakes in mind?"

"The most important one was joining the President's re-election campaign. It was my biggest blunder ever." She tried to say "blunder," but the "d" got lost somewhere. "After that, everything went straight down."

"Down to where?"

"To where we are now."

"Where's that?"

"To a dead congressman."

Her words hit like a sledgehammer.

"You're not telling me the White House had something to do with Van Deventer's death?"

She stubbed out her cigarette. "I don't know."

"That's one hell of a charge to make," Trey said. He got up and paced in a tight little circle between the chair and coffee table. "When you charge people with murder, you better have more than a 'maybe' on your side."

She picked up her glass and headed for the bar, but he had had enough of her little performance. He reached out and grabbed her by both arms.

"If you've got any evidence Longstreet was involved in Van Deventer's death, I want it now. I'll have him busted so fast he'll never know what hit him."

"I don't have any evidence, but I know it in my gut."

"That's not good enough!" He nearly spit the words. "I need names, places—facts the police can work with."

"I don't have anything." She pried herself loose and stepped back, folding her arms across herself. She rubbed where his fingerprints showed in her pale skin.

"You invited me here to say a high government official may be involved in the murder of a congressman—and you've got nothing to prove it? What the hell am I supposed to do?"

"I thought you'd want to know, that's all."

She sat down and began to rock back and forth, arms clinched tightly together. Trey took a deep breath and tried to get hold of his growing anger. Maybe if he took this a fact at a time, he could piece together the disjointed story.

"What makes you think Longstreet was involved?"

"It was what he told me."

"You mean, he *told* you he had Van Deventer killed?"

"No, it was more the *way* he told me."

Obviously, pulling this story out would be like extracting impacted wisdom teeth.

"What did he tell you *exactly?*" He sat down and leaned in to hear her precise words.

"Last night," she started, "after we heard about Van Deventer's death . . ."

"Yes."

"We were here for a strategy meeting. The news came in

299

late. Everybody panicked. We *knew* Maine was a lock for the President."

Trey reached over for his whiskey glass, deciding a quick sip might not be such a bad idea.

"Everybody went crazy," she said. "Everybody but Arch. When he heard the news, he smiled that creepy smile of his and poured himself a drink. It makes me shiver thinking about it. The man can be so cold."

"Go on."

"He said—and these are his exact words—'We're better off with Van Deventer out of the picture.' "

Trey tried to hide his shock. "Why'd he say that?"

"He said Van Deventer was planning to switch his support. I asked him how he knew. He said, 'I've got better connections to Stone than you do.' Jeez, it was scary."

Trey sat back and rubbed a hand over his forehead, feeling perspiration gather. When he spoke again, his voice was shaky around the edges.

"What did he mean, 'better connections'?"

He was afraid he knew the answer even if she didn't.

"He said you met with Van Deventer and devised a strategy to force a second ballot." She leaned forward and rested a hand on his knee. "Is it true? I've got to know, because if it is, Longstreet knows everything. It was as if he was there with you. It gives me the shakes just thinking about it. You've got to tell me, did it happen?"

Trey drained his glass, then got up and moved toward the bar for another.

Laura jumped up and stood behind him, laying a hand on his shoulder. She spoke in a low, conspiratorial voice.

"It did happen, didn't it?" she said. "Longstreet knew everything."

His mind was reeling. The room spun around him, the

colors and shapes swirled through his head like an out-of-control carnival ride. He raised the ice tongs up, then slammed them on the counter and spun around.

"Yes, goddamn it. It happened just like he said. We had it worked out. I met Van Deventer at his cabin night before last."

"Oh, Trey." She clamped both hands over her mouth and stumbled back to the couch. Slumping on the edge, she stared at the residue of her own cigarette smoke curling up from the ashtray, watching with a look of sheer terror.

Trey tried to pull himself together. He walked over beside her and sat down, speaking in a low voice. "How did he know? Van Deventer wouldn't have said anything. We were in sync on this thing."

Laura lit another cigarette. "Arch was half drunk when he told me. He said more than he should have. It's one of his many character flaws. He's always got to take credit, even when he knows he shouldn't."

Trey dropped his hands by his side. "What do you mean, 'take credit'?"

"He wants everyone to know just how smart he is, how 'connected' he is. He bragged about being *tapped* into you—that was his word, 'tapped'—twenty-four hours a day, seven days a week. He claimed to know your every move. He said, 'Stone can't sneeze without me offering a handkerchief.' "

"That's impossible," Trey said. "I've had the house and office swept for bugs constantly. I've had the phone lines checked every day."

"But he's got access to the best equipment—and the best people. Unlimited resources."

"My people would've found any bugs, I'm sure of it."

She shrugged, as if his words ignored the obvious truth:

301

Longstreet was fully capable of exactly what he said. She got up and went to the bar for a gulp of water, then went on with the rest of her tale.

"Longstreet told me about a conversation between you and Jazz. The two of you were on the boat, or on the beach behind the house. He quoted you directly . . . something about meeting with Van Deventer, going to Maine. Plan A, plan B. I don't remember it all. He laughed like a little kid. It was really disgusting. The guy's such a prick."

Trey felt the hair on the back of his neck stand up. Then he remembered the fishing barges anchored offshore, and his mind connected the dots. "A few boats were in the bay, about a half-mile from the house. It's possible the bastard was using long-range mikes to pick up my conversations." He looked up at her incredulously. "Why didn't I think of that before? What an idiot I am."

She came back to the couch and sat down, her hands spread out beside her as if holding on. "I'm scared, Trey. I never wanted it to be like this. You've got to believe me. Why'd I get involved in this damn election? I knew Longstreet was trouble from the start. Now Jack's dead and a congressman, too. All because of this insane vote. Can a fucking political office be worth all this?"

She bowed her head and began to sob. He reached out and took her into his arms, letting her cry on his shoulder, her body racked by emotion. Her robe fell open, exposing one perfect breast. He tried to pull the garment closed, but it wouldn't stay. She seemed oblivious, crying uncontrollably.

When she finally quieted minutes later, he got up to get her another glass of water. But she waved it aside and reached for her tumbler of scotch. Her voice sounded calm again. "The question is, what do we do?"

He was at a total loss. Everything he had tried so far had

failed. Why would anything work now?

He walked over by the sliding glass doors that led out to a patio overlooking Washington at night. Patches of darkness in the distance hid the city's scars that were all too visible during the day—the shuttered government buildings, the poor sections with littered streets, the homeless sleeping on benches along the National Mall. Washington could be so dirty underneath the marble façade.

"We've still got one option," he said. "We have to go to the police."

"With what? We've got nothing."

"We'll tell them just what you told me. It's their job to investigate, not ours."

"They won't find anything. Longstreet covers his tracks too well."

"We'll let the police decide that for themselves."

"Do you realize the firestorm we'd cause in this town, charging the President's man with murder before the biggest House vote in history? We'd be crucified by the Administration, the press, the public. Besides, Van Deventer's death was ruled 'natural causes.' The man did have cancer."

Trey leaned against the couch and went through her points, one by one. She might be half drunk, but she was also right. The timing was all wrong.

"We'll wait until after the vote," he said, "then we'll go straight to the authorities."

She moved in front of him, forcing him to look her in the eyes. Her gaze was remarkably clear for someone who'd been crying her eyes out only moments ago.

"I'm less concerned with what happens a week from now than I am with today."

"What do you mean?"

"If Longstreet *was* involved in Van Deventer's death, he's capable of anything. If he believes you're going to throw the election to Wardlow, God only knows what he'll do next." She set her drink down and grabbed him by the jacket, pulling him to her. "You've got to be careful."

"Don't worry about me. We need to get some protection for you, though."

Her face was so close he could feel her hot breath on his skin. In her bare feet, hair tousled, she looked like a little lost girl.

"I've got two bodyguards outside," he said. "I'll have one of them stay with you tonight until we can make better arrangements."

He moved toward the door, but she wouldn't let go.

"I can't be with a stranger tonight."

"Then come back to the house with me."

"Not like this. I'm . . . not ready for that."

"We'll send you home. You'll be safe there. The governor's got security."

She ignored the question and stared deeply into his eyes, pulling herself even more closely to him.

"Can you ever forgive me, Trey?"

"The fault here lies with Longstreet—and with the President, not you."

"I could never hurt you, Trey. I love you."

"I love you, too."

Standing as high as she could, she kissed him full on the mouth, then asked: "Do you? Do you really?"

"Of course I do."

"Then stay with me. Let me make up for everything. We're a lot alike, you know. We can be even better together."

"Oh, Laura, don't. Please. Not now."

She released her grip and stepped back. Holding his eyes with hers, she reached down and untied her robe and shrugged her shoulders. The silk garment slipped to the floor, and she stood before him in nothing but red panties, a patch of blazing color stark against her unblemished skin.

Trey wanted to turn away, but couldn't. He found himself kneeling at her feet, fumbling with the robe.

"You're drunk. This isn't the time."

"I've been drinking," she said, "but I've never been more sober."

She reached out to him, her magnificent breasts swaying with the motion, enticing him like never before.

"We need each other, Trey. We always have, ever since that first time we made love. It was the best ever. We can have it again. No one has to be hurt."

He stood up, and she threw her arms around him, pressing her naked skin against his chest, her softness enveloping him.

"I've got no one else now," she said. "I need you—and you need me."

She turned her head and buried her face in his chest. The force of her against him made him stumble back against the bar. He felt trapped, the warmth of her body wrapped around him, the sweet aroma of her hair.

He brought his hands behind her and draped the silk robe over her shoulders. Then he kissed the top of her head, and gently pulled away.

"You're a gorgeous woman," he said. "If this were another time, another place—maybe we could have had something together. But I'm not the man you want me to be. Not tonight, not ever."

She looked into his eyes for the longest time, not moving, not responding. Finally, she stepped back to the couch and lit another cigarette. Her hands were steady once again.

"I've always loved you. That'll never change. Even if you don't love me back."

He turned and walked to the door, speaking over his shoulder. "You've been through a lot. Give it time. You'll find someone again."

"I've given it time," she said, looking away. "Too much time. I'm through with giving. Now it's time to take."

Chapter Thirty-Six

It took nearly thirty minutes to get Laura dressed and on her way. Trey sent a security guard with her and asked the other guard to wait in the lobby while he checked his private voice mail, wondering if Charlie Harris from Maine had called.

He hadn't.

Trey hung up in frustration. Then he heard a knock at the door and tensed, unsure of what—or who—to expect. Before he could answer it, the lock turned. When he saw who it was, he felt his hands grip into fists.

He watched in amazement as Arch Longstreet stepped in and closed the door behind. He rested back against the doorjamb, and Trey's impulse was to race across the room, grab the bastard and beat him beyond an inch of his life.

He took a step toward him, raising his arms in anger. But Longstreet put his hands up defensively.

"Think again, Congressman," he said. "Imagine tomorrow's headlines: *Representative Attacks Presidential Aide at Watergate*. On the eve of your biggest vote ever? It'd make a sensational story, *Trey*." Longstreet said his name with a tinge of mockery.

"A bigger story might be your involvement in the death of a congressman," he replied.

"I'd like to take credit for Van Deventer's timely demise," he said, walking further into the room. "But it was simply a stroke of fortune for both of us."

"You really expect me to believe he just collapsed and

307

died?" His eyes followed Longstreet like a target, watching him move toward the bar.

"I don't really care what you think." Longstreet reached behind the bar, pulled out a martini glass and poured a straight vodka. "Even if Van Deventer's death wasn't from natural causes, you think the police and press are going to believe the White House was involved?"

"If they hear what Laura has to say, they might."

He sipped his drink. "Ah, excellent vodka. Russian. The best. Always go with the best." He crooked his elbows on the bar, looking more comfortable as the edge came off Trey's urge to attack.

"Let's talk about Laura for a moment," Longstreet said. "This is speculation, mind you, but let me try out a story on you: Laura meets with you a few days before the election in her hotel suite. She's not in the best of shape—I think your own security guards would testify to that. She tells you an extraordinary tale about White House involvement in murder. She has no facts, of course, no evidence. *'Gut feeling,'* I think she would call it."

He got up and moved over by the double-glass patio doors, vodka in hand, obviously relishing this opportunity to play the leading role.

"Before the evening's over, this lovely, somewhat tipsy young woman—the wife of your dear, departed friend—comes into your arms and expresses her love for you. You express your love for her, too."

He tossed back the rest of his drink and held the glass to the light, like a jeweler inspecting a diamond.

"Did I forget to mention our lovely, shapely Mrs. Weddington is in your arms *naked as the day she was born?*"

Longstreet reached inside his jacket and pulled out a photograph. He flipped it on the table in front of Trey.

"I think I *did* forget to mention that," he said, going back to the bar to freshen his drink.

Trey stared down at the picture on the table. He sat down hard on the love seat where Laura had been earlier. The picture showed her unclothed and wrapped in his arms. From the back, in thong panties, she looked nude, snuggled comfortably against his chest with her face turned in full profile. Trey started to reach out for the photo but couldn't bring himself to touch it. He sat back and rubbed his hands over his face, feeling perspiration gather there as if someone had turned up the thermostat.

Across the room, Longstreet pulled out a barstool and sat down facing him, looking fully at ease now.

He spoke with a disturbing calm.

"Let's forget about little Miss Weddington for the moment and go on to other, more important matters."

Trey sat unmoving, arms by his sides, feeling like he'd just been run over.

"Let's talk about—what did you call it?—plan 'A.' The one where you decide to join your fellow Maryland Democrats in voting for the President. That's the plan I like, Congressman. That's the one I want to see implemented in January. Do we understand each other?"

Trey didn't respond. He struggled to find some words, any words, but his thoughts kept coming back to the photograph on the table. How could he explain to Jazz what he was doing alone in Laura's hotel room with her nude in his arms? It didn't look good no matter what the explanation. And what about his expression of love for her? He hadn't meant it the way she had, but try to explain that one away. And didn't Laura say something about their having made love before? No one knew about that—least of all Jazz. This was no way for her to find out. Longstreet would have everything on tape, of course. Artfully edited, it could be devastating.

Looking up, Trey found the only words he could manage: "You're the slimiest bastard I've ever come across."

Longstreet ran a finger around the edge of his martini glass. "It's called 'knowing your enemy.' I can be your friend, or I can be your foe. It doesn't really matter. After the vote on Monday, no one'll ask 'how.' They'll only ask 'who.' *Who won.* That's all that counts. That's why you'll do exactly as I've said. Any more resistance from you is not only useless, it's dangerous."

Longstreet finished his drink and stood up, steady as a rock. "We will have your support, or we'll destroy you. Simple as that. We'll ruin your political career, your financial standing, your reputation—even your marriage. I've got all the ammunition I need."

He brushed at the sleeves of his suit jacket, then moved over by the door.

"In case you're wondering, *Trey,*" Longstreet continued in that mocking tone of his, "I told Laura about Van Deventer because I knew she'd run straight to you. We were ready for her. We're always ready." He shook his head in pretend sympathy. "Poor Laura. Just an innocent woman in love, I'm afraid."

He opened the door and stepped out, speaking from the hallway. "We can do great things together, when you help us. But when you turn on us, we'll just roll over you. We'll grind you so far down, you'll never get up again." He tossed off a sarcastic little salute. "Pleasant dreams, Congressman. Oh, and . . . God bless America."

Trey listened to the door close, then looked back to the coffee table and stared at the photo of Laura in his arms.

He struggled to his feet and picked up the photo, pinching it between his thumb and forefinger like a trapped insect. He went to the bar and tossed it in the sink, then found a match and set the picture on fire. Standing over it, arms braced on the counter, he watched it burn, and washed the ashes down the drain.

The ritual did nothing to help. He knew Longstreet had plenty more where this one came from. He tried to hold himself steady, but he felt his knees go weak and his arms shake. He leaned into the sink and threw up.

Chapter Thirty-Seven

Trey stood on the patio at the rear of his house, hands in the hip pockets of his jeans, and watched the Chesapeake stir angrily. The water was a sickly green topped by dirty foam. The tide was way up, too. It rushed into the defenseless cove with a vengeance, sucking back sand with impunity.

A powerful nor'easter was on the way. It would pound the coastline the entire weekend. He watched the water crash against the weakened dock and wondered if the pilings would hold. This would be their most severe test.

Further offshore, he saw that the fishing trawler was now gone. Apparently Longstreet had all the information he needed.

Trey breathed in deeply, taking all the air he could, as if fresh oxygen might help reinvigorate him after yesterday. Following his confrontation with Longstreet, he had called back to the house to tell Jazz he'd be later than expected. He went to his Washington office and sat in the dark, trying to calm himself and figure out what to do next.

Despite Longstreet's warnings, he couldn't bring himself to support Forsythe. One thing he had learned over the past few weeks was to follow his conscience, even if it meant hurting himself—and Jazz—beyond anything he had ever expected.

Funny, he thought. In a couple of days, he would go from being the man at the center of the political universe— the up-and-coming congressman who held the future of a

President in his hands—to an accused criminal and adulterer with his best friend's widow.

This would be the public's view, at least. But he cared less about what others thought than the effect on Jazz, especially after she had talked about their trusting each other.

All of this, he thought, *for trying to do what was right.* Maybe "right" wasn't all it was cracked up to be.

By the time he had gotten home, everyone was in bed. He tried to sleep, but his tossing and turning threatened to wake Jazz. So he got up and tried to anesthetize himself with a couple of shots of brandy. Hell, he didn't even like the stuff. It didn't like him much either. This morning, his head felt like the bay—bloated and roiling.

He ran a hand over his chin and felt a stubble of beard. He usually shaved and showered first thing in the morning—a habit learned at Annapolis—but today, he couldn't bring himself to lift a razor that close to his skin, not in shaky hands.

He decided another cup of coffee might help, even though he knew caffeine was the worst thing for a hangover.

Going back inside, he warmed up his cup and chased the coffee with a couple of aspirin. Then he went to get the morning paper. As usual, the security guards had placed a copy on the front porch, wrapping it carefully in a waterproof bag.

He took the *Post* into his office and opened it to a front section filled with nothing but articles on the election. Every angle, every speculation, every possibility was explored in depth. Historians rehashed previous votes of landmark importance. Spokesmen from both campaigns discussed where their strategies went right and wrong.

In the op/ed section, the *Post* editorial board—going against its traditional liberal bias—recommended support for Wardlow, using the same reasoning Trey had used, the only reasoning that made sense in all this senselessness.

He put the paper aside and clicked on the television. More news and commentary on the election. The publicity had reached a fever pitch.

He watched as one correspondent—perched beside a broadcast van outside Trey's own home—reported live. Other vans were parked at the end of the driveway as well. Carloads of journalists milled about everywhere. Trey had given up trying to keep the crowds down. He wasn't going anywhere anyway.

Jazz came into his office, rubbing sleep from her eyes. "You look rugged," she said. "Tough night last night?"

"You could say that. I hope I didn't keep you awake."

"Not much." She yawned and stretched, her actions belying her words. She glanced at the television. "You haven't had enough of this election yet?"

"Yes." He clicked off the set. "There's fresh coffee in the kitchen." He tried to sound as cheerful as possible, under the circumstances.

"I could use a cup or two," she said.

He followed her down the hall, watching her slippers shuffle over the floor like two dust rags poking out from under her floor-length robe. It caused him to flash back to another woman in another robe. He shook the vision away.

"You were out late," she said. "How'd it go with Laura?"

He waited a long time before responding, too long.

"Not all that well."

She knew things were worse than he let on.

"Laura thinks the White House had something to do with Van Deventer's death," he said.

314

Jazz's mouth fell open. "He's a bastard, but I didn't think he'd go that far."

"She's got no evidence—just a 'hunch.' "

"You need more than that to bring charges. What gave her this 'hunch'?"

"He did. He's playing with her mind. He's playing with all of our minds."

"But no sane person would want to be suspected of murder."

"Who said Longstreet was sane?"

She blew on her steaming coffee. "But that's extreme even for him. What're you going to do?"

"Nothing for the time being."

"Shouldn't you go to the authorities and let them investigate?"

"If I leveled charges now with nothing to go on, I'd be accused of the worst kind of politics. I might even be guilty of it. Waiting a few days won't hurt. Van Deventer's dead. Nothing's bringing him back."

Jazz took this in for a moment, thought-wheels grinding inside her head.

"If Longstreet *is* involved," she said, "and Forsythe wins, it would cast doubt on the election. I mean, a President who won office because an opponent was killed? What would that say about the system?"

"It'd cause a constitutional crisis the likes of which we've never seen." Trey stirred in his seat, wondering if now was the time to tell her about last night—*all* of last night.

"The problem is," he said, "we've got no evidence, and an investigation could take months. The vote's going ahead on Monday, charges or not."

She didn't respond, even though he could still see her mind cranking. But he had already been through the same logic and knew he couldn't point a finger at Longstreet without more to go on. The charges were too explosive. By waiting, of course, he could be accused of withholding critical information. Either way, he was wrong. It was a choice he faced a lot lately.

"After the vote, I'll propose the House open a formal investigation. I'm sure we can find evidence somewhere. Right now, all I've got is the word of a highly emotional campaign assistant who has a 'hunch.' "

"You think she's okay?"

"I don't know, Jazz. I really don't." He looked away, trying to work up the courage to go through the gruesome details, to explain how a naked woman wound up wrapped in his arms; how he and Laura had expressed love for one another and spoke of past episodes. "I sent her home with a security guard and told her to stay at the governor's mansion until after Monday. She'll be okay."

"Maybe I should call her," Jazz said. "She's been through so much."

"I wouldn't do that." He felt guilty telling her to stay away from her once-best friend, but Laura was over the edge right now; he didn't know what she'd say or who she'd say it to. "She needs rest and to be with her kids and family. She'll be all right."

Trey got up and poured them both another cup of coffee, knowing he had to stop drinking this stuff, but he needed something to do with his hands.

Irma came into the kitchen ready for the day—fully dressed, make-up on, hair done. She always looked put together, even on a dreary Saturday morning.

Katie trailed behind in her new Christmas pajamas, looking cute as could be.

"Hey, pumpkin," Trey said. He lifted her up and kissed her on the forehead.

"Hi, Daddy."

When he set her down, she scurried over to Mom.

He watched them hug and thought how amazing it was that this little girl could brighten the darkest day just by walking in the room. Then he leaned over and pecked Irma on the cheek. "Good morning," he said, as cheerily as he could.

"Good morning, Mr. Stone," she said, touching where he had kissed. "You need a shave!" She appeared surprised at her own comment.

He grinned. "You sound like my drill instructor at The Yard."

"It's just that you always . . ."

He kissed her again. "Take that," he said. "Any more complaints, and I'll kiss you again."

They all had a good laugh, and Irma started in on breakfast. Trey walked over to the French doors that led out to the patio. The rain, a sprinkle moments ago, was coming down in torrents now, smearing the glass, obscuring the objects outside. He listened to the sounds of family life behind him—Irma with her pots and pans, Jazz and Katie chatting at the table, making plans for the day. He wished things could be just like this forever. But the world outside, twisted and unforgiving, kept rushing in.

It was all he could do to keep pushing it away.

As forecast, the rain continued unabated the entire weekend, pounding at times. Squall-like winds lashed the house like Trey hadn't seen in years. At least the dock held against the tide. Dad's years of attention were paying dividends.

317

Twice over the weekend, Trey shut himself in his office to work on separate documents: a letter to his constituents, and a "diary of events." No matter what happened on Monday, he knew he'd feel better with his version on paper.

He started off chronologically, outlining the "assistance" he gave to Jack and the reasons why. He made clear that his decision-making was flawed, but not illegal. He in no way prevented an investigation from going forward or submitted false or misleading information.

The more Trey wrote, the more he believed Longstreet would have a tough case to make. But Longstreet's charges were less about reality than appearances. In Washington, appearances *are* reality—and an accusing finger pointed by the White House is often the equivalent of conviction.

Then, Sunday afternoon, he took time to write a letter that was, at once, the easiest and most difficult of his life. It was a note to Jazz, a declaration of his love. Like too many people, Trey never took the time to tell those closest to him how much they really meant.

He talked of the time they first met, when he saw her sweep down that marble staircase, radiant in a full-length gown, and how he knew that night they were destined to be together. He talked of how his love for her had only grown since, and how it would never stop growing. He thanked her for dedicating her life to him and to their daughter, and he told her his love for her was unending and—no matter what—she had made his life complete.

It was the *"no matter what"* part where he struggled. He wrote of the incident at the Watergate with Laura and of their interlude so many years ago. The words came one at a time—hard, painful, depressing words strung into awkward sentences and rambling paragraphs.

After working on the explanation for hours, he erased it

all, realizing this was no way to tell her what had happened. He could only do that face to face. Besides, he wanted the earlier part of the letter to stand alone, pure and unequivocal, just as her love was for him. Or at least it always had been. After Longstreet was done, she would be tested like never before.

Sunday evening, they had a casual dinner and retired to the family room to watch television, read and relax. Some time after nine, they got Katie off to bed.

Trey and Jazz then put on some music and sipped wine by the fire. The longer they sat together, the more he re-laxed. Before long, they were asleep in each other's arms. It was almost midnight before Jazz roused him, and they both found their way to bed.

Crawling under the covers, he reached over and set the alarm for five. He always set the clock and never needed it. But the way he felt now, he could sleep until Tuesday and never regret the choice.

Chapter Thirty-Eight

On the top floor of the Old Executive Office Building, Laura slipped her access badge into an electronic lock and stepped inside Longstreet's private office.

He wasn't there, but she could still feel his presence like an over-charged energy field, a pulsing sensation he always left behind. Maybe it was the sickly sweetness of his cologne, or the utter cleanliness and sterility of his surroundings: Everything was precisely set, not a piece out of place. Even his over-stuffed desk chair sat perfectly in front of his spotless desk.

She checked her watch: nearly one a.m. She knew this would be a long night for all of them. Longstreet and the President were encamped in the Oval Office next door, making last-minute calls to key congressional leaders, assuring their votes were still in line. After all, there was no sense taking any chances this close to *the big day*.

She walked slowly across the room in the darkness, finding her way by memory to the cabinet behind his desk. Longstreet never left out papers or files, having learned long ago that confidentiality and secrecy were preeminent in Washington politics—it was the one key to success in a town of lies and half-truths. This was a lesson Laura was still learning. In the process, she had committed the cardinal sin: She had revealed a secret that led directly to her own husband's death and was about to destroy the career of a man she loved more than life itself. How could she have been so naïve? How she could have trusted the likes of

Archibald Longstreet, the slimiest bastard this side of the Potomac? Or any side of the Potomac!

She was slow to learn sometimes, but she always learned well. Longstreet was about to get a taste of his own poison. He had left her alone in his office only once. But it was more than enough to imprint the desk key he protected like a dirty family secret. She bent down to the bottom-right drawer and used her duplicate to open the lock. Reaching inside, she searched for the critical file and found it quickly—a manila folder stuffed with dog-eared papers and a few black-and-white transparencies.

She got up and went straight to his private copier, running the entire package in less than ten minutes.

Then she re-filed the folder where she had found it.

When she was sure everything was precisely back in place, she stepped quietly into the hallway and re-locked the door behind.

Under her breath, Laura thanked Arch for instructing her so well. Little did he know his lessons were about to pay dividends neither of them could have ever expected.

Chapter Thirty-Nine

Trey sat at his desk, hands clasped in front, staring straight ahead, not really seeing the bare wall across the room. Standing, he felt the tightness in the new wingtips Jazz had gotten him for the holidays. He'd have to remember to walk carefully; new leather soles were always slick.

Looking down, he pushed aside the bundles of newspapers tossed on his desktop. He had had enough of the news. Now was the time for reality.

He gathered up a few loose papers and stuffed them into his valise, then clicked off the desk lamp and headed out.

No more delaying.

He met Jazz as she walked into the family room looking for him. They hugged and kissed more formally than usual.

"So this is it," she said. "Long time coming."

He nodded. "Seems like forever."

"You'll call me after the vote?"

He nodded again and picked up his briefcase, but didn't move immediately for the door. "Give Katie a kiss for me. Tell her I'll be home early."

"You're sure?"

"Yes, I'm getting the hell out of Washington as fast as I can."

"We'll be waiting."

"I know you will."

He took a step away, but then came back to her for one more kiss and a long passionate embrace, before he turned away without looking her in the eye and hurried out the door.

At the front of the house, he crawled into the back of a waiting stretch limo for the interminably long ride to D.C., knowing today might be his longest ever—the beginning of many long ones to come.

In his top-floor suite, resplendent in a charcoal gray suit, Longstreet closed and locked the double doors behind his visitor.

They did not speak.

Longstreet turned and walked purposefully across the room to a small office at the back where a copier, printer and fax were kept. Stepping inside, he knelt in front of a floor safe tucked in the corner, as if genuflecting at a shrine. He dialed a three-number code.

The electronic lock whirred and buzzed, then popped open with a gentle, percussive sound.

Longstreet reached inside and pulled out a legal-sized manila envelope. Opening it, he extracted a small, pen-shaped syringe. He held the object in the palm of his hand and inspected it closely, as would a chemist viewing his latest experiment. Without getting up, he reached behind and held out his open palm, the object laying there innocently for the taking.

Hesitating, his visitor picked up the silver syringe between thumb and forefinger, then turned and walked back into the main office.

Seconds later, Longstreet followed, dusting his hands. When he spoke, his voice was unusually soft and tight.

"You simply press the pointed end lightly against him," he said. "The needle goes right through clothes, so you don't have to worry about hitting bare skin. He won't feel a thing."

His visitor nodded, still not having uttered a word.

"In a matter of seconds, he'll go down. It's that fast. No pain—very little, anyway. Just a freezing sensation in the extremities."

More nodding, still no words.

Longstreet realized more convincing was required.

"My mother was a nurse," he said. "She told me about this drug when I was young. It's used in surgeries to numb the muscles. With the right dosage, it's perfectly safe."

Smiling to himself, Longstreet thought: *Yes, with the right dosage.*

The visitor turned and stared out the wide set of windows overlooking Ellipsis Park just across the street, realizing—like Longstreet himself had long ago—that things had come full circle, as they always did in politics.

"Any questions?" Longstreet asked.

A subtle, almost imperceptible shaking of the head.

"You'll know when to use it," Longstreet said. "We'll make sure of that."

He led the way out, opening the double doors with a flourish. Standing aside, he let his guest pass, speaking softly as the person moved by. "Let's just hope it's not necessary."

The visitor stopped. "It's *never* necessary, Arch."

With that single statement in strained tones, the visitor disappeared.

Longstreet turned and went back to gather his papers and personal effects for the walk next door to the Oval Office. There, he would join the President to celebrate their most unexpected victory.

Chapter Forty

In the back of the limo, Trey wished once again that he had driven himself, knowing it would help him relax before the insanity to come. But the security people suggested—demanded, really—a bulletproof car and chauffeur. There was no reason to take any chances this close to "the moment," as the security chief had called it.

Trey had to admit he was better off with darkened windows and a professional driver; he couldn't argue with the chief's reasoning. Besides, he wanted to do a little more polishing on his after-vote remarks and draft letter to his constituents.

The driver pulled through the gate and into a milling crowd. Clearing the onlookers expertly, he gunned the engine, but the pack wasn't far behind.

Everyone jumped into vans and cars and onto motorcycles to follow. A few vehicles attempted to pull in front to get a camera shot, but the driver fended them off easily, until they reached Route 50 and the entourage spread across four lanes.

Trey watched out the side and back windows, wondering why dozens of people would follow a car they couldn't see inside of. He shook his head and smiled, realizing he should know better than to try to figure out the press.

He grabbed the car phone and dialed into the office. Miss Landers answered, as he knew she would.

"It's a madhouse here," she said. "I've never seen anything like it. Not since Nixon resigned."

Trey expected as much. "I'm going to the Capitol Building first. I'll come to the office after the vote."

"Will you be available for interviews? We've got a hundred requests, maybe more—all the networks, the dailies, wire services. Everyone."

"No interviews. I'll issue a statement in the Rotunda and take a few questions. That's it. This'll be a moment for the President-elect, not for me."

"Yes sir."

"Also, I've got a constituent letter to get out today," he said. "I'll fax it from the limo."

"I'll have the staff ready."

He tried to think of other items to cover.

"I guess that's it for now."

"We'll hold down the fort."

He smiled. "When you hear me coming, open the gates."

He could almost see her smile on the other end. There was a brief pause, then she spoke again. "Mr. Stone," she said. "Trey . . ."

It was the first time he could remember her calling him by his first name. He liked it. It made him feel a little more human.

"Yes?"

"Good luck."

"Thanks, Ellen. We're all going to need it today."

He hung up and went back to his paperwork, trying to stay as distracted as possible. In what seemed like seconds, the car pulled off the Beltway and onto the streets of Washington. At first, the town appeared deserted, until they passed Union Station, nearing the Mall. He saw a few small crowds moving quickly toward the Capitol, scurrying on foot. By the time the limo got to Louisiana Avenue, the small crowds had become a crush, spilling out into the

326

streets, making it difficult to pass. Police on foot and horse-back helped clear the way.

The driver turned left on D Street and made a quick right onto First, past the east entrance to the Capitol, fig-uring it would be less packed than the west side that faced the Mall. But he was wrong. The car got trapped near the intersection at Maryland Avenue.

Trey decided to walk from there.

Normally, it would be a two-minute stroll to the front of the building. But surrounded by four bulky bodyguards, several police officers and a crowd numbering a thousand or more, it was all he could do to get through.

Ten minutes later, he arrived at the steep, marble steps. Fighting his way through the hordes, he kept his eyes on the magnificent white dome high above the Greek and Roman facade. The Statue of Freedom perched atop always in-spired him, kept him focused on the job ahead.

The police cleared an aisle, and he jogged up to the second-floor entry without looking back.

Inside the two-hundred-year-old building Trey found a refuge. For one of the few times in history, the public was prevented from visiting today. They would be barred until the closed House and Senate sessions were completed.

Trey took careful steps into the center of the building, his new shoes slipping ever so slightly on the highly pol-ished floor. As he moved under the nearly two-hundred-foot-high canopy, it was like walking into the Pantheon or Sistine Chapel. The curved sandstone walls appeared to rise up around him like a steeple.

Turning in a circle, he viewed the massive plaster frieze high above, which reproduced scenes from the signing of the Declaration of Independence to the Surrender of Corn-wallis. Below that, statues and busts of U.S. Presidents from Washington to Jefferson to Lincoln were scattered around the perimeter, forming the foundation of the country's history, just as they had in real life.

As he stood there in the center, peering slowly around the room, he heard someone coming—soft, slow, sure steps.

He looked down and saw the reassuring face of his old friend and confidant, Bobby Buckland.

"Morning, Congressman," Trey said. "Ready to make history?"

Buckland shook his hand. "Ready as I'll ever be. How about you?"

Shrugging, Trey said, "I'm not sure if I'm making history, or it's making me."

Buckland put an arm around his shoulder and turned toward the broad, curving stairs leading up to the third-floor House Chamber.

"We'll find out soon enough," Buckland said. "One thing's for sure—Van Deventer's death added an element of suspense no one expected."

"That's the understatement of the year," Trey said.

Buckland glanced at him and spoke in a more serious tone. "Are you all right? You seem kind of . . . distant."

Trey stopped and stared at his shoes for awhile, searching for a way to tell Buckland about everything that had happened over the last few weeks, to explain to his good friend and mentor how he'd gotten himself into an untenable position, how he'd made mistakes, but never with the intention to deceive or defraud. He wanted to explain the extraordinary pressure he was under, the underhanded tactics by the White House and why this vote was about to be his undoing.

He sighed deeply. "Bobby, I'm switching my support," he said. "I've decided to vote for Wardlow."

A look of shock and concern swept over Buckland's face. He seemed at a loss for words. He managed to stutter, "Tha . . . That changes everything."

"I'm afraid so," Trey said. "I've got to talk with the other Maryland representatives right now."

"But why?" Buckland stepped back and grabbed the heavy wooden railing, as if he might topple over. "Has this got anything to do with Van Deventer's death?"

"It's got everything to do with it."

"He was planning to support Wardlow, wasn't he? You two had worked a deal—"

"It's a long story, Bobby. Suffice it to say Forsythe was trying to steal the election. With Van Deventer's help, I thought we had him stopped."

Trey could feel Buckland's eyes searching him out. The elder congressman reached out a hand and drew Trey closer, conspiratorially.

"Take it from an old political warhorse, Trey. Now's not the time to do this. You've made your commitment to Forsythe. Change now, and you'll be crucified."

"I understand the stakes, Bobby. It's something I've got to do. You'll understand why later."

Trey turned and started up the stairs, but Buckland didn't follow. He looked up and spoke out haltingly, almost angrily. "No! *You* don't understand the stakes. A lot of people in this town owe that Southern Mafia. They're dangerous people. They'll . . . they'll crush you."

Trey stopped and looked down at Buckland, wondering if the White House had gotten to him, too. Was no one in this town untouchable? For a long time, rumors had been rampant of Bobby's political debts to the Administration, but he had always counseled Trey not to get caught in silent deals.

"The Administration can't hurt me any more than I've hurt myself, Bobby."

Buckland stepped up next to Trey, tears welling in the old man's eyes. He reached out and held Trey by the lapel of his suit. Then he dug inside his suit jacket and pulled out a tiny silver, pen-like object. He lifted it high above his head in a trembling hand, tears streaming down his face, his voice hollow and weak. "You don't realize how far these people will go," he said, his words rising in volume. "You don't understand what they've asked me to do!"

Trey leaned back, staring up at Buckland's hand hovering above him. He couldn't comprehend what his good friend was talking about, or why he was holding this tiny metallic object pointed at his chest.

"Wha . . . What are you doing, Bobby? For Christ's sake." Trey grabbed Buckland's wrist, and the two men stood like this for several seconds, their arms extended high above.

Despite his age, Buckland was a strong man. He stepped around to one side, gaining the upper hand as they struggled, their arms locked together.

Trey's shoes began to slip. He fought to regain his footing, but the new leather soles wouldn't hold on the slick marble floor. One foot went out from under him, and he tumbled back. Then, looking up, he saw the tiny needle come down swiftly at his shoulder.

Chapter Forty-One

President Forsythe sat behind his Oval Office desk inspecting his hands, his fingers spread out on the blotter, as if detached from his body.

He looked from one large, vein-knotted hand to the other, staring intently at the carefully trimmed nails. The cuticles seemed to smile up at him in stark contrast to his own facial expression. Arch Longstreet, standing to one side of the fireplace, knew all too well that a manicure was the last thing on the President's mind.

"You're sure we're lined up?" Forsythe said, glancing up. "Absolutely sure?"

Longstreet moved over by the coffee cart and poured himself a fresh cup of tea. "Sure as I can be," he said, "in this unsure world of ours."

Forsythe slammed his fist on the desktop. "That's not good enough. We should've had Stone in here like I asked—to get a firm commitment. This is no time for guesswork. I don't like it when a man won't face me square on and tell me who he supports."

"He wouldn't have come even if we'd asked—not the night before the vote," Longstreet countered. "Everyone in town would've screamed conflict of interest. It could have threatened the support we already had."

Forsythe sighed deeply. "All that support won't matter if we lose because of one man."

The President returned to staring at his clipped nails, while Longstreet sipped his tea and slowly moved back to his place by the fire, resting against the wall.

"We won't lose," Longstreet proclaimed. "You've got my word on that."

The President's Southern Mafia—seated in their usual spots around the room—watched four televisions simultaneously, each tuned to a different network.

Vice President McNally, on the remote, turned up the sound of one broadcast or another when something important appeared underway. But everyone knew nothing critical would happen until the House completed its session this morning. They also knew the President wouldn't find out his fate by television. The top House and Senate leaders would pay a personal visit to the White House with the final results. Until then, everyone hung on the news reports, hoping someone else might know something they didn't.

Longstreet smiled at their intensity. To him, the broadcasts were like watching a taped delay. He already knew the outcome, having reaffirmed Maine's vote with Harris right after Van Deventer's death. He also knew Maryland was in line. The squeaky clean Trey Stone would never risk his reputation, his marriage, his office, his future, his fortune—everything—simply to deny Forsythe's return to office.

Longstreet reached inside his jacket and pulled out a photograph and stared at it for the longest time, knowing it was exactly the leverage he needed to assure the President's return to office.

Funny, he thought, *how politics always came down to the basest of emotions: money and sex.* Not even the naïve, red-white-and-blue, holier-than-thou Trey Stone could overcome that.

And if he tried, there was always the syringe.

The Vote

★ ★ ★ ★ ★

On the steps of the Capitol, Trey's eyes opened involuntarily. The ceiling fresco high above came slowly into view, the colors merging into a surreal image; the swirling shades soothed yet disturbed at the same time, appearing both real and unreal.

He realized he was flat on his back looking up, wondering what had happened in-between. A moment ago, he was on his way to cast the most important vote of his life. Now he was immobile on the stairway with another person hovering above, holding something shiny in his trembling hands.

Then the object fell away. It bounced on the step beside Trey and down the curved stairway.

Buckland's face slowly came into view.

He was sitting beside Trey, holding his head in his hands. Tears were running down his weathered face, spilling onto Trey's freshly starched shirt, leaving tiny spots that seemed to dry almost as soon as they touched.

Shaking his head, Trey tried to clear away the last of the dream-like images floating around him. He realized his body was still in one piece, but it seemed disconnected from his consciousness.

He struggled to raise an arm; it did not cooperate. He couldn't seem to make his limbs respond. He felt a tingling sensation everywhere, as if his body had fallen asleep while his mind remained awake and aware.

He could feel the hardness of the marble stairs beneath his back, pressing into his spine. He coughed and took a deep breath, making sure he still could. Then, summoning all his strength and resolve, he commanded his body to move. Straining mightily, he tried to bring his head up first, hoping his arms and torso might follow.

They did.

With Bobby's help, Trey sat upright and shook away the last of the cobwebs. He brought a hand to the back of his head and rubbed where a welt had risen up from his encounter with the marble steps.

He turned to his mentor. "What the hell happened?"

For a long time, Buckland didn't respond. He sat holding Trey from behind, one hand pressed to his back, the other hand covering his own eyes. Without looking over, he began his sordid tale. The words came haltingly at first, but soon gathered momentum, as if Bobby had been mute for far too long, and now that he had found his voice, he couldn't stop listening to the sound of it.

"I never could do what Longstreet demanded," he said. "I told him I would, just to make sure no else did."

As the story evolved, Trey put the fractured pieces together. Slowly, the realization struck home: Buckland had been instructed by Longstreet to "disable" Trey, whatever that meant, if he planned to switch his vote.

As Bobby went on, Trey leaned down and picked up the small syringe, placing it inside his briefcase next to the pistol he had been carrying for weeks now. Turning back, he laid a hand on Buckland's shoulder as he finished his story of a Presidential election gone murderously wrong.

According to Buckland's recount, during his own re-election campaign, his personal life began coming apart. His wife had filed for divorce; he was nearly bankrupt from bad investments. He began to drink heavily. Then, driving home from a fundraiser, he fell asleep at the wheel. Only a few seconds passed, but when he awoke, he found his car buried in a hedge in someone's front yard. He jumped out to inspect the damage and saw something dark and crumpled lying on the ground several yards back. He ran over and found a smashed bicycle. Not far away, a young co-ed from Georgetown University was on the ground, her textbooks scattered amidst her twisted, unmoving limbs.

It didn't take Buckland long to realize she was dead. Looking around and seeing no witnesses, he panicked and left the scene. The next day, a witness came forward. But he wasn't interested in justice. He wanted blackmail. Bobby turned for help to the only source he knew who could deliver with total secrecy: Longstreet.

As expected, he agreed to take care of everything. Buckland thought the offer of help meant a financial payoff. But when they went to deliver the bribe, Buckland wound up an accomplice in murder. After that, he knew it was only a matter of time before Longstreet would ask for a "payback" of his own.

Then, a few weeks ago, Longstreet came to him with the order to "disable" Trey if he tried to swing the Presidential vote to Wardlow.

Trey blanched at Bobby's second use of that word. "What the hell did he mean by that? Do you know what's in that syringe?"

Buckland shook his head. "Longstreet said it'd cause a blackout of some kind, like you had a heart attack. But no permanent damage. It'd just take you out long enough so you couldn't change your vote."

Trey thought about this for a moment, then asked, "Did you believe him, Bobby?"

For the first time, Buckland looked him straight in the eye. "No, I didn't," he said.

Trey shook his head. "Neither do I."

With that, the two men helped each other up. Trey checked his watch and realized they still had to gather Maryland's delegation together to tell them of his changed vote. "We'll deal with Longstreet later," he said.

Buckland smoothed his mussed hair and brushed at his rumpled suit. "I better clean up. I'll meet you there."

Trey hesitated, not wanting to leave this highly emotional man alone. "You sure you'll be all right?"

Buckland forced a smile. "This is the best I've felt in a long time. It's amazing what honesty can do for you."

Trey reached out a hand, and they shook more forcefully than usual.

"I'm just glad Longstreet came to you and not some other people I can think of," Trey said. "They may not have been so charitable."

Buckland shook his head. "I haven't done a whole lot right lately. This one time doesn't make up for the rest."

Trey thought about this for a second. "Maybe not, but you sure picked a good place to start."

They laughed uneasily.

Then Trey turned and jogged up the steps, more determined than ever to permanently eliminate this criminal Administration.

Chapter Forty-Two

At the chamber entry, Trey wound his way through a crowd of colleagues gathered in small clusters everywhere. All the congressmen were dressed in their finest suits and ties, hair neatly cut and combed, faces freshly scrubbed. A sense of electricity permeated the room. Even conversation was louder and more animated than usual. Everyone shook hands enthusiastically and laughed nervously.

Trey greeted several friends, then maneuvered inside the cavernous chamber, finding his fellow Maryland Democrats in their usual spot—on the left of the main aisle. He joined them there, along with the state's Republicans. Normally, the two parties sat on opposite sides. But today they would vote as a state, so the Rules Committee had asked all delegations to sit together for this one-time-only occasion.

The Maryland representatives gathered around Trey when he asked them to join him in a nearby cloakroom. Looking at each other nervously, they wondered what this last-minute conference was all about. Reluctantly, they trooped inside the conference room, and Trey closed and locked the door behind. Turning around dramatically, he announced his decision: "I've had a change of heart, gentlemen. I've decided to support the Republican, Wardlow."

A momentary hush swept over the room for a moment, then everyone burst into animated conversation and argument.

The Democrats chastised Trey for waiting until the last minute to reveal his true intentions, leaving them no time for counter-argument or debate. Conversely, the Republicans expressed relief, knowing their man was now sure to win on the second ballot.

Trey tried to apologize for making his announcement so late. "By tomorrow, you'll understand why," he said.

Buckland showed up a few minutes later, and several Democrats tried to convince him to "talk sense" to his young charge. But without explanation, Bobby said he supported Trey's decision. This did little to calm the liberal wing. They continued to debate the decision heatedly. But with time running short, they agreed it was too late to negotiate a compromise. They took a quick show-of-hands, and decided the state would have to cast a "divided" ballot.

With this decision made, a loudspeaker blared out the start of the voting session. The Maryland delegates straggled out to rejoin their fellow representatives.

In the jam-packed chamber, the drone of voices threatened to overwhelm the room. In an attempt to restore order, Speaker Howard Clay banged his gavel furiously and surveyed the chamber with an angry stare.

By force of will alone, the room quieted.

Clay began the session with a quick swearing-in of all newly elected Representatives. Then he hurried through the fastest formal balloting ever for congressional officers.

With the preliminaries out of the way, he raised his eyes to the gallery above the chamber floor and welcomed the guests there—all one hundred members of the Senate. After the Presidential voting was official, the Senators would retire to their own chamber to elect the Vice President.

Clay waved to the ninety-six men and three women senators seated above. The hundredth member—the President Pro Tem of the Senate—sat beside Clay on the podium to oversee the formal counting of Electoral College votes. The two men shook hands and turned to the roll call.

The Sergeant-at-Arms called out: "All members present and accounted for?"

A roomful of voices called back: "Present."

Clay spoke again. "I declare the required two-thirds present. If anyone disagrees, speak now." He paused an instant, then banged his gavel dramatically. "The Electoral College count can proceed."

Trey watched all this with a sense of awe. He would never admit it, but he loved all the pomp and circumstance passed down through generations of congressmen. The procedures were more than mere flourish. They created a sense of higher purpose. Whatever was decided in these chambers would stand for all time.

As the President Pro Tem called out the state-by-state Electoral results, Trey's eyes swept across the walls from left to right. On either side of the towering Speaker's Rostrum, life-sized portraits of George Washington and the Marquis de Lafayette dominated. High above them, the official seals of the fifty states were prominently displayed in the order they had joined the union.

Trey's gaze came to rest on the gigantic glass eagle dead center, outlined in bronze. He had forgotten it was there, it had been so long since he'd looked up. He'd have to remember to do that more often.

In a matter of minutes, the formal Electoral count was completed. As expected, the tally followed the results reported in November exactly. The President Pro Tem announced the results "official."

Clay took over from there. His voice reverberated throughout the hall as he ran through the rules of Hinds' Precedents. A designated spokesperson from each delegation was to step to the podium, hand two envelopes to the

Sergeant-at-Arms, then call out the vote of his or her state. Inside the envelopes were signed certificates affirming the voice tally. This assured each delegation's decision was recorded accurately.

"We'll proceed in alphabetical order, beginning with Alabama," Clay said. "Is the great Cotton State prepared to cast its vote for President of the United States?"

The senior congressman from Alabama, nearing eighty years of age, frail and infirm, stood and spoke in a gravelly voice: "We are, Mr. Speaker."

"Let's proceed."

Representative Thornton Akers, cane in hand, began his way down the aisle, helped by a junior congressman.

Shuffling to the podium, Akers held out his state's envelopes in palsied hands. The Sergeant-at-Arms took the envelopes, and Akers pulled out a folded paper from which to speak. He then talked for nearly three minutes, extolling the seriousness with which Alabama cast its ballot.

"In summation," he said finally, breathing hard, "we cast our vote for the next President of these United States— Mr. Carl Wardlow."

Tucking the paper inside his jacket, he leaned down to the microphone and said, "God bless America."

With assistance, he headed back to his seat. The whole ordeal took more than five minutes.

Trey thought, *at this rate, we'll be here all day.*

Alaska came next, then Arizona and Arkansas. On it went. Each spokesperson took one to five minutes to regale everyone on the virtues of their state and its commitment to reflecting voters' wishes.

All the votes fell perfectly in line. California, Colorado, Connecticut, Delaware, Florida, Georgia.

One by one, each state voted exactly as everyone knew

they would, following the nationwide results from November.

Hawaii, Idaho, Illinois . . . Indiana, Iowa, Kansas.

The closer it got to the "M's," the more tension grew all around. People began to stir in their seats. The Speaker banged his gavel and demanded silence.

Then Kentucky and Louisiana reported in.

And the time had arrived.

"Next," Clay said, clearing his throat, a tremor in his voice, "the great state of Maine."

A hush fell over the hall as all eyes came to rest on the lone figure of Charlie Harris, sitting in the front row by himself, the state's only representative now. Harris had entered the session at the last possible moment, appearing from a side entrance.

Now, he rose and moved slowly toward the podium, holding his official envelopes and a set of three-by-five cards in trembling hands.

Halfway back in the room, Trey tried to slow his breathing. It had all come down to this, a single moment for all posterity. Even if he hadn't been through all the insanity and crisis over the last few weeks, he would feel the same right now. Without the pressure from Forsythe, without Camp David, without the car accident, Katie's disappearance, Longstreet's extortion, Laura's betrayal, Van Deventer's death, Buckland's confession, this was still a landmark moment, and Trey was nearly overwhelmed by the significance of it all.

The Sergeant-at-Arms stepped toward Harris, who was a tall, gangly, balding man of unremarkable appearance. The sergeant reached out for his envelopes. But Harris did not reciprocate. He held up a hand and leaned into the microphone. "Mr. Speaker. May I ask your indulgence?"

"Mr. Harris?"

"The state of Maine respectfully requests," he paused and glanced around the chambers, "*I* respectfully request . . ."

"Yes . . ."

"I request a temporary pass on my vote."

A combination roar and moan went up from the crowd. Clay banged his gavel furiously. Several House officers signaled for silence. The representatives calmed down and listened for Clay's response.

"Are you sure, Mr. Harris," Clay said, disappointed, "that a pass is best at this time?"

"Yes, Mr. Speaker. A *temporary* pass, of course."

Everyone wanted more of an explanation, but Harris offered none. Clay mumbled something to a clerk at his side. "All right, Mr. Harris. Pass granted." He slammed his gavel once, and Harris went back to his seat.

The Speaker sighed and went on. "This brings us to . . . Maryland."

More whispering and rumbling swept the hall. Clay hammered on the desktop, his ruddy complexion pulsing red. "Ladies and gentlemen, if we continue with these outbursts, today's session'll never end."

The crowd quieted and looked toward Maryland. All the state's representatives looked to Trey and Buckland, their strategists-by-default. Buckland whispered loud enough for everyone in the group to hear. "We didn't think of a pass. What do we do now?"

Trey smiled, enjoying the drama of it all. "We follow Maine's lead," he said, looking around the group. "We pass, too."

Everyone's heads moved up and down.

Clay shouted out: "Can we have a representative from Maryland? We've got a President to elect."

Buckland got up and stormed down the aisle to the podium. "Mr. Speaker, I thank you for your patience."

Laughter swept across the chamber.

"Maryland also requests a temporary pass."

Clay pounded his gavel once. "Hell, pass granted. Massachusetts!"

The next thirty states went quickly, the spokespeople delivering their votes perfunctorily, wanting to get back to Maine and Maryland as quickly as possible. With each state's vote, the balloting matched the November results perfectly. No surprises, no deviations.

Three hours after the session began, Wyoming's congressman recorded his state's support for Wardlow.

He was the last.

At the Speaker's Rostrum, Clay turned slowly in his chair and looked at the lighted tote board. Everyone in the room stared silently with him: Forty-eight votes cast. Twenty-four for the current President. Twenty-four for his challenger. Clay turned back to the room, saying nothing for a long while. Everyone watched him fumble with paperwork on his massive desk.

Trey wasn't sure if Clay was confused about how to proceed, overwhelmed by the occasion or allowing the weight of the moment to build. Maybe all three.

Finally, Clay looked up and spoke. "Mr. Harris," he said. "Time has come. Can we have your vote?"

Harris lifted himself up a section at a time. Walking slowly to the podium, he handed over his envelopes.

No one in the chamber made a noise. The only sound was the Sergeant-at-Arms shuffling across the thick carpet, the papers rustling in his hands. He delivered the envelopes as Harris began to speak.

"Ladies and gentlemen of the House and Senate," he said, "my fellow congressmen and women. As you know, we lost a colleague last week, and the great state of Maine lost one of its sons."

Hesitating, he reached down, poured water into a paper cup, and sipped slowly.

"This happened at a most inopportune time. Congressman Neil Van Deventer was a highly dedicated man. He was dedicated to his home state, yes, but equally dedicated to his country. He was a true patriot." Harris glanced down at the note cards in front of him, his hands gripped like pliers on either side of the lectern. "Because of the fragile nature of his health, Congressman Van Deventer also took special precautions."

Trey and Buckland shot glances at one another, then their eyes returned quickly to Harris, standing slumped shouldered in the well of the room.

"Knowing the importance of his vote today," Harris continued, "Neil entrusted to me, the day before his untimely death, a confidential letter. I won't go into the details now. A full text of the document is available for all here to view. The letter outlines his position—and mine—on the vote to be taken here today. Our decision was not an easy one to reach. In the end, we agreed to cast our ballot for the man who—apart from partisanship and party—most deserved the office of the Presidency."

Clearing his throat, he scanned the chamber, letting the emotional moment swell. "That man—the next President of the United States—is Carl Wardlow of California."

A roar went up from the crowd. Everyone came out of their seats. Forsythe supporters gasped in surprise and shock. Wardlow supporters jumped up and down, shaking hands, throwing their fists in the air. Clay beat his gavel repeatedly, calling for quiet.

In the midst of all this, Trey was the only congressman

344

still seated. Hands in his lap, he smiled to himself, marveling at the announcement. For all intents and purposes, a dead man had just elected the new President.

Buckland sat down beside Trey and spoke to him under the noise. "Maine just took us off the hook."

Trey smiled, remembering Van Deventer's last word to him: *"Dirigo. I lead."* It seemed so appropriate now.

"We can vote for Forsythe," Buckland said, "then get Wardlow confirmed on the second ballot. Your strategy's working perfectly."

Trey nodded and put an arm over the older man's shoulder and pulled him close. "We could do that," he said, "but it's time we stood up and told everyone who we support, Bobby. To hell with a second ballot, let's confirm Wardlow right now."

Buckland held Trey's eyes with his own. "I like your style, Congressman."

They shook hands and looked around to the rest of the Maryland representatives, who were nodding solemnly. "It's done then," Buckland said. "We'll put him over the top."

Miles Ogle, entrusted with the state's envelopes, reached inside and registered their final tally.

Buckland stood up, and the crowd quieted.

Clay's voice filled the arena: "We've got one last vote, ladies and gentlemen," he said. "Can we have your results, Maryland?"

"You can, Mr. Speaker," Buckland said. "The honor goes to my esteemed colleague." He gestured to his left. "Mr. Thomas Josiah Stone."

Trey looked at him, startled. "You don't have to do that, Bobby."

"Yes I do. You're our spokesman. Go on up there and make history."

"Gentlemen, please," Clay implored, "we're trying to elect a President *today*."

Trey stood up and started down the aisle, feeling a new respect for his colleagues and for his own role in arriving at this monumental decision. He understood better than ever what his dad had said—that doing right is not always easy, but it's always right. No one could ever take that away.

Arriving at the podium, he handed over the envelopes and looked up at the more than five hundred congressional members gathered throughout the chambers. They leaned forward in their seats, wondering whether Maryland's vote would force ballot two, or end the process here.

As Trey looked around the chamber, he felt enormous pride in the men and women around him. Some of them could be inordinate pains, true. Others were not as well informed as they should be. And all of them were too dependent on lobbyists and big contributors. But when they came together, the individual flaws disappeared. As an institution, they could still accomplish good things, even when it was so much easier to go the other way.

Trey spoke out in a strong voice: "My fellow congressmen—and especially my colleagues from Maryland—I thank you for this opportunity to speak. I promise to take only a moment of your time. I don't have a formal statement to read, but I'd like to say we've honored ourselves today. We've upheld the dignity of this House and preserved the integrity of our offices. Our system, as designed by the nation's founders, has worked. The system always works when good men and women come together in service to their country."

He allowed the words to resonate within the massive chamber, filling it.

"Ladies and gentlemen," he said, "the Chesapeake state

of Maryland casts its vote for the next President of the United States of America—Carlos Wardlow. God be with him and with us all."

As one the roomful of representatives and senators stood and applauded. There were no unseemly demonstrations, no shouts of support or disagreement, just a swelling of applause that went on for several minutes.

Trey, working his way back up the aisle, shook hands as he went. Finally, he stood by his seat to join the ovation, feeling like a victor for the first time since the entire process began nearly two months ago.

It was the longest two months of his life. Until now. He knew many more long months were yet to come.

Chapter Forty-Three

For the next thirty minutes, the entire House stayed locked in session. All electronic links to the outside world were shut down while the Senate retired to its own chambers to conduct what turned out to be perfunctory balloting. With a Republican majority, no one but Wardlow's running mate stood a prayer of getting affirmed as Vice President.

Afterward, the House Speaker, President Pro Tem of the Senate and minority leaders went to the White House to deliver the news to the candidates. In less than thirty minutes, the officers called back to the Capitol Building and formally closed the two sessions, ending one of the most incredible congressional voting episodes in U.S. electoral history.

It didn't take the members of Congress long to exit their respective chambers. The senators and representatives left en masse, spreading out to various locations around the Capitol facility—meeting rooms, conference halls and briefing centers—to talk with the press.

Trey agreed to make a statement in the Rotunda where a selection of pool journalists had gathered. He offered a short statement outlining his reasons for backing Wardlow. He restated key points about the general election balloting and how, except for an historical anomaly, Wardlow would have won outright in November. Trey declined to criticize or even discuss the current Administration.

"This is a time to show our respect for the institution of the Presidency," he said, "and to honor our new President-elect. Let's keep the focus where it should be, ladies and gentlemen. The voters deserve no less."

At the close of his comments, reporters shot up their hands with follow-up questions. Trey answered a half-dozen or so, then stepped aside to let other congressmen have their time.

As he walked off the podium, another representative followed behind, catching up with him in a private area behind the stage. Trey felt a hand on his shoulder and turned around to find Maine's Charlie Harris. They had only met once before—at Camp David.

"Mr. Harris," Trey said. "It's a pleasure to see you again."

"Likewise, Mr. Stone."

"Call me Trey, please."

"If you'll call me Charlie."

They moved toward the curved Rotunda wall, near a bust of Thomas Jefferson, where they were sure no one else could hear. Trey went first.

"I must admit, I was caught off guard by your vote today. I had no idea about Neil's letter, of course."

"I apologize for not returning your calls. Neil filled me in on your discussions of White House threats, and I decided to be extra careful about all personal contact."

"I understand your concerns—better than most."

"I was especially worried after being confronted by an Administration official."

"Let me guess: You were contacted by a gentleman named Longstreet. . . ."

Harris smiled. "You use the term *gentleman* loosely."

Trey nodded, and Harris went on.

"I found out firsthand why you had approached Neil. This Longstreet character is intimidating. I decided to leave him with the impression his tactics had worked. It seemed safer that way."

"That was the right thing to do. But one part still bothers me, Charlie. Do you think Longstreet had something to do with Neil's death?"

"Neil was very sick, much more so than he let on. A reliable physician performed the autopsy, and he believes Neil hung on well past what most men could have tolerated."

"That's reassuring," Trey said. "But I still wonder if we should get a second opinion."

"I'm afraid it wouldn't do any good."

"Why's that?"

"His body was cremated."

Trey looked down and shook his head, realizing Longstreet was off the hook for sure. The only evidence against him was the syringe, but to use that meant exposing Buckland, a man who had just saved Trey's life; the conflicting choices in this whole sordid affair were getting more difficult by the moment.

He looked up. "When are they scattering the ashes?"

"Tomorrow afternoon at Nicatous Lake."

"I'd like to be there."

"We'd love to have you."

"I'll fly up in the morning."

With that, both men looked away, not sure what to say next. It had all been said, all been done. Glancing toward the podium, they watched a number of congressmen from states around the country holding forth on their roles in electing the new President, maintaining the integrity of the Constitution, serving the public good.

When Trey looked back, he noticed Harris was not a particularly handsome man—kind of spindly and drawn, and his eyes were a little rheumy, like a professor who had spent too much time poring over test papers. But in the reflected light of the Rotunda, he looked magnificent. Here was a man who had honored the memory of generations of representatives before and after him. He had done this simply because it was right, and for no other reason.

Trey stuck out his hand, and Harris shook it enthusiastically.

"You're a good man, Charlie Harris," Trey said. "I'm proud to serve with you."

"Thank you, Congressman. Same here."

Without another word, they parted, walking off in opposite directions. In the future, Trey knew, the two men might disagree on the issues and wrangle over legislation, but whenever principle was at stake, they would find a way to come together. The system wasn't perfect, but it *worked*— most of the time, anyway.

This was one of those times, and it felt good.

Chapter Forty-Four

Trey walked quickly across the Rotunda floor to where his small security force was waiting. They clustered around him as he moved toward the elevators leading to the basement subway that connected the Capitol and Cannon Building offices. Before they got there, Trey caught a glimpse of a familiar face approaching through the east entryway. A bodyguard held up a hand to stop the intruder, but Trey said it was okay. He turned to the visitor and spoke solemnly.

"Hello, Laura. How are you?"

She struggled to find the first words they had spoken since that fateful day at the Watergate. Finally, she whispered, "I'm much better, thanks." He took her by the arm and stepped to the side where they could talk more privately. Glancing away, he said, "It's finally over. The only thing left now is dealing with Longstreet and the criminal charges he'll bring."

Laura shook her head, her long, thick hair sweeping luxuriously over her shoulders. "Just remember you did the right thing, and we're all proud of you."

His first reaction was to say thanks, but underneath her words, the remark seemed so insincere. Here was a woman who had thrown him over for political gain—not once but twice in the span of a few weeks. He couldn't simply accept her compliment now and let it go at that. He wasn't that *Washington* yet. He grabbed her by the elbow and led her to an empty conference room off the main hall, his security force trailing behind.

He turned to them. "We'll be just a moment, gentlemen." He slammed the door.

Inside, she moved away from him, her back turned. He stared at her, searching for the words to convey his disappointment that she had betrayed him so callously.

"Why'd you do it, Laura? I thought we had something special between us. I, I—" he stuttered, frustrated by his inability to understand her treachery. "It *was* you, wasn't it? You told Longstreet about my meeting with Jack. You betrayed me *and* your husband. Do you realize the pain you caused?"

He dropped his briefcase on the floor and moved past her, looking out the window onto Independence Avenue. Outside, supporters of President-elect Wardlow were out in force, carrying placards, blowing horns, throwing streamers—it looked like a political convention gone mad. A light snow was falling, too, but the cold and wet did little to dampen their enthusiasm. Then Trey felt a hand in the middle of his back. Tensing, he listened for the words he didn't really want to hear.

"Yes, it was me," she said, softly. "It was the biggest mistake of my life."

Spinning around, he saw her face streaked with tears. She did nothing to wipe them away. He wanted to reach out and hold her, to make the pain stop for both of them, but he couldn't do that. Not any more. Nothing would ever be the same between them. To survive in this town, he knew, he could never again place loyalty to others above loyalty to himself and his family.

He spoke softly but firmly. "In that one act, you destroyed your husband and nearly destroyed me. I'll never understand why. For a goddamned election? Was it worth it? Just answer that one question for me."

She held onto his arm tightly, looking deeply into his eyes. "Do you really think I could do something like that for an election? God, no—I did it for you. For us." She lifted a hand to brush away a lock of his dark hair spilled across his forehead, but he pulled away.

"Don't you understand? There is no *us,* Laura. There never was; there never could be."

She stepped in front of him, and he could feel her eyes penetrating his. "Oh yes there was an *us.* I could feel it and so could you. We had something. We could have gone places around here."

He laughed. "And to do that," he said, "you exposed me to prosecution. You revealed my private conversations with your husband and made my actions appear like something they weren't. If that's 'going places,' leave me out."

She sat on the edge of a conference table, head down, hands folded in her lap. "I thought if I got you to support Forsythe, you'd lock up a White House position—maybe even a run at the Presidency." She shook her head thinking about it now, realizing how everything turned out. "I was trying to save you from yourself. That's the God's honest truth, Trey. I never believed it would go so wrong." Her tears had stopped; she appeared too drained to cry.

Trey sat on the windowsill, wondering why so many people in D.C. felt compelled to control the fates of others, when they could barely handle their own.

"The only person who can save me from myself is me. Over the last few weeks, I've learned a lot about who I am. I'll admit, yes, I was attracted to you. You're an exciting woman who likes to play for big stakes. I admire that, even envy it in many ways."

She brushed a streak of hair away from her face; even with make-up smeared, she was stunning, but the hardness in her eyes belied the softness of her features. Trey knew no matter what happened to him, Laura would be all right. She was a survivor. More so than she realized herself.

"You don't need me to make a name for yourself," he said. "You don't need anyone. Maybe that's what makes you so damn attractive."

Standing, he faced away from her, watching the snow gather over the crowded streets. "What you don't understand is I *do* need people, Laura. Most of all, I need Jazz and Katie. But I also need to be who I am inside—not who others want me to be."

He turned back to her. "A lot of people think my style doesn't work that well in Washington. They think I'm too damn honest for my own good. Call it naïve, call it stupid. I can't change who I am."

She looked up, trying to smile through her tears. "I don't want you to change. You're wonderful just as you are—better than you can ever imagine."

They both suddenly realized there was nothing left to say, nowhere else to go; the relationship had outlived its usefulness for both of them.

Reaching down, Trey picked up his briefcase. "After Longstreet's through with me, I hope the public's as sure about my future as you are."

"He might be through with you already," she said.

He hesitated. "Why do you say that?"

She reached inside her valise and pulled out a manila folder, handing it over to him. He quickly thumbed through the file. It was filled with hastily-made copies of what appeared to be pilfered documents stamped "Top Secret" and "Highly Proprietary."

"They're files from the personal records of one Archibald Longstreet," Laura said. "Illicitly obtained FBI files, transcripts from illegal wiretaps, spying records, campaign tactics based on extortion. It's all there—enough to hang him several times over."

"Where'd you get these?"

"Arch taught me the value of never trusting anyone. When he got called out to an emergency meeting one day, he left his desk key behind. I had a copy made." She smiled. "He never suspected. He never believed I could be as dirty as him." She looked away, her eyes glistening. "I proved everyone wrong."

Trey continued to review the documents, realizing they showed a clear paper trail of criminal campaign tactics, dirty tricks, abuse of federal agencies and broken privacy laws. There was enough here to put Longstreet away for a long time.

"Maybe you were caught up in something you didn't fully understand," he said. "We all were."

Laura fumbled inside her pursue, looking for a fresh tissue. "When Arch contacts you—and he will—show him these records. He'll think long and hard about coming after you."

Trey pulled a handkerchief from his breast pocket and handed it to her. "I'll do that."

He watched her wipe meticulously under each eye and thought back to the night at the Watergate when he held her in his arms. He knew such temptations would always be an occupational hazard. Power and position attracted admirers—wanted and unwanted. The hard part was deciding which was which.

"I owe you, Laura," he said. "You may have just saved me."

She scoffed. "You don't owe me anything. I got you into this, remember?"

"No, I got myself into it with a combination of stupidity—and even more stupidity." He shoved the folder into his briefcase and locked it securely. "But I'm a lot wiser now. I won't be caught like that again."

She smiled through her tears. "You mean you won't be caught in the arms of a drunken, naked woman again?"

He grinned. "Not unless it's Jazz."

They laughed together. Then a long silence slipped between them.

Laura checked her make-up in a compact mirror; Trey fiddled with his briefcase, switching it from hand to hand.

"I better get to the office," he said. "I just realized I've got a fax to intercept."

"One more thing, Trey," she said. "For what it's worth, I didn't know anything about the hidden cameras at the Watergate."

He nodded. "Longstreet told me. For once, I believed him."

"But what I said that night, I did mean. I do love you. But I know we can never be together. It was crazy of me to think so. I can't believe I came so close to hurting someone I love so much."

He stepped up next to her. "Don't ever stop loving the people close to you, Laura. That's the best you can do. But remember to love yourself, too, and those incredible boys of yours. They're the spitting image of Jack, and they adore you. They need you."

"They're my life from here on out."

Leaning over, he kissed her lightly on the cheek. "Don't be a stranger. It's been too long since you've been to the house."

"I'll call Jazz," she said, "and set something up."

He knew she wouldn't, of course.

"I'll hold you to that."

She reached inside her purse as the tears threatened once more. "Go on." She shooed him away. "You've got work to do—and a man to see."

He opened the door and stepped out, Laura following right behind. The guards gathered around him again. As they moved off, he glanced back over one shoulder, looking for her, but she had already disappeared into the crowd.

Chapter Forty-Five

The congressional tram took less than two minutes to arrive at the Cannon Building. A few journalists and camera crews were still wandering the halls, but Trey managed to avoid all comment and rushed straight to his office.

He found his staff consumed by phone calls, faxes and courier deliveries. Twenty or more admirers had sent bouquets of flowers. Arrangements were stacked everywhere—on desks, windowsills, the floor.

Miss Landers hung up the phone and came to him. "We're swamped. Everyone's calling—reporters, voters, party leaders. Governor Wardlow tried to reach you several times, too. He left a number at the White House."

"He moves in fast."

"President Forsythe gave him an office for the day."

"How gallant." Trey picked up a handful of faxes and glanced over them. They were mostly notes of thanks from political officers around the country. Then he looked up to his long-time secretary.

"Get the President-elect on the line for me, will you?" he said, moving toward his office.

Miss Landers grabbed him by the sleeve. "You've got a visitor in there—from the White House."

He stared at the closed door, knowing who waited on the other side.

"Longstreet," he said.

"Yes, he told me you had an appointment."

"We do." Trey handed the faxes back to her and the

359

sheaf of documents from Laura. "Make copies of these and bring them in. Lock the originals in the safe. I won't be long. Hold off on the Wardlow call until I'm done."

"Yes, sir."

He grabbed the door handle and looked back. "Miss Landers—that fax I sent in earlier from the limo. . . ."

"Yes."

"Hold off on it, too, would you?"

"I already locked it in your top desk drawer," she said, turning away. "I thought you might want to review it again."

He shook his head, wondering how she always knew his next move better than he did. The fax was a letter of apology to his constituents and an offer to resign from office in advance of the criminal charges to come. It was his way of getting out in front of the White House publicity machine. But now with the papers provided by Laura. . . .

He reached down and turned the knob to his office door and marched in.

Longstreet was standing by the window watching the boisterous celebration below. He didn't even glance back when Trey entered.

Trey went to his desk and slammed down his briefcase. Opening it, he sat back in his chair, hands laced together behind his head. And waited.

Slowly, Longstreet swung around. Leaning against the sill, arms folded across his chest, he looked as dapper as always in a navy blue suit. Behind his thick glasses, his eyes were bright and sharp, almost dancing, as if he took a perverse delight in the final outcome; it gave him the opportunity to do what he did best—pillage and burn. He motioned toward the scene outside.

"You made a lot of people very happy today."

Trey shrugged. "I take it you're not among them?"

Longstreet grinned. "You could say that. The President's less than ecstatic, too. But you probably knew that."

"I assumed as much."

Longstreet stared at the floor for a moment. "Mind if I take a seat?"

Trey gestured at the chair in front, and Longstreet sat down, sighing melodramatically. "It's a shame," he said.

"What is?"

"That we lost such a good congressman today—a darling of the Democratic Party, a man with a future as bright as could be. It's a crying shame, I say."

"You're not referring to me, are you?"

"Ah, but I am." Longstreet leaned forward, his eyes narrowing as if he were trying to bore a hole through Trey. "Damn you, Stone, we had it all right at our fingertips. We could've owned the world. You, Forsythe . . . me. We could've done great things. You had a shot at the White House. The goddamned White House! You realize what you threw away? For the life of me, I can't understand it."

Trey stared back just as hard, leaning in toward him. "You're the one who threw away everything—your integrity, your honor—if you ever had any. You trashed the office of the Presidency and all it stands for. You guys don't deserve to run a student council, let alone the White House."

The smirk on Longstreet's face didn't change.

"When we hold a press conference tomorrow, you'll realize honor and integrity are for losers. You think just because we're out of the White House we don't have power? You'll learn the meaning of power. We'll drop you like yesterday's garbage. From here on out, your life'll spell misery. You'll never forget the day you turned on me—and on the President."

Miss Landers knocked lightly and leaned inside. Trey motioned for her to come in.

He took a handful of copies from her and flipped them on the desk in front of Longstreet.

"Look at these documents, then let's talk about press conferences."

As Miss Landers left, Trey stepped over by the window, looking out at the steady stream of partiers below. Traffic was backed up along Independence like a parade. The snow was falling more heavily now. It looked like a ticker-tape blizzard welcoming the start of a new year, a new regime. He checked his watch. It was nearing three-thirty. He'd have to get on the road soon, or it'd take him half the night to get home.

Turning around, he saw Longstreet sitting on the edge of his seat, looking down at the pile of papers, his hands clasped in front. It was as if he couldn't bring himself to touch the offending documents. His face was as white as the flakes outside. Trey went back to his desk.

"Look at me!" he commanded.

Longstreet's eyes lifted up, large as half-dollars.

"You disgust me," Trey said. "You're the worst of what our system has to offer. You want to come after me? Go ahead. I'll take a few hits, sure, but my actions are defensible. Yours are not. There's enough evidence here to put you away for years. I'm not talking Club Fed, either—I'll see you do hard time."

Trey placed his hands on his hips. It was all he could do to calm the shaking inside. The adrenaline was pumping full out now. For the first time in weeks, he knew exactly what to do and how to do it, as if a sudden white-hot light had shown the way.

Longstreet tried to speak, but the words wouldn't come. He tried again.

"Wha . . . Where did you get these documents?"

"Where do you think they came from? *Your* office. They've got your mark all over them. Signed, sealed, and delivered."

Longstreet tugged at his suit, trying to regain composure. "You'll never make the charges stick. These are fakes. I never authorized this activity. Forgeries, that's all you've got."

"Names, places, dates," Trey said. "Eyewitnesses, too. Fellow conspirators. What do you think will happen when these people are called to the stand? You think they'll hang themselves to save you? I doubt it. It's your call, though. Go ahead. I'd like to see you under cross-examination."

Longstreet grabbed hold of the arms of his chair, his eyes darting around the room, unable to focus for more than a fleeting second. He opened his mouth and tried to speak, but no words came.

Trey sat across from him. "Remember, I've got a friend in the White House now. President Wardlow would love to burn your ass—you and the entire Southern Mafia."

Longstreet stood up with some difficulty. Moving to the back of the office, he paced in a tight little circle. His suit jacket billowed out, exposing his small, silver-plated pistol. As he walked, he laid a hand against the gun through his suit jacket. But Trey knew Longstreet would never have the nerve to use the weapon. The man was a coward. He might ask others to do violence for him, but he would never risk it himself. Still, just in case, Trey didn't move far from his open briefcase where his own pistol was stored.

"I've got as much on you as you've got on me," Longstreet said. "You want a war of attrition? I can hold up better than you. You've got more to lose."

Trey reached inside his briefcase and picked up the

small, silver syringe, holding it up for Longstreet to view.

"You told me once to 'always know your enemy.' But you broke your own rule. You didn't know Bobby Buckland, and you sure as hell don't know me. I can withstand any charges you want to bring. I'll admit my mistakes, apologize, and move on. The voters and my colleagues will forgive me—because we respect each other. That's something you wouldn't know anything about."

"How long will it take that little wife of yours to forgive the 'mistake' at the Watergate?" Longstreet asked, gamely smirking again. "The tabloids'd love to splash those photos across their front pages."

"My wife's a smart lady." He stood and moved around the desk toward the door. "She knows a setup when she sees it. She also knows *her* enemy, and it's not me. It's you."

He laid a hand on the doorknob and spoke in controlled, carefully measured tones, giving the words even more of an impact. "You're a weak, sniveling coward. You sicken me. I want you out of my office and out of this city."

He opened the door and walked back to his desk. "Now get the hell out of here. I've got a President-elect to congratulate." He hit the intercom. "Miss Landers, get Mr. Wardlow on the line for me, please."

Trey looked up just as Longstreet moved toward the door. When he stopped and glanced back, Trey froze him with an expression that seemed to say: *One word, and I'll draw and quarter you on the spot.* Then he heard Miss Landers' voice.

"The President-elect's on line one," she called out.

Trey sat down and punched the blinking light. When he looked up again, Longstreet was gone.

Trey knew he wouldn't be back.

Epilogue

Later that evening, the road back to Annapolis was remarkably clear. The snowplows were out in force as a light dusting continued to fall over the heavy blanket laid down earlier. It was only five o'clock, but the skies were already darkening under a low layer of clouds; the early evening light reflected reddish-pink off the white.

Red sky at night, sailor's delight.

Trey smiled inwardly, feeling at ease for the first time since he could remember. He drove with his right hand on the wheel, left arm crooked through the open driver's window. The wind was like ice, but it didn't take long to feel only the cleansing effect.

He drove carefully along the two-lane road toward home, slowing when he came to the spot where the "accident" occurred nearly two weeks ago. It seemed like a lifetime had passed since then. The thought of nearly losing Jazz still gave him a chill.

He closed the window and cranked up the heater.

Then he glanced into the rearview mirror and saw nothing but empty road in back. Same in front. Trey knew he should have let the security guards accompany him, but he needed time to himself and his own thoughts, without the distraction of other people and things outside. That's why he rented a car for the ride home. It gave him the chance to do something he should do more often—pause to reflect, take his own counsel and stop listening to those with their own purposes and agendas.

As he neared the entrance to their compound, he was surprised to see all the media trucks gone. A lone security guard sat on the side of the road.

In a matter of hours, all the focus had shifted to Wardlow and his new Administration. This was how it should be, of course. The vote was over. The people's will had been done. Despite the compromises and aggravations of democracy, a smooth transition of power was underway.

Trey waved to the guard as he pulled through the gate. Driving over the unpaved portion of the driveway, he listened to the crunch of tires over gravel, then gunned the engine and pulled up in front of the house.

Climbing out, briefcase in hand, he trudged over to where Jazz and Katie had built a five-foot-tall snowman. They had placed an Annapolis school banner in one stick hand and a tiny American flag in the other. The snowman's smile, constructed out of buttons, was as big as could be.

"This better not be who I think it is," he mumbled to himself. He stepped around to get a better look. As he did, his foot bumped against a lumpy object in the snow.

When he glanced down, his stomach leapt into his throat.

There in the pure white drift between the snowman and the house, half hidden by an evergreen bush, was a mass of long, red hair lying in pooled blood. Trey knelt down and reached out to smooth the matted strands. He felt warm blood oozing from a gaping wound.

It was their family pet, Red Dog.

He was dead—shot by a high-powered weapon that had left an exit hole the size of Trey's hand in the dog's chest. The animal never knew what hit him, Trey was sure. At the same moment, he thought: *Where are Jazz and Katie?*

He scrambled to his feet when he heard the crunch of heavy boots across the snow behind him.

Swinging around, he looked up into the gray sky at a massive figure towering over him.

A man's shaved head and diamond stud earring reflected what was left of the fading light.

It was Steele. He held a huge handgun—an automatic of some kind—in one steady hand and pointed it directly at Trey's forehead.

Trey wrapped one hand into a fist, thinking: *Gun or not, if this son of a bitch has hurt Jazz or Katie . . .*

"Where are my wife and child? If you've so much as touched them, I'll rip your heart out."

"If there's any ripping to do," Steele said, "I'll be the one doing it." He motioned toward the front of the house. "We've got a little paperwork to do."

Trey had no idea what Steele was talking about, nor did he care; he only prayed he would find Jazz and Katie safe inside.

He stepped through Steele's crushed footprints toward the front porch. When he reached the first step, Steele ordered him to halt.

"Drop the briefcase," he said.

Trey did as he was told, and proceeded carefully up the slick steps to the double-door entry. He shoved the door open and moved inside. The place was eerily quiet. He took several steps down the hall, hoping to see his wife and child, but afraid of what he might find.

He stopped and glanced back to see Steele come up the steps behind, the briefcase clutched in one hand and the pistol in the other, still aimed at Trey's head.

Trey continued toward the family room where he heard the crackle of a fire and smelled burning wood. Near the corner, he pulled up short when he saw blood splattered on the marble floor by the step-down into the Great Room. He could barely control his heartbeat now. His mouth was dry;

he could hardly catch his breath. He tried to calm himself, then turned around the corner and looked inside.

There, sitting on the couch in front of the fire as if relaxing on a weekend afternoon, were the three ladies of the house, their heads side-by-side. Katie's hair was barely visible over the top of the sofa.

Trey rushed to them. But as he neared the couch, he saw someone else off to the side. Ridge Franks was sitting by the maple table—a sawed-off shotgun lying across his lap. Rocked back in his chair, he chewed on something that looked like leftover meat. He appeared as comfortable as could be, like the uninvited guest who wouldn't leave.

Trey ignored Franks' leer and went to his wife. He moved to the front of the couch and noticed all three had their mouths taped shut. Their hands were tied behind their backs and their feet were linked together with an electrical cord. It looked especially absurd for a little, harmless girl to be bound and gagged.

This was so typical of Longstreet's overkill.

Trey reached toward Jazz's mouth to pull off the tape.

Steele yelled out, "Leave 'em as they are," he said. "I'm running this show."

Trey ignored him. What could Steele do? Shoot him? He was going to do that anyway. It might as well be under Trey's terms. He leaned forward and gently lifted off the masking tape. Jazz grimaced. The adhesive left red splotches around her mouth.

He knelt down in front of her.

"You hurt, babe?"

She shook her head, but she couldn't summon up the words to answer him without dissolving into tears. He was on the verge himself, but he knew he had to hold himself together for them.

Steele came around and bumped him aside. He reached down and began to reapply the tape. Then Trey caught Katie's frightened eyes with his and tried to smile to calm her. He looked over to Irma and discovered the source of the blood in the hallway. She had been rapped alongside the head. Her ear and cheek were covered in red. She nodded ever so slightly, trying to show she was all right. But her complexion was pallid, and Trey thought she was about to pass out.

He sat there for a long moment trying to figure out how this could have happened. He hadn't released the property's security force. They were supposed to be on the grounds, armed and ready. Longstreet's men must have overpowered them. With their highly specialized equipment, they probably had the element of surprise on their side, as well. Trey wondered who the security officer was at the front gate—undoubtedly one of Longstreet's men, too.

Steele continued to work on Jazz, and Trey looked around the floor for a weapon of his own, something he might use to knock the gun out of Steele's hand. With Franks leaning back on two legs of his chair, it might take him a moment to recover, giving Trey a chance to attack.

But Steele had his gun leveled at Jazz's chest. Now wasn't the time.

"Get up," he growled. "Like I said, we've got paperwork to do." He motioned toward the maple table. "You're going to write a letter of explanation, about how you sold yourself out on the vote today and tried to frame the White House—how you tried to steal a national election." Steele laughed. "Did you really think we'd let you just roll over us? We didn't get to where we are by being patsies for the likes of amateurs like you." He pointed toward the table. "Start writing, Congressman. This is going to be the confession of your life."

Trey knew Steele meant that in more ways than one. This would be the *last* confession of his life, too.

He got up and walked slowly forward, watching Franks gnaw on his day-old beef, the juices running down the corner of his mouth and dripping onto a napkin stuck into his shirt collar. Just below that was the sawed off shotgun, lying there for the taking.

But as Trey neared the table, Franks grabbed the gun with his free hand.

This guy may be sleazy, Trey thought, *but he's no dummy. He won't leave himself vulnerable.* Trey knew it would take a bold move on his part to seize the upper hand.

He sat down across from Franks.

Steele threw down the briefcase. Kneeling in front, he tried to figure out how to open the lock. "What's the combination?"

Trey shrugged, but Steele pointed his pistol at the front of the valise. "We can do it the easy way, or my way. Whichever you prefer."

Trey sighed and gave him the four-digit combination. It took Steele two tries, but he finally popped the lock. Inside, Trey's pistol was lying in plain view. Steele pulled it out and pretended to admire the gun, which had never even been fired.

"Like to play rough, do we?" he said, tucking the .22 in his waistband. He pulled out a pad of paper and a pen and handed them over. Trey sat frozen in front of the stationery while Steele reached inside his jacket pocket and pulled out a sheet of paper torn from a legal pad.

"Longstreet's done the writing for you," he said. "I'll dictate."

Trey could see the note covered three-quarters of the page. He had hoped it would be longer; he needed more time.

"Put today's date in the upper right corner," Steele said,

"and the time, too." He checked his watch. "Five-nineteen."

Trey started to write, but then pretended the pen was dry, shaking it a few times. "I need the gold pen inside the right pocket of the briefcase."

Steele picked up the valise and tossed it on the table. Trey reached inside and pawed around, while stealing a glance at Franks, who had stopped eating and was staring down at his lap. His complexion was as gray as Irma's.

Steele watched his partner for a moment, then asked, "What the hell's with you?"

Franks shook his head, unable to respond. Perspiration dotted his forehead and upper lip. It was obvious he was about to throw up. Leaning forward, he took the shotgun from his lap and set it aside. He then covered his mouth with both hands and vomited through his fingers.

"What the fuck!" Steele bellowed. He looked down at his boots, covered with greenish bile and flecks of undigested beef. "I told you not to eat that stuff."

Steele grabbed a loose paper from the table and reached down to wipe himself.

Then Trey found what he was looking for. He grabbed the tiny silver syringe and, in one motion, lunged toward Steele, jabbing the point of the needle into the side of his bulging neck.

Steele froze immediately. It was eerie. This giant of a man simply stared straight ahead with the look of a frightened child; he knew something bad had happened but couldn't quite comprehend what. He tried to move but was unable to lift a finger. Slowly, his eyes turned toward Trey. Then he dropped to one knee, still holding the pistol out in front of him, pointed aimlessly at the wall.

Franks looked up from his retching and realized what was happening, but he was too weak to respond. He couldn't even find where he'd put his gun. Glancing around, he saw the weapon standing against the back wall. As he reached for it, Trey snatched Steele's pistol from his hand. He got the .45 under control and pulled the trigger.

When the gun erupted, the side of Frank's face exploded against the wall.

He collapsed off the chair into a pool of blood.

Trey stood and watched the two men resting beside each other, staring up through fixed and dilated eyes.

Slowly, Trey dropped the pistol on the rug and fell to his knees. He waited for the anguish to come. But it never did. With a sudden sense of calm, he realized all the insanity had stopped in the only way it could from the beginning.

The next morning, Trey pulled on a light jacket and stepped outside to see if he could find his wife and daughter. They had gotten up early to play in the fresh snow. He found them putting the finishing touches on their huge snowman, adding an old Navy muffler and worn seaman's cap.

Earlier in the morning, Trey had taken Red Dog's lifeless body away from where Katie might find the remains. This was done with the approval of the police and FBI, of course, many of whom were still onsite, combing over the crime scene.

The investigation had gone on through the night. When the first officers arrived, they discovered the security guard at the front gate was one of Trey's own men; he had been shot and propped up in the driver's seat. Two other guards on the property were killed, as well.

Reconstructing the events, the police felt Steele and Franks operated alone when they took Jazz, Katie and Irma hostage. While waiting for Trey to arrive, Franks had demanded something to eat. Irma fixed him a plate of food laced with an odorless household cleanser. Irma wasn't sure what the reaction would be, but she knew it couldn't be good.

She was more right than she ever expected. . . .

In the morning's chilled air, Trey watched Jazz and Katie finish up the last of their snowman's wardrobe—a pair of old Navy boots stuck at the bottom.

He couldn't resist asking, "Who's this supposed to be?"

"Who do you think it is?" Jazz said.

"The snowman's *you*, Daddy!" Katie yelled. She ran to him and grabbed him by the hand. "It's you!"

He inspected their creation and announced his decision: "This thing outweighs me by forty pounds. I haven't got a paunch like that! And where'd this triple chin come from?"

Jazz packed another handful onto the mid-section. "Have you checked a full-length mirror lately, buster?"

He smiled and reached down to scoop up a handful of clean snow. When she wasn't watching he let it fly, catching her in the leg. She grabbed two handfuls and threw them both, grazing him in the arm. Katie got off a shot, too, before he wrestled her to the ground. Before Trey knew it, his wife and daughter were on top of him with double handfuls of snow. They were all laughing uncontrollably by the time he finally gave in.

"You win," he shouted. "The snowman *is* me. It's beautiful. Perfect."

Irma stepped onto the front porch, shivering in little more than a housedress.

"Hot chocolate on the stove," she called.

"I want marshmallows," Katie said.

She scrambled up and ran to the house. Trey and Jazz helped each other up and walked back slowly.

"I'm surprised you're out of the house so early today,"

she said. "I thought you'd be on the phone all day with reporters."

"They'll be there tomorrow," he said, "and the next day."

She nodded. "I heard the news reports about Longstreet," she said. "I'm not surprised."

"I knew he'd take the easy way out," Trey agreed.

"Do they have any idea where he went?"

He shook his head. "They're watching all the airports. The FBI figures he'll try to get to the Far East. Apparently he's got connections there."

"When they searched his house," Jazz said, "they found a hidden basement that looked like a dungeon."

"I understand it was more of a torture chamber with weird sadomasochistic equipment. The guy's a real nut case."

Jazz took a deep breath and changed the topic.

"Irma said the White House called this morning."

"I guess I'm going to have to set up a direct line," Trey said, grinning. "Wardlow's working out of an office in the East Wing. He said he'd like me to join his Administration, but I'm not sure that's a good idea."

"Why not?"

"With the charges pending against Forsythe, the next several months will be an unbroken string of legal proceedings. I can't do justice to investigating Forsythe and serve Wardlow's Administration, too. Besides, I just got re-elected. I'd hate to desert Maryland's voters now."

Jazz nodded again. "It's nice to have friends in high places, though."

"Republican friends, too," he said. "Who would've thought?"

He stopped and turned to her. "You know, it's easy to

forget how many good people there are, and to just see the bad side at times like these."

She smiled and kissed away a speck of snow on the end of his nose; she didn't have to respond verbally. They communicated better by touch and feel, anyway.

Turning, they walked to the front steps.

He hesitated at the bottom as she moved halfway up. Watching her, he said, "When I met with Van Deventer, he told me about a promise he made once."

She glanced back, eyebrows raised.

"When he entered politics, he followed one rule: Compromise on the issues, but never on principle."

"That makes sense," she said.

"Will you make me a promise?"

"What?"

"Never let me forget that."

She thought for a split-second. "I promise."

He stepped up next to her and kissed her deeply.

Then Katie appeared at the front door.

"Come on," she said. "The chocolate'll get cold."

"We're coming," they said together.

As Jazz went inside, Trey paused to look around the property. It appeared so peaceful in the new-fallen snow, as if frozen in a time and place before all the insanity of the last few months.

He smiled at the scene, but he couldn't shake the nagging thought that Longstreet was still out there somewhere—and bent on revenge. The world was full of good people, but a few bad ones like him could destroy it for everyone else. Trey knew, even if Longstreet were found and prosecuted, he would never forget.

And that was all right. Trey wouldn't forget, either.

About the Author

T. D. Patterson is a long-time professional writer who lives and works in San Diego, California. Over the years, he has served as a journalist, public relations consultant, corporate executive and occasionally, an informed voter.